P9-AFA-606

Before the Reef

Eleanor Swanson

Plain View Press
P. O. 42255
Austin, TX 78704

plainviewpress.net
sb@plainviewpress.net
1-512-441-2452

Copyright Eleanor Swanson, 2007. All rights reserved.
ISBN: 978-1-891386-96-1
Library of Congress Number: 2007942844

Cover Photo ©Jack S. Grove, *Florida Keys Reef Scene*,
www.jsgrove.com

Acknowledgments

Thanks to Kelley Young for invaluable editorial assistance, and to readers of earlier drafts of this book, including Chris North and Carol Rossini, whose suggestions guided me in the revision process. Special thanks to Alice Reich, who has always been stalwart in her support of my writing, and in particular of *Before the Reef*.

To Bud, and in memory of Helen, Carl, and Carl Eric Swanson

Part One

"Between the outer reef and the shore of the Florida Keys there are many surreal formations of sea whips in the murky water. This is a haunting world of half-seen shapes and fading shadows. One of the soft corals found here is commonly known as deadman's fingers, *Biarcum Asbestinium*. I cannot help think that the person who coined the common name must have been nervously exploring such a habitat at the time."

Reef
Jeremy Stafford-Deitsch

For Lisa —
With all best
regards,

One

Rachel stepped onto the damp tiles of the front porch and looked up at the sky. Heavy clouds rolled over one other, giving off weak glints of light as they twisted along above the rooftops and trees. The faintly rotten smell of wet earth and leaves hung in the air. She could just make out her father's voice echoing from a distant room of the house—a ghostly sound, like wind stirring the mango. Rachel's mother had already scolded her, saying "you get ready now," each word sharp as a handclap.

Her stomach ached. Fear had taken shape and swum into her, like the dark thing in the Black Lagoon pushing against her ribs with slick hands. Jumping into the yard from the second step, she bent over to pick up the *Herald*. The grass held beads of dew that sparkled with the same colors as her mother's opal ring. The ring was bad luck. That's what her mother said. Her mother thought a lot of things brought bad luck. Rachel snapped the rubber band off the paper and searched the front page. Her face burned when she saw the column in the lower right hand corner: "Colgrove Murder Trial Begins Today." As she walked slowly up the steps, she heard the sound of her name, the way Miss Fowler called it, two hollow syllables—*Rae-chul*—and she saw the faces of her classmates turned to stare at her. What was murder anyway?

She *wouldn't* go back to school. Like Margo Rosenberg who'd gotten rheumatic fever from playing in the rain, Rachel could learn at home. No one could make her go back to school, not even police with guns and handcuffs, like the ones who'd arrested her father and asked her whether her mommy and daddy ever fought. "Sometimes," she'd answered. "They close the bedroom door when they do," she'd told the policeman, hoping that was the right thing to say.

"You're not even dressed yet." Her brother Gibb, a year younger, stood in the living room in his dark blue Sunday suit, hair combed, bow tie in place. Arms at his sides, he looked at her sternly. "You'll make us late." His suit sleeves fell to the middle of his hand. He looked like a midget at the circus. Last night he'd cried and cried—mashing his face into the pillow so their parents wouldn't hear—so she was sorry when a tiny smile grew on her mouth in spite of herself. She touched her lips to hide it.

"It's not funny. We'll be late and everyone will look at us," he said, stomping into the room they shared. She raised her hand to the half-closed door to push it open and taunt him, but instead went to the bathroom and locked herself in. Standing at the mirror, she teased her hair, and then worked the tangled mass into what the older girls at school called a French twist. She stuck in hairpins all around the bunched up hair, the way she'd practiced. Leaning close to the glass, she rubbed a few dots of her mother's lipstick on her cheeks and mouth. She wanted to look pretty because she felt so ugly inside, ugly and ashamed.

Just as she pulled her dress over her head in the bedroom's dim light, she heard the shrill sound of the horn. "Shut up!" she cried out loud. The neighbors would hear and peek through the slats of their blinds, spying on her, last to the car, the nosy neighbors keeping watch on them. Everyone watched them now. She ran out the door and slid into the back seat of the Ford, next to Gibb. He sat stiff, looking straight ahead, as if his clothes were made of cardboard. With a roar of the engine, her father backed the car out of the gravel driveway, shifted and spun into forward, making the tires squeal and rocks spray into the road. The sound made her want to scream. Did he want everyone on the whole block to hear them leaving? She hated him.

They flew past the vacant lot, but still she saw the high golden weeds sway, the fast-moving air passing over their feathery tops like a wave. She and Gibb had found a secret way into the lot, a path that went right to the dark, dirt-smelling center no one else in the neighborhood knew about. Deep inside the thicket of weeds they were safe.

Smoothing her skirt down over her crinolines, she looked at her chewed nails, then out the window at the sun coming up with a glittering hard light that had already begun to burn away the clouds. Her mother's hand beat at the air. "Don't. Of all the...times to speed," she said with a hard little gasp at the end like someone who'd been holding her breath underwater. When she turned to look at Rachel, her eyes flashed with anger. "Take down your hair and brush it out."

Her mother's own usually unruly hair was set and sprayed, and it sat on her head like a dark hat. Rachel liked her mother the other way, when her hair flew in the wind, curly and wild. Her mother watched as Rachel took the pins out one by one, searching among the tangles. "Wipe off the makeup, too," she ordered, before turning around and facing the road. Her mother leaned toward the windshield then, swaying with the turns, her shoulders square and her hands in her lap.

"This isn't a party we're going to, Sis," her father said, glancing back at Rachel.

"I know!" she said angrily, feeling the tears rise. Gibb gave a snort of stifled laughter and she flicked his thigh with her index finger.

"Ow," he shouted. "She hit…"

"That's enough!" her mother said without turning around, but the fury in her voice frightened them both into a silence that lasted until they reached the courthouse.

Rachel looked up to the pyramid top of the Dade County Courthouse, the tallest building downtown. Walking up the steps behind Gibb, she squinted to focus on the row of windows just under the pyramid. That's where the prisoners were kept, so they couldn't escape unless they jumped. Her father hadn't had to stay very long, because he'd paid money to get out. *Bail.* Now she knew what that meant. Before her father came home, her mother said the word to a lot of people on the telephone and sometimes cried. Before her father had gotten out of jail, her mother had cried every night after Rachel and Gibb had gone to bed. She closed their door and her own, but they could still hear her sobs, like sad far-away music. How many tears would it take until dark streaks of mildew grew down the walls of their house and cracked them? Even as Rachel reached the top step, the building looked far away, as if she were seeing it through the wrong end of a telescope. Pigeons floated down lazily and pecked near her feet. Rachel and Gibb and her mother and father walked close together, so close she smelled her mother's dusting powder and felt the edge of her father's jacket brush her arm.

Gibb bumped against her as they moved toward the giant column near the door. Rachel counted the people trudging resolutely up the steps. A woman carrying a screaming baby; a man with a gray suit and a bulging briefcase; an old lady with a built-up shoe, pulling her leg clumsily from step to step. Rachel had already counted nine people when she saw her father's lawyer, Mr. Lachon, striding down the steps toward them, smiling. He wore a tan suit and brown oxfords. She remembered the night he'd come to the house and sat with his sleeves rolled up. He told them, "It'll be all right, don't worry." But she worried anyway, and did most of her own crying when she was in the backyard and no one could hear her.

Staring up at the sky again, she imagined herself flying straight to the jail near the top of the courthouse. She could set someone free up there. Someone nice who hadn't really done anything wrong. Morning traffic screeched around her, making her head hurt. She stuck her fingers in her ears and heard the roar of her blood, like the sound of the ocean caught in a shell. She listened keenly. What if the sound stopped? Would she die?

Soon—Mr. Lachon had told them—everyone would know Noel Colgrove was not guilty. If "guilty" meant someone was a murderer, then "not guilty" meant he wasn't. She said the words in her mind and let them echo—*not guilty not guilty not guilty not guilty*. She made herself stop and counted off the good things to remember. Soon she'd be ten. After that—maybe before, maybe even on her birthday—they'd have a new baby. Rachel looked at the roundness of her mother's body, then up at her face as her mother listened intently to Mr. Lachon. Beads of sweat lay on her mother's forehead and temples. As Rachel watched, her mother nodded at what Mr. Lachon was saying, and the drops rolled down her cheeks and hung for a moment, shining at her chin before falling, just like her tears.

"Today we'll get through jury selection and that'll be about it. But I want the jurors to *see* you." He spoke to her father. "You, the children, and you too, Elizabeth." He turned to Rachel's mother and gave her shoulder a quick pat. "The family. New baby coming. Then in the next few days we'll show those twelve folks that the prosecution lacks any persuasive evidence." He said the last word more firmly than the rest, the way Pastor Nielson said the final words of his sermons. She started to spell out the word in her mind, struggling for a meaning. E-V-A-D-E-N-S-E. Another good thing, she thought firmly, something to trap a criminal, like a robber's fingerprint. But the notion confused her. What if they'd found her father's fingerprint where it shouldn't have been? Was that enough evidence to mean someone was guilty?

Gibb held their father's hand. Staring up at him, Gibb slowly blinked, his mouth open a little. With that smooth, pale face he looked like an angel boy in a painting. Which he wasn't. Just last week she'd seen him holding lizards by their tails and trying to burn holes in grasshoppers with the magnifying glass. As if he knew she was thinking about him, he looked straight into her face. "I'm scared," he whispered.

She could tell he was ready to cry. "Me too," she said in her own quietest voice.

"Let's go in now," Mr. Lachon said. He glanced for a moment at his tie, and then straightened it carefully, with a small tug at the knot.

On her fourth day in the stifling courtroom, Elizabeth Colgrove fanned herself with a folded newspaper and glanced at their lawyer, Sam Lachon. He'd worn a different suit every day. Suits with fine, tailored jackets. Soft silk ties. Soon he'd be buying his clothes with their money. Elizabeth stared at her husband's back. Noel faced the witness, his head tilted to one side. His white shirt was wet with perspiration and the cloth clung darkly to his broad shoulders. Even though an air-conditioner droned in the room, the air was heavy with humidity that tasted thick in her throat every time she took a breath.

She scanned the faces of the jurors. Some looked out toward the row of dingy windows or studied their hands. A few faces showed alertness in a raised eyebrow or mouth set hard. By accident she found herself looking into the eyes of a dark-haired woman about her age. For a moment they stared at one another. At first, the woman's gaze seemed merely curious, but for just an instant, before she turned away, Elizabeth saw another expression flicker across the woman's face. Pity. She's sorry for me because my husband is on trial for murder. Elizabeth caught her breath. *Murder.* The word tore at her like a barbed hook, a searing companion to the dull pain that always throbbed inside her. *My children,* she thought, *my poor children.* She imagined the children at school, shunned as though contagious. After the second day of the trial, she'd made them go back. Rachel had cried, then shouted, her face finally turning to a mask of hatred, the kind of pure hatred only children feel, uncorrupted by motives or conscience. Gibb had gone quietly, staring at her with the veiled look of a grim adult in those old posed photographs, a little old man already, as if he'd lived a lifetime wearing that tired, blank face.

She commanded them to be gone, those wretched faces. The future was what she had to see right now. The world hosed clean as shiny tile. They'd all march courageously into the future. She saw Rachel and Gibb—her unborn one, too, Martha or Jess, depending—three healthy children with sports letters and gleaming school medals at their chests, standing larger than life, hugging books and smiling, as if in the news cavalcade at the picture show. Time would pass and they'd all forget. Even nightmares faded after enough time passed, didn't they? They'd forget the whole ugly thing, this circus of a trial, grown men shouting at each other or asking one silly question after another. It was all show business, like in the wrestling matches Noel watched. There was no truth to the law—she saw that—just a matter of who could put on a better show. For a moment she ached with love, the first pure love she'd ever felt for Noel. She had not been young or pretty when they'd met, yet he had treated her tenderly. There had been no one else for him ever. No other woman. No…murder.

The witness stepped down and the judge called a brief recess. The shuffling and the screeching of moving chairs rose up around her like animal noises and people crashed about blindly, a harsh conjunction of sounds. She was suddenly so tired. She struggled to keep her eyes open. How she longed for the refuge of sleep.

Noel stood up and came to her. His own eyes were wide and shining with some instinctive alertness. The rest of his face amazed her—the uncontaminated blankness of his expression. "How are you?" he whispered, reaching for her hand and grasping it firmly.

She forced herself to smile. "All right," she said quietly. Then Sam Lachon stepped to Noel's side with a thick folder and Noel turned away.

When the judge returned to the courtroom, Elizabeth rose heavily to her feet. The baby had been kicking steadily all morning, but when Elizabeth stood, a foot lodged under her ribs, pushing hard, as if to break its way out. The pain stunned her. Yet even as things began to grow dim around the edges, she continued to stand.

The judge spoke to her. "Are you all right, Mrs. Colgrove?"

She nodded slowly in the direction of the judge's deep whiskey voice. Noel turned, his face floating far away in some sourceless light, his body grown massive and shapeless.

"I'm fine," she said firmly to no one in particular, sitting down. In a moment, furtively, short of breath, she pushed at the stubborn foot. Had she been alone, she'd have spoken aloud to the misbehaved creature inside her. *Don't be in such a hurry*, she'd have scolded. *We're safe together now, you and I, so just stay put.*

The next witness swore to tell the truth, the echo of his oath ringing out. *So...help...me. God.* God? Was God listening? She put her fingers to her lips. Noel would say she blasphemed. But how impatient she'd grown with these rituals, the endless repetition, the waste. Here, precious time flowed through silences between the droning voices into nothingness. Her impatience turned to anger. *Just ask him if he did it*, she wanted to cry out, *the way I did. I'm married to him. I'd know.*

"Mr. Ottawell, how do you happen to be acquainted with Noel Colgrove?"

She watched the prosecuting attorney's face in profile as his thin lips formed the words.

"We're neighbors."

"Have you ever gone fishing with Mr. Colgrove?"

"Yeah, a few times."

"About how many times a year?"

"Oh, one or two times, maybe. I'm more of a fanatic, I guess. Noel likes to take his boy...piddle around a few hours."

"How many times a year do you go fishing, Mr. Ottawell?"

"About sixty. I'd go ever'day if the wife'd let me." Several people in the courtroom laughed.

"Where do you usually fish, sir?"

"Objection." Sam Lachon began to stand up.

"Overruled."

"Depends on what's runnin'. I check the papers, you know, talk to folks over at the marina, but I go out to Bache Shoal a lot. Fowey Rocks is close in, too, about three miles south of Cape Florida, so I usually fish the patch reefs between Fowey Rocks and Triumph Reef. I don't like to get out in the Straits much. My boat's on the small side."

The prosecutor turned and looked out at the spectators in the courtroom, deliberately catching Elizabeth's eye for a moment before he glanced at the jury. She felt her face burn, as he'd intended, she guessed. In a smug, practiced way, he put his hands in his trouser pockets and smiled a little. "How large is your boat?"

Mr. Lachon rose. "Objection. I don't see the relevance..."

"Overruled." The judge looked down at Joe Ottawell. "Answer the question."

Ottawell crossed his legs and rubbed his jaw. "Sixteen foot."

The prosecutor rocked on his heels, then stepped closer to the witness box. "How large is Noel Colgrove's boat?"

Joe Ottawell shifted in his chair. "I'm not sure." His thinning hair was carefully combed across his scalp. His suit looked borrowed. The shiny brown cloth made his sunburned face look even redder. Elizabeth and Jean Ottawell used to talk across the hedge of Florida cherry that separated their lots. Now Jean scurried about the yard to do her chores like a frightened dog, not even glancing toward her neighbor's house.

"Mr. Ottawell, there's not a fisherman around who doesn't know the size of another man's boat."

Joe Ottawell looked down at his hands. "Noel's boat's fourteen foot," he muttered.

"Mr. Ottawell, in the last year, say, what's the farthest you've ever gone to fish?"

"I heard the yellowtails was running down by Old Rhodes Key and I went down there. That's about twenty-five miles from Dinner Key."

"And that's nautical miles, right?"

"Yes sir."

"Okay. Let's focus in on May 30. Was there anything unusual about what happened that day?"

"Well, Noel called me up about four that afternoon and said his boat quit."

"Where was he calling from?"

Joe wiped his forehead on his sleeve. "Rattlesnake Key, just up from Largo Sound."

"Pretty good fishing down there?" The prosecutor took another step forward and stood near Joe with his arms folded.

"Objection!" Sam Lachon brought his hand down flat on the table.

The judge looked at him, annoyed. "Take it easy, Mr. Lachon." He peered at the prosecutor. "I'll overrule in hopes you're going somewhere, sir. Answer the question, Mr. Ottawell."

"Depends. Could of been Noel had a tip..."

"Had you been out fishing that week?" He raised his voice almost imperceptibly and pronounced each word with care, as if he were talking to a man slightly hard of hearing.

"Yeah, just over to Soldier Key."

"Had you heard any tips about good fishing in the Rattlesnake Key area?"

"Objection. Just because he didn't hear a tip doesn't mean..." Sam Lachon started to stand, but the prosecutor turned to face him and raised a hand.

"It's all right. I'll ask you this way: Did Noel Colgrove tell you why he was some twenty-eight nautical miles away from Dinner Key Marina?"

"No sir."

"Did he ever mention fishing or tell you what he was hoping to catch out there?"

"No sir."

"What *did* he tell you?"

"He said the boat cut out on him. The weather was gettin' bad. Some young fellas stopped to help, and he asked for a tow. They didn't have no rope, it wasn't their boat, this and that. Anyways,

13

they couldn't tow him, but he hitched a ride in with them and called me from Key Largo."

"What else did he tell you? Did he tell you why he didn't wait for a boat that could have towed him?"

"Yeah, he said it was lightning and he was worried...he thought his wife would be worried." He looked at Elizabeth and met her eyes before glancing away.

Elizabeth remembered how the storm had come up that day, heavy, black-streaked clouds gathering everywhere she looked, and an onshore wind blowing in hard gusts. She'd been glad when Noel phoned, but she hadn't thought to be worried before that. It was true; he wasn't much of a fisherman, but he never took chances on the water. But sometimes he took chances with people. He trusted them too much and they took advantage of him.

"Sir, are you aware the body of the victim was recovered off Carysfort Reef, only six nautical miles from Rattlesnake Key?"

The body of the victim. A violent shiver passed over her. She thought of the newspaper stories and the picture of a pretty blonde girl who'd been struck across the face, hit on the head and had a concrete block tied around her ankles so she'd sink. Her blood had mixed with seawater and her battered face had been rinsed clean by the same water. Before she'd even digested her breakfast, she'd drowned. Spear fishers looking for black grouper had found her body at the base of the reef. Hardly anyone dove Carysfort Reef, but this was a new charter company, trying an out-of-the-way place. Elizabeth felt something knotting in her throat like she'd swallowed a stone with jagged edges.

"Objection. The witness's awareness of these distances has no relevance."

"Sustained."

"Okay. Mr. Ottawell, what happened when you reached the boat?"

"It was raining real hard by then. Good thing I got a cover and lights. We tried to start the engine. No spark. Maybe a bad distributor, I thought at the time. Noel told me later it was just a grounded wire in the distributor cap. Anyways, we rigged up a tow line. Couldn't hardly stand up, there was so much chop. Rain poured down the whole way back to the Pennekamp marina. When we got there we hitched up my boat and I drove Noel back to Dinner Key to get his car."

"That's more than an hour's drive. Did he seem upset?"

"Well, sure. The damn engine quit on him out there. He had to leave his boat in Key Largo, drive down again."

"Where was the boat anchored, sir?"

"Just about two miles northeast of Rattlesnake Key, in Hawk Channel."

"What did you talk about on the drive back to Miami?"

"The weather, mostly. Hurricanes. Whether we'd get the big one this year."

"Was Mr. Colgrove upset for the whole drive? Nervous?"

"No sir, not really. He was more relaxed, relieved, maybe, once we got on our way. He kept thanking me for coming out."

Elizabeth glared out into the room, hoping one of the reporters might look in her direction. Her husband wasn't a murderer. She remembered him holding Gibb. Gibb was only a few hours old and Noel had taken Gibb's tiny hand between his own thumb and forefinger with the lightest grasp she'd ever seen.

"Just a few more questions, Mr. Ottawell." The prosecutor walked to a table where his assistant sat. No conversation passed between them, but the young man reached out and handed the older lawyer a folder.

Elizabeth imagined the two lawyers outside the courtroom, walking together, afternoon sun falling through the trees to crisscross the sidewalk with shafts of light. Did they discuss their strategy over drinks, ice tinkling in the raised glasses? How they could win a conviction? "Win a conviction," wasn't that how the lawyers said it? They'd written a plan, like a script for a play, of how they'd convict Noel.

Bill Davis was the prosecutor's name. Elizabeth had an idea he was related to the Davises who owned a mansion on Brickell Avenue and half of Coral Gables. As Davis turned away from the table she saw his face straight on. His short hair was pale, almost colorless, and clipped to glossy perfection. He nodded slightly at someone he knew in the courtroom and his mouth opened in the briefest of smiles, the expression disappearing as quickly as the flick of a camera shutter. Turning to Joe Ottawell, he held the folder in front of him importantly. She could see him sitting at the tiled side of a sparkling blue pool, his smooth, rich man's face angled up toward the sun. Noel "should die for his crime." That's what he'd said the first day of the trial. For an instant, rage rose in her like a wave of sickness.

"So did Mr. Colgrove catch any fish that day?" Davis looked at the jury and flashed his perfect smile.

"No sir, not that I saw."

"Did you see Noel's rod and reel, or bait bucket? Anything like that?"

"No sir."

Sam Lachon half-stood, his hands on the table in front of him. "Your honor, I don't see the relevance..."

"A man tells his wife he's going fishing. He just happens to be within a mile of where the body of a murder victim is found..."

"Your honor..."

"That's enough, Mr. Lachon. Mr. Davis, I'm overruling Mr. Lachon's objection, so proceed with your questions."

"Now, when you climbed into Mr. Colgrove's boat to see if you could give him a hand, help him start up the engine, did you find anything unusual?"

Joe Ottawell said nothing. He looked blankly at Davis.

"Mr. Ottawell, did you hear me?"

"I...you said...would you repeat?"

"I said, did you find anything unusual in Noel Colgrove's boat?"

"I'm not sure what you mean."

"Sir, did you find anything in the boat that you brought to Mr. Colgrove's attention?" Bill Davis began to speak more slowly, more softly, as he asked the question again. Elizabeth strained to hear. His voice was patient, and between each of the words the courtroom grew quieter.

"I found one of Elizabeth's...Mrs. Colgrove's earrings, a little gold earring."

"Did Mr. Colgrove say anything to you about the earring?"

"He said 'thanks,' and put it in his pocket."

Davis opened his folder and pulled out a large photograph.

"Mr. Ottawell, I'd like for you to take a look at People's Exhibit H. This is the photograph that's already been identified by police divers and by the examining pathologist as being a picture of the deceased, Neoma Kelch. Only one earring was found on the body. Does the earring you can see in the picture look familiar? Does it look like the earring you handed Noel Colgrove?"

Joe Ottawell took the photograph Davis handed him. For what seemed like several minutes, he held it motionless in front of him. "I can't remember," he said finally. "I don't know much about women's jewelry." He shrugged his shoulders.

"Was it a small ring, like the girl in this photograph is wearing?"

"It was a little gold hoop, yeah, but I wouldn't say..."

Sam Lachon rose from his chair, his long body unfolding in a single movement. "Objection. There are hundreds of earrings..."

"Overruled. Enter Mr. Ottawell's response into the record." The judge looked at the court reporter.

Elizabeth searched for the eyes of the dark-haired woman on the jury. The eyes wouldn't judge, would attach no significance to a trinket found in a boat. But the woman's head was down. She was writing quickly in a small black notebook that lay open on her lap. Elizabeth gazed at the back of her husband's chair, as if it were an idol that would protect her from that sea of curious and accusatory faces.

The woman did not glance at her again. After the next witness was called, she continued to write in her notebook. Elizabeth turned away and watched the man move toward the witness stand. He walked as if he were used to being watched, especially by women. He was handsome, in a rough way. He had sun-streaked blonde hair and a deeply tanned face, and his short-sleeved white shirt stretched taut around his muscular arms. As he sat down, before he was sworn in, he smiled at the jurors and the spectators as if he were in a play. Elizabeth felt her scalp prickle. Here was the kind of man who liked to gamble and fight. After a fight some girl who'd been watching would come to him and hang on his arm, whispering. Steve Mc-Grath was his name, and he worked at Dinner Key Marina. "Bix," he said rather loudly. "I go by Bix." She imagined him standing on the dock, sea spray at his back. He watched the people who came and went and thought indecent things about them. How could anything this coarse man said be believed?

Mr. Lachon had told them that Bix was one of the prosecution's key witnesses. She leaned forward in her chair and listened.

"Mr. McGrath, were you working at the Dinner Key Marina on May 30 of last year?"

"Yes sir, I was."

"Now, I know it could just become a blur, all the people you've seen at the marina. But is there anyone you saw at the marina that day, May 30, who's in this courtroom?"

"Yeah, the guy at the table over there." He pointed at Noel.

"How can you be sure?"

"He was standin' right next to me while I was gassin' up his boat."

"Was he alone?"

"Yeah, at first."

"What do you mean?"

"He was joined by a young lady."

"Mr. McGrath, I'm going to show you Peoples' Exhibit H, a photograph that previous witnesses have identified as the deceased, Neoma Kelch. Is this the young lady you saw at the marina on May 30?"

"Yeah, that's her."

"And when did you first see her?"

"She came over and started talkin' to that guy, like they knew each other."

"Objection. Speculation. Move to strike the witness's last remark."

"Sustained."

The testimony stretched on, with the prosecutor trying to link Neoma Kelch and Noel through their conversation and "knowing looks."

But Sam Lachon's final questions seemed to make everything that had gone before irrelevant.

"Did you see them leave in the boat together?"

"No."

"You didn't see the girl afterwards, but you didn't notice Noel Colgrove's boat leaving either. You might have stepped inside for a time and missed seeing the girl simply go on her way and Noel Colgrove take off for his day of fishing. Is that possible?"

Bix McGrath shifted in his chair, then sat up straight and leaned forward. He stabbed the air with his forefinger. "They took off together sure as I'm sittin' here."

"Answer the question, Mr. McGrath," Sam Lachon said calmly. "Could you have missed seeing them go their separate ways?"

For a few seconds, Elizabeth watched the muscles of his jaw twitching. Had someone in a bar made Bix McGrath this angry, he would have fought, drawn blood.

"Yeah," he said finally in a voice with a rude edge to it. "It's possible."

Elizabeth stared out the kitchen window at the backyard. The late summer sun burned down through the clear air as if through an enormous lens. They hadn't had a drop of rain for weeks. She brushed damp hair from her face. The grass was brown, dying slowly in the fiery heat.

When Sam Lachon had talked to them about the earring, he'd told them to expect it to be brought up at the trial. But with each discussion, the tiny gold ring had become smaller, until it was no more than a glint of light in the palm of a large hand. So Elizabeth had been shocked by the furor that had come—muffled cries of outrage, the mock calm of the courtroom ritual shattered—with the introduction of this evidence, evidence that seemed to link Noel with the drowned girl. Elizabeth hadn't been prepared, even after all their talks. Of course she knew...how Joe had found an earring on the boat. Only Joe had ever suggested the trinket belonged to her. It did not. Noel had never seen the thing, whatever it was, before the day on the boat. And before another living being had seen that mysterious gold ring, it slipped out of a hole in Noel's pocket and disappeared forever, as if it had never existed.

But Bill Davis had stood there, waving a large, slightly blurry photograph, focusing attention on a small, ordinary earring that could never be matched to the one the dead girl had worn.

Feeling the child inside her turn, Elizabeth ran her fingertips comfortingly up and down her belly. Sam Lachon had talked to them, too, about the prosecution's "star witness," a woman who claimed to know Noel and Neoma Kelch. This woman had picked Noel out of a police line-up, then disappeared the day before the trial was to have begun. Bill Davis had gotten a delay, but the woman hadn't turned up, was nowhere to be found. She'd simply vanished. Sam Lachon had told them that without her, the missing witness, the prosecution didn't have a case any longer. Elizabeth shuddered. What if this woman, whoever she was, had gotten up on the stand and told her lies? How many innocent people had been put in prison by liars...or sent to their deaths?

She walked slowly from the kitchen to the dining room and looked out across the patio at the tangle of deep ligustrum bushes, frangipani and crepe myrtle trees that fringed the yard. It needed tending. If only she could do it herself. But she was so tired. Thank God Noel could sleep. He slept now; he'd been sleeping for hours. For her, real sleep had become an impossible pleasure. Each night she lay down exhausted and closed her eyes, to watch the trial replay, word by word. She listened more keenly now than she had on the first days, took notes of her own. Noel had never lied to her; she believed that. The marina employee who testified, even the mysterious prosecution witness whose blabbing had gotten Noel charged in the first place— they'd been mistaken, caught up in the hysteria of the prosecutor's portrayal of Noel as a heartless killer and an adulterer. She wound a strand of hair around her finger. Music came to her, slow tunes she and Noel had danced to, their bodies so close, she'd felt their hearts beat together, felt Noel's blood move silkily through his veins. The words of a song came to her unwanted, cloying now as they'd once been perfect in their sweetness, in capturing their love. They'd sung the song together, softly, as they'd danced. "Before the Reef," was the title. With a small shiver, she passed a hand over her eyes, willing the now-bitter memory of the song to fade. She saw the words reel and swim away, like a school of dusky fish.

A single brown sock lay curled around the leg of a chair, like a snatch of fur from a half-starved animal. Rachel and Gibb shouted in the front yard. She hoped they weren't quarreling as usual. The trial had made them wild. Day after day they scrapped and bickered, cried out in their sleep, woke up puffy-eyed, and asked a hundred questions she couldn't answer. The phone rang and she reached for it warily, her hand feeling leaden. Sometimes her sister Carlene from Alabama called on Saturdays to say she was praying for Elizabeth and to complain that her three-year-old twin boys were wearing her to the bone. The ringer was loud, a fractured sound that set her teeth on edge. "Hello," she said, waiting.

"Murderer's wife!" the voice hissed. "Hope he gets the chair for what he done to that girl. Hell's too good for 'im."

"Leave us alone!" She cupped her hands around the phone with a sob, felt her own breath sticky-warm on her fingers, listened to the click and dial tone. Reporters and cranks called every day. Police had asked their neighbors all kinds of questions. Homicide detectives had talked to her for hours. Do you and your husband fight? Have you ever suspected him of stepping out on you? On and on. They'd asked Rachel and Gibb questions, too, sitting alone with one of them at a time in the backyard. She remembered how police had searched the house, drawers and closets, cabinets and shelves, the garage, the car. They'd dusted everywhere for fingerprints with a fine, sticky powder that clung to surfaces, even after she'd scrubbed them. They'd impounded Noel's boat. But he'd washed down the boat. He always washed it down after he'd been fishing.

She thought of the terrible thing Noel had read in the paper just a day before the story of the Kelch girl's murder had appeared. One of his friends from night school, Jimmy Youngblood, had been stabbed to death in the Keys, in the parking lot of a Marathon bar. Robbed. She'd known Jimmy just well enough to dislike him. A slick, handsome fellow who'd done prison time for writing bad checks. When he came to the house, he would smile at her in a way that made her think he was seeing through her clothes. She'd always seen something vile beneath Jimmy's good looks. What had he done to be flashing so much money that he'd gotten himself killed for it? She tried to hold back the thought that maybe he'd been more than just a petty criminal. The news had made Noel physically sick. He'd vomited and shut himself up in their room. She didn't know they'd been that close. Then the Kelch story and Noel's arrest. All these things she hadn't expected to face in her life. Her heart thumped like the heart of a small, frightened animal, and she struggled for a deep breath, willing herself to be stronger.

She got up and began to clear the dining room table, littered with bills and magazines. The Waterford fruit bowl that had been her grandmother's was filled with dusty odds and ends—jacks, a spool of thread, safety pins, rubber bands, a stub of pencil. Dusty things lay everywhere she looked, things out of place. Dust glazed the table and the rungs of the chairs. Noel had left his shoes in the living room. Gibb yelled something. She made out the words "no" and "stop it." The front screen door slammed and Gibb ran into the dining room, stopping short in front of her. Tears mixed with the grime on his face.

"Rachel...pushed me," he sobbed, breathing hard. He could barely get the words out. "...down, tickling, she tickled me. I told her to stop. It hurt." Elizabeth sat down and held her arms open for him to come, and he stepped to her and laid his head in her lap, still crying. She stroked his hair and watched a cardinal hop halfway across the yard, then strut in a zigzag line, crest feathers straight up, as if showing off for a hidden female.

The screen door squeaked faintly and Rachel walked past without looking at her.

"You can go to your room and stay there until dinner."

Rachel faced her. "I was going to my room anyway."

"Don't you talk back to me."

Rachel continued to stand as if fixed to the spot where she'd stopped, looking defiantly at Elizabeth, daring her to become angrier. But suddenly she turned and half-skipped down the hall, swinging her arms.

Gibb had stopped crying and stood beside Elizabeth with a grimy hand resting on her lap. "Rachel's mean."

"She's just showing off because she's bigger."

"She's a meanie," he said solemnly. He leaned against her and put his hand across her back, looking into her face. His eyes were a bright, clear blue and his blonde hair was thick and curly. But he was too thin and serious to be a really handsome child. "Is Daddy going back to jail?" His eyes locked hers, his jaw set.

"Why do you think that, honey?" she asked gently. On Mr. Lachon's suggestion, they had taken the children to court on the first and second days of the trial, but she'd been troubled about them being there. She wanted them to know as little as possible about what had happened to their father. Why should they learn so soon that the law wasn't always fair?

"Somebody told me he was."

"No," she said, stroking his hair, "he's not."

He looked away and began to walk around the table, his small hands touching the edge and leaving faint patterns in the dust.

"Who told you?" She caught his arm. "Someone at school?"

"No, Rebo, the man from the vacant lot."

She knew no one with a name like that, clownish and foreign-sounding at once. In a moment of panic, she imagined the children with a bum, a vagrant smelling of whiskey who slept on a filthy mattress in the center of the lot, among the high weeds, where she knew the children played. "Who's Rebo? What does he look like?"

Gibb smiled and fixed her with an expression of solemn pleasure, as if she'd asked the right questions, finally. "He's my friend. He has black hair and a beard. He wears two diamond rings and carries a big bag full of bubblegum and cars and some other toys. He gives them to kids when they're good."

She nodded, listening. His imaginary friend, of course. Gibb needed someone like Rebo now. She wouldn't discourage him. "You and Rebo don't have to talk about Daddy. You must have lots of other things to talk about."

"Are you sure Daddy's not going back to jail?"

"Yes, I'm sure." She reached for his hands and leaned forward to kiss him on the cheek, feeling the terrified beating of her heart.

He pulled away. "Rebo says he is because he killed a lady and put her in the ocean."

She grabbed him and held him close to her but he stood in her arms like a life-size doll, stiff and unresponsive.

A wave of fear pushed through her to her fingertips. "Now look, don't you pay any attention to Rebo," she said, straining to control the tremor in her voice. "Everything's going to be okay."

"Rebo said Daddy pushed her," his voice was muffled, his breath warm against the front of her dress, "and she went down. 'Splash,' like a rock."

Two

"Before the reef where the sea is dark and cold, / My love has gone / And our dreams grow old. / Someday I know he'll come back again to me."

Phil Louis

On the last day they spent in court, her father wore his white Florsheims. Rachel knew how to spell the name. Showing her off to the salesman, he'd taught her when she was six and he was buying new shoes, a "church pair," he said. The polish on the leather was powdery now, after so many coats. Rachel would remember those shoes forever, she'd stared at them so long, frightened to look up at her father's face. While they were waiting for the verdict, he took her hand and pulled her over to him, to sit on his lap. Rachel felt too big, but came anyway, to please him. He seemed almost ready to smile, his eyes lively and distant at the same time, like when he carried her on the wheelbarrow, on top of the sweet-smelling grass clippings. After a while, though, he gazed off into space, as if he'd forgotten she was still on his lap. His hands rested idly on the arms of the chair. She remembered the way he'd looked the night he'd come home from jail. His face had been dark and rough, and without his hair tonic, his hair fell across his forehead in limp strands. Her mother had gone to bed with one of her sick headaches and Gibb was already asleep. In her nightgown, Rachel peeked into the living room where her father sat, still, like he sat now, except for his arm. She'd watched, engrossed by the sight of that moving arm taking a cigarette to his lips again and again until the room was filled with smoke. He'd looked like he was sitting inside a cloud.

When Rachel got up and went back to her place beside Mother, her father reached into his briefcase for the Bible and opened it, not to any special place, for the red ribbon—sticking out like a snake's tongue—still lay in the book some pages forward.

It was the afternoon of the fourth day of jury deliberations. Finally, the jury walked in together and sat down, twelve tired, serious faces that made Rachel shiver deep inside. Her mother had kept her and Gibb out of school for a week. "We have to be together now," she'd told them. "It's almost over." The judge leaned toward the jury, moving his lips in words she couldn't hear. One man stood up. "Yes, your honor." He held a piece of paper in front of his face. "Not guilty," he read, and Rachel felt the words like soothing hands even before she heard them. Her heart beat wildly, then grew bigger in her chest until it was full as a balloon that could float away, up into the sky. Her father wouldn't go to jail. Her father wouldn't die. He was *innocent*.

A scream rose behind her that ended with a sob, and Rachel turned. She saw a big woman in a flowered dress half-collapse into the arms of a man in a pork-pie hat. Then people closed around the woman until Rachel couldn't see her any longer.

The courtroom filled with the noise of shuffling feet and voices growing louder and louder. The woman's sobs echoed in the background. They stood. The lawyer Mr. Lachon was there and everyone hugged. She hugged too but felt tired and far away. She was an ugly girl with sticky sweat dripping down the backs of her legs. She wanted to put her hands over her ears and crawl under the seats, but everyone was watching and the reporters stood around with flash cameras. One went off with a huge burst and she shut her eyes to the fiery wave. She tried to make her face belong to someone else, a nice girl who loved everyone and would be an honor to her family. But her tiredness grew into a pain wrapping around her middle like a tight belt. She smiled, so as not to shout, *go away! Stop staring at us!*

A man with a notebook came up and asked her father what he thought of the verdict. How did he feel? Rachel moved away to stand by Mother and at that same moment Gibb stepped forward between her father and the reporter and held his thin arms up like a shield. Gibb babbled and cried in his sleep these days and even sleepwalked. Rachel woke up one night to see him with his eyes wide open. She'd been so scared she'd almost wet the bed. "Gibb," she'd whispered, "are you asleep?" "Find killer," he'd muttered. "Gotta find 'im." But now he looked so grown up, protecting their father like that. More flashbulbs popped.

Her father patted Gibb's shoulder. "That's all right son," he said, bending down to whisk the Bible out of his briefcase. His voice came out loud, causing a silence around them and more staring. As he talked, his face twisted into angry lines. "All my life I've been a Christian. I asked myself, 'Why did this happen to me?'" He opened the Bible. "This is what Matthew says: 'Love your enemies and pray for those who persecute you so that you may be sons of your Father who is in heaven; for He makes your sun rise on the evil and on the good, and sends rain on the just and on the unjust.' Pray for those who persecute you. That's my comment," he said, clapping the book shut and looking at the reporter and the spectators who had gathered—a blur of colors and bobbing heads. Rachel smelled sweat and perfume mixed with the reek of cigarettes. "Now leave us alone!" He strode away and they followed. His Florsheims clicked like tapshoes on the tile corridor.

Rachel took big steps to catch up and reached out to him. "Daddy?"

Without stopping he took her hand for a moment, squeezed her fingers hard, then let go. "See Sis," he bent his head toward her, his lips close to her ear, the sound wet, an unpleasant tickle. "I'm ruined no matter what. It's up to you and Gibb now. You have to take over."

She wasn't sure what he meant, but she thought of Gibb's sleepwalking—his fierce little face, blank eyes and voice raspy as a ghost's. *Find killer.* Is that what their father wanted? She was afraid. Maybe the killer out there would come after her next...or Gibb. They walked outside the courthouse, the people around them beginning to disperse. Lazy pigeons still strutted about, pecking at nothing. Her father leaned against a pillar, holding his coat, his arm around her mother. His long-sleeved shirt clung to him in dark patches. A few last blinding flashbulbs exploded and died out, but three or four reporters lingered. One of them called out, "Are you going to stay in Miami?"

"Why shouldn't I?" Her father called back angrily. "Weren't you just in court?"

Mr. Lachon stood between her father and the last of the reporters. "Why don't you fellas get going and let these folks go home?"

Mr. Lachon walked them part way to the parking garage then stopped, shook her father's hand, hugged her mother and wished her

well with the baby. "Call me if you need anything," he said. He patted their shoulders, Rachel and Gibb, and was gone.

On the way to the car, her father spoke to her mother in the
wrung out and pitiful voice of someone weeping, but his face was
dry of tears. "Murder," he said. Her mother's words came back firm,
each one solid as a wall. *We'll put this behind us. . .*

Later, silent, they sat at the dining room table under the yellow
light and ate scrambled eggs, with milk to stretch them, cooked to
rubbery tastelessness. Right after the meal, Rachel and Gibb were
hurried off to bed and their door was closed. Still, they could hear
the muffled sound of their parents' voices. Sometimes the words
were almost loud enough to understand. Rachel and Gibb peered at
each other across the darkness of their room and whispered, "Are
you asleep?" "No, are you?" "No." Then they began to talk, too,
about how scared they were, still. About what would happen to
them. They whispered and listened until the voices stopped and the
dusty light of morning squeezed into the room through the tightly
closed blinds.

In early August, less than a month after Noel Colgrove was acquitted of the murder of Neoma Kelch, Elizabeth DeLile Colgrove
gave birth to her second son, Jess Taylor. Almost before she had
touched the baby's tiny hands and feet and stroked his silky hair,
dark as her own, she felt herself grow distant. At first she shrunk to
no more than a speck, lying invisibly on the sheets. Then she grew
larger, till she'd become gigantic, a woman in whose huge hands the
baby—delicate as a mockingbird's egg—had no business being.

"Mrs. Kelch?" Elizabeth was small again. A voice wound its way
from a dark, ragged hole. The nurse hovered over her. "Are you having trouble feeding the baby?" *Mrs. Kelch.* Something was wrong.
No, she felt herself saying firmly. "I am Elizabeth *Colgrove.* The
nurse reached down, took the baby and left the room. Soon she was
back. She stuck a thermometer in Elizabeth's mouth and laid an
icy hand on her forehead. Then Elizabeth slept until the heat grew
dreadful. She realized that she lay outside, covered with blankets,
under the burning sun. Why had they put her outside? But there
was no light. Her eyes were sealed. The bed rocked like a boat and

fish flopped over her like wet hands. Where was her baby? He'd fall overboard and drown. Gone from her forever. He was much too small to be on the boat. He'd been born tiny, no bigger than a thumb. The slightest wave...She called his name. *Jess, Jess.* He'd drown, like that slut. She opened her eyes and tried to get up but the cold, wet hands held her down. Then the pain came. At first she had only the suffocating heat to deal with, but now there was pain, someone pressing jagged rocks into her chest and stomach. And the screaming. She tried to cover her ears, but her hands were fastened with rope. She was a prisoner.

"Elizabeth."

Finally a voice she recognized. She opened her eyes. Noel stood beside her and bent down close to kiss her cheek. Tears streaked his face. Rachel and Gibb were with him. They hung back until Noel pushed them towards her. "Momma." Gibb was crying. Rachel held his hand. Elizabeth looked at Noel. "Why are these children dirty?" she whispered. A nurse stepped out of the shadows of the room. She motioned them away from the bed.

"We'll call you," the nurse seemed to say to Noel, but her voice was faint. Like a puff of smoke it drifted into a corner and disappeared.

The nurse walked out with Noel and the children and closed the door, leaving Elizabeth alone in the room where faint yellow light wavered like a hooded flame. She noticed that the walls were streaked with stains, slender fingers of dirt moving up towards the ceiling. She lifted herself up in the bed and saw that dirt lay piled in the corners, too. She looked toward the ceiling to find that dust was drifting down like ashes, covering her. No wonder she was sick. The place was so filthy no amount of scrubbing would clean it. The whole world was full of such filth.

No one had to tell her she'd almost died. Part of her *had* died, died completely away, but that had happened because of the trial, not her sickness. At any rate, when she felt the children slipping from her, dark shapes edged in ragged light, she'd willed herself back into the solid world. Her children needed her. After three weeks in the hospital, her milk was gone and she'd hardly seen her new baby. "Toxemia," they'd said. Gibb and Rachel were probably going to school looking like ragamuffins.

For the last week Noel had come to the hospital every night. Everything was fine, he said, taken care of. He'd gotten into the habit of reading to her from the Bible until her head ached.

"Home tomorrow," he said, fluffing a pillow. He leaned close, but didn't touch her as he slipped the pillow behind her head.

"Are you working?"

"Working? Yes, dear. In a position soon to move into management. You'll see for yourself. Don't think I'm completely ruined, that I can no longer take care of us." He opened the Bible. "Ruination," he said majestically, and started to read. "Though a man gets praise when he does well for himself, he will go to the generation of his father who will never more see the light."

She explored his face for a moment, but finding nothing, closed her eyes and feigned sleep. Turning her head into the pillow, she imagined him gone, the droning of his voice replaced by silence, the chair empty. The sheets smelled of bleach and harsh detergent. She lay very still, waiting for sleep and darkness.

Elizabeth was grateful for the quiet house when the baby was sleeping. Gibb and Rachel were in school and she'd done all the housework she could do for the day, her strength was coming back so slowly. She walked to the back door and stepped outside. The breeze carried the smell of the ocean. Pink blossoms from the crepe myrtle near the door drifted down and scattered on the steps and grass like bits of tissue. She sometimes could call forth an image of herself when she'd been a young girl, her hair done up in a bow, her organdy dress shining with starch. After what she'd been through, remembering that good little girl was a comfort somehow. But today she tried for the memory and the picture came out blurred and faded; the dress was stained an indecent red right down the front, as if she'd been doing something she wasn't supposed to be doing. She sighed and took down some towels from the clothesline. When Jess woke up she'd put him in the carriage and walk over to the Kwik Chek supermarket, where everyone always made a fuss over him, touching his tiny fingers or his silky thatch of dark hair. Such a pretty, good-natured baby, they said. Such blue eyes! Do you think they'll change? When Jess woke up, no matter who he saw, a smile would light his plump face like the sun coming out; that's how people described his smile. The way everybody spoiled Jess, you'd think he was the one who'd almost died.

The trip downtown to the bank where the safe deposit box was could wait until tomorrow. Yesterday, Sam Lachon had dropped off the trial transcripts she'd asked for. She'd paid dearly to have them, from money she'd saved for years from this and that, and secretly put away. No matter how much they needed the money for bills, this was something she had to do. She would not tell Noel, not ever. She had a whole secret life now. Going through the trial had made her someone else. In the bank, she'd lock away the transcripts. She'd hidden the stories she'd clipped from the newspaper, too. Their pictures had been on the front page! Story after story had followed until Noel's acquittal. For some reason, she had saved the story of Jimmy Youngblood's murder too. Two unsolved murders. Two killers on the loose. The back of her neck prickled. There was more to know, to find out.

Elizabeth looked down at the grass, imagining that even now old Mrs. Ellis was peering out her kitchen window, watching her. She raised her head defiantly. Go ahead, stare and whisper about us all you please, she thought. Time would pass. Time would do its work and wear down the knife-edges of their memories—fade the gawking faces of strangers, their mouths opening in accusation, police at their door. Would she ever forget the sight of Noel in handcuffs? Would she ever be able to get rid of her anger? *Yes*, she said to herself firmly. *I'll put the story away in that box, in the cool vault.* Maybe in a few years, she'd give these things to Gibb. He would be the one to want them most, her little old man. He could read about what had happened as if it hadn't happened to them, as if it had been no more than a sad story from a book. He could write a story of his own and send the ghosts away.

Rachel sat on the beach, digging her toes in the hot sand, remembering how Billy Singer's mouth had felt against hers. His lips touching hers. She was almost eleven and a half now, old enough to learn how to kiss. She thought of her parents, how she studied them when they weren't watching. They didn't even look at each other, much less kiss. Maybe they used to kiss before her father's trial.

She watched the clouds drifting together and drifting apart across the streaks of blue, the sun disappearing and rolling out again. The clouds were dark bluish-gray and fluffy like the dyed hair of old ladies. When the sun shone down full for a minute, it was so hot it made the skin on her face and arms tingle. She watched Gibb and her friend Rona playing in the big inner tubes they'd brought to the beach, kicking their feet like outboard motors and raising a froth of water all around them.

Her father had laid out their towels, and then gone walking down the beach. She stepped to the edge of the water. The rush of breaking surf sucked at her feet. Just in front of her Rona and Gibb were hanging onto their inner tubes and laughing, playing some kind of stupid game. She lay back lazily with her arms stretched out and floated, letting the warm water lap over her face. She thought of Gibb, how he talked all the time about "crimes" and how someday he'd be as powerful as Batman and fly all over the city. He'd see all the bad people. No one could hide from him. She smiled a little, but then she felt afraid. What if someone hurt him? What if he went away someday and never came back?

"Rebo," Gibb shouted. "Rebo did it. Rebo's a killer." Rebo was the dumb imaginary man her brother had invented. Gibb was ten and a half but he still made up stories about Rebo. He woke her out of a sound sleep one night and told her Rebo was standing in the closet with a knife. She'd been scared silly and hadn't fallen back to sleep for hours.

Rachel lay down again to float, listening to the gurgle of water in her ears and the muffled sound of voices. Then Rona's screams. Rachel stood up to see Gibb dunking Rona under water. He held her down by the shoulders until she burst up out of his grasp, coughing.

"The drowned girl, the drowned girl, look at the drowned girl," Gibb sang out, jumping up and down in the water until a wide ring of froth encircled him. Rachel started towards them.

When she caught her breath, Rona started screaming. "I swallowed water. He held me under. I couldn't breathe."

The lifeguard blew his whistle. They were too near the line of buoys.

Rachel held out her hand to Gibb. "Come on," she yelled. "We'll get in trouble." He grabbed for her and caught her wrist in a strong hold. His fingers dug into her skin.

"Play the drowning game first!"

She tugged free. "Stop it, you little jerk. I'm telling Dad."

But there was no need. Her father had jumped in the water and was swimming toward them. He stood up next to Gibb, water rolling down his arms and chest, his hair dripping water. He held Gibb by the shoulders. When Gibb tried to break free, Noel shook him and Gibb's head lolled weirdly back and forth. "What were you doing?" he shouted. "What kind of game was that?"

"The drowning game. I was just playing."

Noel's hand rose above the water quickly as a fish leaping and caught Gibb across the face. The red print of his palm rose on Gibb's pale skin. "Don't ever play that again. Go up to the beach and get your things together." He turned to Rachel and Rona. His face frightened Rachel, all twisted into dark, ugly lines like a Halloween mask. "You too, girls."

Clouds had covered the sun and lightning struck in a jagged line at the horizon where several gun-colored freighters headed out to sea. When the thunder sounded, all four of them were on the beach, silently gathering their shoes and towels. As they walked across Ocean Drive, rain began falling in big, warm drops. By the time they'd scrambled into the car, a downpour drummed the car roof and swept the streets. They couldn't even see as far as the end of the block. The only sound in the car was the steady clacking of the windshield wipers. When they got to Rona's house, Rona's good-bye was short and barely polite.

At school the next day in the hall Rachel said hi and Rona said hi back. But during lunch Rona walked past Rachel's table and sat with some other girls. From then on that school year, Rachel was marked. Rachel was different. Her secrets, or what everyone took to be her secrets, clung to her like the mist that rolled across the Everglades canals at night. The rumors began, whispered voices in rooms she'd just left, a curious silence in rooms she entered. Her father was a gangster. No, the Colgroves were too poor for that. He carried a gun. Someone had seen him in Kwik Chek with a policeman walking beside him. He'd robbed, beaten, set fires, molested. He was...a murderer. Rachel wore her badge of shame hidden next to her heart. *They said he wasn't guilty!* But she kept her story to herself.

Soon after that day at the beach Rachel's wide-awake nightmares began, hours of sleeplessness after bedtime prayers, a ritual their parents required.

One night they had recited "Our Father" and "Now I Lay Me" as usual, and Rachel lay awake listening to Gibb's and Jess's breathing, soft and rhythmical. She tried to stay calm. Her mother had left the door open only a crack and beyond the half rectangle of light Rachel saw dark shapes. Her heart began to pound. If I should die before I wake. I pray the Lord my soul to take. She imagined herself dying in her sleep, her soul a shining glob with wings, being snatched away by the hand of an unseen god. Where would the hand take her?

Before Jess was born, her mother had stayed a while by each of their beds, her hand moving softly across their backs, her voice comforting. But now the goodnights were short. One kiss from her father, one from her mother. Some part of Mother had been left somewhere. Her fingers were thin and cold and the shine had gone from her thick black hair. She smelled of medicine. Maybe it was the Listerine she swished in her mouth so many times a day. Rachel had seen her, standing up close to the bathroom mirror, stretching her lips back to look at her teeth, and pouring the golden liquid in the bathroom glass. Once, Rachel had tried a small sip and spit it out instantly, amazed at the awful taste of something so beautiful.

Each night Rachel watched the room grow dark with the inevitable closing of the door. As soon as she shut her eyes, she saw her soul flying through darkness filled with the voices of dead people. How many of them had been murdered? Then she lay with her eyes open—this was the nightmare—hour after hour watching the shapes in the room, the parade of animals from some underground world. Rebo in the closet with a knife. The white-faced ghost girl came almost every night. She wore a dripping, raggedy white dress and had black holes where her eyes should have been. Her brother's drowned girl had seeped into her own brain. She put the pillow over her head so she could scream. *Ahhh.* She watched the shadows until nausea swam through her. She'd try not to be sick, but sometimes it was no use.

Gibb would sit up in the darkness. "Don't Rachel," he'd call to her softly. "Please don't. You'll be okay."

The first few times her parents ran quickly to the bathroom after her. But after a week or so they began to come more slowly, her father sometimes not at all. When he did appear, he stood in the doorframe, filling it. Once, when the gagging stopped and Rachel's mother wiped at her face and mouth with a washcloth, Rachel caught a glimpse of her father, his arms folded. He looked down at her, his mouth fixed in a stern line.

"Stop giving her so much attention," he said. "That's what she wants. For heaven's sake. She's too old for this."

Rachel's mother turned to face him. The light in the bathroom turned pink, then gray, and the floor tiles swam close to her face, their pattern in crazy motion. She lay on the cool floor, curled next to the tub. Her mother started to cry. She heard the sounds of her father's footsteps in the narrow hall. She felt herself falling asleep, her mother's hands tugging at her shoulders, touching her through layers of cloth.

"Rachel, what is it? Tell me." Her mother's voice floated into Rachel's consciousness, thick as water. Tonight she'd close her eyes and her soul would be taken. In the morning her father would find her, thinking she was just sleeping. Just her shell would be left. She'd be hard and brittle as one of her dolls. He'd be sorry then. *My little girl was only eleven when God took her*, he'd say, crying.

The jalousies were wide open to catch a hint of breeze and Gibb heard Rachel's voice ringing through the house. "Come in, Gibb. Daddy's got something he wants us to see."

Gibb pushed the screen door open and let it bang behind him. The sun had made a band of pink across his thin nose. "What is it?"

Elizabeth walked out of the bedroom.

Jess tugged at the hem of her dress. "Daddy brought bag."

"Aren't you home early?" she said to Noel.

"Yes ma'am. I'm home early to watch my kiddies have some fun." He pulled the something out of the bag with a flourish.

"Looks like a pool." Rachel nudged the bright blue plastic with her toe.

Jess clapped his hands and sat down next to Noel, watching him unfold the pool and smooth out the wrinkles in the plastic.

"It's big," Gibb said. He glanced at the deflated pool, then at his father.

"It sure is, so I'm going to need some good lungs to blow it up," Noel said, his eyes resting for a moment on each of his children.

"Don't blow it up in the house and don't drag it across the floor," Elizabeth called to Gibb and Rachel, who had gone outside with Jess between them. They turned on the hose and Jess whipped bright plumes of spray through the air, the way Rachel and Gibb had shown him.

Gibb walked back into the house to find the camera. He stopped when he heard the sound of his parents' voices in the kitchen.

"It's the last thing we need," his mother said.

"Need." His father spoke the word slowly. "It can't always be need, need. Sometimes it has to be *want*. I want to see the children have fun. I want to hear some laughter."

"That's all right for you, but I'm the one who has to count out the pennies, to make the money last."

"You're telling me I'm not a good provider. Is that it?"

"Don't start."

Their voices were low.

"You wouldn't let me take the accounting class. Or take the time off work to study for the real estate exam. How do you expect me to make something of myself selling refrigerators?"

"The bills have to be paid. Nobody waits."

"I'm ruined, aren't I? You never let me forget."

"Stop."

"I want to talk about it. The trial. All of it."

"I don't. It's over, in the past. We have to forget."

"You've never forgotten. You hold it against me every day of my life but you won't talk about it."

"That's right. It's best that way. Be quiet and don't bring it up. Don't bring it up," she hissed. "Haven't you hurt us all enough?"

"Please...I need...I need you."

"I've given you everything I have to give. For the sake of the children, we have to go on."

Their voices fell silent and Gibb waited for one of them to leave the kitchen and find him eavesdropping. He listened to the still air and took a silent breath.

Finally his father spoke again. "Is that what we're doing? I can't live like this. I need someone to talk to. Someone to hold at night. Someone to...make love to."

"I don't know what you're talking about," his mother said. "Make love? Most of the time I even can't bear to have you touch me."

Gibb had heard enough. Quietly, he walked outside, past Rachel and Jess, who were running in to get their suits. Already, they were half soaked, but no one scolded them for tracking water through the house. Their bare feet left a trail—three faint sets of prints on the terrazzo, rugs and wood—as the aroma of coffee slowly began to fill the kitchen. Gibb stood in the backyard for a minute looking at the half-empty pool. He turned on the hose and watched the water ripple above the cheap blue plastic of the pool's bottom. Then he wiped his face and walked inside. He carried a chair over to the hall closet. The camera was on the top shelf. He could just see one dark corner of it. He stepped up onto the chair and eased the camera out of its space. As he pulled the old box Kodak free, something wedged against it, wrapped in a towel, started to fall. Gibb caught it and the towel dropped open. He stared at the photograph in his hands, a framed black and white image of his father beside the boat. His father wore a baseball cap, so that his face was mostly in shadow, and stood with his hand on his hip. New tears welled in Gibb's eyes and he brushed them away, angry. No one would see him cry again, not ever. He wrapped the towel securely around the picture, put it back in its place and checked the window on the camera. Six photos were left on the roll.

Gibb watched Jess smack the water, and then hang onto the side of the pool and kick, pretending he was a motorboat. When Gibb was ready for the picture, Jess stood up primly in the center of the pool, hands at his sides, smiling his best.

"This is a formal portrait," Gibb said seriously. After the click of the shutter, Jess collapsed into giggles and put his face underwater to blow bubbles. Poised at the edge of the pool, Gibb snapped another picture of Jess as he burst up for air. Then Gibb held Jess on his lap and water sloshed around them, the ripples forming patterns that caught the sun and reflected beams of light like polished swords pointing to the sky.

Their mother called them in to dinner. Sunburned and dripping, they stepped from the pool, one by one. Because there was no breeze, the surface of the pool quickly settled to calm in the reddish twilight. Its surface a hard mirror of the evening, the water reflected the cooling sky, the topmost branches of the crepe myrtle and the three Colgrove children silently toweling themselves dry.

At dinner, Gibb watched Jess's eyelids flutter half closed between bites of tuna casserole. Elizabeth's face was set into reproachful lines. She served portions silently, her hands at work, her eyes meeting no one's as she set the plates down. Gibb glanced at Rachel questioningly. His father's face was blank. He heaped a large serving of casserole onto his plate and chewed steadily, gazing above all of their heads.

Taking another serving, he asked Gibb for the salt. As Gibb passed the shaker slowly across the table, above the casserole dish where a few dry, brown-edged noodles clung to the sides, he looked at his father intently. He thought of the boat, his father beside it, tan and slim. The way some boys counted the days till they could drive a car or a motorbike, that was how Gibb longed for a boat of his own. The boat would take him across the bay and out into the ocean, far from the tainted house.

As they ate in silence, Gibb thought of the boat he'd have, a small boat at first, with an outboard motor. As he imagined the purr of the motor through the blue water, he knew suddenly —what he wanted passionately, and what he needed with the same measure of passion. Between the two was a fathomless gap. He didn't know which was more important.

"I remember the time you took me fishing. We caught twenty-three fish," Gibb said finally, looking at his father. "We counted them. Remember? What were they called?" The word *fishing* echoed eerily. There was something defiant about the way Gibb had broken into the silence to speak of the forbidden past.

Noel drew a paper napkin roughly across his mouth before answering. His face was surprised. "Snook."

"I'm going to get a boat. We could all go out together. Wouldn't you like that, Rachel?"

"*I* would!" Jess said excitedly, wide-awake now. "I got toy boat."

"I want to learn to dive…and explore the reefs. I'm going to get a paper route and save money," Gibb said, looking at Rachel. "I'll get my own boat. Anyone who wants can come out with me."

"I hate to tell you, Son—it'll take a lot more than you can earn delivering papers," Elizabeth said, gathering up the dirty dishes.

A deeper flush rose in Gibb's already sunburned face. "You don't think I can do it, but I can. I'm getting a boat and I'm learning to dive. You'll see what I can do. I'll change things," he said mysteriously, looking at each of them. "You'll see."

A few weeks after he'd said he was getting a boat, Gibb had caught Rachel reading from the black loose-leaf notebook he always wrote in. She remembered the last two lines. He said he'd find out who killed a girl named "Neoma"— the one they'd accused her father of killing. They'd fought afterwards, and she'd cried till he'd finally come to comfort her. Why had he been so angry? She didn't think she'd read anything personal, just something about the trial Gibb could never stop thinking about. "You can't read things without people's permission, things that aren't finished," he'd said. Gibb just liked to keep secrets. But he had told her one: He'd already saved five hundred dollars from mowing lawns and delivering the *Miami News* after school. Soon he would be able to buy scuba gear.

She shivered and thought of her nightmares. Neoma, that was the drowned girl who stood dripping at the foot of her bed. Suddenly she remembered a lawyer asking her father questions, over and over. *Did you know her? Where did you meet her? Did you love her?* She remembered a woman's loud sobs. She clapped her hands over her ears. "Stop it!" she said out loud.

From somewhere in the house Jess screamed "Teddy, teddy," and she thought she heard a floorboard creak outside the door. She guessed the sound was only the house settling, as her mother called it, but she was afraid, thinking someone stood outside her door. She lay face-down on her bed. She did *not* remember the trial. She had told Gibb that, and it was true. She did remember the father who had carried her on his shoulders at parades and the smell of his Old Spice. She remembered the father who had gone away, and the one who had come back.

Rachel walked to the window. Gibb was in a low branch of the jacaranda, his back to the trunk, writing in his black notebook. He wasn't figuring sums now, for his hand moved steadily across the page. She wondered what he found to write about day after day.

Gibb had been spending most of his time alone lately. She thought of the differences between Gibb and Jess. Jess never kept to himself the way Gibb did. Anytime they went anywhere Jess could be counted on to walk up to someone and start babbling away, or to pull a perfect stranger over to a toy or book or even a can on the grocery shelf. Whoever it was would always come, smiling.

But the way people felt about Gibb was different. "Don't you think he's weird, Rachel?" one of her friends had whispered. Maybe it was the way Gibb sometimes appeared from behind a bush to glide by them at play, not even glancing in their direction, as if they were invisible. More than once they'd been in the middle of a hushed conversation about a certain boy and had heard that pecu-liar whistle of his—just high notes, never a tune—and they'd looked up to see him high in the Royal Poinciana tree or the jacaranda. Sometimes they'd hear only the whistle, drifting on the breeze, Gibb nowhere in sight.

At these moments Rachel was ashamed of herself for saying nothing, but somehow she wasn't able to find the right words to describe Gibb. She reasoned that the way she might have praised Gibb's talents and mysterious nature would simply have established their silly opinions more firmly.

The fragrance of the jacaranda came to her and she looked up. Gibb was in the same spot, still writing, his elbow stirring the purple blossoms as he turned to a new page. But while she watched, he closed the notebook and put it under his arm. Swinging his legs over the branch, he jumped down from the tree, springing up a little when he hit the ground, like a cat. He saw her at the window, smiled and motioned for her to come out. The bright afternoon sun shone through his pale hair. She turned from the window and heard his whistle, trilled out like a mockingbird's call. The image of Gibb in the sunlight had squeezed its way into her as a sadness and lodged deep in her chest. "I'm coming," she called, making her voice light. "Wait for me."

Three

The year Jess started second grade Elizabeth took a part-time job in a bakery just a few blocks from the house. She left at a quarter to four in the morning. Since she never slept past then anyway, she told them, it was better to be doing something. And besides, they needed the money. Rachel sometimes heard her mother leave, and she imagined Elizabeth walking erect in the scented darkness, facing straight ahead, not even noticing the breeze rustling the palm fronds, the warm gold of the first lighted windows or the sounds of birds. What did her mother think about on those solitary walks?

By eight o'clock Elizabeth was home, just in time to be sure everyone had lunches ready for school. She wore a white uniform of crinkly material, thin as tissue paper, and she smelled of sugar and yeast. Lines of dough stuck under her fingernails. Her hands were still nice, even with all the bleach and scrubbing.

Sometimes when the morning was particularly fine, Rachel wanted to hug her mother and take in the rich warm smell of her, but her mother was always in motion, slicing meat, rounding up books, putting things away. Rachel saw that the course of each of her mother's days was already charted. There was never a moment to waste, not a moment to spare. No time for idleness or idle talk.

Rachel rolled over and looked at the clock. Ten-thirty. She'd only been asleep half an hour. She heard the creak of the heavy wooden ironing board and the thump of the iron. Lying in the darkness with her eyes open, she listened to her brothers' breathing and the louder, more insistent sound of the iron, rhythmic as the bass beat of a lonely song. A memory came to her of her parents long ago, dancing to the record player in the living room. Rachel had been seven or eight. Her mother and father had held each other tightly as they slowly circled the room. She got up, pulled on her robe and crept out of the bedroom. Her mother stood in the kitchen, framed by the door. The bright light had washed color from the objects in the room and given them sharp edges. One of her mother's hands deftly moved the iron, the silver point swooping down on a collar to smooth away the tiniest wrinkle. Her other hand quickly moved the shirt here and there on the ironing board. She bent her head a little, eyes fixed on her hands, and didn't notice Rachel watching.

"Why aren't you sleeping?" Rachel finally asked.

Her mother raised her head and stared for a moment as if she were looking at someone far away, whose voice she'd barely heard. Then she met Rachel's eyes with her own light blue eyes, the color of ice frozen thick.

"Can't sleep. Anyway, I'm getting behind."

"I'll help you."

Her mother smiled faintly as her arm slid up a shirt's back pleat in a single motion. "You have a life. You're young. When I was your age I didn't have time to be young. I was already working for a family." She put the iron down, but still grasped the handle. "I was a DeLile you know. That meant something once." She looked away, shook her head. When she turned again to face Rachel, her eyes shone with tears. "There are so many things I haven't told you. Where have the years gone? My father was a lawyer but he died of TB before he could even get his practice going. I can only remember what he looked like after he was sick. His face got thin and paper-white. Then he died. My mother must have caught it from him. She died about a year later. I was ten. Her sister took me in for awhile but then she said she couldn't keep me anymore." She shrugged her shoulders. "So I went to an orphanage. After that I was on my own until I met your father." She looked out the kitchen window into the darkness. "Your father and you children are my whole life. Despite what you might think when we argue, no matter what, I will always love your father." She turned back and picked up the iron. "You should go to bed. You need your rest."

"I'm not tired."

"You're a stubborn girl," she said. "I know that much about you." She pulled another shirt out of the basket. "You're guarded. You work at it. We're all like that except Jess. We'll go to the grave with our masks on." She moved the iron in and out along a row of buttons. "What would it be like to really know another person? To look into someone and see everything there was to see?" Putting the iron down, she folded her arms. "Even then, would you understand anything? Do you know what I'm talking about?"

Rachel nodded. She wanted instead to say *stop stop. I don't want to remember.* But she stood in silence and listened.

"Your father...people believed he killed someone." Her eyes blazed up, darkening the blue unnaturally, like dye poured into water. "The crime was never solved. I don't believe it ever will be. That's broken your father, the doubt lingering in people's minds," she murmured. She positioned the collar of another shirt on the ironing board and began to work again, the motion deliberate and measured, the iron once more making the sounds Rachel had heard in bed. "Goodnight, Rachel," she said without looking up again.

"Goodnight." Rachel walked out of the kitchen and through the darkened house, the light of the room behind her. In the bedroom, she took off her robe and lay down, remembering what she didn't want to remember—that out there, somewhere, was a murderer. He lived in her mind, at the edge of her consciousness. He possessed her. He possessed all of them, especially Gibb. Rachel listened to her mother ironing, the sound going on and on, even after she'd fallen deeply asleep.

Rachel closed her trig book. She was sick of working math problems. She walked out of the bedroom, stood where her father couldn't see her and watched him ease the bottle of Old Crow from the cabinet, fill half a glass and take a long swallow. He shuddered a little. She imagined the bourbon burning its way down his throat to his stomach, a heat gleaming with the liquor's rich syrupy color. Pushing himself away from the counter, like a man shoving off from a dock, he made a steady course for the living room. Her mother sat in a triangle of light, reading. When her father stepped into the room, her mother turned the page of her ever-present book, but didn't look up. Gibb squatted on the floor with his diving gear spread on an old sheet. Her father's hand found its way into his pocket for a mint, and he brought the candy to his lips.

Gibb stood. "Dad, this's my scuba gear. What do you think?"

"It's your money," Noel said loudly, glancing in Elizabeth's direction, "you can do what you want with it."

"I'll show you how the mask and regulator work."

"Not now, son, I've got to read brochures on the new Amana. This Frigidaire should be in everyone's home." He pronounced the sentences carefully and they came out sounding almost the way they should have. These were words he'd practiced over and over again during the day. He didn't drink at work. Rachel thought he had a certain sad dignity when he talked about his work. He walked slowly to the cluttered table where he kept his papers, held up a flyer with a glossy black and white picture of a refrigerator, unfolded it like a map, then slowly put it down and smoothed the paper flat. Rachel couldn't see her mother's face behind her book, and Gibb's head was bent low, as he worked to adjust his face mask. She saw her father turn slowly away from the table, and with careful strides, walk back to the kitchen. Neither Gibb nor Elizabeth looked up.

Rachel slipped from her hiding place and went into the bedroom she shared with Jess and Gibb.

The little milk glass lamps on either side of the room cast a weak light, but they'd been a bargain, just three books of Top Value stamps for the pair. She remembered the day Gibb had helped paste the stamps into books before he and their mother had gone to the redemption store on the bus—how he'd licked yellow stamps, hundreds of them, until his mouth must have grown dry and sour-tasting from the glue. For two ugly lamps that didn't give much light.

Jess sat on the floor in the middle of the room working on a puzzle. The small part he'd put together so far was no more than a patch of random shades and colors, an irregular stain against the gray cardboard of the box.

"Hey," Gibb said, coming into the room and sitting down beside Jess, "what's this going to be?" He peered at the jagged confusion of lines, looking for a pattern.

Jess showed him the shiny picture on the box's cover, a four-masted schooner on a frothy sea. "I can finish by tomorrow, I bet."

"Say, Jess, I can't find the string. Do you know..."

Jess bounded up. He was the finder of lost things, with a drawerful of trinkets he'd seen gleaming deep in grass, spotted on the street, coins and medallions, tieclips, broken necklaces and buttons.

In the house, nothing could be lost for long. "I know!" he cried, half-running down the hall.

They watched him disappear and closed the door.

"Dad's drunk again," Gibb said.

Rachel looked up from the table where an algebra book lay next to a notebook filled with problems. "So what else is new?"

"We've got to do something."

She watched Gibb slip a brown piece of the puzzle into place. Part of the mast or deck? The hull or the cabin, according to the picture. But couldn't the pieces form something else? A giant beetle crawling along a blue wall, maybe.

"Why? He doesn't yell, he doesn't bother us."

"Don't you think it's weird he and Mother hardly ever say anything to each other anymore? At least they used to fight once in a while."

Jess threw open the door, a ball of twine held in both hands like an offering. "Found it," he said proudly.

"Wow, you did, thanks," Gibb said, putting out his hand.

"Are you gonna dance?" Jess clutched the string to his chest, suddenly shy.

"Yeah," Gibb said. "Pick something, Rachel."

Rachel took her box of forty-fives from under the record player and sat down at her desk. Jess came up to her and put his hand on her knee. His palm was warm against her bare skin. She touched his hair and vowed to keep him safe, always.

"Play 'Hound Dog,' please."

"We danced to that last night," Gibb said, pushing the beds up against the walls and rolling the braided rug to stand it on end. "It's old."

"I like it."

"Okay," Rachel said. She and Gibb got ready for the first line, their hands loose in one another's, faces taut with looks of concentration that would disappear at the first guitar break. She and Gibb danced together better than anyone they knew.

Well, they said you was high class
Well, that was just a lie

They liked to imagine crowds in the bleachers on American Bandstand watching the two of them doing all the new steps, like the kids Dick Clark smiled down on—the cheerleaders and quarterbacks whose fathers played golf together and smoked Cuban cigars. Jess played the judge, practicing his printing skills. *Very good*, he wrote, *you win*.

They put on another record and danced again. At that moment, their minds were washed clear of everything else. Jess sang along. Even though he was just in second grade he knew the words to the songs they danced to. Most afternoons they'd come home and find him playing his toy piano in time to the radio. They clapped then, and praised him.

Rachel and Gibb danced for an hour, sweating and heady with stifled laughter, the silent living room forgotten, Jess tugging on their clothes to make them read what he'd written. They both saw his sturdiness, his face already grown strong in its features, and handsome. They shared a secret as their eyes met—their pride in him. The Colgrove children would always be together. Nothing could part them.

They put Jess to bed at nine and took a walk, slipping out the garage door into the scented darkness, feeling the fresh air in their faces like wind off water, like a suddenly granted freedom. The rustle of lizards and the grating, broken sound of crickets rose up around them. They talked in hushed voices, stepping silently in their bare feet down the still-warm sidewalks.

Rachel talked about high school, how sick she was of the ordinariness, the teachers who did not teach at all or those who lectured in the twilight of advanced age. Each boring day was another obstacle between her and college. And Gibb talked about diving, always, the other world. She saw in his descriptions the platinum sunlight filtering down, a hundred glittering fish darting by in a single motion. "Aren't you afraid?" she asked.

"Sure," he said, "sometimes. But the only monsters down there are dumb humans." He paused and crossed his arms, staring down at the sidewalk. "They'll spear a moray or take a shark as a trophy." He shook his head. "Those creatures belong to time," he said, "not to assholes like that."

"What're writing in your journal these days?"

He didn't answer for a long time. They walked and she waited, listening hard in the darkness, hearing the faint sound of them breathing in unison. "I'm trying to unravel a few mysteries," he said finally with a harsh laugh. "Isn't that funny? I'll be able to tell you more someday."

"Tell me now," she pleaded.

"No," he said. "I can't."

She saw her own sorrow captured in his face and didn't ask again. When she reached out and grabbed his arm, he turned to her in surprise. "Promise you'll always be my best friend," she said.

"Yeah," he said, smiling. "You know I'd do anything for you."

She would do anything for Gibb, too. She studied his profile and saw the features they shared. She didn't care anymore that people thought they were odd—all of them. She wore her oddness like a flag, for everyone to see, dressing in her mother's old fancy dresses with brass buttons, in moth-scented jackets with grosgrain piping, clothes saved from another age, bought at rummage sales. Arraying herself in these sometimes mad, out-of-style costumes, Rachel had let her dark hair grow long and go wild. "That mane would stay healthier if you trimmed it once in a while," her mother said at least every other day. But Rachel cherished the image of herself wild as her wild-animal hair.

Rachel did what she wanted in spite of everyone. She ringed her eyes with black pencil, smoked Old Golds at lunchtime without getting caught and was haughty with the teachers, causing them to rasp out her name in two exasperated, disapproving syllables. She read, made A's, and went on her way alone.

Standing in the archway between the living room and dining room, her hand on the cool plaster, Rachel watched her mother and father read. She'd caught them between pages and they sat still as wax figures, butter-colored light spilling over them. She held the letter she'd gotten in the afternoon's mail, her acceptance to the University of Florida on a scholarship. She'd come to show them, but now she no longer wanted to bother. They'd nod approval be-tween the ticks of the glass-domed clock and the turning pages and would whisper, "That's nice Rachel, good for you." Cocking her head to one side, she squinted to see the lettering on the spines of her mother's books: a new assortment weekly, borrowed from the library — *The ABC's of Old Glass*, *Gardening in Containers*, biogra-phies of Helen Keller, Mary Baker Eddy, Charles Lindbergh, Isadora Duncan, and *A Man Called Peter*, never a novel. Her mother didn't approve of novels. Rachel wondered if beyond that solemn counte-nance her mother's mind was lively with activity, like a house where a spirited party was in progress, rooms furnished with the things her mother read about, the revelers and conversations, too, straight from her books.

Watching her father's motionless form, Rachel suspected he slept tonight instead of reading. He held his favorite book in front of his face, *The Best Loved Poems of the American People*. He'd marked the ones he most admired with newspaper cut into neat rectangles: "Death is a Door," "Invictus," "We Are Seven," and "How Did You Die?" From the spot where she sometimes studied in the dining room, she'd seen him many nights close the book, fold his arms over his chest and stare at the bare wall across the room. She'd learned to take her homework then and disappear, knowing what would hap-pen next, her father's eyes streaming tears, his cheeks and nose soon mottling to the color of an overripe plum.

Rachel glanced at the mantelpiece where five faces—a photo-graph of each of them—gazed politely from their separate frames, into the room. When she went away to college, she'd pack her own photograph, and then throw it in the first trash bin she could find, to leave no part of her to see and hear what went on in this house. The shadows hovering in the corners of the living room were full of secrets, and stories clung to the hallway dust like the hulls of in-sects. Lies, like tiny black ants, visited the kitchen at night when no one could see them. Yet they all went on and did nothing. Rachel turned.

"Sis?"

She paused before glancing back at her father, who had already started to get up and walk towards her. She waited.

"Have a minute?" he asked, tilting his head to one side, coyly as a child, the book of poetry pressed to his chest. "Something I'd like you all to listen to."

Rachel waited, the letter behind her back.

Her father stopped at her mother's chair and tapped her on the shoulder. "You too," he said.

Her mother stood up at once, as if she'd been struck, her eyes alert, but the rest of her features slack with indifference.

Rachel and her mother walked behind him to the bedroom. She searched her mother's face in profile. Rachel's cheeks felt suddenly warm and taut. She was ashamed at the thought her mother no longer loved her. She wanted to turn, to feel her mother's arms around her and to breathe in the sweet powder smell her mother's body had once worn so long ago. But she only stood straighter and stubbornly fixed her eyes on the dark slab of her father's back, moving steadily toward the bedroom door.

Her father opened the door to his children's bedroom and took a step in, staggering slightly, then striding firmly to Rachel's desk where Gibb and Jess sat side-by-side, as Gibb read aloud from *20,000 Leagues Under the Sea.*

"Now listen," he said, "all of you. We better start acting like a family again before it's too late."

Taller than anyone, he hovered in the room, stealing the air, until Rachel felt her lungs ache with the effort of breathing. *Get out,* she wanted to scream. *Take the shadows and sadness with you and leave us alone!*

The record Gibb had been playing stuck on a scratch and the same line came again and again—

Twistin', twistin', twistin' the night away.

Rachel walked to the record player and moved the arm from the disk. Her father seemed not to have noticed the music. As he looked out the window into the darkness, his gaze locked upon something. A sudden breeze lifted the pages of an open notebook lying on the desk, and he turned from the window, his eyes wide and brilliant. He passed his hand across his face and began to read. "No shamefaced outcast ever sank so deep / But yet might rise and be again a man. / Art thou a sinner? Sins may be forgiven; / Each morning gives thee wings to flee from hell, / Each night a star to guide thy feet to Heaven." He paused dramatically, looking at each of them. "You see?" he asked, sweat beading on his forehead. "Here, listen to this." The pages flew by his thumb to a marked place. "Beautiful lives are those that bless / Silent rivers of happiness, / Whose hidden fountains few may guess." Noel closed his eyes for a moment and slowly shook his head. "I wish one of you children would take an interest in writing." His eyes fluttered open. "It's a gift to be able to write, to express yourself." He glanced backwards at Elizabeth. "But at least we can talk to each other. We can converse if we try."

A look of anger flickered across Elizabeth's face, but in a moment the lines settled and her expression fell away to blankness. "It's a lot easier to talk about being a man than to be one," she said calmly. "Go on and recite your poems, but you'd be better off reading the Bible again if it's forgiveness you want." She turned and walked to the door. "I'm going to sleep," she said, disappearing into the shadowy hall.

"You see," he said, shrugging his shoulders, his voice half a whisper, "what I've had to put up with all these years?" He leaned toward them confidentially. "I'm not a pariah," he said hoarsely. "I've done wrong, but I'm not an evil man."

Gibb and Jess still sat at the desk and Rachel stood beside them. Gibb got up and walked to his father. "Why don't you go to bed, Dad?"

"I want one of you to save me," Noel said, his voice thin and high as an old man's. "Do you know what I mean? I want one of you to save me. Please." He grabbed Gibb by the shoulders and wept. "I'm sorry," he said, "I'm sorry for all the trouble I've caused you."

Four

On his last day of school, Gibb spun the knob on his combination lock, swung open the locker, pulled out a wadded-up gray sweatshirt and threw it in the grocery sack he'd brought from home that morning. A few pieces of orange peel lay in a corner of the locker, dry and rigid as curls of wood. He started to scoop them into the bag, but it didn't seem to matter. Orange peel left a better smell than dirty socks or rotten baloney sandwiches.

Before he pulled out the two notebooks, he glanced around to see if anyone else was in the hallway but he was alone. He dropped the notebooks into the bag. In a storm of banging lockers, hoots, whistles, and laughter, most of the kids had left the school at least half an hour ago. He'd watched the parking lot empty, souped-up cars trembling as drivers revved their engines, girls resting their smooth, bare arms on car windows, waiting for a last goodbye. Then he'd strolled down the halls, past each silent classroom with its overflowing wastebasket and jumble of empty desks.

Gibb slipped one of the notebooks out of the bag again and opened it to a page where he'd carefully mounted a glossy 8 x 10 photograph on heavy paper. The black and white print was grainy; he'd had it made from a snapshot. He studied the girl's face, the dark spot in part of her smile. Maybe she was missing a back tooth or the negative had been damaged. Her hair was light—a mass of fine hair—the kind so delicate it floats instead of getting tangled when the wind catches it. He bit his lower lip and frowned, tracing the line of Neoma Kelch's small nose, as if the picture were three-dimensional. Who could have killed a pretty girl like that? After a couple of years of research, he finally had some information, some clues. With luck, he'd find out who did it. But he needed more than luck.

After a minute he closed the notebook and put it back in the grocery bag, folding the top of the bag over so he could carry it inconspicuously under his arm.

He heard footsteps, echoing down the tiled hallway, getting louder. He glanced at his watch. Russ was right on time for their meeting. Russ Patterson had delivered papers with him a year ago.

The lights were dimmed already and Gibb squinted to be sure. It was Russ all right. No mistaking that walk. Russ whistled softly and the sound reverberated in the empty hall.

"Hey, man," Russ said as he approached Gibb, his voice low. He was a good three inches taller than Gibb, thin and bony. He had rounded shoulders and a loose, lazy way of walking. "Don't you wish you were a senior," he said, hovering over Gibb. "You could leave this dump forever." Russ had already graduated from Palmetto High in South Maimi. He opened his mouth wide to laugh and threw his head back a little, but hardly any sound came out, not more than a rasp of air. "You could join the living," he said, fixing his eyes on Gibb's. His features were small except for a full and shapely mouth, which redeemed his face, making him almost handsome.

"I don't care about having to come back," Gibb said, taking the lock off and closing the locker. "I'm part of the living already." He turned to face Russ and watched his mouth open in another silent laugh. "What did you want to tell me?"

"Like I said on the phone, I found out something for you, man. I found somebody." Russ slowly shifted his weight from one foot to the other. "Sorry to ask you for dough. I'm kinda down on my luck right now."

Ever since Gibb had known him, Russ had been down on his luck. Gibb wondered how long it would take Russ to end up in Raiford Prison for some petty crime. Gibb got out his wallet and put two ten-dollar bills in Russ's palm. Russ was one of only a few people who knew how involved Gibb was with trying to exonerate his father, how much time he had spent combing through newspapers and trying to find people who had had something to do with the trial or who had known Neoma Kelch. Russ had promised that his lead was a good one.

"Who is it?"

"This guy, he'll want some dough too. He's a loser."

"Who is it?"

"It's that guy who worked at the marina. That McGrath guy. Turns out he's a hoddie for one of my cousins. I met him out at a job a couple days ago. Recognized the name from that clipping you showed me. I'll take you over to his place. I told him I was bringing you by. He'll talk to you for money. Give him thirty and he'll talk to you."

"Where's your car?"

"Over by the side entrance." Russ turned and began to walk down the hall.

They passed the rows of lockers and stopped a minute at the glassed-in case where both shiny new and tarnished trophies stood among five decades of Miami High team pictures. How many of the football heroes were dead, Gibb wondered, with a touchdown pass or game-winning yardage having been their life's most glorious moment?

"Ever go in for sports?" Russ asked, turning to Gibb, his eyes glinting in the dim spotlights above the trophy case.

"Just diving."

Russ thumped his chest. "Me, believe it or not—as in Ripley's—I broke the quarter mile record for the butterfly at Palmetto." He dropped his cigarette on the cement floor and ground it out with his heel.

Gibb could not imagine Russ ever moving rapidly, especially in water.

"My lungs are probably shot now. Couldn't save myself if I was drowning." He laughed his silent laugh again, shoulders moving up and down.

"What are you boys doing?" The voice came from a distance, echoing a little.

Gibb turned. A stocky man approached them from about fifty feet away, taking quick, small steps and swinging his arms aggressively. It was Mr. Grover, the assistant principal.

His manner became friendlier when he recognized Gibb. "I'm surprised to see you here so late. I thought all you kids wanted to do on the last day was get away as fast as you could." He cast a suspicious glance at Russ.

"Russ used to deliver papers with me and he's never seen our school. Russ, this is Mr. Grover."

Russ raised the tips of his fingers to his forehead in a half-salute. "Hey," he said.

"Pleased to meet you, Russ. Glad you came by." Mr. Grover put his hand in his pocket and began to jingle his keys. "I'm locking up, so I'll have to hurry you fellas along."

"That's okay, Mr. Grover, we're on our way out."

"See you in the fall then. Have a good summer."

"Thanks. You too," Gibb said as he and Russ turned to walk away.

"Say, Gibb?"

Gibb glanced back.

"Rachel Colgrove's your sister isn't she?"

"Yes sir."

"Tell her good luck. Wish her all the best in college for me. I hope she's looking forward to it."

"She sure is." Gibb thought of the date for freshman registration that Rachel had already circled in red on the calendar. He tried to imagine the house without her, silence where her voice had been, the whole of her gone.

"Well, don't let me keep you."

"So long, Mr. Grover."

When they were in the car Russ gunned the GTO's engine a couple of times and they pulled away.

McGrath's duplex was at the fringe of one of the poorest sections in north Miami. Russ pulled into a dirt driveway adjacent to the rundown building. A jagged crack traveled the length of the foundation, close to the ground. Someone had planted hibiscus bushes on either side of the two concrete slabs in front of the duplexes' doors, but they hadn't flourished in the silty soil. Each bore only a few misshapen red blossoms. Russ knocked on the jalousies, and the door swung open. A man stood in the dim light of the tiny living room. The furniture was sparse—a sagging couch, a couple of folding chairs, a single end table and a dinette set. Russ jerked a thumb at the man. "This here's Bix."

Gibb slowly said his own name while Bix squinted at him, as if he were closing his eyes by habit against the relentless sun. Bits of dried mortar spattered his thin white t-shirt, and he gave off a smell of smoke, sweat and dust.

"Russ told me who was coming," he said, after taking a deep drag on his cigarette.

Gibb reached for his wallet, but Bix waved him away. "I don't want your money. I want to tell you what I have to tell. You can listen. Nobody remembers anymore, but my picture was in the newspaper." He pointed to the table and chairs. "Sit down," he said.

Gibb studied Bix's weathered face and faded, unkempt hair. He could not remember seeing him at the trial. Bix was close to his father's age, or maybe a little older, and he could tell the man had once been called "handsome." Just as his father had been.

Their chairs scraped across the bare terrazzo floor, and they sat. "Git yerself a Schlitz, there, Russ. Bring out a couple for us, this kid and me." Russ disappeared into the deeper gloom of the kitchen. "I want to talk," Bix said. "I never got my day in court, not the way I should have." He put his big, scarred hands on the table. "Flashbulbs goin' off," he said. "People askin' me what I thought. That never happened to me before and it hasn't happened since. So I'll tell you if you want to know so bad." He drank from his beer, and a bit of foam dribbled down his stubbled chin. He pushed the can closer to Gibb. "Drink," he said, "drink up."

Gibb took a swallow. He had never tasted beer before. It was cold and bitter.

"I had a lot of women before that day. Some after. I even got married once, but she left me. I still know what their looks mean. Them sweet looks, how they find your eyes and lock on. They dip down just a little bit and show themselves, just enough of their titties to make your mouth go dry. They sway when they walk and look back at you, over those thin white shoulders." He pulled another cigarette from the pack on the table. "Those two, that girl and your pop, they were an item...I swear it. I watched them long enough to see how they looked at each other. Anyone would know what them looks meant. I tried to swear it in court, but that lawyer guy made me look like a dummy." He put the cigarette in the ashtray and seemed to ponder it a while before picking it up again. "After the trial I had some girlies who were really interested in gettin' to know me. They'd seen my picture in the news. We drove on down to the Keys together for some good times. I missed a couple days of work and they fired me!" He lifted his weathered hand. "I was a popular guy back then, but after that trial, it was like a curse was laid on me, like *I* was a murderer or something." He drank more beer and brought the can down hard on the Formica table. "Talk to your old man, kid. Ask him straight out what he did that day. See if he blinks or turns away. Now get outta here."

Gibb looked into the man's small, watery eyes. They seemed about to close against the world. It would make no sense to tell McGrath that he already had asked his father "straight out." His father was a weak man, but he was no liar and no murderer. This man was a liar, Gibb could see that. A liar and a loser, just as Russ had said. Gibb finished his beer. "Do you know anything else? Did you find out anything more after the trial?"

"Rumors. Lots of rumors. Folks who knew what your pop did after night school. Some might have truth to them. Why don't you try to find the mother, that Kelch woman, and see what she knows about the old days?"

But Gibb was a step ahead of Bix. He had found Bertha Kelch, and her granddaughter, Amanda. Now he needed to find a way to meet her, to meet both of them. He savored the name. *Amanda.* He had followed her, saw how much she resembled her mother, yet with features even more delicate and beautiful.

Gibb asked Russ to drop him off a few blocks from his house. Russ pulled to the curb.

"I hope you got what you wanted," Russ said, leaning over and grabbing the door handle.

"Everything helps," Gibb said

"Keep in touch."

Gibb nodded and tucked the shopping bag with Neoma Kelch's picture firmly under his arm. Russ screeched down the street, the silver car rocking a little when he shifted gears. Gibb looked up and down the empty block and blinked, his eyes still not used to the bright afternoon sun and the intense green of early summer.

An unsolved crime.

The words sounded in his head like a series of skipped heartbeats. He'd find what he needed to find, to step from the knife-edge he walked, between the past and the present. Time would make sense to him again. He'd make sense to himself. He would keep unraveling the mystery of what had happened those long ago days, thread by thread and seeing each new piece of the whole would continue to bring him the near-delirious pleasure he felt at this moment. He pushed past the drooping branch of an orchid tree and headed down the sidewalk for home.

"I love you," her boyfriend, Gene, breathed into Rachel's ear. "Don't go. I'll only be able to see you on weekends." He pressed his mouth over hers and kissed her for a long time. She felt herself falling in the darkness, swirling away, losing the part of her mind that said "don't" and "can't." Once, such kissing had frightened her, but now she welcomed the deep languidness of the feeling, as if she were slipping into a pool of soothing water.

"Don't go," Gene said. His hand lifted her blouse, and then eased under her bra. She pushed his fingers from her nipples, but the sharp, sweet pain had come already, an ache that gathered in her like a knot. He brushed her lips with his and drew back to look at her. "I won't hurt you," he said softly.

"I know." Rachel remembered the time she'd first seen Gene, coming into the White Castle from the rain, walking the same carefree way he always walked, a tall, lanky boy, with sandy hair and honey-brown eyes. He was soaked, but he stamped his feet and brushed his shoulders as if that were enough to dry him. He'd flung drops of water everywhere, leaving a puddle around his feet on the black and white tile. Grinning at her and the girl she was with, he'd gotten his order and he'd winked before pushing open the door and striding out. They'd watched him retreat with a bag of burgers and fries under his jacket, blurred by the rain rolling down the plate glass window. Then her friend ran to the jukebox before Rachel could stop her and played "He's So Fine," by The Chiffons. Rachel had hidden her face in her hands, laughing.

But Gene wasn't smart and he wasn't going to college.

Rachel pulled away gently and straightened her blouse.

"What did I do?"

She heard the hurt in his voice and wished she could comfort him. But what could she say that wouldn't be a lie? "Nothing. I just have to go." She turned to look into the darkness. The scritch of the crickets rose up all around, loud as the gears of a huge machine, turning and grinding. If the crickets stopped, the night would stop too, and the darkness would drift away aimlessly as if it had been no more than black smoke, a magician's trick. Was that why Gibb liked the night so much, and the blue light of the reefs? Things didn't look as ugly in the darkness as they did in the relentless sun—shacks with scrawny abandoned dogs scratching in the dirt, or the drunks who lay in Bayfront Park sleeping it off. She was young. She could still escape the ugliness. A bullfrog grunted in the distance and something splashed into the canal near where they were parked. "What was that?" she said.

"A coconut." He slid away from her and started the car. He sounded so unhappy that she wondered what harm there would have been in letting him hold and kiss her a while longer. In a week, she'd be gone.

A good person would have told him straight out that once she was gone to college she wouldn't be seeing him anymore, that she'd let him fade to a sweet memory kept only faintly alive in the single photograph of them together, the one taken in April under a crepe-paper-streaming archway before the Spring Follies Dance. But she wasn't a good person. When she searched beneath her confident facade for evidence of goodness or kindness all she found was her intractable self, hard as a chunk of coral rock, full of secrets, acting as she had to act.

"If there's anything I can do...," Gene said. Instead of driving as he usually did, with one elbow carelessly jutting out the window, he hunched over the wheel, steering with both hands, eyes fixed on the road.

She thought of the weather, glad for the mild night and the velvety blue-black sky prickled with starlight. The windows in both doors of Gene's old Ford were cracked and he always kept them rolled down so he wouldn't get a ticket.

"You could go to junior college," she offered hopefully. "Then transfer." How casually she lied, her voice gentle. But she couldn't stop herself, faint-hearted, almost breathless in the face of his sadness. Gene, along with her brothers, was one of three people in the world who really loved her. She didn't dare take love for granted.

"I'll love you forever, Rachel," Gene said, as if reading her mind. "Whatever happens between us, I'll always be around if you need me. Just remember that."

Despite the warm air, a shiver passed over her shoulders like the touch of a bony hand. Some of the girls she knew were engaged, a speck of diamond on a thin band showing on their ring fingers. They'd get married and *then* go to college; that's what they said. Any of these girls would gladly have exchanged their dependable husbands-to-be—all doggedly ready to settle into trades or steady jobs as produce managers at the nearby Kwik Chek—for carefree Gene. Yes, thinking of the beautiful babies they'd have and the nights of love promised by his deep and thick-lashed bedroom eyes, those girls would walk right out on their Dwaynes and Bruces and Eddies if Gene—Rachel's Gene—beckoned.

"I mean it," Gene said, looking at her finally, and Rachel looked back in a kind of embarrassed surprise.

"I know," she said, as the lights of a car passing from the other direction washed over his face, making it ghostly, a face from a dream. Watching the light fade, the set of his jaw, she forgot for a moment what he'd just said. Yes, he would be there if she needed him. "Thanks." She bit her lip. If she bit down hard enough she could cause herself pain, feel enough to cry, maybe.

He waited at the light to turn onto Dixie Highway, staring into the intersection.

"Green," she said.

He took the turn slow. "Why do you need to get away from home so bad?" He glanced at her. "Look at me," he said. "My father hasn't been around for a couple years, my ma's got a new boyfriend every week, she's never home. I'm the one should be leaving."

She thought for a moment of her small house, the room she still shared with her brothers. Four or five years ago, her father had built a desk and put it in the room. "Her place," he'd called it. Because she was a girl, he said, he'd painted the desk a bright, hideous pink.

She never asked kids over after school or to spend the night, so most of them thought she was stuck up and didn't try to get to know her.

"I just do," she said finally. "It's haunted."

Gene laughed. "I don't believe in ghosts."

"You would if you lived in my house," she said, putting her feet up on the seat and drawing her arms around her knees.

"Just be glad you don't live in one of those places." He pointed to the frame shacks just off the highway, windows broken, the wood unpainted and cracking, clumps of weeds poking up out of ash-gray dirt.

"People could love each other in those houses as well as anywhere," she said wistfully.

"You don't even want to know what goes on in those places. Roaches thick on the walls. No bathrooms in some." He shrugged. "You're crazy. What's so bad about your house...except the ghosts?" He tried to smile.

"What do you know about me? Once my parents went a month without talking to each other." Rachel twirled a strand of hair around her finger.

"Not talking's better than throwing things at each other like my folks did when they were together. Screaming, cussing. Once my dad gave my ma two black eyes."

"You can see black eyes."

Gene's face was quizzical. "What?"

She thought of her father, moving through the house in the darkness, night after night when he couldn't sleep. If people were crippled or blind from the war, like fathers of kids she knew, you could tell what was wrong with them right away. What about things that didn't show on the outside? Things that had happened, that people carried around with them like dead legs and heavy braces. They were there just the same. You just couldn't see them.

"Up north like that in Gainesville won't even seem like Florida anymore. No ocean."

No ocean. She'd miss that. She thought of Gibb, who would never leave the ocean. The great, forgiving sea had taken him in as if it was his real country and land was the foreign place.

"Were your parents ever in love, Rachel?"

Rachel thought of the snapshots she'd seen of her mother and father on the beach before they were married. There was something easy about the way her father's arm draped over her mother's shoulder in those old pictures. And her mother's smile was full of life, as if she'd just taken a breath of the sweetest air in the world. But then, they were not yet her parents. "No," she said finally, "they never were."

The morning they all were to drive to Gainesville, Rachel flicked on the bathroom light, blinking as her eyes adjusted to the bleached, bare gleam of the walls and tile. She'd hardly slept, imagining all night the road winding out in front of her like a worn ribbon, the steady drone of the car's engine in her head, hour after hour.

Last night, she'd finished packing, stuffing just a few more things she wanted to take into one of her suitcases, looking one more time at the things she was leaving behind, things that belonged to all three of them, like the records and shell collection, the scrapbooks. Everything she was bringing fit into two string-tied cardboard boxes and two brown paper-peeling suitcases that her parents had had for twenty years, from the looks of them.

Some time after dinner, her father had taken her aside. Her stomach tightened as they'd walked out on the porch and into the warm darkness. The dim yellow bug light turned their faces and their clothes colors that were sickly and harsh. He hadn't said good luck or that he'd miss her.

Trying to remember his exact words, she ran the water on her hands and rubbed them together until the heat soaked into her skin. "Don't come home till you've finished school," he'd said, his face so close to hers she'd smelled aftershave and his breath, sweetish and stale, and seen in his features and the line of his jaw the shadow of a man who'd once been handsome. Turning away from her, he'd stared up into the sky, at the stars twinkling through fine clouds, at the sickle moon, something dangerous and fragile at the same time. A breath of wind could break it in two and shards would fall that could cleave buildings.

"Look at all this," he said, his hand sweeping above his head. "It makes me feel like a nothing." He looked at her. "I was a proud man once. I knew who I was. Somebody with drive, a life…. His voice trailed off, then he laughed harshly. She stood silent beside him until his own silence seemed to dismiss her. Walking back toward the house, she felt damp grass brush the sides of her sandaled feet and heard his voice behind her, soft. "Goodnight, little girl."

She turned on the shower and checked her watch: 5:20. Was she wrong to leave Gibb and Jess? She pushed the question out of her mind. They'd leave too, soon enough. Already she could feel a hollow spot, like a hunger, a loneliness for them she'd never get over. Stepping into the shower, she raised her face to the hot water, letting it soak her hair and warm her whole body. With her eyes closed, she imagined herself gone, standing in the dormitory shower already, no longer home.

A wheat-colored haze hung over the flat highway. They sat at a train crossing, fanning themselves, as one boxcar after another clacked by. In less than an hour they'd be pulling into Gainesville.

Her father stared ahead, his jaw tight, a muscle twitching just below his ear. Jess slept, slumped down in the back seat, his face against Gibb's hip. Gibb had come only because she had begged him. He sat with his arms folded across his chest, looking out the window, his long, pale hair blown into tangles by the wind. Her mother, too, gazed out the side window, shading her eyes once in a while as if to focus better on some point of interest near the car. But in her field of vision was only a lot overgrown with weeds and sprinkled with rusty cans that people waiting for never-ending trains had thrown there.

The sun had shone fiercely all day, robbing the landscape of color and shade. Rachel had watched the last of Miami spill out into the Everglades until finally the thick black-green curtain of Australian pines rushed past them, nearly screening the canal, so that she caught only tiny glints of sunlight reflecting off the water's surface.

Gibb gently punched her on the shoulder. "I bet you can't wait to try out for a sorority, huh?" he said softly, almost in a whisper, mocking.

She turned to him and smiled. Seeing his face full on startled her. His eyes were bloodshot and his face was pale and puffy, even though Gibb was thin as a stick. It was August and he should have been tan, the sun and heat of late summer showing on him in a flush of health. Instead, his skin looked bleached. At the beginning of the month he'd been diving practically every day, but now he spent hours away from home or sitting in the backyard writing in his notebook. Too much solitude, she decided. He smiled back at her, his mouth twisting up in a half-grin, but his eyes weren't on hers. He looked beyond her. She wanted to grab his hand and make him tell her what was wrong. *Nothing*, he'd say. She imagined him going down into the green and silvery water, bright at first, then cloudy as he swam deeper. *Tell me, tell me now*, she'd coax, insist. And he would finally confide in her as always, tell her some troublesome thought. Just last week he'd asked her: *Who really killed that girl? Wouldn't you like to know?* She hadn't wanted to talk about it, but she'd answered anyway. *It was a long time ago*, she'd said. *I try not to think about it.*

Gibb's smile faded. His eyes focused on her face and searched it in a way that was fearful and puzzled. But before she could decide what his curious expression meant, the look vanished. Folding his arms, he smiled again suddenly, "College," he laughed softly, shaking his head. "Oh boy." He paused and looked at her a moment longer before turning once more to the window to rest his forehead against the glass.

Rachel leaned forward, away from the seat's torn vinyl. Her thin blouse was soaked. She pushed the thought from her mind that she wouldn't see Gibb tomorrow, wouldn't be able to ask him, *What were you thinking about yesterday, when you looked at me like that?* Sweat rolled down her neck, between her breasts. The car smelled of sweat.

Her mother still stared out the window, hands in her lap, twisting her thin wedding band. Her hair, which had started to turn gray a few years ago, was dark again, a flat, toneless color. She kept it short now, permed and sprayed stiff.

Rachel saw that the road ahead was patched, the asphalt carelessly splattered down and never leveled. Her father hit one of the black mounds, jolting the car.

"Noel!" Elizabeth cried sharply. She held her face in her hands.

"What's wrong?" Noel glanced at her, drawing his hand across the back of his neck as he turned.

Her voice came muffled. Her hands still covered her face. "I have a headache."

"What can I do?" Noel pronounced the words slowly, his voice quiet, so that the sentence didn't sound like a question at all.

"You can take it easy on the road." Elizabeth dropped her hands and straightened in her seat so that she faced directly forward. She rubbed her forehead with her fingertips, then clicked her purse open and shut, open and shut.

Rachel stared from her window at the sky, bleached out by the afternoon sun. She waited for the argument to start. Air from the passing car stirred the wayside grasses, but the trees stood motionless, as if they had been pasted flat against the white-hot sky. Everything seemed about to burst into flames.

"I put the patches on the road," Noel said, raising a hand off the wheel and clapping it down again. He turned to the back seat and smiled sheepishly.

"I ask the smallest favor..."

"I'm sorry your head hurts, Mom." Jess had woken up and stood in the back seat, leaning forward between his parents in the front seat. His face was red and wrinkled on one side from sleeping on Gibb's lap. He put his hand on his father's shoulder.

Rachel slid forward and playfully put her arms around his waist. He squirmed and laughed. "That tickles," he said.

For a moment she laid her head against his damp, warm back and he turned slowly in her arms and faced her. She brushed a strand of sweaty hair from his forehead.

Tilting his head, he fixed her with an intense look and put his small hand on her cheek. "You're pretty," he said.

"Pretty as what," she teased, "an old witch?"

"No, silly," he said, his face breaking into a smile, "a girl."

"Okay." She looked down at her bare knees, blinking back sudden tears. Jess, if ever she was lost, he could find her. Someday, whatever she needed to know, he'd tell her. His voice calling her, even his baby laughter, already she'd followed those sounds up out of sleep, out of other dark places. Jess was the thread that held them all together, that kept each one of them from falling and breaking into a thousand pieces. She pulled him toward her again and held him gently.

"We're almost there, aren't we?" he asked, turning and resting his chin on the front seat.

"Only a few more miles." Rachel looked toward Gibb, but he still peered out the window and gave no sign he'd heard her at all.

"A few more miles," Jess echoed, "then you'll be gone. I'll miss you."

"I'll miss you, too," she whispered.

Five

At dawn Rachel had watched the sky show its first color, then turn crimson between the trees across the road from the bus terminal. All morning, looking out the bus windows, she had waited for a storm. But the sky was clear now, and the air shimmered over the asphalt, heat turned liquid. She had just finished her junior year in college.

On the long bus ride from Gainesville to Miami, Rachel thought about her first few weeks at school. After more than three years, she still remembered Jess's damp hand in hers as he walked with her to her dorm room, and the grief-stricken look that had flashed across Gibb's face as he'd said goodbye and turned away. She had introduced her family to her new roommate, Mona Rook. They had talked about the university for a while, then Rachel had gone out to the car with everyone and stood waving till they'd disappeared from sight. Back in the room, she'd sat on her bed, smoking and chewing her nails, while Mona chattered about high school and what the parties would be like now that they were in college. "I can't wait to rush a sorority," Mona had said. Mona unpacked, boxes and boxes of clothes and shoes. Rachel watched the sky through their square of window. Orange clouds drifted by before the square faded to gray. She saw Mona's lips moving, her voice going on and on, using up all the air in the meager space. Rachel caught her breath, mumbled something about taking a walk, and hurried out of the room. She breathed hard in the darkness, searching the air for the tang of salt. Unfamiliar trees towered up. The air smelled only of trees and dank earth. She walked fast, feeling the tears on her face before she knew she was crying. She found a phone booth and called Miami collect, hoping that her family was back from the trip to Gainesville. "Answer, Gibb," she said out loud. "Answer." He was on the line then, accepting her call. "You have to come get me." She wept into the phone, strangled tears. "I can't do it. I miss you. I miss Jess."

"Listen," he said.

"Please."

"No." His voice was firm. "You have to do this. Be...away."

"I can't."

"You have to." He listened while she cried. "It's going to be okay," he said. "You can do it."

"I love you."

"I love you, too. Call me tomorrow."

She hung up the phone and walked in the darkness across the sprawling campus. Her dorm room was dark when she got back, and Mona was snoring softly. Rachel stared at the sooty square of window until the sickle moon rose, and she finally slept.

She lived alone now, in a small, shabby house. The solitude suited her. No one could disapprove of her or give away her nightmares.

As they pulled into the Miami bus terminal, Rachel pressed her face against the bus window, looking for Gibb in the small crowd. She saw him and waved her hand back and forth, close to the glass. He spotted her and waved back, smiling, but his face was drawn and sad. She felt the familiar tightening in her chest, closed her eyes and took a deep breath, hoping she wasn't walking into trouble at home. She got up and pulled her bag from the overhead rack.

Stepping off the bus into a wave of June heat, she walked to where Gibb stood and they hugged. He drew back and gently held her by her shoulders, at arm's length, gazing at her head to foot. "You look great," he said.

"You too," she lied, making her voice light. He needed a shave and his dungarees were stained. The pocket had ripped from his blue T-shirt and a patch of darker fabric showed there.

"I've got some bad news."

"Not Jess," she said suddenly. She held her breath and waited, watching his face.

"No." He took her hand and held it. "Jess is fine, just great. I guess you haven't heard, being on the bus and all," he said.

She shook her head.

"Bobby Kennedy was killed last night."

"No," she cried, "no one else." Gibb had written her a long, despairing letter after the assassination of Martin Luther King. "I'm trying to make sense of things that don't make any sense," he'd said. "The world's like a snake devouring itself."

70

He shook his head, stooped down to pick up her bag and walked to the car.

"Gibb," she called, taking long steps to keep up with him, "what about you, the draft?" She was half-breathless and the last word caught in her throat like something rough she'd swallowed. "What's the latest?"

He threw her bag in the back seat without answering and slid in behind the wheel.

She got in beside him and stared at his face in profile. "Gibb?"

He drove without looking at her, peering into traffic. "I'm talking to a draft counselor at Miami-Dade. I don't know...I can get a psychiatric, maybe. I can't go to Canada and leave Jess." He took a deep, slow breath, and turned finally to face her. "Don't worry," he said with a tight smile, "I'm not going to kill anyone. That's not going to happen." He glared at the road. "I'm not going to go, no way. I've got too much going on here."

"I went to a protest downtown last week, a draft card return." Rachel remembered the faces of the locals, twisted in anger, and a sign that had bobbed in the crowd: "Draft dodgers are yellow, like gooks."

"Did you get any eggs thrown at you? I did the other day at the courthouse." He glanced over. "Some of my friends in the theatre department organized a thing—half street theatre, half protest, you know. They asked me to be one of the speakers." He shrugged his shoulders. "Here's what I said: 'People get a false sense of power from doing violence to weaker people. This country gets the same false sense of power by dominating and doing violence to weaker countries.' Then somebody threw an egg at me and yelled, 'Commie! Try saying that in Russia.'"

"Please," Rachel said, "Why don't you come back with me, bring Jess. We have rallies all the time. You'd be so good..."

"Hey, hey, slow down," he said, patting the air. "It's not that easy. I go to college too, remember? Jess is in school..."

"It's summer," she broke in. "We could go back together, get a place."

He pulled in the driveway and turned off the engine before answering. Facing her, he put his arm on the back of the seat. "I love you, Rachel. I miss you. But I have a job here that pays pretty good money. I'm trying to help the folks out."

She felt herself blushing, embarrassed. He gave her money, too, every other month or so, checks tucked in his letters. "Buy yourself treats," he wrote, "and get a good meal."

"I'll come back," she said.

"No, you won't," he said sharply, then lowered his voice to half a whisper. "No. You can't do that." He shook his head slowly. "Let's go in," he said, making his face smile for her. "We've got the house to ourselves another half-hour or so. One of the neighbors took them to a church bazaar and Jess is at a friend's house playing."

The front sidewalk was cracked and the window screens were dark with age. Only a few green leaves still clung to the skeleton of the jacaranda.

"Our tree," she cried. "What happened to it?"

"It's dying," he said. "It's old and sick inside, rotting from the inside out."

She wanted to ask him if he was all right. His ragged looks shocked her. They stepped into the quiet house and walked through the rooms together, hearing only their footsteps and the ticking of clocks. This had become the house of clocks—seven clocks at least, and not one of them set to the same time, so that as they walked from room to room, the whole day seemed to change on Rachel somehow, these different hours and minutes beating away, as if no one cared what time it was. Late or early? Maybe an hour off, she forgot from one room to another.

"Gibb," she said, her own voice surprising her, "what do you do here, day after day?"

He tugged at his stretched-out T-shirt and smiled a thin smile. "It's not what the boys you know do, I'm sure," he said impatiently. "I didn't blend in too well with the college crowd those times I visited you in Gainesville, did I?" He took a quick breath and looked at her. "I work part-time at the dive shop during the week and on weekends I teach morons who thrash around through sea fans as if they didn't know they were living things." He shook his head. "They stand on brain coral even after we've told them over and over again 'don't stand on the coral, don't even touch it. It's fragile.'

I go to school part time and take Mother to the doctor so she can renew her prescriptions for painkillers. I try to keep Dad out of fights with the neighbors when their dogs shit on our grass. I've got a part in a play. I take Jess to swimming lessons, piano lessons and Little League." He stopped himself. "I'm sorry, Rachel," he said softly. "I've had bronchitis and I'm worn out." He looked up and touched her shoulder gently and smiled. The smile grew wider as he looked into her face. "I've missed the hell out of you. I know I've said that already. Forgive me, okay? Everything's going all right here. It's just been a hectic week. How're your classes?"

"Oh, they're fine," she said quietly, hearing the frightened beating of her heart.

"Listen," he said, "I've gotten you upset. I'm okay. Stop looking at me funny."

"All right," she said.

Later, on their way to the backyard, they walked down the hall and stood before the hall mirror, gray and speckled with age. Rachel tried to remember if she'd ever once seen herself clearly in any of the mirrors of the house, their silver flaking away like ancient, glittering dust. Gibb stood behind her, his face so much like hers, yet so ghostly in the mirror's dimness, she had to turn to look at him for a moment, to be sure he was really with her, really there.

Rachel looked out the Peacock Cafe's front window and straightened her apron. The cloth was as stiff and slick-feeling as plastic. A boy of about Jess's age pedaled by on a red bicycle. The last time she'd seen Gibb and Jess she'd driven to Tampa to see Jess play in a Little League All-Stars game. His team had lost, but Jess had made a base hit that gave the team two runs. That had been just after the Republican convention on Miami Beach and the riots in Liberty City, about five months ago. During the riots, a boy in Jess's class had been knocked to the sidewalk by a police water hose. Four people had died. She hadn't been back to Miami since she'd visited Gibb last June.

"Come on, Rach. You're sleeping. Did you get those two girls at table four yet?" Bill's voice was breezy, but lines of annoyance showed on his thin face. His seersucker jacket brushed her arm as he squeezed past.

She looked at her watch and picked up two menus. The girls sat at the table in front of the window, behind the sign a local artist had painted years ago—a stylized peacock, blue and green curlicues of feathers forming letters: "The Blue Peacock Cafe. Breakfast, Lunch, and Dinner. Closed Mondays."

One of the girls lit a cigarette. A cloud of smoke rose over the table, sunlight from the window diffusing through it. As the girl who smoked talked, she tilted her head. Sleek blonde hair fell across her perfectly symmetrical face and hid one blue eye. She looked up at Rachel.

"Coffee?" Rachel laid the menus on the table between the two girls.

The blonde girl wrinkled her face into a frown. "I hate the taste," she said in the lilting drawl of north Florida. "Milk and a number four with poached eggs. Make sure they're not watery." She looked at her friend. "Eggs are disgusting if they're not right."

Her friend glanced up. "Just coffee," she said, pushing the cup toward Rachel.

Rachel caught a glimpse of her nose—small and upturned as the nose of a cartoon animal. The rest of her face was broad and athletic, and the cute nose didn't seem to belong to her at all. She stared at them for a moment. She knew that the fathers of these girls had played tennis with their daughters and bought them charm bracelets and debutante gowns. The fathers of these girls had never been tried for murder. Her face burned as if they knew her. She turned away.

She looked at her hands. Two of her nails were broken and her hands didn't feel clean, though she'd just washed them before waiting on the table where the two sorority girls sat. It was eleven-thirty. She'd brewed so many pots of coffee, poured so many cups of coffee since six, that its odor— stale and acidic now, permeated the cafe. Her hair, her clothes, had that smell to them too, along with the intermingled odor of cigarette smoke and grease.

Rachel brought the order to the blonde and poured more coffee for the kitten-nosed girl. She laid down the bill. "Anything else?" she said quietly.

"No thanks," the blonde murmured.

Fortunately Rachel wasn't the cashier too, but that's where she'd started two years ago. During the first two weeks of her sophomore year she'd been all over town looking for a job. She had come to Bill twice and the second time he had hired her. Maybe he'd felt sorry for her. She'd been desperate for a job then, and desperately tired, too excited to sleep, studying fervently, as if she had never seen a book before.

She took off her apron and threw it in the closet where all the waitresses kept their things. Placed very neatly on the floor side-by-side was a pair of white shoes, the much-polished leather dusty and starting to crack. The shoes had been there since Rachel started work at the Peacock, probably left by a former waitress who never wanted to see them again.

Rachel walked through the kitchen and out the back door. She kicked a rock and watched it arc and tumble into the grass and disappear.

She patted her pocket to see if her house keys were there, and felt the shape of the ring and keys against her hand. Something crinkly, too, her mother's letter, asking her to come home for a while at the end of the semester. "Please think about someone but yourself for a change. Your brothers miss you." Not "I miss you" or "your father and I miss you." For the rest of the letter her mother complained about how the Cubans were taking over Miami, how they'd brought crime and gotten jobs that should have gone to other, more deserving people. They couldn't leave their door unlocked anymore, her mother said, or they might be killed in their beds. Robberies everywhere, shootings, rapes. Murders.

Over the last few years, Rachel hadn't been home much. Her mother had practically stopped writing, especially after Rachel had dropped out of school for a semester to work two jobs so she could afford her own place, but Gibb still wrote her once a week. Although she'd begged him to come see her, even to go to school here, he'd only visited her once or twice a year. Too much was going on, he said, for him to get away very often. He was finishing college, diving, acting in plays, still writing. He described dives and different dive sites in the Keys. He wrote about Jess, too, sent school pictures. He talked about the war; he'd gotten a hardship deferment after Noel lost his job in November. "But the shrink was ready to certify me—mad, mad, mad. And the ones who volunteer? Aren't they the crazy ones, poor fuckers? Not to understand what's worth dying for and what isn't?"

Where did that prickle along her spine come from when she read Gibb's words?

"What are you writing about these days?" she'd written back. "You're writing about us, aren't you? Our crazy family."

In the next letter he'd answered her. "Funny that you want to know what I'm writing. I *am* writing about us. What happened to us so many years ago. How it changed our lives forever."

Then she was sorry she'd asked. She stepped across the street and through a vacant lot to a path that was a shortcut to her house. The ground gave a little under her feet—a layer of leaves the color of dark water, mottled by the light seeping in ragged patches through the thick trees. The air always smelled wet along the path. If she put her ear to the ground, she was sure she'd hear a rush of underground water, constant as a river. She thought of the conchs she'd pressed to her ears when she was little, giant pink shells filled with the hollow rising and falling roar of wind and surf. But the sound of underground water was different, a steady drone, none of the mystery to it that ocean water had.

Your brothers miss you. She knelt down and poked at the ground, moving away the surface layer of leaves to find the dark, fibrous humus. Gibb was fine, busy, hadn't he said so? *Give me a sign, Gibb, right now. Say you hear me.* When they were younger, they'd called out to each other that way, picked numbers, held cards, tried to read each other's minds. Clairvoyance, ESP, synchronicity. *Gibb, damnit.* Cicadas droned and clicked their wings. She remembered when she and Gibb had danced, night after night. "Gibb," she said aloud, staring at the brown earth. But he was silent. So many miles stretched between them.

Sweat dripped down the backs of her legs. Each time she took a breath the humid air saturated her lungs, as if they were sponges steadily growing heavier. A tiny barbed hook laid half-buried in the dirt. About a mile or so down the path was a lake where she sometimes went swimming. Walking on the thick, cool mud of the bottom was like stepping in chocolate pudding. People always sat at the weedy edge of the lake, dangling cane poles. Once, her father had fished. She'd seen a photograph on a shelf in the closet of her father standing by his boat.

The pines smelled sweet. Sap glistened red-gold on the rough trunks. Touching her finger to a drop, she brought it away, trailing a transparent strand. She rubbed the resin against her palm until it was no longer beautiful and all that was left was a sticky black streak.

Rachel opened her historical geology text to a chapter she needed to study for her final. "In Devonian times," she read, "the Choanichthyes included two great tribes, the Dipnoi and the Crossopterygii. The living examples belong to the Dipnoi and like all the fossil representatives of that group, they are deficient in having very weak fins, in lacking true teeth and in other respects which indicate that none of them could be ancestors of the higher animals."

She turned back to an early chapter on the cosmic history of the earth. She thought of Dr. Rayburn lecturing, his thick mustache moving up and down like a dark brush, his hands beating the air emphatically, like the hands of a conductor. Outside of college how much did people really think about such things? The beginning of the earth, the monstrous steam-filled world? The world before humans. She closed her eyes and tried to imagine the earth cooling in the black backdrop of space, then she stared down at the page again, at a picture of an Ordovician fossil, *Byssonychia radiata*, that looked like a pure white scallop she'd found once on a field trip to Sanibel Island with her fifth-grade class—a shell she'd saved for years and foolishly counted on for luck.

She underlined "deficient," stood up and stretched. Her geology final was tomorrow. The chapter Dr. Rayburn had told them to study especially carefully was entitled, "Precambrian History of the Earth," and she printed "Cryptozoic Eon (hidden life)," in her notebook. On the first page of the chapter, the textbook author had quoted *The Tempest*: "What seest thou else / In the dark backward and abysm of time?" She liked the eerie sound of the lines and said them out loud, hearing them echo faintly in the room. "The dark backward and abysm of time." Yes. She wanted to see the mysterious history of the world captured in stones and fossil fish, skeletons trapped in tar, proven things that wouldn't slip away and change on her.

An hour and a half later she had filled five pages with notes, and she began to reread them, the afternoon hot and silent, so quiet every sound in the house was magnified—the workings of an old electric clock, water trickling somewhere down a drain, the rustle of birds in the big live oak. With a few more hours work she'd be ready for the hardest test Dr. Rayburn could dream up. If she aced the test, she'd have an A in the course. She was counting on A's in all of her courses this semester. She remembered her father telling her not to come back home until she had accomplished great things, learned enough to explain his life to him, was that how he'd put it? She'd never understood what he'd meant for her to do, why he'd hurt her. But her father didn't matter, the sting of her mother's words didn't matter, because she wasn't going home again at all. They wouldn't have another chance to heap their bitterness on her.

A sound woke her, something outside, and she lifted her head from the table, her neck and shoulders stiff and aching. The room was dark. She felt her way along the edge of the couch and peered out the front window. The street was empty. A single streetlight cast a pale halo around a cluster of large, dark trees. Was someone out there, hiding in the shadows?

She remembered the dream she'd been having, of eons of time moving through her head. "The time of the great dying." That was Cretaceous. Ichthyosaurs marching behind plesiosaurs, mosasaurs, all gone, never to see the dawn of the Cenozoic era. She had been swimming with a blue jellyfish, and she reminded herself of its name in case it appeared on the test: coelenterate—big as a car, transparent as a balloon. Through its one and only all-purpose orifice, coelenterate had sucked her into its blue-lit world and spit her out again in a stream of slimy flotsam. The fossils and rock strata proved that the world was ancient—proved that there had once been a past empty of humans and all their mistakes.

*

Rachel put her hands on the windowsill and looked out at the empty street. The semester was over and she'd gotten A's in all of her courses. Sun falling through the big oak trees made irregular patterns on the sidewalk, like light shining through tattered cloth. Nothing moved. She sat on the edge of her rumpled bed and slipped two of Gibb's letters from the drawer of the nightstand. One was about diving; she'd gotten it a couple of weeks ago. He wrote more than ever about diving. She felt the thrill of danger, understood in Gibb's words the allure of fear mastered. He described decompression, nitrogen narcosis, free-diving. He wanted her to dive with him someday. "Whenever I'm underwater, I feel humble," he'd written. "Today the sound of my own breath seemed to come from far away, as if it belonged to the whole of the sea. I listened to my steady intake of air, and looked below at a school of blue tang with some bright yellow young swimming among them. I was at Grecian Rocks, and the Gulfstream had moved in, so the water was as clear as I've ever seen it. I swam back and forth between the cascades of elkhorn and staghorn colonies, watching the photographer I was diving with try to get a shot of a Spanish hogfish that kept darting away and hiding under a huge star coral head. I've never stopped being conscious of my breathing—not since my very first dive—but today I felt a special sense of mystery, hearing myself breathing in the place I feel most at home—down in the first world."

"Jess is fine," he'd written in the letter she'd just received. "He's still taking piano lessons. Willingly!" She felt like a distant relative, reading that. Missing her brothers had depressed her for days now. She'd imagined their faces on people who passed her as she walked through the town. She'd found herself staring at children Jess's age on their bicycles or playing hide-and-seek in overgrown lots. She'd remembered the long-ago games they had invented, just for the three of them so that Jess always had a part.

Gibb hadn't mentioned their parents, except to say he was sorry they weren't helping her with school anymore. She pulled her feet up on the bed and sat cross-legged. She should take a long bath, a walk maybe. But it was so sultry hot and she couldn't imagine meeting the raking eyes of strangers, seeing lovers with their arms entwined.

The floorboards squeaked and groaned as she walked to the bathroom. Her face was thin as a bone, and the skin under her eyes sallow-dark. She took her hairbrush into the bedroom and plopped down on the bed again.

She'd written to Gibb four times since May and called him twice, but he hadn't made it up to visit her. Gibb had gone to school during the summer, too, and was seeing someone. That was the surprising news. She traced her own name on the front of the envelope in Gibb's neat handwriting and tried to imagine the girl's face, but images shifted and displaced one another in her mind as though she were looking through a kaleidoscope. She felt a twinge of jealousy.

After the bar closed last night she had gone over to her friend Phil's to listen to music and try some Jamaican weed he'd just gotten. A few of them had stayed past three o'clock, listening to *Electric Ladyland, John Wesley Harding* and *Abbey Road*, and talking about the story on the front page of the newspaper, on television, too. A young woman had drowned when Senator Kennedy had driven a car off a bridge. Rachel had listened to Phil and Russell talk about what had happened when, the car, the darkness, the bridge. What had really happened? *What really happened,* they said, until their voices bounced off the walls, the floor, the sound getting louder, making her dizzy. In a sudden panic Rachel had pressed her palms to her eyes, imagining the woman, floating hair, dark water...newspaper headlines of long ago. She'd been old enough to read the papers, to see her own last name in the stories. Her picture had been on the front page of the newspaper. The fear she'd felt so many years ago came back to her exactly as she had felt it then—a bright, stinging panic. A deep shame. Her mother had taken the papers away, but always too late. Rachel had already read every word.

Darkness, music. The electric guitar breaks raveled through her brain as if it were made of a mass of wires. She closed her eyes, her head spun, she felt sick.

"Are you all right?" Russell had whispered. She'd looked up and nodded, and he'd smiled and nodded back, teeth white against the curly auburn of his heavy beard. She'd stammered something about "good music," pushing the memories away, pushing them back to where they had come from as if they were no more than ghostly images from a dream.

She felt groggy now, as if she'd slept all day. But it was only noon. So hot, she didn't feel like moving. She was sick of the heat waking her, her pillow wet with perspiration. She stared out the window. A gangly boy rode by on a bicycle, pedaling fast, his knees making outlandish angles with each push. Somewhere in the distance, a baby cried.

Afternoon shadows had already begun to gather in the corners of the room, this room with peeling paint the color of false white calm and hot skies, where a thousand cigarettes had been stubbed into ashtrays during hours of studying by students like her. The walls had taken up the sound of tears and love cries. Had the idea ever occurred to any of the occupants that they were part of something larger than their own lives? The room wasn't very big but it was still was larger than her own life. History and memory reverberated through this meager space. To live, to make a real life, she needed to understand such intersections.

She would not live a life of pain and suppressed longing the way her mother and father did, smothered by a private history. She wouldn't let that happen to her.

Part Two

I sit listening
To the surf as it falls,
The power and inexhaustible freshness of the sea,
The suck and inner boom
As a wave tears free and crashes back
In overlapping thunders going away down the beach.

It is the most we know of time,
And it is our undermusic of eternity.

    . . .

Across gull tracks
And wind ripples in the sand
The wind seethes. My footprints
Slogging for the absolute
Already begin vanishing.

"Spindrift"
Galway Kinnell

Six

Prompted to my revenge by heaven and hell…/ For murder, though it have no tongue will speak…/ I'll have these players / Play something of the murder of my father / Before mine uncle: I'll observe his looks…/ I'll have grounds…/ The play's the thing / Wherein I'll catch the conscience of the king. The words ran through Gibb's head as he pulled the Valiant into a parking space near the entrance to Lum's Restaurant. He felt the anxious rhythm of the lines as he committed them to memory. Time was left on the parking meter, nearly twenty minutes. Opening the glove compartment, he read over the notes he'd prepared for his talk in Dr. Wesley's class tomorrow. "Why have I quoted *Hamlet* in the conclusion of my senior history thesis? As Tillyard has noted, the order of this particular drama is an antidote to history's chaos—'time out of joint'—history public and private. In *Hamlet*, human experience is presented in the largest possible cosmic setting. *Hamlet* is an antidote to reading history narrowly. As the play clarifies, truth is an unworthy end in itself." Gibb found a pencil on the dash and changed the last lines to read: "As the play makes clear, and as the title character's suffering confirms, truth is an unworthy—even a dangerous—end in itself." He added: "The truths of history can reveal themselves only in conflict and struggle, both personal and public. The path to the truth is littered with ambiguities. Even after Hamlet confirms the truth of the Ghost's words, he disobeys the Ghost's commands. Hamlet finds that the relationship between intellectual mastery and consequent action is untidy and illogical."

He glanced out the window. After he'd spoken the last words of his senior thesis, he'd have nothing more to do but to stand in the heat in his heavy graduation gown. He'd be attending the ceremony only because his parents had asked him to, each of them with a tender dignity that had moved him. He'd stand in the heat—watching the afternoon clouds gather and the tall line of Australian pines sway in the breeze, moving the air without cooling it—one of the first to graduate from Florida's newest university, still half a sandlot of a school halfway to the Everglades. Rachel had gotten her degree, but she'd left Florida before her graduation ceremony. She'd been wandering ever since. He'd written to General Delivery addresses from Vermont to Utah. "You earned it," Rachel said in a long letter congratulating him. "What will you do now?" He'd smiled a little, reading that. He'd do what he'd been doing, what he loved. Work in The Dive Shop. "I've been asking myself the same question," she wrote. "I'm confused. No matter where I go, I want to be somewhere else. *Need* to be somewhere else."

The meter's red flag clicked up and he searched the glove compartment for change. A dime would do. That would give him more than an hour to wait for Amanda's shift to begin. Over the years he and Rachel had grabbed a week here and there to visit, and spent a small fortune on long distance calls. He felt a settling of pain in his gut. He was alone; he knew that, so this was no occasion for hope or self-pity.

He closed his eyes and his sister's face floated into his consciousness, splendidly detailed, as if, when he opened his eyes again, he'd find Rachel there, on the seat beside him. How he missed her. He looked at his watch: 2:45. Lum's had a shift that started at 3:00. He was sure the car he'd followed yesterday had dropped Amanda off here, but when he'd gone in, standing pressed against by a crowd of people waiting for tables, he'd caught no sign of her. He stayed to have a meal anyway, watching, waited on by a girl who popped gum while she talked. Her makeup was heavy, theatrical and odd in its shading, as if applied by air brush to disguise the real contours of her face. Was she covering scars? He had stared at her when her eyes were averted, wondering what secrets lay under the layers of powder.

Gibb checked the rearview mirror, seeing nothing but the dark, intertwined wall of cocoplums, dense as the end of a blind alley in a dream. A rearview mirror, though, that was the important place to discover things otherwise missed. People didn't think of being observed in rearview mirrors. Small things, things half out of sight, like people hurrying stealthily by or looking about nervously, those were the ones to watch. He was in the habit of watching people surreptitiously now, looking for clues of human behavior everywhere. He watched instinctively. How often he saw violence coming from the smallest provocation, faces growing red, the middle finger shooting up. For what? Someone cutting into a lane on the highway maybe, a dented fender in a parking lot.

He glanced up again, imagining he'd seen light, glimpsed movement on the periphery of his vision. Making her way across the street, her reflection tiny in the rectangle of glass, was the crippled girl who hung out at Lum's with the long-haired freaks and small-time dope dealers. She swung her stunted legs out in front of her and planted the metal crutches in the same slow pattern, again and again. She got around town by hitchhiking. He'd even picked her up once, watching from the corner of his eye as she hoisted her steel-braced legs into the car. Her shoes were incongruous, small and pink, like dancing slippers. He'd wanted to tell her...She was especially vulnerable. She shouldn't be hitchhiking. But her manner of speaking was coarse and aggressive, sprinkled with four-letter words; she wouldn't have listened. He watched her join a group of people on the lawn, most of them wearing various parts of military uniforms—army jackets with black-stenciled letters, combat boots, or fatigues.

A bus pulled past the Valiant and to a stop near the corner. He watched the people step off slowly—a cleaning woman with a Richard's shopping bag, slow and stiff-kneed; a young black man wearing a shiny black shirt, a woman dragging two squirming kids by their elbows, purse swinging at her wrist. The bus pulled away, trailing dirt and exhaust. It was 3:05. The dopers in army clothes had left the crippled girl sitting on the grass alone. He saw the exit door to the restaurant open and a young woman half skip down the steps, untying her apron at the same time, a long blonde ponytail trailing down her back. She was nearly out of sight in the deep green of the trees before he recognized her, but he didn't need to follow her—he already knew where she lived. So she worked the lunch shift, or maybe came in on call. He'd be at Lum's again tomorrow, and the next day, until they finally met.

Gibb had changed clothes once, but his shirt was already clinging to his back again. In the last week the temperature hadn't dropped below eighty-five, even at night. He brushed hair out of his face and took the restaurant steps two at a time, glancing at his watch. It

87

was after one-thirty, yet a few of the usual lunch crowd from Coconut Grove lingered at Lum's—realtors, dentists, secretaries and the people who worked in the shops—the sun streaming through the windows and spilling over the varnished tables.

"Excuse me," Gibb said to the plump woman who had started to show him to a table. "I'd like to sit by a window."

She turned, her eyes resting on his for several disconcerting seconds, then searching his face. Chewing at her bottom lip, she tilted her head, the white, abundant flesh below the line of her chin shifting like a mound of thick cream. "I know you from somewheres," she said finally.

His face grew warm at first, as if he'd been discovered spying and tailing the girl he'd waited for more than two weeks to meet, but then he shrugged his shoulders and smiled. "I come in here a lot for lunch." Four times in the last week, without luck.

"I'd remember you from here," she said, a hint of irritation in her voice. "Somewheres else." She put the menu on the table, glanced out the window that faced Grand Avenue, and then stared at him again.

He slid across the vinyl seat, looking at her blankly. He saw that she wasn't as old as he'd first imagined. There was something coquettish in the way she stood gazing down at him, hand on hip.

"Well," she said finally. "Have a good lunch."

The hostess turned and Gibb's eyes followed her heavy, swaying hips as she walked back to the front of the restaurant. He scanned the room until he saw the girl—Amada— finally, coming towards his table. Feeling the quick beating of his heart, he took a deep breath and opened his menu, staring at the wrinkled crease of the center fold until she stood at the table's edge, the fabric of her skirt touching the wood.

"Can I get you something to drink?" she asked, the voice tired, the pleasant inflection mechanical, like the sound of phone company recordings.

He looked up, startled to find that she wasn't pretty at all, as he'd supposed, seeing her from a distance. He opened the menu again, stalling. She shifted her weight from one foot to the other impatiently. "Uh, yeah," he said, "let's see, Heineken's, is that on tap?" A series of small shocks rippled through him as he studied her face and found each of the features familiar, matching a face he'd memorized, her mother's—a woman dead almost twenty years now.

"Yes."

"Okay, a Heineken's." His plan had seemed so surefire, but it was already falling away into a confused jumble of singles' bar phrases.

"You can get a glass or a mug. Mug's a better deal."

"Mug it is." He tried to sound light-hearted, accommodating. She was tall, five nine at least, and the lines of her face, nose, the curve of lips were austere, almost sharp, the kind of face that can be called beautiful at one moment and severe the next. Her hair was pulled straight back into the long ponytail he'd always seen her wear.

"Dark or regular?"

"Uh...regular."

"I'll be back in a minute to take your order," she said, leaving him to watch her disappear into the darkness of the bar.

He was still watching when she came back with the beer, walking quickly, not looking at him but checking, he supposed, her other tables. She set the mug down. Foam sloshed over the top and trailed down the side of the glass. Pulling out her pad and a small pencil, she met his eyes with a look of cool indifference.

"I guess I'll try the combination seafood platter. Is it any good?"

Her lips curved slowly into a small, wry smile. "Sure," she said, reaching behind her head and lifting her hair off her neck for a moment. "Everything was still swimming this morning."

"Okay," he said. He smiled without meaning to, wanting to make some witty remark of his own, but she was already gone, her ponytail swinging as she walked.

She set down his food in the same indifferent manner, glancing behind her, allowing him to see the white curve of her neck and the fragile bones at the hollow of her throat. "Would you like anything else?" she said, and it was the mechanical voice again, recorded politeness.

"Yes, I'd like to take you out." He was surprised, half-annoyed at his own bold voice. There wasn't any place for ego in his plan. He'd intended to move slowly, to be sure that nothing would foil his chance to get to know her. She looked at him hard then, mistrust flickering onto her face.

"Where?" she asked, no waitress-polite inflection this time. Her voice was flat yet mocking in the one word.

"To the beach." He shrugged his shoulders, embarrassed by the look she fixed on him. "I like the ocean. I dive," he said foolishly.

She laughed then. "I've got to go." Starting to turn, she stopped and faced him again, and put her hand on the table next to his plate. He sat, stunned by the presence of that slender, appealing hand, as if she had touched him.

"The beach," she said with a small sarcastic nod. "I haven't been to the beach since I was in high school." She laughed again, a laugh that was musical, almost merry, and had nothing to do with him at all.

"I'll pick you up after you're finished working." He made his voice bold now.

"Nine," she said, walking away without looking back.

He and Amanda were diving. They'd been together for three weeks. He watched her pale hair floating up toward the surface of the water, like the delicate plumes of a sea feather. He motioned her toward him. When she was close, he took out his regulator and mouthed her name. He wanted to carry her on his back as if he'd stolen her from the world above. He wanted to unfold the whole story of his life and hope she'd forgive him, love him. That was impossible, of course. He'd fully deceived her, even using a false name, Gil Conover. He even deceived himself with the name he called her, "Ama," pushing her real name from his mind. She pointed to her wrist, then up, towards the gleaming surface of the water. The sun was right over them now. He shook his head. They had at least fifteen more minutes of air. Pivoting around with a few small kicks, he headed down to an open spot on the bottom where the sand was particularly white and fine, halo sand from the coral, and turtle grass, fringing a large head of star coral.

He glanced back at her. She hadn't learned to relax yet. She trusted him, though, knowing he'd been diving for nearly eleven years. Just last week, a four-foot nurse shark had circled them curiously for a while. Even after the shark swam away, she'd clung to him, panicked, and he'd felt the frantic beating of her heart, and the warmth and life coming through her skin like a current.

He'd told Ama where he'd come up with her nickname: the Ama were female divers in Japan. He'd described how the sounds of whistling echoed across the water when the Ama were preparing to dive. They whistled to be sure it wasn't too cold. She'd laughed that beautiful, austere laugh of hers. Amma means mother in Latin, she'd said. You don't think of me as your mother, do you? she asked. No, he'd said, running his hands up her bare arms, gently holding her shoulders, I don't.

They were driving to Tarpon Springs for the weekend. They'd see the sponge divers in action, do some more diving themselves and eat good Greek food. He wanted to be close to her. It didn't matter any longer what she knew or didn't know about her mother. What mattered was her, Ama.

"Why do you like that stuff?" she said, looking at Gibb's glass of ouzo.

He took a sip, wondering himself as he swallowed, feeling the heat of the liquor rising immediately to his face.

"I can't believe they just hold their breath and go down there for a sponge," she said. Her hair hung loose and she twisted a thin strand around her finger. "Free diving scares me." She gazed out over the inlet, shading her eyes. "You asked about my mother the other day," she said suddenly and the sentence reached him like a slap, rousing him from the state of drowsiness that had come from the liquor and the humid afternoon. Light rose from the wavelets like gleaming knife-tips. Her hand lay on the table and he covered it with his own.

"You already know my grandma raised me," she said softly. She was no longer the worldly cynic with him. She had a childlike optimism that her wariness had at first hid. But she was tough, too, the way a hand gets from work, feeling less pain the more work it does.

"My mother drowned when I was a year old, in an undertow at Haulover Beach. I don't remember her at all. My father was killed in a car wreck before I was born. They weren't...married." Her eyes brimmed with tears. Turning away, she wiped roughly at her face.

Her grandmother had lied to her and he'd lied to her. If this was what she believed about her mother's death, he had betrayed her trust for nothing. Already, he knew far more about her mother than she did. But he'd been entrapped by his greed to know still more, to read back into her mother's life from Ama's own to find something, some clue overlooked. He struggled to imagine a way to tell her the truth.

"Gil," she said suddenly. "You don't know how hard it's always been for me to talk about...her. With most people, that is." She looked into his face and smiled. "I care about you. I really do."

He stood, nearly upsetting his chair. She still held his hand. "Excuse me," he said, slipping his hand from hers, his voice thick. He walked quickly to the men's room and into a stall. He gagged. He wanted to heave up his whole life. To forget he'd swallowed a poisonous sea. Sweat ran into his eyes, down his neck, but he lost nothing more of himself at all.

They'd intended to drive home down the coast that afternoon, but after he'd come back to the table—not just pale, she'd said, but white, his face drained of color—she insisted on driving. Drive to Dunedin Beach, he'd said, wanting to swim.

"You shouldn't go in the water. You haven't stopped shaking." She kept her eyes on the road, watching for the turnoff. He traced the line of her face in profile, as if with a fingertip, laid his head back on the headrest and closed his eyes, her image still with him. For as long as he lived, he'd remember her face that way, set in exquisite focus by the late afternoon sun and the blurred green and blue of the passing landscape.

"Please don't swim." Her voice wavered into a higher register, becoming a child's. He opened his eyes to see if the elegant face had changed, but she still looked steadily forward. "I think you should see a doctor."

"No." He touched her, unable to help himself, gently running his hand up her arm to her shoulder, feeling through the smooth bare skin, veins and muscles, the vitality poised in her as in the crouching sprinter or bird ready to spiral into flight. "What, for a stomachache? I got some bad fish, that's all." Panic gripped him, the nausea coming again. What was he doing? He'd go away for a while, take Jess on a trip. Rachel would come. He would tell Ama the truth in a letter. No, he had to meet her grandmother first. He had gone too far to stop short of that. He imagined himself speaking to the old woman, saw her fix smoldering eyes on him as he visited, as if she found something familiar in his face—familiar and despised. He imagined her revealing his duplicity, calling him by his hated name. Ama would despise him then too.

He looked down the road to the tall Australian pines that fringed the strip of public beach. "Turn there," he said. "Just ahead."

She looked in the direction he pointed, and then glanced at him. "I wish you wouldn't swim."

"We'll both swim," he said. "You'll stay with me and I'll be safe. I feel fine now." His stomach pained him as he spoke. His lies had taken shape in him. They clawed at his insides. The huge orange sun filtered through the trees, hovering near the horizon. She stretched out her hand to him and he took it, squeezed it and gently let it drop.

They got out and he opened the trunk. He gave her a mask, snorkel and flippers. "Come on," he said. Walking beside her to the edge of the Gulf, he pulled on his flippers and mask and waded in, put his face in the water and swam, breathing through the snorkel, looking down at the coarse bottom-sand. With the setting of the sun, darkness slid into the water like dye poured in a huge vat, diffusing slowly. He stood, took off his mask and turned to find Ama swimming near him. Gently, he took her shoulders and raised her from the water. Wrapping his arms around her, he laid his wet face against her hair, fragrant with the intermingled scent of her perfume and salt water. He put his mask on again, helped her pull on her own and they moved together underwater holding hands. He felt the warmth of her skin against his, waited to feel the whole pulse of her. But he felt only his own frantic heart working to burst and have done with it.

*

Gibb rehearsed the story as Ama knew it. She didn't remember her mother, who'd drowned off Haulover Beach. Ama had been just a year old. Her mother hadn't been married and Ama, her mother, her grandmother and grandfather had lived in the same house that Ama and her grandmother lived in still, a white Oolite bungalow with a red-tile roof and Bahama shutters on the windows. An allamanda in full bloom climbed a trellis up the side of the garage. A single yellow flower lay in the driveway. Picking it up, Gibb touched a petal's fleshy, delicate surface. They'd had such a bush in their own yard when he'd been nine or ten. He'd cried to see it broken at the base, a profusion of shiny leaves and yellow flowers, the morning after the torrential rains and gale-force winds of a near-hurricane.

He crossed the front yard to the door and rang the bell, hearing it sound somewhere deep in the house.

Ama opened the door wearing a yellow sundress the color of the allamanda blossom he'd just held in his palm. She kissed him on the cheek and he followed her into a dim living room. A large photograph of Neoma Kelch sat on a glass-topped coffee table. A lace doily spread under the glass like a web. Before he had heard her enter the room, an older woman emerged from the shadows to stand behind Ama. Ama took a step back and placed her arm lightly across the woman's shoulders.

"This is my grandmother."

"Glad to meet you," the woman said flatly, her eyes fixed on Gibb's face, and her voice bearing the unmistakable twang of old "Miamah"—as the natives still called it.

"The same."

They stood for an awkward moment, looking at one another. Bertha Kelch wore her steel-gray hair braided atop her head. Her eyes were black as a parrot's with a gleaming intensity exaggerated by pince-nez glasses. Her shoes were black oxfords with stocky heels, of the style that older women had ceased to wear more than ten years ago. She wiped her hands on a starched white apron and stretched her thin lips into a smile. "Sit down," she said, gesturing toward the couch.

He sat in its center, alone, facing the photograph of Neoma Kelch, Ama and her grandmother in chairs across from him. Bertha

Kelch began her story almost immediately, as Ama had warned him she would. "She tells everyone," Ama had said. "It's so embarrassing, how she acts."

"My husband died less than a year after my daughter drowned," she said, her voice steady, even the emotional timbre of the words sounding practiced.

Gibb remembered reading her trial testimony and imagined this persuasive voice behind the words, words that had almost sent his father to prison. Given her rage, he wondered how she had managed to conceal the facts of Amanda's mother's death from her. Did her grandmother lie out of a need to control? To protect her? From what? Life's sordidness.

"I've raised my granddaughter and kept my house alone since then. I want to know who she goes with."

"Grandma," Ama interrupted, but Bertha Kelch took her grand-daughter's wrist in her hands and stroked it lightly.

"Shhh," she said gently. "Grandma's talking. Sometimes you never get over a heartbreak, sir," she said, leaning forward in her chair a little. "Neoma was our only child. After she died my husband took pneumonia. He couldn't get better. He didn't care to get better."

"Grandmother, *please*." Ama slipped from Bertha Kelch's hands and stood.

"How..." Gibb started, but couldn't force his lips to form the rest of the words. How did she drown? He felt himself getting warmer, his pounding, resonant heartbeat becoming diffuse. Queasiness snaked from his stomach to his chest and up to the back of his throat. "I...may I have a glass of water?"

"Why sure. Or some limeade? I squeezed some fresh limeade from the key lime trees out back." Bertha Kelch's eyes fixed him to the spot, twin needles.

He heard the sound of ice against glass, the faucet running. Ama brought him water, and when she handed him the glass, their finger-tips touched. She sat down on the couch beside him.

"Look at her," Bertha Kelch said, handing him the framed por-trait, a face so familiar. "She wasn't a prom queen but she wasn't a nobody either. She was beautiful. Smart, too. She would have made something out of her life, I know it. But she got on the bus one day and I never saw her alive again."

Ama took the photograph from his hands and put it face-down on the table. "I'm sorry," she said to Gibb. "Grandma, can we please talk about something else?"

He regained his composure while they talked about his work. Mrs. Kelch asked about sharks.

"Crossing the street during rush hour in Miami's more dangerous than diving with sharks." He forced a laugh, his voice slipping into a high, phony register.

She shook her head, disbelieving. "They're devils," she said. "Come from another time."

"They're due our respect, because of that—because they're ancient beings." He looked at his watch, stood up.

Bertha Kelch walked to stand near him. He felt exposed, as if she saw through his skin to his heart beating hugely in his chest, sending waves of blood to his eyes, his ears. Could she see his father's young face in Gibb's own? As he turned toward the door, she peered at him as if reading his thoughts, her eyes flickering over his face, studying his features. She walked close to him, so close that he could smell her body's aggressive scent—a smell of bleach and stunning cleanliness mixed with the odor of primitive anger, an odor no washing could ever mask. He took a last look at her face, seeing there, too, the rage shining in her coal-dark eyes.

He got in his car and pulled away. Ama waved to him from the sidewalk, her dress bright as a flag, an uncanny, too-bright yellow that absorbed the intense sunlight and made his eyes sting.

On the way back to his apartment, his mind cast about wildly. Ama's image—her hand raised in that goodbye wave—showed itself in the windshields of passing cars, on the sun-struck glass of office buildings. He blinked and tried to focus on his driving. The bridge was open and causeway traffic was backed up. He glanced at a nearby car. The young woman at the wheel was young and blonde. She smiled at him. Then her car slipped forward until he could no longer see her face, only her long hair, stirred by the wind. A sigh shuddered through him. He couldn't see Ama again. He risked too much—her finding out about his deception, her love turning to hate.

A month passed and he had said nothing, done nothing. He'd been with Ama every week, made love to her, grown more in love with her. They had sat together at night in a park near her house and he'd told her more than he'd ever told anyone about himself, all that he could. He described Rachel, praised Jess's precociousness, talked about diving. She had drawn his picture a dozen times or more. It was her dream to go to art school. "I don't look that good," he'd said, laughing at his rather sharp features rendered softer by the charcoal, his expression made tender, a smile sketched that he wished she'd really once seen on his face. He forced himself to wait a day, two days, between his calls to her, but he was full of the old loneliness without her. When they were apart, he thought of her constantly, yet when they were together his pleasure was tainted by pain and guilt. He had started to plan how he'd tell her the truth and beg her forgiveness. But he was tormented by the thought that she would never forgive him, that she would always despise him for what he had done.

One night she phoned him, crying as she spoke his name.

"Gil, I'm sorry, I'm so sorry."

"What," he said, alarmed. "Are you all right? Can I meet you somewhere? What's wrong?"

She sobbed into the phone.

"I have a...chance," she said catching her breath, "to get out of here. Can you come with me? Do you remember Carol?" Her words were tumbling out now; he could hardly follow her. "She's in San Francisco. She has a place. I can stay for free," she said, "until I get on my feet. There's an opening where she works. I'll start art school, like I always said I would. I can't stay here. I can't live with Grandma anymore. She hates everything. I feel sick when I go home at night, and when I wake up in the morning, I feel like I've been breathing poison!"

She paused, and then her voice came soft across the line. "Come with me, Gil," she pleaded. "I love you."

"I love you too," he said. He imagined himself packing, his apartment empty, a late afternoon, salt-smelling breeze fluttering through the silent rooms. *Why not?* a voice inside him cried.

"Gil," she whispered. "Are you there?"

"I can't...I...my work," he faltered.

"Oh, Gil. I know. I know how much your work means to you. I'll earn money and come back. You can visit me."

"Let me pick you up. Spend the night with me."

"No," she said, "No. I couldn't stand to make love to you again and then just say goodbye."

"When are you leaving?"

"Tomorrow. I already have a bus ticket."

"Let me take you to the station."

She began to cry again.

"Please don't..."

"I'll...call." She caught her breath. "When I get there."

But the weeks went by until she'd been gone a month, and another, and Gibb heard nothing from her. Desolate, he was haunted by her face, so sweetly familiar. Unexpectedly, the light perfume of her skin floated to him in the darkness. He imagined her body's soft curves. He heard the mysterious whisper of her voice in the lisp of his breathing as he dove. Yet even as he missed her desperately, he was angry with her for leaving him. Night after night his anger left him shaking in the dark of his bedroom, afraid, full of the old loneliness. He convinced himself then of the danger of their loving one another, and came to believe that her decision to leave had somehow saved him, had saved them both.

On a cool February day, months after Ama left, Gibb went to court and sat among thespectators at a first-degree murder trial. He wanted to see what it would feel like, being there. He wanted to kindle memories. He wanted to have the details right. He had the transcripts from his father's trial, but he needed more than those two-dimensional words. He watched the expressionless face of the "accused," and studied the tears of the victim's family, saw the emotions sweeping across their features. He thought of his mother as he watched—his mother, who had been instantly widowed to the good life she'd imagined for herself and for all of them. He thought, of course, of Bertha Kelch and her husband who'd died of grief. He'd never have children, because he believed her. He'd die of grief, too, if he lost his only child.

Seven

On their way to visit Rachel in Denver, Gibb and Jess sat in the Miami air terminal, looking across the runways at the streams of glittering cars on the nearby highway, the rush-hour traffic they'd missed by leaving so early. Noel had taken them to the airport. Gibb and Jess had met at the house. Their mother, still wearing her robe, opened the door, and Gibb stepped from the damp predawn darkness into the warm living room where he smelled coffee and saw Jess sitting on the couch. Jess had moved out of Gibb's apartment several months earlier to share a house with two women. Gibb had met them when he'd helped Jess move. Gibb suspected Jess was in love with one of his roommates, but Jess talked about them both with the same unselfconscious affection. Sally was a grade-school teacher and Carey worked at a health-food store. "They're both just friends," Jess insisted.

Gibb hugged his mother, her body stiff in his arms.

"You haven't been over to visit for weeks and you're flying to Colorado," she said.

His father came into the room dangling the car keys and Gibb didn't answer.

"Okay, let's get going so's we don't hit the traffic," Noel said, picking up a bag.

"Tell Rachel to write once in a while," his mother said, standing in the doorway, her body framed in light.

The air grew brighter as they drove and when they stepped from the car at the airport Gibb could see his father clearly—the last dark streaks in his hair faded, his chin's white stubble. Around his eyes clung a web of lines and folds, a face to be studied like a map. A face in the early light offering itself to be read. *I want to do something to give my father back part of his life.* Gibb smelled the dampness of soil and trees on the morning air, and the intermingled acrid odor of jet fuel. He listened to the distant rumble of rising planes. He'd willingly entered a labyrinth long ago, an elaborately confusing place. He saw himself inside, moving forward towards the center. At the center—if there were a center—would be revelation, the journey half-completed, the way back certain. To be confounded by a single turn…No. He would risk being overcome or lost forever. He thought of Ama, his beloved Amanda, pain and desire mingling cruelly in him, the pleasure of the time they had spent together diminished by his feelings of shame. But she was safe from him now. He had used her, lied to her. He was no longer angry at her for leaving him. As Gibb looked around at the scattering of cars unloading suitcases and passengers, his father walked over to the trunk.

"Give Sis my regards," Noel said, starting to lift a bag out of the trunk.

Gibb put his hand on his father's, and then took the bag. "I will. Thanks for the ride."

His father stepped back. "I'll see you two on Sunday the twelfth, then. Flight 515." He wiped his face with his handkerchief and looked away.

"Right."

As they stepped into the terminal, Gibb glanced behind him. His father still stood next to the car. He lifted his hand. Gibb waved back.

They sat on the concourse waiting, Jess staring out toward the runways, elbows on his knees. Gibb looked at Jess in profile. Jess wasn't like any of them. He was taller than everyone else in the family, yet his build was slender, powerful. Jess walked, played music, studied, did everything Gibb had ever seen him do with a kind of energy Gibb couldn't quite describe. It wasn't the aggressive energy of athletes, though Jess soundly trounced Gibb at their one-on-one basketball games. It wasn't a nervous energy, either. No. Jess had an unselfconscious trust in his instincts, his body. Gibb remembered a line from Dostoevsky one of his English teachers had quoted again and again. "One must love life before loving its meaning." Jess had gotten the order of things right, even if Gibb hadn't.

For a moment Gibb longed to tell Jess everything, to tell him about Amanda, about the mystery he'd inevitably unravel, no matter what it took. Passing a hand over his eyes, he imagined he heard the hiss of his breath, felt the water bearing him and the metallic taste of nitrogen in his mouth, which meant he was going too deep.

He had to correct now, to focus. Maybe sometime in Denver he and Jess and Rachel could talk. This wasn't the time, not yet.

Smiling, Jess glanced at Gibb and turned back to the window. The metal skin of a taxiing plane glittered, and light shuddered down the length of it, spilling onto the runway like fire.

Gibb remembered the hollow notes of the piano in a practice room, Jess at an early lesson, a simple rondo played again and again, note by note, until the notes connected and became fluid, a first recital, applause. His teacher Mrs. Benuto saying, *he has talent. Try the Beaumont School of Music. They have programs for gifted young musicians.*

As he studied Jess's profile, Gibb saw Jess the child and the teenage Jess, still lingering familiarly in his features like benevolent ghosts. Jess was studying music and mathematics on a scholarship, and at the rate he was taking courses, he'd have his degree a year early. Gibb had seen Jess angry, but he'd never seen him lose his temper. There was a difference. His father's outbursts of temper had taught Gibb that all too well.

"Okay," Jess said, pinning him with a curious look. "You're just sitting there staring at me. What's up?"

"I was thinking of that club you joined at school. What's it named?"

"It's not a club," Jess said mildly. "I'd call it a group, I guess, a group for change: "Jobs and Lives with Justice."

"What does that mean?"

"If you wipe the cynical smirk off your face, I'll tell you." Jess glanced out the window.

"Sorry."

"It means what it says." Jess didn't turn around at first, but when he looked at Gibb his face wore an expression of earnestness that made Gibb remember himself and something he'd done years ago, a speech he'd given on the Dade County courthouse steps. People had jeered him, someone had thrown an egg, but nothing could have changed the feeling of hope he'd had then.

"We're dealing with justice issues in the community, racism, for one—police brutality, homelessness," Jess went on, "students and some professors, too. It's hard to know where to start in this city.

We've got a meeting coming up on racism. Our next one's on police brutality. Homelessness? You'd be amazed if I told you how many people were homeless here." Jess put his hand lightly on Gibb's arm. A muscle in his jaw twitched. "I get angry. I'm sorry."

"Don't be. I want to hear more." Planes in their noisy ascent rumbled in the background and Gibb recalled a story he'd read once about a person on a plane who'd been swept through an emergency door that had suddenly sprung open. She'd fallen—doomed—all the way to earth. Why hadn't there been a way to save her, Gibb wondered. Until the last moment, the person falling would have hoped to be saved somehow. Everyone wanted to live, in spite of the perils, the suffering. There were so many things to hope for. He listened keenly as Jess talked about the group's last meeting. Jess had hope, Gibb was convinced of that, hope that would last.

Rachel wasn't at the gate. Gibb searched the faces among the waiting crowd, looking for hers, wondering if she'd changed so much that he'd missed her. He peered down the concourse, expecting to see her walking toward them. But the flight emptied and the waiting relatives and friends and passengers gradually disappeared.

"I know I gave her the right flight number."

"She'll be here," Jess said. "Let's go get our bags and see some mountains."

They started down the concourse and suddenly Rachel stood in their path, smiling. Where had she come from? Her hair was shorter than Gibb had ever seen it, and she wore dangling earrings that caught the light. She put her arms around both of them. "I can't believe it." Shaking her head, she took a step back to look at them. "Your hair is *long*," she said to Gibb. "I like it. You're grown up, Jess." She sighed. "Just like that."

Gibb felt himself staring, not smiling, wanting only to fix his eyes upon hers and to study her face, each feature and quality. He wanted to tell her how much he'd missed her, but the words snagged somewhere and he made up a smile, made his face look as happy as everyone else's.

At the baggage carousel Rachel talked for all of them. She'd drive them to the mountains, to the national park. The weather was warm. They could hike, camp, she'd borrow sleeping bags. She glanced at Gibb through her chatter, her face changing for an instant. Rachel, I've missed you, he wanted to say.

Rachel was working full time, coordinating a consumer advocacy program, training volunteers, taking the last class for her master's degree. She'd gotten a few days off to spend with them. Her voice rose too high when she talked, and through the smiles her face was drawn, her eyes tired.

Gibb's pulse beat in his head until it became the sound of a dull bell, then pain. Did she notice? He heard Jess say his name, then "diving." He looked toward them, forced himself to focus.

"That must have been hard," he heard Rachel saying.

"Yes," he said, thinking of Ama leaving, knowing his answer would be right, no matter. ·

"Salvage work pays great," Jess said, "but the diving's dangerous."

"No," Gibb said, "it doesn't pay that much, not always." ·

"Gibb," Rachel said, her eyes on his, "I've missed you."

"It's been a long time, hasn't it?"

"Yes," she said, her voice straining again, pressing him to take the first few moments of their being together again lightly. "Let's not waste a minute catching up."

Gibb fell silent and followed a step behind Rachel and Jess. He blinked as he walked, the air bright and so hazy at the same time. At the top level of the parking garage, he looked for the horizon, the sky's clean meeting with the edge of earth. But here the sky slipped curiously behind the jagged, distant edge of the still-snowcapped mountains. He sat in the back and Rachel drove with the windows down, her hair flying crazily. The hot, dry air blew across his face. He looked at his watch. It was 5:30 at home. The palms would be casting long shadows across the St. Augustine grass where he always walked after working in the shop or coming back from a charter, where he passed old men and women with sun-leathered faces, overhearing snatches of conversation, each a door opened onto the simple mystery of another life. "Oh, he said...he'd...let her go... peacefully."

"Gibb, you're so quiet back there. Tell me about commercial diving. What kinds of jobs are you getting?"

"Wait until we get to your place," he said, peering out the window at the low, blunt-topped mountains they drove towards, no snow on these, and a cornfield next to a farmhouse, too close to the highway, its edge ragged and dusty, trash-scattered. "I brought some photos to show you."

She talked to Jess then, about her work, his classes, her voice purposely low, he thought. Was she angry? He noted the peculiar color of the sky. Intensely blue, without a trace of clouds, the color a painter would use whose imagination was as spare as the landscape this false-looking sky arched over.

They pulled into the driveway of a brick house.

"Here's where I moved. Three weeks ago." She gestured up toward the tall elms, across the small yard, defining the whole of the place with that sweep of her hand, a gesture, Gibb thought, of someone coming up through water, slowly finding the surface. His heart ached with something he couldn't name.

"I saw the picture you sent to Mother," Jess said, looking up toward the peaked roof. "I'm sorry," she said. "That wasn't much of a photo."

Gibb took his bag from the trunk and walked up to the front steps.

"Wait," Rachel called. "I want to go in with you. Jess, come on with us. Jack's waiting to meet you."

The door swung open and Gibb stepped in first.

Rachel followed, and stood beside Gibb. "Jack, I'd like you to meet my brothers, Jess and Gibb."

The man held out his hand to Jess, then Gibb. "John Kellogg," he said, "Jack for short. Glad to know you. Welcome to Colorado."

Gibb looked at Jack's broad, confident smile and studied his face.

Jack held out his hand to Rachel and she came to stand beside him. He kissed the top of her head. She looked up at him, then at Jess and Gibb. She took a quick breath. "We got married two weeks ago," she said.

Maybe Gibb had known, within a second of her telling them, what she was going to say, and this made his manner easy, helped him smile. "Congratulations. We'll have to celebrate." Inside he was angrier at Rachel than he'd ever been.

Rachel spoke almost before he'd finished. "You each have a room," she said brightly. "They're small bedrooms, but you each have one. Jack, show Jess. The basement, is that okay Jess?"

"Sure, great." Jess walked to Rachel and put his arms around her. "Neat," he said. "What a surprise."

Jack picked up Jess's bag and Jess followed him down the steps.

"Gibb," she said, "you're here, right down the hall," her back to him already. She pointed into the room with its neatly made bed, walked in with him and shut the door. "Gibb," she said, "I'm sorry. I'm really sorry."

"For what? Getting married?"

"For not telling you."

"Why didn't you tell me?" Gibb turned away, snapped open his suitcase, looked at the confusion of his clothes. *Once I was closer to you than anyone in the world. You could read my mind, remember?* He glanced back at her.

She ran her hand over the top of the dresser and looked at it. "Dust," she said. "It's been dry."

"I know, I feel it every time I take a breath."

"That's the altitude." She paused and looked down at the carpeted floor. "I was going to tell you, and then you said you were coming. Maybe we should come to Miami and have a ceremony."

"Why do you need another one?"

"I just don't want you to be angry."

"Are you in love?" he asked, turning away from her and putting a shirt in the drawer.

"Yes." Her voice was soft. "I am."

"I'm happy for you then."

"You're really angry at me, aren't you?"

"No," he said. "I just need a shower."

"Then we'll go eat. I know a place you'll like."

"Okay. We'll celebrate."

After she closed the door behind her, he sat for a minute on the bed, and then slowly walked down the hall to the bathroom. He took off his clothes and turned on the cold water faucet until the tub was half-full. The water was icy, not like the near tepid water that came from the tap at home. He turned on the hot tap, let the tub fill, then lay down. His body stretched out before him, bloated-looking under the water. Drawing up his knees, he slid down until water covered his head, exhaled and held his breath for a long time, as long as he could.

At the restaurant, Gibb listened. He watched the angle of menus, the length of fingers, observed the manner each of them used with the young waitress who introduced herself as "Serene." He wondered if her parents had given her that name, or if she'd made it up. Even before he felt it on his skin, he smelled the evening's cooling on the air. A wavering oval of light reflected from the new gold of his sister's ring. They ate outdoors and he noted a certain kind of brightness reflected on the faces of the passersby—the last of the sun coming through such thin air. He'd try to describe that odd light— the whole scene—in his journal, when he was back in his room.

Rachel's glances questioned his long silence. He touched the napkin to his lips and remembered he'd once acted—small parts, mostly, but still, he had learned to pull up the lines at will, to devise convincing gestures and expressions. He faced Jack. "What a change for us, Jess and me," he said. "I'm looking forward to hiking in the mountains." Turning to Rachel to see her smiling at him, he reached for more words, easy words that wouldn't betray him. "We've had a heat wave," he said finally, realizing this fact of the weather barely touched him on the boat. He was always busy getting ready for dives, or he was under water. He'd learned of the record-breaking heat only by reading headlines in the *Herald*.

Satisfied, Rachel nodded, asked Jack something about his dinner and looked around absently. Gibb waited for her eyes to meet his and tell him he was shamming. But she turned to Jess and didn't look in Gibb's direction at all. "So are you taking any summer school courses?"

Gibb didn't hear Jess's answer. He glanced up to find that Jack Kellogg had been himself engaged in scrutinizing Gibb. When Gibb met his gaze, Jack didn't look away.

"I'm looking forward to hearing more about your job, Gibb. Rachel's filled me in on a few things about diving, but it's all exotic to me. My family took a vacation at Myrtle Beach when I was seven."

He laughed. "And I had nightmares about whale-sized jellyfish. That's the only time I've ever been in the ocean."

"I do commercial salvage, including so-called medical salvage— at least my certification covers that—scuba tours with advanced divers, that sort of thing." Medical salvage. Why had he mentioned that? The words came back like an echo.

"Medical salvage. I'm guessing that's looking for accident victims? Drownings and such?"

"Yeah. As I say, I've never done any. A few other divers with the outfit have."

"Whew, that would be tough."

"So what line of work are you in, Jack?"

"Unemployed at the moment." He ran his hand through curly blonde hair in a gesture Gibb took to be affable. He was a man who'd grow old gracefully. His hair would thin unobtrusively, because of its color, and his body always tend toward a leanness a few drinks and rich food wouldn't easily undo. "I just finished my Ph.D.," he said, offering the explanation, finally, into the silence that Gibb hadn't filled. "In Public Administration. I'm looking for a job." He put his hand over Rachel's where it lay near her plate. "But first we'll take a camping trip or something."

He didn't say "honeymoon," Gibb thought. And of course, he'd been gracious. Gibb and Jess had come right at the time they would have been on such a trip. Jack was clever and well-bred. For what other reasons did Rachel love him? Gibb glimpsed the rich brown of Rachel's eyes, the firm line of her chin. She had always been tough, in her own way—tough and eccentric and single-minded, going off like that, living in five different states. Would she settle into a peaceful life with Jack Kellogg so easily? Gibb heard her laughter and raised his wine glass. "To you both," he said gaily, leaving the matter ambiguous, even to himself.

Gibb stood in the kitchen listening to the sound of their voices, laughter. A splash of bourbon hit the countertop as he poured himself another drink. Adding an ice cube, he drank half of what was in his glass. He refilled it and walked into the living room to sit cross-legged on the rug. Jess was telling Rachel and Jack about the course he'd just finished in music theory. Rachel leaned forward towards him, her eyes sparkling. They'd all had a little too much wine with dinner. Rachel's dark and lustrous hair was so unlike Amanda's. When Amanda was tired, Gibb had lifted her hair's delicate silken bundle and stroked her neck and shoulders. He pushed her image from his mind. With an effort, he turned his attention to Jess. A cool breeze drifted through the open door, carrying a flower scent he didn't recognize.

"Harmony versus rhythmic structure," Jess was saying, his hand sweeping an imaginary horizontal plane. "Chinese music theory depends on a single note, the *Chuang chung*. Twelve notes come from that and each of those twelve notes is the basis of a pentatonic scale."

Gibb smiled in spite of his dark mood. A crazy happiness ran in Jess like a current of pure, deep water. One night about a week ago Gibb had stopped by Jess's place. Jess was playing the piano while his roommates Sally and Carey sang. "We're celebrating," Jess had explained, grinning. The women were festooned with blue and green crepe paper. All of the lights were on and the little duplex glowed like the head of a match. "Someone bought one of Sally's drawings today," Carey said. "It was Jess's idea," Sally crooned tip-sily, "to sing and dance the night away."

Rachel came to where Gibb sat on the floor. "Hey," she whispered. "You've never changed, have you?" Her lips curved in a half smile. He remembered she had protected him against something unnamable once, something he'd long since taken into his body like an extra heart.

"Let me show you the garden."

The nearly full moon had risen to cast its luminous blue light over Rachel's overgrown yard. "We've got a lot of work to do," she said, pulling a twining weed off the fence. "Bindweed." She yanked off a piece and the heart-shaped leaves dangled along the slender vine. "It's everywhere." She turned a white face upon him, "I'm worried about you, Gibb."

Ah, sisterly concern, he thought bitterly, annoyed by her tone. But he wouldn't hurt her by saying so. He forced a laugh. "You should be. I've been working like a dog. I took out a group of divers every day last week. They tell you they're advanced—they've got their certificates—but you go down with them and you know different."

"I'm glad you came."

"I wish you'd told me you were getting married."

"Would you have come then?"

"I don't know."

She walked to the edge of the yard and he followed her. Resting her hands lightly on a strand of barbwire that ran atop the chain link fence, she spoke softly without turning. "Jess is incredible," she said. "How could he ever have ended up such a good person?" She looked at him behind her. "So..."

"Happy?" He laughed dryly. "Stable?"

"Yes." She nodded, solemn.

"Because we raised him not to be screwed up like us." The liquor warm in his chest, he wanted to put his arms around her then, to talk the way they used to. Moonlight poured over her hair like shimmering liquid.

She pivoted, faced him and held his shoulders. "You've always been...so...weird," she said. "In a good way...the best way."

The pressure alarmed him, not pain, but the feeling of her fingers, the power of her grasp. "Rachel..."

"What?"

"Thanks for having us."

"Don't be silly." She dropped her hands and turned back toward the fence, looked up at the moon. "How are Mother and Dad?"

"The same."

"I'm glad I don't know what that means anymore."

They had gone hiking, just the three of them. Jack was job-hunting. Gibb followed Rachel across the boulder field, to where the trail took up on the other side. She stepped easily from one huge, lichen-spattered boulder to another. The larger stones were like prehistoric eggs that malformed creatures might spill out of—stegosaurus and triceratops and brontosaurs that could wake at any moment from their interminable sleep and amble off into the pines.

Hunching over, crablike, Gibb used his hands as much as his feet. What if they slipped down the rock field into the jumble of trees and brush below? Jess was ahead of them. He stepped out onto the path, into half shadow, and turned to look back expectantly, his face eager as it once had been when he shared in their games, the innocence of his excitement drawing them out of their seriousness. The trail opened to a meadow, dotted with flowers—orange, blue, white, yellow. Rachel named them—paintbrush, harebells, mountain aster, firecracker weed. She took Jess by the hand. Gibb imagined them lying side-by-side in the grass, their faces against the roots and soil, the joyful beat of their hearts rumbling down into stone, causing the earth to tremble with their sudden, cumulative happiness. The crazy Colgrove children together again. A wisp of iridescent cloud, filmy as a shred of fancy cloth, floated above him.

They sat cross-legged in a rough circle, close enough to touch one another. Rachel pulled a bottle of wine from her pack, sandwiches, oranges. They drank and ate without conversation, their meal accompanied only by the insistent twittering of birds, whole trees of chiding, love-calling, for-the-pure-joy-of-it-singing birds.

Later, the sky paled as they watched, to a faded, silky blue. They sat overlooking a creek several hundred feet below that ran like a shiny ribbon, winding smaller, out of sight. Gibb heard the rush of water, faint but constant among the other sounds of evening.

He and Rachel sat against the rocks. Jess had decided to hike down the trail a ways before it was too dark.

Rachel looked up at the sky and spoke quietly. "What do you do for fun these days, Gibb? Are you going out with anyone?"

"No," he said, and felt the word on his tongue for a moment like a drop of burning liquid. "Just working." He managed a smile.

"What about that girl you wrote me about, Ama?"

His throat tightened. "She moved to California. Quite a while ago."

"It doesn't seem that long since the last time you wrote about her."

He pulled up a piece of grass and twisted it around his finger. "Somehow time gets distorted in letters."

"You keep saying things like that."

"Like what?"

"Things that make me feel guilty." She looked down, moved a small rock by her knee.

"I'm sorry." He saw her in profile and wanted to say more, heard himself telling her more than she'd be able to understand, more than it was fair to tell her. "I'm a..."

"A what?" She turned her face toward him. "You're a what?"

Bats had begun their fluttering descent into the valley below, emerging from some darkness he could not imagine. "I'm a jerk, I'm sorry...I'm not very thoughtful of your feelings, I guess." *When we were young, we played house, you and I and Jess—who'd just started walking— all of us together in the echoing rooms of the backyard. The secrets of children, do you remember? I thought we'd never be parted. Now, if we sit here long enough, you'll disappear; you'll change into a rock or tree as if you'd never existed. Without you, how will I know who I am?* He expected more of Rachel than she could give, any longer. He picked up a small rock and threw it into the brush below.

"You're angry," she said, "or terribly sad. Or something's happened you're just not talking about." Her voice was low. She kept her eyes on some spot in the distance, the mountains, perhaps, that had blurred to dark blue uncertain silhouettes in the early twilight. He noted her profile, seeing his own face there—nose, chin and jaw—both of them shaped by the same scattering of genes, the same fierce rush of blood. "What's going on?" she asked finally, still not looking at him.

"Not much. Not much more than I've said." He felt his hands suddenly grow cold, to the wrist, as if he held some small, frightening object just arrived from another world. "I'm a little preoccupied, I guess. I'm still doing some research that might help exonerate Dad."

She turned to him with a quick motion, interrupted. "You can't still be thinking about that." She snapped a twig into smaller and smaller pieces. "That's not just a preoccupation. Don't you think it's gotten to be more like an obsession? You can't change the past. You have to forget it. You've got to come out of this private history you're living in. It's not the world. Believe me, I know."

Her voice spilled over him, echoed below and circled behind him through the trees. He had no time to break into her earnest speech, or he might have asked, *What world? How do you know?* They had been through so much together; he wished he could have heard her answers.

"I never tell anyone," she said. "I never talk about it. I've never even told Jack. I don't want to tell him. 'Jack, guess what? My father was tried for murder. He was acquitted, but the murder was never solved.' It's like a disease I had and now I'm over it. Don't you see? You don't have to keep on being sick with it."

Gibb watched her mouth, the white glint of her teeth in the deepening twilight, and gave the appearance of listening patiently to every word. He understood that Rachel thought she'd convinced him of something, that she meant well, trying to cure him with reason, imagining him helpless in the grip of his "obsession." If only he could persuade her that *he* was ultimately the reasonable one. Naturally the past couldn't be changed; that wasn't the point. But the past was an arrow, flying into the future. To know who pulled the bowstring, to see the arrow's flight and imagine the target—to grasp all these things was to shape the future. Finally he'd understand where to find the arrow, spent and harmless. His course of action was quite sound. He started to explain.

"Rachel, hey, Gibb, the moon's rising." Jess half-ran up the trail, reached their niche in the rocks with a few long steps.

"Where?" Rachel stood up, wiped her face with both hands and brushed the twigs and leaves off the backs of her legs.

Jess pointed.

Gibb looked up. The edge of the moon was keen as a blade, a white disk that gave off a ragged circle of light in the darkening sky.

"We'd better start back," Rachel said. "Jack will be wondering what's become of us."

They gathered their things in silence and walked down the trail, the strawberry moon slowly rising over them, slicking the rocks with light and filling the woods with shadows that changed shape in the wind. Gibb savored their quiet steps down the mountain, for they were together again, the three of them, and he had spared Rachel pain. He was grateful for that.

More than a week later, back in Florida, Gibb paced his apartment, thinking of his visit with Rachel. Had he been rude? Had she ceased to love him, even a little? She seemed so tired. Wasn't she well? Did she regret the marriage? He thought of Amanda, how he missed her. His physical desire for her was often so overpowering that it shamed him. Walking into the bedroom, he switched off the light and lay atop the bed without pulling back the sheet, hearing the murmur of voices on the sidewalk below. He took a deep breath, and another, smelling the salt in the air, and then he slept.

Touching her delicate nipples, he felt them grow firm under his fingers, felt her ribs under his palm, the wedge of bone that formed her hip. He slid his hand to her knee and down her smooth calf. She cried, softly at first, then in great shaking gasps. "Ssshh," he said gently. She sat bolt upright then, her hair tangled, her face crimson with rage. "Murderer," she screamed. "No," he said, "not me. It wasn't me." He opened his eyes. His hair was soaking, as if he'd just come up from under water, the sheet beneath his back wet, his heart pounding. Squeezing his eyes closed, he saw the face of the girl in the dream clearly, as clearly as if she stood before him. It wasn't Amanda. It was her mother. He closed his eyes, opened them again and walked across the room in the darkness. Without putting on the light in the bathroom, not wanting to see himself, he turned on the shower.

When he stepped from the tub, he was still sweating. Running the towel over his body roughly, he laid it beneath him on the bed and stared at the ceiling, half-afraid to close his eyes again.

His heart drummed in his ears and his neck muscles were taut, his back stiff. The voices of the gulls rose to screeches as they always did after a storm, when there was so much to scavenge from the shoreline debris. He hadn't heard the rain start during the night, but he saw it was raining still, jagged rivulets streaming down the windows. The morning light was flat and gray.

He fixed coffee and sat at the table. He and Jess had made plans to visit their parents that afternoon. The prospect began to fill him with the familiar dread, which shamed him even as he gave in to its rising hold on him. His parents were like robots. They sat still and silent in the darkened and airless house until human voices roused them into motion, his father beginning, then, his unsteady trips to the refrigerator for beer. When had his mother finally stopped screaming at his father for each of these trips? Gibb didn't know. Now she merely fixed a stony gaze on Noel as he passed her, and then turned her attention once again to the droning television. Their hair had turned gray together, they walked on the same painful joints, and age had inscribed the same lines on their faces. They both wore sweaters in the stifling house, no more than cracking the windows so as to prevent the entrance of drafts or thieves. They had, in short, declined simultaneously and identically into old age.

Gibb stood up and refilled his cup. Maybe he had exaggerated the dreariness of their lives. Sometimes when he and Jess visited, they all sat together in the shade of the avocado trees and threw breadcrumbs to the birds. He saw the joy with which his father and mother both looked at Jess, grown robust and tall, the one of their children, surely, who'd make something of himself, the only one of their children who treated them with gentle indulgence.

He walked to the window and saw that the clouds were breaking apart. The sky had begun to show blue. Through the years, Gibb had talked to his father, watched him, listened for some slip of the tongue, some accident of speech, anything. But his father had never wavered. He had been dignified in his indignation that his son, of all people, questioned him, when he had been absolved by a court of law. How often he'd heard his father say those very words—*I've been absolved by a court of law.* But Gibb needed to be certain that his father was innocent. He lived with a rage, with a decent passion, to know. It wasn't any longer simply a question of exoneration for his father or punishment for Neoma Kelch's killer. It was a question of knowing the truth of something. With each interview, letter or telephone conversation he had come closer to that goal: Bix McGrath, Bertha Kelch, Sam Lachon, his father's lawyer, the district attorney, the few members of the jury he'd been able to talk to. The trial transcripts he had read and reread. All of his work was recorded in his journals.

He had a sudden urge to strike something, to find the proof of himself in head-clearing pain, in the flow of his blood. For a moment, he stood in the center of the room, eyes closed, feeling, absurdly, that if he moved he'd step headlong into air. He opened his eyes, half-dizzy, picked up his keys and hurried quickly down the stairs, eager to be out of the close, sour air of the landing.

The dark, knotted clouds near the horizon meant another storm. Gibb took a deep breath and smelled salt on the slight breeze.

When Gibb crossed Ocean Drive, he could see the blue sky and water meeting. The St. Augustine grass, still wet from the rain, crunched under his feet. He sidled over the low coral-rock wall. He took off his thongs, walked to the tideline, and stripped to his trunks. He waded to waist level then dove and swam far from the shore with strong, even strokes until, when he turned, the people who scattered the beach were indistinct dots of color. He raised his arms and jumped up with a cresting wave, remembering as he'd remembered a thousand times, lying in bed as a child after a day at the beach, still feeling himself rocked by the breaking surf.

He swam to shore. As he was toweling himself dry, an old woman walked slowly toward Gibb, wearing a bathing suit with a skirt. Her body was wiry, sun-dark and oddly firm beneath the drooping skin of age. She turned her back to him and to the sea, and began to touch her toes, slowly—one...two...three...four. Pivoting to face him suddenly, she smiled and nodded. As he raised his hand in reply, a sudden pain rose in his chest. She was very old, but in her face he saw contentment and perfect peace. He imagined her someday swimming out farther and farther, until the water took her.

As they turned onto Bird Road, Jess flipped on the radio. WQAM, the oldies station, was playing a Van Morrison song, "Brown Eyed Girl." The words conjured for Gibb an image of his younger self, a body so eager to be satisfied, to satisfy; he remembered crazy lovemaking in the apartments of several women, and later, in the woods near the lighthouse delirious hours in Ama's arms...

"Gibb."

"What?"

"You just passed the turn."

"God, I did. Sorry."

"Are you okay?"

In the periphery of his vision, as he made a U-turn, Gibb saw Jess watching him. He briefly met Jess's curious eyes, a darker blue than their mother's, and saw beyond his handsome features a maturity of expression he'd never noticed before. Gibb had so often thought of Jess as guileless, and perhaps naïve. But at this moment he understood that Jess was far more complex than Gibb had ever realized.

"Yeah. I was thinking about the time I first heard this song. I was probably driving somewhere near here in this same kind of sticky heat." The asphalt up ahead gleamed like melted silver. Jess was the kind of person to have in the water with you, someone who never panicked. There was something more to Jess than all that, something Gibb struggled to put words to—how Jess found the redeemable in circumstances Gibb dismissed as hopeless. A sensuous intelligence worked in Jess, worth a truckload of minds like his own, minds that toiled laboriously along, remote from the living, peopled world.

"Hey," Jess said. "I feel like I'm riding with someone having an out-of-body experience." Jess grinned, but his voice was serious.

"I enjoy these visits less and less," Gibb admitted. "And I'm thinking about you, how...tolerant you are of things that drive me nuts."

Jess gave a snort of laughter and hung his head out the window, looked up toward the sky and back at Gibb. "Can't you see I'm only a dumb kid who doesn't know any better? Give me time and I'll be as cynical as you are. That's what it takes, right? Time and a few gut punches."

"Okay, you're young and crazy," Gibb said, smiling and shaking his head slowly. "I admit it."

"No, I'm just stupidly happy. Let's go to the Y and shoot some hoop after we leave the dark mansion." He jerked his thumb down the street, toward their parents' house.

"Sure," Gibb said. "It's a plan."

A flock of green parrots flew overhead as Gibb swung the car into the driveway. When he switched off the engine, his mother appeared in the doorway. She smiled and raised her hand. Gibb had only a few photographs of his mother smiling. In one, she wore her hair permed and pulled back from her face with two clips. She'd just taken an unfiltered cigarette from her dark lips and it bore a smudge of lipstick. The picture had been snapped at the factory in Miami where she'd been a riveter. Elizabeth of long ago. The face from the photograph that had for a moment replaced the one of the old woman at the door disappeared, and his mother stepped off the porch toward the car. Jess blocked Gibb's view of her as they hugged. Gibb got out of the car and stood, waiting, hands in his pockets, until Jess stepped away.

"You're so thin," his mother said.

"I'm fine. It's good to be thin." She turned her cheek to him and he kissed it. He'd seen her less than a week ago, and already she seemed smaller. Oddly, when he thought of her, she always towered above him, her once-dark fall of thick hair blocking the light like a curtain as she bent over him, to say goodnight or tend him in an illness.

"Your father's clipping the bushes in back."

They followed her through the house to where their father stood with his hand clippers near the back fence.

"I can't understand why the damn neighbors..." He stopped and made his hand into a fist. "They don't have any right to call themselves neighbors. Why can't they keep their goddamn bushes trimmed?"

"How're you, Pop?" Jess put his hand on his father's shoulder.

"I'm crummy. My hip aches from something. No doctor can tell me what." He lowered his voice for a moment. "Your mother's driving me crazy with her nagging. What's a matter, Gibb, shark gotcher tongue?" he boomed suddenly in a voice that could be heard in the next block.

Gibb smiled faintly. "Hey, how's it going?"

"I thought I just told you," he said, peevish as a child.

Gibb saw the irritable cast of the jowly face before him, and tried to dismiss a lifetime of insults and cruelties suffered at his father's hand. Looking into his father's face, he worked to decipher it, to see in his father's expression, as he just had in Jess's, something he'd never observed before. Cunning, perhaps, slyness.

His father looked back, revealing nothing. Gibb felt the heat of the afternoon, his hair limp, his face slick with sweat. His father had turned to speak to Jess. Bluejays sang their four-part throaty call from the avocado trees and swooped down near his feet for the bread his mother and father had thrown in the grass. He stood apart, near the edge of the yard where he'd so often played as a child, alone with his thoughts. This was not the day to tell his parents that Rachel had just gotten married.

Later that afternoon, Gibb called Jennifer Lehndorff, a juror who had told a reporter she had been one of the hold-outs for a guilty verdict. Her name was in one of the newspaper articles about the trial that his mother had clipped and saved. "I took a lot of convincing there was 'reasonable doubt,'" she'd been quoted as saying. Tom Mullen had found her unlisted telephone number as quickly as only a private detective could, Gibb guessed.

He listened as her phone rang, expecting her to hang up on him, or, at best a short conversation ending in a "No," after he'd asked if they could meet. But she readily agreed to see him—at her home, another surprise. She lived on San Remo Drive in Coral Gables, so he expected to find himself in a nice place. In fact, the house was lavish—planes of glass and chrome, sleek Scandinavian furniture, a plush white carpet, French doors leading to a stone patio where she decided they would talk. The patio overlooked a deeply green sloping lawn, bordered with red rose bushes. Her hair was dark and shiny, even though she must have been over sixty. She wasted no time. "I took careful notes," she said, "on everything. I remember how distraught your pregnant mother looked. Your father's show of politeness...all 'yes sir' and 'no sir.'" She seemed oddly eager to tell her story, which somehow made her less credible to Gibb. She'd brought them a pitcher of lemonade, and she took a sip from her glass before speaking again. "I was sure your father had lied when he denied knowing Neoma Kelch."

"What persuaded you to change your mind?" Gibb asked.

She brushed back a strand of hair with a lacquered nail. "At the time, I believed I'd been convinced by your father's attorney—he was very good—that there was 'reasonable doubt.' I'm sorry to say I'm not so sure anymore. I'm a strong woman and I'm not in the habit of being emotional, but the other jurors did everything in their power to wear me down. Even to the point of meanness. They said the prosecution's case was flimsy. They liked your father, whereas I was absolutely certain I was listening to a liar."

"I've been gathering evidence to solve the murder and absolve my father of doubts like yours," he said when she paused.

Before he'd finished his sentence, her eyes filled with tears. "Finding out it was someone else would give me relief after all these years. I've lived with such guilt thinking we let a murderer go free. I don't envy your task, but I wish you luck."

Eight

Already the Miami winter had been unseasonably cold. In the late fall, most of the citrus crop had been lost to a hard freeze. Last night the temperature had dropped to forty-five and a thirty- to forty-knot on-shore wind blew across the water, turning it to foamy chop. Diving, he was used to cold, chop, lousy visibility. But outdoors, walking, he could hardly stand the way the wind bit through him and the ugly, ragged clouds that scudded across the sun. Trash and sand blew through the streets, and the faces of the people he passed were grim, their lips held in tight lines. He thought of Rachel, unable to imagine how she stood the snow in Colorado.

He crossed the road to his car, leaning sideways in the full force of the wind. He doubted if Jon, his boss, would want to go out. But an hour later, by the time he'd arrived at the Key Largo shop, the wind had subsided. He walked across the parking lot to the small office, the sun warm on his face.

"Hey Gibb." Megan Sanchez put down the phone and looked up at him, smiling.

Megan's long black hair hung down her back in a braid, showing off her slender neck and the fine bones of her face. He'd seen her hair loose for the first time last Friday when he'd taken her out to dinner at a small Japanese restaurant in Coconut Grove. She had picked the place to go later, Monty's, for dancing. Gibb didn't dance and she'd left him at their table to dance with some other diver friends who were there. He hadn't minded, seeing Megan move with an athlete's grace—if not a dancer's—across the floor and hearing the pleasure in her laugh when she returned to the table, her cheeks flushed and tendrils of damp hair curling around her face.

Jon stood at the edge of a cluttered desk checking the map. "What's goin' on, guy?" he said, glancing up.

"Not much." Gibb walked over to his gear, to check it before loading it onto the boat.

Jon let out a snort of laughter. "What the hell were these dudes doing out by Carysfort? Not exactly anything to fish for there now. Who's out joyriding when it's this cold?" He folded the map and looked over at Gibb. "Except us, of course."

"How deep?" Gibb asked calmly, feeling a sudden confused mixture of embarrassment and fear, as if shame marked his face like a brand. *Carysfort Reef.*

"A hundred feet, maybe less. These guys didn't know shit. But they have money and they want us to haul up anything that's salvageable."

Gibb carried his gear out back and on board the boat. Two men with Coral Gables addresses had gotten a gas leak at the fuel filter in their powerboat, a 38-foot Sutphen with twin 400 hp V-8's. They wanted the engines salvaged, plus the prop, drive train and hull.

The Coast Guard had rescued them just before the boat had gone down, less than a nautical mile east of Carysfort Reef, the site of the grounding of the HMS *Carysfort* in 1770. Gibb had never been near this reef, not once in fifteen years of diving. At the thought of being underwater where Neoma Kelch had died, he grew cold inside.

The conditions were good after all, since the wind had died down to a slight breeze. As the boat pulled away from the dock, Gibb zipped up his jacket and watched the foamy wake, the poured-silver surface of the ocean under the early sun. He glanced aft to where Jon and Megan stood at the helm. They'd get their LORAN coordinates and haul up what they could, while the weather held. Gibb would be diving with Pete, a Key Largo native Jon had hired just a month ago. Pete was a stocky man a few years older than Gibb. His hair was bleached colorless by the sun and a patch of raw-looking skin scarred the bridge of his nose. Pete fished when he wasn't diving, and wrote a fishing column for the *Key Times*. He worked a toothpick around in the back of his mouth. "I can't ever be out this way without thinking of that story. I was just a kid, probably eleven or twelve at the time. It's always stuck in my mind," he said, staring out across the water. "I guess because my uncle told it so many times I got to know the whole thing by memory." He laughed uncomfortably.

Gibb knelt down to adjust the strap on a flipper. "What story?"

"Somebody drowned a girl out here." He turned and glanced down at Gibb.

Gibb stood up and looked into Pete's face, feeling the blood rush and throb in his skull.

Pete shook his head. "I've never seen a waterlogged corpse, have you?"

"What do you remember?"

"My uncle knew one of the divers who found her. Day, day and a half maybe, after it happened. Can't pinpoint the time of a drowning death too well. A few more days, she'd have been gone. Right out here off the reef, some guys spear fishing. They'd never seen a body before either. Blue as a periwinkle. Eyes wide open." He threw the toothpick over the side. "I remember the headlines on the trial. Guess the guy got off. You're probably too young. Maybe you couldn't read yet." Pete smiled at him.

"Yeah, right." Gibb made himself smile and touched his hands together where the sweat had already turned icy. He pulled on his wetsuit, bending over so that Pete couldn't see his face.

They made it to the reef in good time, and Jon secured the boat to a mooring buoy about 100 feet east of the light, and looked across the water. Another diver's down flag was hoisted a quarter mile or so northwest of where they'd moored. "If it isn't Dives Unlimited with some sucker tourists who don't know it's cold." Jon turned back to Pete and Gibb. "Okay, we should be pretty close. I'm guessing you'll find that crate at 50, 60 feet or more." He snorted and shook his head. "Jackasses," he muttered. "Look," he said. "Why don't you see what you can do in about thirty or forty minutes." He and Megan checked the repetitive dive worksheet.

"Yeah," Megan said, "if you guys have to go down again today, even for another half hour, that'll keep us out here four more hours." She shrugged her shoulders and looked at Jon. "We might lose visibility, depending on the current. What do you think?"

"I'd rather not have to come back here tomorrow. See what you can do."

Gibb and Pete checked their watches and the worksheet, and Gibb was in the water right behind Pete, swimming down on the seaward side of the double reef into the dwindling light. Along the near wall of the second reef, lettuce coral cascaded down the reef face. A queen angelfish passed Gibb's facemask and angled away, its blue and green coloring shimmering with iridescence. Pete and Gibb descended slowly, planning to move parallel to the reef line till they located the boat, which would lie somewhere to the east of where they'd moored. They were about a mile off the light, so the powerboat might be even deeper than Jon had guessed.

The body of Neoma Kelch had been found quite near where they swam. Gibb told himself to stay calm, to swim, to breathe slowly. The tidal current was stronger than he'd expected. As they gained more depth, at about twenty-five feet, the brilliant colors of the reef began to fade in the filtered light, until the greens and blacks were gone, leaving only blue. He checked his depth gauge: fifty feet. As he descended down along the coral wall, the hydraulic winch cables trailing behind and above him, he looked ahead, to the east, for the sunken boat.

Pete had already seen it, and was motioning to him and pointing. They swam down toward the boat, where it tilted, partially covered by the fine sand, at a greater depth than Jon had guessed, 75 feet. A ragged hole marred the stern of the fiberglass hull. When they reached the bottom, it became half-bright again because of the light reflected from the sand. Gibb sent up a marker. As he and Pete made their way together slowly around the Sutphen, Gibb reached out and ran his gloved hand along the sleek finish of the hull.

For a moment, without thinking, he closed his eyes, and the calm, blue face of Neoma Kelch floated into his consciousness. He opened his eyes and heard the lisp of the regulator grow faster. Struggling to regulate his breathing, he took small amounts of air and followed Pete to the engines. Pete got out the tools and began to unbolt the first engine while Gibb secured the winch cables. He looked up. Several feet above him a spotted eagle ray beat its seven-foot wing flaps and disappeared into blue-gray shadows.

They worked together steadily, and at thirty-five minutes sent up the mangled prop.

Pete made an okay sign and pointed up with his thumb. Gibb nodded and followed, checking the pressure gauge on his wrist. He had used much more air than usual for this kind of salvage and his body felt stiff and knotted with cold.

At ten feet below the surface, his twenty-five minute stop seemed to stretch for hours. He took little pleasure in the things he usually savored as he recompressed...an old grouper hovering just above the reef floor, smelling out a meal on the coral wall, a school of damselfish, drifting above the silky surface of the water. As Gibb watched, they suddenly reeled, changed direction in a single motion and were gone, sensing some lurking predator. But he had seen nothing. Maybe they'd sensed the presence of that dark shape, forming in his imagination, a weighted body floating down. Fighting nausea with every shallow breath, Gibb glanced across the water at Pete every now and then, feeling the other man's eyes upon him.

Jon met him at the boarding ladder. "Hey, good job! How's it look down there?"

"Pretty," Gibb said, pulling off his mask and feeling his breath catch. "Piece of cake." He managed a tight smile, looked at Jon.

Jon peered at his face. "You look like hell. See a few of Her Majesty's crew down there?"

"Yeah, sure," Gibb patted his stomach. "The paella last night. That was a mistake," he said, feeling his panic start to ebb.

Megan came from aft and smiled at them. "Did I hear paella? I could go for that, I'm starved."

"Yeah, well you missed your chance," Pete came up the ladder and Jon turned to him. "Good job," Jon said, glancing back at Gibb.

"Look," Gibb said, pointing. The Dives Unlimited boat was heading toward them, its two faded red and white flags looking ragged as they fluttered in the wind. Someone was leaning over the starboard side and waving his arms above his head. When the boat was within a hundred feet or so, a bearded man in a windbreaker shouted at them.

"We've got an emergency." He cupped his hands around his mouth. "Do you have any oxygen?"

"We sure do," Jon yelled back into the wind. He looked at Gibb. "This could be one for you, iceman." Jon was the Dive Master and had the most experience, but he deferred to Gibb in medical emergencies. Gibb had more first aid training and a cool head. He could quickly staunch the flow of blood from a bad gash or calm a novice diver who was panicking after a brush with fire coral. "What's the problem?"

"Don't know yet." The voice faded on the wind.

Gibb saw a woman wrapped in a blanket, several people huddled around her. He boarded when the boat was close enough and squatted next to her. "What happened?"

She had both hands pressed to her chest at the breastbone. "Stupid," she half-whispered. "God, it hurts. I...I'd been down a while photographing...got cold...too worn out I guess." She looked up at Gibb and smiled weakly. "Dumb ass thing to do...I wasn't breathing...right...when I swam through that current."

Gibb gave the woman oxygen and stood up.

"We called the Miami Recompression Chamber and the Coast Guard. Ambulance'll be waiting at the Rattlesnake Key Marina. Sounds like an embolism," Jon said.

"Yeah. We better get her aboard our boat," Gibb said. "That'll give us an extra fifteen minutes or so."

"You bet."

Two Dives Unlimited crewmembers stood at a distance with their arms folded. They could get their charter license yanked for this one. The man with the beard turned and spoke to them, and Gibb leaned down to the woman. "What's your name?" he asked softly, moving the mask away from her face enough so that she could talk.

"Cindy."

"Cindy, you're going to need to recompress for a while at about 165 feet. In the hyperbaric chamber on Virginia Key. My name is Gibb. Do you think you can stand up?"

She nodded and he helped her into Jon's boat where Pete and Jon were waiting to get her aboard.

Megan opened throttle and Pete radioed the Coast Guard again to let them know the change in plans.

Gibb and Jon knelt by the woman, tucking more blankets around her.

She took off the mask, whispered. "Gibb," she said. "I know you. Gibb Colgrove. High school." Her voice was faint. "I was Cindy Moore then."

He looked into her blue eyes and remembered a younger face... Cindy Moore, cheerleader, Homecoming Princess, pinned to the president of Key Club. *Who are you now?*

"You...were in my English class. I called you a weirdo once. I'm sorry."

"Look, Cindy, it doesn't matter. That was a long time ago. Don't try to talk."

"I'm going to die, aren't I?" she asked, pushing the mask away. "Or be paralyzed." She started to cry.

"Please don't," Gibb said. "You've got to try to relax." He took her hand, stroked it, pushed wet hair from her face. She closed her eyes, opened them and blinked, stared. Then her eyelids fluttered down and were still.

She had died. Panic gripped Gibb as though a wide band of steel had suddenly tightened around his chest. She was dead. He looked at Jon, who stared back, puzzled. Gibb held her shoulders, and her eyes popped open like a doll's, her pupils dilated with fear.

"You're not going to die," Gibb said, blood surging in his ears, his heart pounding. He could barely hear the sound of his own voice. "Listen to me, Cindy. Relax and breathe. Tell yourself you're going to make it."

The ambulance was waiting at Rattlesnake Key, lights flashing. Two paramedics hurried down the pier with a stretcher, oxygen, IV. They worked fast. In less than a minute they were on U.S. 1, sirens screaming. On the boat, Cindy hadn't let go of Gibb's hand the whole trip, and his knuckles were red and sore.

"She never lost consciousness," Pete said, clapping him on the back. "Good job, guy." Shaking his head, he grinned with a clenched jaw, his eyes meeting Gibb's. "We've worked together a month and I just found out your last name today." He looked at Gibb quizzically, then pulled a cigarette and matches from his shirt pocket. He lit the cigarette, took a deep drag, and exhaled a thin stream of blue smoke. "Whew," he said. "Hope she makes it."

"Let's go home," Jon said, running a hand through his hair. "We've had enough excitement for one day."

Megan held Gibb's forearm, walked with him to the boat. "You all right?"

"Me? A little cold, that's all." He still wore his wetsuit.

"A weirdo in high school, huh?" Megan looked up at him and smiled.

"Once a weirdo, always a weirdo," he said, while the pain inside him grew, as if he had been the one with the bubble. His ribs and legs ached. The rigging on a nearby sailboat clanked in the wind, like the sound of a wrench on a tank underwater. Megan talked to him on the way to the boat and he nodded to her voice, the sound coming from somewhere far away. The pier stretched before them, very long, tapering to thinness, as if he'd walk off the toothpick end of it, straight into the sea. He was bone-tired. The edges of things shimmered and wavered, the curving hull of the boat, the line of sky and horizon. He prayed not to die, not that way, lying in the back of an ambulance. He spoke to no god but recited, simply, a rambling string of entreaties, for what, he wasn't sure. For Cindy's life, if not his own.

"She's all right, but are you sure *you're* all right?" Rachel asked, as they were about to say goodbye.

"I'm fine. I'll call you in a couple of days."

"I love you," she said, before Gibb hung up. Gibb's words had been cheerful, upbeat at first, but she'd heard the tension in his voice and asked him what had happened. He told her about the dive then, the woman with the embolism. Rachel recognized the name, saw a fall of sleek hair flipped up at the ends, bright blue and golden pompoms framing the face. A lovely face, a smile made for photographs. Gibb had just gotten back from visiting her at South Miami Hospital. In a day or two she'd be fine, he'd said. "I thought she'd died," he'd said on the phone, his voice shaky then. "I didn't say anything to the others, but I really didn't think she was going to make it."

Just after Gibb called her, snow began to fall. Over the long afternoon, the light faded, dwindling into the grays and blacks of dusk.

Moving through the house, Rachel turned on lights in every room but the living room, where she stood in shadows, looking out at the falling snow. Wind flung the heavy flakes upward, swirling eddies of snow that sparkled under the streetlight. Jack had taken a plane to Chicago that morning, before the storm had started. Off to another conference. Although she missed him, she also enjoyed the solitude.

She sat on the bed and took off her shoes, remembering Gibb's voice in her ear, the image of him rising to the surface of the rough water, the boat carrying a woman she'd known in high school, so long ago. And words of danger—extraordinary words—*emergency, pain, ambulance, death*—delivered in so ordinary a manner.

The weather had been fiercely cold. A sudden gust of wind rattled the windows, startling her. "Gibb," she said out loud. She laughed a funny little laugh just for him as if he stood before her, the only one who could understand what the laugh meant and why she'd said his name like that.

But Gibb wasn't there and the ringing of her own voice in the empty house made her feel hollow inside. Something had frightened her when Gibb had told her about the Cindy's eyes, wide and fixed upon him. "I thought she'd died in my arms," he'd said. She shivered.

She thought of her work and of Ann Kramer, a patient at Chautauqua Institute, where Rachel was a social worker. Ann had at last begun to respond a little, since Rachel had discovered the storytelling. Ann Kramer was twenty-six. Her translucent blonde hair was wispy as a child's. She was so thin and pale she seemed invisible in a room, unobtrusive as a chair. Ann had been sexually abused for years by her stepfather and beaten up so badly by her first and only boyfriend that he'd broken her jaw and cheekbone. She had attempted suicide four times, trying, as she put it, "to get to the heaven where the animals are." The last time she'd tried was at the veterinarian's office where she worked as a helper, cleaning out cages and feeding the dogs and cats. She had injected herself with a syringe full of the euthanasia drug they used for dogs. A security guard had found her, and now she was at Chautauqua.

The next morning, Rachel stepped onto the elevator at Chautauqua. The elevator sighed to a stop on the third floor, the locked wards. Rachel walked to Ann's room to look in on her. Ann slept fully clothed in a Care Bear's T-shirt and pink jeans, knees drawn to her chest, her thumb in her mouth and a Princess Shirra doll in the crook of her arm. Ten or more stuffed animals and dolls lay on the bed and the floor. For a moment, Rachel felt she was looking at a child of eight or nine, locked in the profound and peaceful sleep of late morning. But the door glass stood between them and the room was austere and windowless, and no child ever slept quite as Ann did, her body rigid as a carving, her mind turned blank and dreamless by Thorazine.

Rachel stepped away from the door and down the corridor to her office. The images of her own dreams came to her. She remembered a small boy standing on the concrete edge of a huge aquarium, a boy in some kind of trouble, who'd stepped from deep bushes, coming too near the edge, Rachel taking his arm. She and Jack were trying to have a baby. The boy on the edge of the pool, their child, not even born and already in danger?

Sitting down at her desk, Rachel checked her calendar—a staff meeting at eleven, phone calls, routine patient visits and an hour set aside to be with Ann Kramer. Russell Holzman, the supervising psychiatrist, had agreed to let Rachel continue the storytelling sessions, which had started accidentally, with Rachel telling Ann part of a fairy tale and Ann, in turn, telling Rachel about a dream she'd had of her father. "I turned him into a log," she'd said. "then set him on fire." Her telling Rachel the dream was the first response anyone had gotten from Ann since she'd been admitted a month and a half earlier.

Ann's psychiatrist, Sarah Jauss, unlocked the door and pulled chairs near Ann's bed. Rachel followed her into the room, resisting the urge to tiptoe. Ann lay as she had in the morning, but her eyes were open and she followed Sarah and Rachel's movements without expression. The room was cool and silent.

Sarah put her hand on Ann's forearm. "How's Princess Shirra today?"

Ann's eyes darted to the doll, to Rachel, and then fixed themselves again on Sarah's face.

"Would you like to sit in a chair?" Sarah patted the seat of the chair next to her.

Rachel studied Ann's motionless form, her colorless face. Her eyes seemed to hold all the vitality she had, bright eyes snapping with intelligence and rage, irises a pale gray-green, the color of deep seawater. Her lips moved and her forehead drew into lines. Both Sarah and Rachel bent closer to hear. "Go"—Ann breathed, until Rachel felt the pain, ready to burn, in the hiss of the last syllable—"away." Rachel leaned back slowly. Sarah stayed near Ann a few moments more, rubbed her arm, said her name softly. When she finally moved back to sit upright in her chair, Ann's eyes were closed. Sarah motioned toward the door and Rachel followed her into the corridor.

"Russell took away her television privileges on Saturday. She probably thinks I did it."

"What happened?"

"That weekend orderly, Jerry. He let someone working on the telephone lines in her room. The guy was on a ladder and Ann came running toward him. She wouldn't have done anything. But he didn't know that. The guy got real upset."

"I'm surprised Russell's still letting me do the stories."

"I am too." They walked into Sarah's office and Sarah turned to face her. "You seem out of sorts. Is everything all right?"

In the silence before Rachel answered a clock ticked with ferocious intensity. "I'm fine."

Sarah shook her head and smiled a little. "Nobody's talking to me today." She sat at her desk and glanced through a file.

"I'll drop by on Ann again in a little while."

"Okay, see you later." Sarah had begun writing and didn't look up.

Rachel walked past a window and looked out at a parking lot full of snow-covered cars, the gray sky. *A dumb mistake.* She remembered Gibb's words of yesterday, the image of him rising through water, the blue twilight, the blurred images and bubbles, his flippered feet carrying him to the surface. A froth of blood on the woman's lips. He said she'd be all right, and that he was all right, but she couldn't push the incident from her mind.

"Mrs. Kellogg? I'm sorry, I didn't mean to bother you." Bobby Saneven's mother stood behind her, wearing a sweater that was a startling shade of red. She limped on a cane, although she wasn't old. Bobby had had an electroshock treatment that morning. "No bother, Mrs. Sanevan. How's Bobby?"

"Could you come see him for a minute? Also, I just had a quick insurance question."

Bobby lay with his arms at his sides, awake, his eyes sunk deep in their sockets. Under each eye the skin was the shade of a new bruise. Rachel imagined him with color in his face, hair combed. He might have been handsome. "How's it going?" she asked.

"I feel fine," he said tonelessly. "I can't think anymore. I like that."

She answered Mrs. Sanevan's insurance question and walked back to her office. She updated Bobby's paperwork and picked up her file on Ann Kramer. She let herself into Ann's room, wondering why she had come back. Her own mind was blank. She had no stories today. Ann sat on the bed leaning against the wall, arms around her knees, watching her. She had fastened her thin hair on each side with pink, heart-shaped barrettes. "Those are pretty," Rachel said, pointing. "The way you did your hair."

Ann closed her eyes and dropped her chin nearly to her chest, angling her body to the wall. She rocked back toward Rachel and opened her eyes. "Thank you," she said. "Can I have a cigarette?"

"I don't have any, I'm sorry."

"You told me that story about the swan girl."

Rachel nodded.

"Tell me another story."

"I'll tell you a story about people who live underwater," Rachel said, her mind searching for details. "Atlantis. Have you ever heard of Atlantis?"

Ann shook her head.

The beginning felt wrong. She didn't know where to go. "Underwater everything floats."

"Mermaids," Ann said.

"Yes, there're lots of stories about mermaids, but I'm going to tell a story about a little girl who lived on land but who wanted to live underwater." Rachel paused, thinking of Gibb years ago, the day he'd gotten his first scuba gear. "She lived by the sea and every

134

day she walked out to the beach where shells washed up to the sand with each rushing wave. The little girl walked into the water and held her breath to swim near the sandy bottom. She opened her eyes and saw the blue-green of the sea and the silvery fish floating past. She saw the green ferns...She hated her house." Rachel hesitated, lost for a moment.

Ann stared at Rachel's face and squeezed her arms more tightly around her knees. "Don't stop," she said softly.

"One day when the girl was playing on the beach, a giant fish from deep under water saw her and fell in love. He swam back down to the great, undersea city where he lived and told his mother, 'I have a broken heart.' When his mother asked him why, he said, 'I've fallen in love with a human girl.'

"'Ah,' his mother said thoughtfully. She was one of the wisest and kindest fish in the whole sea country. 'I know the one. Before I turned each of her salty tears into emeralds, they were making the ocean rise and all the fingerlings cry with her.'"

"What are fingerlings?" Ann asked.

"Fingerlings are baby fish."

"Okay," Ann said. "Don't stop."

"'I can help you,' said the fish mother, 'but you must do exactly as I say. If she comes with you, you must give her all your love, but if she wants to leave you must let her go.'

"'Thank you wise Mother,' said the fish boy. 'I'll love her as long as she'll stay with me. Then I'll let her go back to the dry world. Will she become strong, here, with our love? Can we make her happy?'

"'We can hope for these things,' said the mother, her eyes shining. 'Here, take my magic cloak of scales. If she'll come with you, the fish women of the realm will make her her own glorious cloak.'"

Rachel stopped.

Ann stared at her, unmoving. "What's wrong?" she asked.

"I'm thinking," Rachel said.

Ann tilted her head, still peering at Rachel, the tiniest of smiles growing at the corners of her mouth. "Okay," she whispered.

"'In her own fish cloak she'll swim in beauty and feel our protection while she's with us. Can you love her this way, my son? So your love will never hurt her or keep her in a place she no longer wants to be?"

"'Yes, Mother,' the boy said.'" Rachel glanced at her watch. It was past five and the roads would be treacherous. Russell didn't like for the staff to stay during patients' dinnertime. "I'll have to finish the story tomorrow."

"Finish it now." Those brilliant eyes caught Rachel's for a moment, and then dropped away. "Please."

"I'm sorry, Ann, I can't. But I will tomorrow."

"I wish I could have a dream about it," Ann said, closing her eyes. She opened her eyes suddenly and sprung to the edge of the bed, so that her knees almost touched Rachel's. "I don't have dreams with the medicine."

"It's better to take the medicine than have bad dreams."

"Yeah."

"I'll see you tomorrow."

"Okay." Ann swung her legs back and forth from the side of the bed. As Rachel walked to the door, Ann said softly, "That was the best job I ever had, at the vet's."

Rachel turned, her hand on the knob.

"The animals liked me. I missed them when they died. They all died."

"Some of them got better and went home."

Ann rested her feet on the floor and looked up, her face solemn. She squeezed the edge of the bed until Rachel saw the tendons in her hands, standing out like cords from the white skin. "They did?"

"Yes, they did."

"You promise you'll finish the story tomorrow?"

"Yes." Rachel nodded.

"Okay. Bye."

"'Bye, Ann." Rachel closed the door behind her and checked to be sure it was locked. She walked slowly to her office. *If only we could transform ourselves as easily in real life as in our fairy tales*, she thought, *just step out of one identity into another*. She touched the wall switch and the room was suddenly washed in fluorescent light. Gathering her things and turning off the light, she took the stairs down, two at a time, and stepped out into the falling snow to the sound of sirens, screaming from the highway.

At home, she dialed Gibb's number. "Hi," she said, when he picked up the phone.

"Rachel," he said, his voice thick as if he was getting a cold. "Did you just get home?"

"Yes, I just walked in. I...wanted to call you. Did I get you up?"

"No," he said, "not really. I wasn't sleeping. Just lying down. I've got a killer headache."

"Oh," she said. "I'm sorry. Should I call you back tomorrow?"

"No. No." He laughed softly. "You can call me in the middle of the night if you want. I'll never be sorry to hear your voice."

"I thought...I wondered about coming out."

"Are you okay? Is everything all right with you and Jack?"

"We're fine. It's just that yesterday, you know...that whole story about Cindy."

"What?"

"It made me feel worried for you...your work...safety and all. It frightened me."

He was silent. Static crackled across the line.

"Gibb? Are you there?"

"Yeah. Listen, I'm in more danger driving on Dixie Highway than I am underwater. I'm with a great, professional outfit. We don't take any chances. Okay?"

"Okay."

There was another silence line before he spoke again. "Hey, I do have some news, though. You know how Jess's been playing more and more jazz and blues over the last couple years? Well, he and some other guys from the university started a group. I forgot to tell you yesterday."

"That's exciting. But he's still in school, isn't he? What about his job at the music store?"

"Yeah, yeah," Gibb chuckled. "He's not ready to give up his day job just yet."

"Why don't I come out for a few days when things settle down here?" She thought of Ann, the stories. She had a full caseload now.

"That'd be great."

"I'll try to make some plans soon."

"Okay. Thanks for calling. And don't worry about me. I love you."

"I love you, too. Take care of yourself."

She waited for the dial tone and then called Jess, counting the rings. Just as she was ready to put the phone down, he answered, slightly breathless.

"Hello." He lived alone now, in a tiny apartment—Gibb had described the disordered state of it in mock horror: "He uses his couch for a bookcase and puts the TV set on the oven door".

She smiled, imagining him there. "Jess, hi."

"Hey Rachel. How're you doing?"

"I'm doing okay. I just talked to Gibb and he told me about your new group. Congratulations."

"Yeah, thanks. It just kind of happened...you know, from all of us playing together, getting a gig here and there, giving ourselves a name."

"What's the name?"

Jess laughed. "We call ourselves 'Crosscurrents.' I'm on piano and there's Cage Evans on bass—I think I told you about him when I was in Denver. The other guys I just met a few months ago...alto sax and drums. I hope you can come out and hear us before too long."

"I was just talking to Gibb about trying to do that. I can't get away from work right now, but maybe in a few weeks...Say, Jess, what's going on with Gibb? Is he okay? He sounded kind of...I don't know how to put it..."

"Removed? Far away?" He paused. "He's like that most of the time. We do things together, when he's not home writing or whatever he does at night. He'll tell me he can't go out because he's busy on a 'project,' whatever that means. I feel like I'm talking to someone on another planet sometimes."

That was how she'd felt tonight. "Something to do with his work?"

"No, I don't think so. I worry about him too."

They talked a while longer about Jess's classes and his music.

"You're so busy," she said.

"Yeah. I'm doing some other stuff too." His voice was excited. "We've been trying to organize garment workers in the northeast section," he told her. "We're picketing a factory this weekend."

"Don't get arrested," she kidded. Miami with all of its problems seemed remote to her now. When she was there she remembered things she didn't want to remember. As soon as she breathed the thick air of the place she felt herself dwindle into an awkward girl again—ugly inside. She hung up the phone and walked to the bedroom, wishing Jack were home. The house was so cold, the weather still bad. Taking off her shoes and her clothes, she felt goose bumps rise on her legs and forearms. A "bad headache," Gibb had said. And Jess's words came back to her..."removed," "far away." She stepped under the shower, which warmed her skin without penetrating to the cold, empty place that her fears for Gibb had carved open inside her.

In the late morning, the sun came out dazzling on the snow and Rachel's day passed in a series of small crises. Paperwork that had to be done immediately, intake interviews with new patients, patients ready for discharge who needed of out-patient support arranged.

"I thought you weren't coming," Ann said when Rachel opened the door.

"But here I am."

Ann sat cross-legged, barefoot, waiting, as if Rachel had left no more than a few minutes ago. "I remember where we are. Where the mother fish gives the boy fish the scale suit and tells him not to ever hurt the girl."

"Right." Rachel took a deep breath, smiled.

"You look sad," Ann said.

"No, I'm not sad. Should I start again?" She'd thought about the story last night and jotted down some notes about how she'd finish it.

"Yes."

"The very next day the boy fish swam up from his deep home, up through the shimmering water carrying the iridescent coat of scales, till he'd made his way to the edge of the sea, near where the young girl waded. His great head broke the surface of the water, and she heard his voice in her mind. 'Don't be afraid,' he said. 'I love you. You are so beautiful. Would you like to come with me to the sea realm? You'll have a safe home with us there, for as long as you want it.'

"She nodded and he covered her with the magic coat of scales. Instantly, she was transformed into a sleek, beautiful fish. She swam alongside him all the way down to the world far under the sea, past the blue and yellow fish, past the colorful reef with its waving fans and beckoning fingers of coral, past turtles and whales, the squeaking dolphins, past stingrays and sharks. They went deeper and deeper, past shipwrecks, temples, palaces and roads, until they were down at the very bottom of the ocean. The girl was amazed. Everything was as beautiful as she'd thought it would be. The fish women made her a splendid scale-cloak of her own, and for seven years, she and the boy fish lived together happily under the sea."

Ann held up her hand, like a child in a classroom. "I've never been in the ocean. Did you know that? Did the girl fish cry underwater?"

"No, no more salty tears. She had the love of the whole fish realm, and she'd become strong and happy. But still, she wanted to go back to land. She wanted to see her parents again, even though they hadn't been very nice to her. She longed to see the blue sky and white clouds. She wanted to fill up her lungs with air, and smell trees and flowers and grass again. She wanted to run.

"So one day she told the great mother fish all her thoughts and the mother fish said, 'It's time for you to go back to the world of humans.'

"The boy fish cried as he swam with her up, up to the dry world, but at the surface, he helped her out of her coat of scales and watched her become a human woman again. When she was free she ran through the shallow water all the way past the tideline to the dry sand on the beach. She turned back and waved, watching as the great fish lifted his head out of the water and cried to her in a pitiful voice, making sounds she couldn't understand any longer. Then she turned again and ran through the grass and fields, past the big trees, all the way back to her home." Gibb would have stayed under water, Rachel thought suddenly. Gibb would have stayed forever.

"Was it still as bad there?" Ann twisted a strand of hair around her finger.

"No. I hope not."

"Are you happy?" Ann asked.

"Yes," Rachel said quickly, wishing she hadn't started the stories, uncomfortable, suddenly, with the responsibility she had taken on, uneasy with Ann's affection.

"So it's crazy like they say…" Ann paused and looked away. Finally she turned back to Rachel and finished her question. "Not to want to be alive?"

Rachel hesitated, looking at Ann's face, a color risen in it she had never seen before, her eyes bright and cool. "If I say yes, it means I think a person who doesn't want to be alive is crazy. It also means that I don't believe a person can hurt that bad—bad enough not to want to be alive." She paused. "But if I say no, it's like permission to give in to all the things that have hurt you. And you're not the one who should be punished. You've asked me a trick question, haven't you?"

Ann nodded, her face solemn, her expression no longer childlike. Averting her face again, she began to speak softly. "He was bigger than me, and he kept hitting me and hitting me," she said matter-of-factly. "I heard a crack when my jaw broke. I passed out." She took a breath and looked at the ceiling. Her face was expressionless. "I know he would have killed me. He only stopped because he thought I was dead."

Rachel's stomach had gathered into a knot. She found her words carefully. "Promise me you'll start talking to Dr. Jauss. She can help you."

"I love you, Rachel," Ann said, calling her by name for the first time. "Can I have a cigarette? God, I wish I had a cigarette."

Ann's voice followed Rachel home, and seeped into her dreams, haunting and disembodied. *I love you, Rachel.* The sound was with her in the morning as she dressed, and now, as she walked down the corridor to Sarah's office, it trailed behind her like the sound of someone breathing. Rachel would see Sarah first, tell her how calmly Ann had recounted her story of nearly being beaten to death.

Though it was a part of her medical record, it was a story Ann herself had never told anyone before.

Sarah was on the telephone. Rachel took a seat outside the office and waited. She looked up and was startled to find Sarah standing next to her. She hadn't heard her approach.

"You were in a deep daydream," Sarah said, lightly touching her shoulder.

"I guess I was," Rachel answered, but she could not have told Sarah what she had been thinking. The daydream had vanished, like a nightmare, leaving only its unsettling traces.

"You've come to bring me good news," Sarah said, as they walked into the office. "I've already seen Ann this morning, and I hope you'll drop in on her when you can. She's quite fond of you. I never thought her prognosis was very good, but I'm starting to change my mind."

"The uses of enchantment," Rachel said softly.

"What?"

Rachel repeated the phrase.

"Yes, the Bettelheim book. I read it several years ago."

"The book and what those words bring to mind."

Their eyes met. "She's had so much of the monstrous. Maybe she's ready to believe in enchantment and transformation. To tell a story of her own where she's the heroine. I'll try it," Sarah said. "Thanks for what you've put into your relationship with Ann."

"It's a bit scary."

"Always."

By the time Rachel was able to see Ann, it was past one. She pushed open the door slowly, surprised to see Ann dressed in jeans and a t-shirt and sitting at the room's small desk, reading a magazine. "Hey," Rachel said.

Ann turned to Rachel and smiled. She gestured towards a page. "*Good Housekeeping*. I like those words. Do you think I could ever have a house?"

"Sure." Rachel pulled up a chair and sat down next to her.

"Did you live in a house or apartment when you were growing up?"

"A house." Rachel saw its shadows, its recesses. Silence alternating with the sounds of her parents' voices raised to quarrel. A place she would not return to willingly.

"If it's not too personal, what's the most tragic thing that ever happened to you?"

Of course it was too personal. A question that burned in front of her like a struck match. With an answer she would not speak. She took a breath. "Nothing…," she said, grasping for words. She would not name it or give it voice. It belonged in the past, meant to be forgotten. Even if others could not forget, she could forget. "Sad things," she managed. "Just the usual. My cat was run over by a car." She lied, so that she would not have to say more.

Ann gasped. "Oh no! I'm so sorry."

Rachel had forgotten how dearly Ann loved animals.

"What was its name?"

"Droopy." An absurd name. Stop. Rachel felt her eyes begin to fill with tears and she looked away. Ann wanted more than she could give.

"Do you have any sisters or brothers?"

"Brothers," Rachel said, relieved. "I have two wonderful brothers—Gibb and Jess."

"Gibb?" Ann looked puzzled.

"It was my great, great grandfather's last name. He was Welsh. My father picked it."

"What do they do?" Leaning forward in her chair, Ann looked at her expectantly.

"Gibb's a commercial diver and Jess is a musician."

Ann slowly shook her head. "I really wish I could meet them."

"Maybe you can someday," Rachel said.

"I hope so. I'd feel lucky." She laughed softly. "I'll invite them to my new house."

Part Three

To what shall I compare this
life of ours?
Even before I can say
it is a lightning flash
or a dewdrop
it is no more.
   Sengai

Nine

Only ten o'clock and already the car door handle was too hot to touch. On the way to his girlfriend Robin's, Jess looked across Biscayne Bay. The sun's reflection splintered the whole expanse of bright water. He remembered the burning cars in Liberty City on last night's news, people silhouetted in the red dark, no overlay of newscasters' voices, just the sound of glass shattering, screams, the crackling of fire everywhere.

"RIOTING OVER," the morning paper had proclaimed in inch-high letters: May 18, 1980. Jess watched a black Firebird race to the bumper of a car in the left lane and stay there for several threatening seconds before gunning past on the right. Heat made people's anger worse. Heat—cloying, hard-to-breathe in, inescapable heat. Heat was the catalyst for turning anger to rage, rage to violence. Last night, a black teenager standing at the perimeter of the violence had screamed into a reporter's microphone. "We're prepared to die. We ain't got no hope."

Jess could still see the teenager's face, contorted with rage and fear. He remembered the mute, staring children one of his education classes had visited. "A Headstart group," the professor had explained with a wry look, "but the funds for this neighborhood have just been cut." Jess gripped the steering wheel hard, angry at the memory. He took a lane and exited onto Brickell Avenue. Royal Poincianas were in bloom along the street, their flame-colored blossoms filling the trees, already lining the gutters below with ribbons of color.

The verdict had come in three days ago. Four Miami police had been accused of beating a black insurance salesman to death with flashlights, then trying to make it look like he'd been killed in a motorcycle accident. This was the story Miami had followed, broken open with a shattering of windows, torched buildings, cars aflame in the streets, looting. Sixteen people dead, hundreds injured. An all-white Tampa jury had acquitted the four policemen.

The first day of the rioting Jess had called his band's bass player, Cage, who had a keyboard Jess wanted to buy, to find out if things were as bad as they looked on the news. "Worse, man," Cage had told him. "Don't even think of coming over here."

Jess pulled into the parking lot of Robin's apartment building, the back of his shirt already soaked and clinging to his skin. Taking a deep breath of the dense air, he wondered, did he just imagine the smell of smoke? The riots were over. Traffic from the highway hummed in the distance, unobtrusive. Shade from a rose apple tree made lacy patterns on the sidewalk. A tabby cat lay drowsing on the grass, ignoring a mockingbird's dive-bombing arcs and shrieks. Jess rang Robin's bell and waited for her voice on the intercom, but only the buzz of the unlocking door answered and he let himself in.

"You probably should've made sure it was me," he said, putting his arm around her and kissing her lightly on the cheek.

"Who else would it be, for heaven's sake? It's ten in the morning." She smiled. "So you got a windfall," she said. "'Most outstanding first-year graduate student.' That's pretty cool."

"With the money Rachel sent, enough for our picnic and that keyboard. Then I'll be broke again as usual." He ran his fingers along the edge of the table. "I'm only going to work half-time in the fall." He paused. "I want to finish by next May. Somehow."

"Oh," she said, glancing toward the window. "I thought...I don't know. You study so much already." She laughed a little. Walking behind him, she put her hands on his shoulders. "Sure you want to go to the Glades? Back out in that heat? I know something we can do right here."

"Let's." He laughed and took her hands, stepped around to face her. "Before the picnic *and* after the picnic."

The highway shimmered in the heat; hot air from the open windows blew across their faces. They drove west on Tamiami Trail, past the farthest suburbs, past developments failed decades ago, past the gun club, a beer joint, several sites for airboat rides, until finally the Everglades was dense on either side of them and the shining ribbon of the Tamiami Canal showed in flashes through the Australian pines. Jess watched an anhinga fly to a power line and spread its wings to dry. Sawgrass stretched across the flat miles, airboat paths crisscrossing through in an abstract mosaic of lines. Scars, Gibb called them. "My brother says the Glades are being destroyed," he said, glancing at her.

"They look the same as always to me. My father used to take me fishing out here before I got breasts." She laughed. "I was about eleven, I guess, and I took off my T-shirt when I got too hot, just like always. He got really weirded out. 'Put your shirt back on, Robin. You're a young lady.' I'll never forget that, 'you're a young lady.'" She stuck her head out the window for a minute. "Looks the same. Smells the same. It's everything around that's changing. Hotels and stuff."

"Yeah."

Where the Everglades became cypress swamp, Jess turned onto a dirt road, stirring up a cloud of dust that lingered behind them. They found a grassy shoulder shaded by the swamp's thicket of vegetation, a green darkness smelling of wet growth and all of the swamp's hidden life. The air was still.

Robin slapped at a mosquito. "I know this is your idea of a good time..."

He spread the blanket and pulled the cooler from the trunk. "No people, no cars, no houses. Just you and me and..."

"Snakes and bugs and wild animals." She gave him a quick smile and glanced toward the dense thicket that fringed the road.

Jess followed her gaze. "Feel like we're being watched?" he asked softly. He dropped his voice to a whisper. "We are. Panthers, most all the Florida panthers that are left are right here in this swamp. 'Coons, possum, armadillo..."

"Stop," she broke in, squeezing her eyes shut and putting her hands over her ears. "You're giving me the creeps."

Later, after they'd eaten their cheese sandwiches and shared some wine, they walked down the road for several miles, watching a stick figure in the distance become larger, its outlines clearer as they came closer. The wood stork regarded their approach calmly at first, before taking a few long steps and flying off into the swamp. They saw a dust cloud in the road grow larger quickly, a truck, from the sound of it, coming toward them fast. Just as they stepped off the dirt and onto the weedy shoulder, a quarter-ton Chevy pickup stopped beside them. Jess saw the gun rack through the driver's window, a 30-30 rifle in place and two men in the cab, a six-pack between them. The driver leaned out the window. "Ya'll better be careful. Y'look like deer off in the distance."

"It's not hunting season now, is it?" Robin said, taking a step toward them.

The man snorted and glanced at his passenger. "Season," he said, "course it's the season, so doncha be standin' out in the road with nothin' but them teeny shorts on." The man gunned the engine and rattled off, leaving a dust swath heavy as smoke from something burning. They watched until they could no longer see the truck, only the plumes of dust, dwindling.

"What was that all about?" Robin shaded her eyes, still staring down the road.

"Just a couple of Collier County rednecks who found us in their territory. Let's go home."

Jess left Robin's apartment after the sky had faded and lit up again with the orange of the late sun. He'd called Cage.

"All quiet," Cage had said.

As he passed through the neighborhoods, Jess watched the colors of the houses darken with the changing light. He drove languidly in a city where such a pace had become nearly impossible, turned corners with a careless ease, watched children playing on side streets and people walking out the last of the daylight. He heard the pop of a firecracker, and suddenly sensed someone very near, beside the car. Before he could turn to see, Jess felt the pain, a burning in his head, and as the car drifted into darkness, he gripped the steering wheel hard and did not let go.

"Jess was shot? What else did he say?" The room seemed unnaturally bright for the time of day, the edges of the sink and countertop, the stove and toaster honed to a fierce sharpness. "Please. What else!"

"He was shot; he's in surgery. That's all Gibb said, Rae. You've got to try to calm down. Can I call the airlines for you?"

"No." She walked the length of the room, turned to look at him, fighting back tears. "I'm sorry. Let me try calling Gibb again."

She let the phone ring ten, fifteen times, but there was no answer. "Shot," she said numbly. "He just said 'shot'?"

"I'm sure Gibb would've told me more if he could have. He was trying to get to the hospital."

Rachel stood at the gate, waiting for her flight to be called and trying not to think. On the plane, she sat rigidly in her seat with a book in front of her face so she wouldn't have to talk to the person next to her, an elderly woman who could surely hear the violent thumping of Rachel's heart.

She took a cab directly to the hospital.

"Are you a member of the family?" the person behind the desk in the lobby asked her.

"I'm his sister. Can you give me any information about what happened?"

"Take the elevator to the sixth floor. That's ICU. They can tell you there." The woman pointed and turned away.

Rachel walked slowly to the elevator, still carrying her bag. The elevator doors faced an empty nurses' station. She put her bag down and stood in front of it numbly, waiting.

"Can I help you?"

Someone stood behind her and she turned. "Yes," she said. "Please. My brother..."

"Jess Colgrove?"

The sound of his name shocked her, as if she'd been expecting a mistake, a puzzled look, the nurse shaking her head and saying, *We have no one here by that name.* "Yes. Can I see him?"

"Let's talk to the doctor first. He was just with him a minute ago." The nurse gestured to a man standing a few feet away.

"This is Mrs. Kellogg, Dr. Spender. Mr. Colgrove's sister."

The man extended his hand. "I'm sorry to meet you under these circumstances. Did you just get in?"

Rachel struggled to keep from crying. She felt numb from the hours on the plane, not knowing what had happened to Jess. "Yes. I did. From Denver. I just got in. What...happened?"

"I performed surgery on your brother late yesterday. Why don't we go into my office for a few minutes before you see him. I want you to know, first of all," he said slowly, "he's in no danger. He's been awake, his vital signs are stable, everything looks okay right now."

Dr. Spender began with X-rays of Jess's skull. He pointed. "Your brother suffered a gunshot wound to the head, right about here. It was a small caliber, high-velocity weapon of some sort, and the bullet passed through this area." He gestured across a mass of brain tissue that showed gray on the film, "and lodged here."

"A gunshot wound? How? Why?"

"I don't have the details on that. It appeared to be random. No witnesses, no apparent motive. That's what I gathered from the detective who spoke with me this evening. I'm sure you'll be able to get more details from the police and Gibb, is it? Your other brother?"

"Yes."

"He left the floor just a little while ago. He may be in the coffee shop."

"What about the wound?"

"Yes, point of entry was here. Because of the small caliber and the trajectory, it did relatively little neurological damage. The bullet left some bone fragments at the point of entry, which we removed, and spent itself near the surface of the skull where we could get to it." He traced the path of the bullet across the X-ray. "I'm not saying it wasn't a serious injury. It was. The bullet could have imbedded itself in the soft tissue of the brain. Give or take a few centimeters it could have been a very grave, possibly mortal injury. All things considered, the surgery went well and the damage was minimal."

"Brain damage?"

Dr. Spender hesitated almost imperceptibly. "Yes, the bullet passed through what's called the 'optic chiasma.' That's where the nerve fibers from each eye divide and cross."

She heard the distant ticking of a clock. "You took out the bullet."

"Yes." He nodded.

"But...the optic nerve. His sight will be affected."

"The nerve fibers were severed." He paused. "Given the point at which the bullet passed through the brain...the capacity for sight was destroyed. I'm sorry."

"He's was blinded?"

"Yes."

She walked to a chair and sat down and swallowed to ease the knot in her throat. An expensive-looking gooseneck lamp cast a small light across Dr. Spender's desk. He wasn't more than a year or two older than she was. He looked at her, hands in the pockets of his white coat.

"Does he know?"

"He was awake for a short time while your parents were here. But no, your brother Gibb indicated he'd like to wait for you. Maybe wait a day or so. Jess is very strong, very physically strong. There are some good rehabilitation programs in the city. In fact, we'll begin rehabilitation here at the hospital as soon as he's out of ICU. Would you like to spend a few minutes alone before you see him?"

"Yes."

"I'll be here a while longer tonight and later tomorrow to answer any more questions you might have. Will you be all right?"

She nodded.

He closed the door behind him and left her in the dimly lit room.

She held her face in her hands, and then looked around the room, at bookcases, diplomas, a large, handsome walnut desk, imagining it all vanished into darkness. Struggling to take a deep breath, she stood, picked up her bag and walked into the corridor. She heard her name and turned.

"Rachel." Gibb was beside her. He put his arm around her shoulder. "You look so tired," he said, his own face washed clean of expression. "Really tired."

She laid her face against his chest. He put both arms around her and she closed her eyes, feeling the odd, bright edge that fear and fatigue had given her body. She stepped back. "What happened?"

"No one has a clue. The woman who called the police heard a noise, that's all. She looked out the window and the street was empty. Just Jess's car up against a tree in her neighbor's yard." He looked at his watch. "About 7:00 yesterday. I talked to the first cop on the scene and a homicide detective. Mother and Dad were here and they were total basket cases. Dad was in no shape to drive. I had to send them home in a taxi. And Robin was hysterical. He'd just left her apartment. He was on his way to buy a synthesizer or something at a friend's place."

"Homicide?"

"Because of the riots they're investigating it as attempted murder."

"What riots?"

He looked at her, puzzled. "I thought it made all the major networks. You didn't hear about it in Denver? The four cops who beat Arthur McDuffie to death last December just got acquitted."

She shook her head. "No," she said. "I...maybe I heard something about it. I don't know." The shrill sound of her voice echoed in the nearly silent corridor.

"I can see it now," Gibb said, with a quick sweep of his hand. "They'll use it to make things worse. 'Man blinded in latest incident of racial violence.'" He stared down at the floor.

"Jess is blind." She whispered it, half a question.

Gibb turned toward her suddenly and put his hands on her shoulders, his eyes filling with tears.

"This is unreal," she said.

"Let's get our five-minute visit," Gibb said, his voice flat. "He's been awake a lot, in spite of whatever they're sedating him with. He's fighting to be conscious."

"What if he asks us why he can't see?" Pain started up under her ribs. She wrapped her arms around herself, feeling a deep chill.

"We'll have to tell him," Gibb said. "We've got to be calm and start right now...helping him through this."

"Helping him through..." Rachel stopped. "I'm afraid. I'm afraid for Jess. I'm afraid for myself."

"Look, I'm afraid too. Someone fucking *died* in there tonight during one of my visits." He pointed toward the pneumatic doors leading to the ICU. "Jess got through the surgery in great shape. He'll probably be in a regular room in a couple of days."

Jess slept through their four and five a.m. visits. They watched his still form, reassured by the steady heartbeat shown on the green line of the monitor. At first light, they drove to Gibb's apartment.

Gibb put clean sheets on his bed for Rachel and made himself a bed on the couch.

Putting down a glass of bourbon, he sat at the kitchen table, hands folded in front of him, as if he'd forgotten Rachel was there. After a few minutes, he turned to where she sat in the living room. "I'm sorry," he said. "Can I fix you a drink? Do you want any food?"

"No." She shook her head. "No thanks." He lifted the glass slowly to his lips and she saw the slight rise and fall of his shoulders, as if he cried through that small, agonized movement. "Gibb," she said softly. "Are you going to sleep?"

"Yes." He turned his drawn face to hers. "Soon."

He seemed so suddenly fragile that she couldn't imagine him underwater then, or stepping outdoors, driving a car, doing even the most ordinary tasks. But the thought of him anything but strong vanished as quickly as it had come and she saw only how tired and sad he was. She went to him and kissed him lightly on the cheek.

He covered her hand with his. "Goodnight," he said.

In the bedroom, she lay down and closed her eyes, hearing the muted screams of gulls just before she entered a dark room she sensed to be round. But she couldn't determine her place in it no matter how hard she tried, running her hands along the curving walls, crawling around on her hands and knees until finally she lay exhausted, hearing only own labored breath.

Less than forty-eight hours after his surgery, Jess was moved to a private room. The day before, Gibb and Rachel had used up almost all of their five-minute-per-hour visits, until evening when Gibb had followed Rachel from the hospital across town to return their father's car. When they'd opened the door, they found him sitting at the dining room table, an empty quart bottle of beer in front of him. He was sobbing, head resting on his arms. Their mother was sleeping, sedated. Before they left, Gibb had walked his father into the bedroom and put him to bed.

Jess's hospital room had a large window that looked out on a dirt parking lot fringed by Dade County pines. Jess was awake when they came in. His bed had been cranked up a little and he turned his face toward them.

"Dr. Spender?"

"No," Gibb said. "It's us."

Rachel walked to the side of the bed near the window and took Jess's hand. She leaned down and brushed his cheek with her lips. "Hi," she said. "How do you feel?"

"I feel like shit," he said softly. "My head hurts. The doctor came in this morning and said I'd been shot. What the hell happened?" Slipping his hand from Rachel's, Jess pressed his palms to his eyes, and then took his hands away. "I can't see," he said. "When am I going to be able to see? Somebody *fed* me breakfast. That's how I knew it was morning. Can you believe that?" He stopped and touched his bandages. "I really got walloped."

Neither of them spoke. Rachel looked across the bed at Gibb. He swallowed and glanced away. Reaching for Jess's other hand, Gibb took a breath.

"When will this heal?" Jess asked. "You have to tell me...What's going on?"

"The bullet passed through the point where your optic nerves cross," Rachel said finally. She had talked to her clients and their families about terrible things before, somehow summoned the words, but this was Jess. She could still remember carrying him in her arms. Tears rose in her eyes.

"So what happens next? More surgery? What?"

"The nerves were severed." The color drained from Gibb's face. He put his hand on Jess's forearm. "You won't get your vision back."

Jess pushed himself up to a sitting position. "I'm blind? Are you telling me I'm fucking blind?" he said hoarsely.

Rachel put her arms around him. "Yes," she said.

"Don't say that. No way. They can do something." Jess shook his head. "I don't believe you."

Ten

Almost six months had passed since Jess had been released from the hospital. Rachel had stayed in Gibb's apartment at first, had flown back to Denver for awhile, then spent two weeks more in Miami to be with him. Jess had grown used to her then, to her voice, which he'd never heard so often for so long, more resonant than the one in her letters. She had taken care of a multitude of details, read him the newspaper every morning, and ordered the books he needed to have on tape.

Gibb had insisted that Jess continue to live on his own, and he'd found Jess a larger place, near shopping and a bus route. After Rachel had gone, Gibb took a month off from work and spent the days driving Jess to the Miami Lighthouse, to other appointments, to practices, staying with him evening after evening, helping him through every detail of the process of reorganizing his life. Gibb had forced Jess, literally, into the street, as soon as the mobility instructor at the Lighthouse had let Gibb know Jess was ready. Gibb still came over almost every night. Jess wondered what was happening with Gibb's "investigation," as Gibb called it, into the unsolved crime their father had been acquitted of. Gibb talked about diving, but that was all. Gibb had begun to be secretive about what he was doing even before Jess had been shot.

"You're alive," Rachel had said in the hospital. "We're so thankful for that." Then she'd kept her hand in his as he slept or just lay there, not wanting to talk, for hours, for days, her hand the only thing keeping him from floating away into the darkness forever. At least I can play, he thought, walking over to the piano and running his fingertips over the surface of the keys. He'd already played for a couple of hours in this morning, again in the afternoon, practicing the ostinatos in Monk's "Epistrophy" again and again without getting them right, the notes sounding hammered, never swelling into overtones the way they should have. He practiced every day and had jammed with the whole group a couple of times, but would he ever play a gig again?

He struck the first few notes of a song he and Cage had written a while back, "Dereliction," the music drifting outside of him, the way people's voices floated around him, disembodied. *Jess, hi, it's....* then the shock of a hand on his shoulder or his arm, a hand come from nowhere.

He thought of Gibb's preoccupied silence that afternoon. *It's like you're not here when you don't talk to me,* Jess had said, trying to keep his voice light. Remembering Gibb's own voice, the flat, distant sound of the words, Jess struggled for the image of Gibb's features, his expressions, wanting so badly to have seen his brother's face, to have been able to read something there.

"What's going on with you, Gibb? Jess had asked. "Work," Gibb had said somewhat shortly. "And the writing."

"Your journals? Will you try to get something published?"

"No," Gibb had said with a dry, mocking laugh that lingered in the room. "I'm not any good. I can't even figure out a story line. I wish to hell I could even figure out the plot of my own life, one day to the next."

Jess walked to the window. How long would his memory of sun-light stay so keen? On the day he had been shot, he remembered a flaming sun, light reflected from windows, from the shiny paint of cars, from a glittering watch face. Feeling sun on his skin now, he could still imagine the huge wavering shape of it, deep shadows, its brightness, changing over the day.

He recalled nothing that had happened after he'd left Robin's apartment that day. His psychiatrist could repeat all she wanted about the "mechanisms" of his forgetting. But there was no fear to understand, no assailant in sight, nothing he could have done. It had been reported in the newspaper as an incident of random violence. The shooting of an "innocent bystander." But Jess didn't think of what had happened to him that way. No one had anything to settle with him, nor had the violence of the act been "random."

Jess remembered the months following his shooting as a series of pictures in the round—a dizzying mosaic of sounds and imagined scenes. Police questions and a procession of visits by Rachel and Gibb, his parents, nurses, orderlies, Robin, Cage, friends from his classes, work. The pictures had great speech balloons floating above them. "Do you have any enemies?" "How do you feel?" "Would you like something to eat?" "Can I bring you anything?" He had tried to create from this jumble of sounds and images, a story subject to the proof of chronology. But only the parade of cartoon-like pictures came to him, never in the same order. His anger burned around the edges of things, confusing even more the matter of what had happened when.

At first, Jess had struggled merely to get out of bed. It had been easier to sleep. His dreams convinced him that he still belonged to the world of the seeing. Those garish excursions had taken him back to his childhood, had given him sights from the past, and the most brilliant landscapes his imagination could create. He was ashamed of his helplessness. Everything he tried seemed risky. He'd feared burns, the voices of strangers, stairs and curbs. Going out alone had made him crazy at first, but Gibb pushed him all the time.

Jess heard someone mowing a lawn nearby. The sweet smell of cut grass drifted up. He took a deep breath. Just a month ago, Gibb and his girlfriend Megan had taken him underwater, starting in a pool, where he'd felt safer than on the street, with no obstacles, nothing but the water, buoying him. "Breathe," Gibb had said. "Hold on to my arm and kick. Float. Feel the water on your skin." Then the three of them had gone on a shallow dive just off shore. As soon as they'd entered the surf, Jess had felt a sudden terror. This water wasn't like the pool. Jess tasted the saltwater, smelled it, elemental as blood. Pulled by the tidal current, he heard the respirator's lisp, the sound of his breath growing ragged, felt things brushing against his skin, Gibb's hand on his arm. Meaning what? Jess pointed above his head, realizing he no longer had the slightest sense of up or down. Gibb had touched Jess's throat. Breathe. That was the signal they'd arranged before going down, and Jess breathed. He listened and breathed, letting the water hold him, letting Gibb and Megan guide his fingers to the bottom sand, to shells and coral. He'd gone down again, kayaked, camped in the Everglades, stepping back into the world with each new thing he tried. His second time underwater he'd heard the whistles and squeaks of dolphins as perhaps no seeing person ever had, heard his resolute breath and heartbeat and marveled. He'd felt the water flow into him and through him. That moment, Jess had known his brother in a way

159

that was beyond words, for the water *was* a kind of blood, the same blood, surging through them both.

Thinking of Gibb saddened him. He walked through his apartment and snapped on the tape of a *Composition Theory* article on harmonics. The reader was a woman, speaking in a beautiful, entirely mellifluous voice that never hesitated over even the most difficult words. Jess turned off the recorder and leaned back in the chair, listening. Contrary to myth, his hearing had not become more acute. Fiercely, he used the senses he had left: the sound of his own footsteps, voices, echoes. The air on his face told him he was next to an open door. His fingertips learned the shapes of things. His hand on the cane connected him to the solid world. The cane found obstacles, steps, curbs, stairs. Using his musician's discipline, he practiced all of his new abilities ruthlessly.

Listening, he discovered things he did not want so much to know. When he walked into a restaurant or shop, especially if alone, he heard conversations stop in midsentence, felt people's eyes turn in his direction, their curiosity and sympathy hanging in the air like a slow-to-disperse gas.

Jess found a shirt he'd left on the back of the couch and carried it into the bedroom. The clutter he used to live in had given way to a necessary and perfect order, his clothes labeled in Braille so he'd know their colors, things put away, always. He'd taught himself to keep track of everything now, even the minutes and hours, which at first had slipped by, diffuse as sand flowing through his fingers.

Jess was reading when he heard a tapping on the door, the rattle of a key in the lock. He heard Gibb's voice at the door and met him there, the air flowing around him—warm, damp air smelling of soil and leaves. The scent of night swept further into the room with the closing of the door. A car alarm sounded and grew faint. Jess touched his watch. "I've lost track of the time. It's eleven. You left hours ago."

"Yeah. I'm going to fix myself a drink. Can I make you one?"

"Sure." They sat at the table.

Gibb rattled the ice in his glass, drank, put the glass down. A cricket started up somewhere close to the window.

"I can't stare you down like I used to," Jess said.

"You're doing a surprisingly good job of it." Gibb laughed dryly.

"What's going on? Did you have words with the folks?"

"I guess you could say that."

"About what?"

Gibb didn't answer. The chair creaked as he shifted his weight. He took another sip and held the glass, swirling the ice.

"About what, Gibb?"

"Unfinished business. And the business of their reclusive nonlife. They don't go anywhere. They don't see anyone." He got up, walked the length of the room. "Mother told me 'just leave us be.' I wonder what would happen to them if I really did that?" Gibb's voice was harsh.

Jess felt the dampness on his arms, smelled the heavy perfume of the jasmine that curled in a corner of the yard. "They haven't had an easy time of it. Mother working at the bakery all those years."

Gibb laughed, walked into the kitchen, shook more ice loose from a tray. "So many stories of their hard life. Dad had to tell me again about our grandfather's being a brakeman, sweating his way through strikes, getting laid off. 'He worked sixteen hours a day just so we could eat. So us kids could have a chance to be someone.'" Gibb paused. "So many hard lives. So many stories. What's the true story? Just change the details and make things sound the way you want them to. Maybe just live an out-and-out lie." He unscrewed the top of the bottle, poured.

Jess got up and walked to where Gibb stood, remembering suddenly a police detective's questions and a reporter's, both of them trying to get a story from him about his shooting. Both wanting two very different kinds of stories. *Did you see anyone on the street? I don't remember. Did you see any of the…rioters anywhere that day? I don't remember.* The detective's questions had taken a clear direction. Jess's shooting was another act of violence the police hoped to pin on a black, especially, but anyone would do. Make causality simple: victim, criminal. And the reporter, she'd wanted to make Jess into another kind of victim altogether. She'd asked him how he felt about what had happened, about the "adjustments" he'd had to make. *What do you mean?* he'd asked. *What do you expect me to say?*

Why don't you find out how many blind people are unemployed and how little money the rehab programs get, if you want to tell a real story. Do that instead of writing a sympathy piece on me. I'm not a curiosity, he'd said angrily. She had been flustered and had soon left, and no article on him had ever appeared in the paper.

"What're you thinking," Gibb asked suddenly. "You look so serious."

"Do I? I was thinking about what you just said, that's all. About stories. Listen," Jess paused, "if there's something going down I can help you with, let me try, okay? Let's talk."

"No," Gibb said after a time. "Everything's fine. What more could I want from my life?" There was a momentary silence, a stopped heartbeat's worth, and Gibb's laugh came. "It's perfect the way it is," he said brightly.

"You're a hell of an actor," Jess said. "But tonight your timing's off a notch. Otherwise you'd have fooled me. You're still working to clear Dad's name, aren't you? What's happening with all that?"

"It's all in order for the moment," Gibb said airily, dismissing him. "A clue here and a clue there, but nothing much...you know? No revelations. Yeah," he said. "Everything's fine with me. Say, how'd you feel about a trip to see Rachel after they have the baby? In a couple of months or so?"

"I'd like that, but don't forget what I said...about talking."

"Oh," Gibb said abstractedly, "I won't." He went on then, his voice tinged with a kind of excitement. "Maybe before too long I'll marry Megan, and you'll marry Robin and we'll all live happily ever after, speaking of stories. There's a good one."

A police siren screamed in the distance, grew closer, slowed. A chorus of neighborhood dogs howled. The sound dwindled and lingered faintly in the background for a long time.

"I can't quite believe in that story, my part in it, anyway. Robin wants to take care of me," Jess said.

"What's wrong with that?"

"You should know better than anybody. You pushed me out the door and into the street. If you felt sorry for me then, you sure didn't let on. Robin flipped out when we went diving. She thinks I'm trying to kill myself when I do some of the stuff I do, but it's just the opposite. I can't spend the rest of my life being scared to do things. Robin would keep me scared." Jess stopped himself.

"I want the best for you," Gibb murmured, his voice so low Jess could barely hear him. "The best...whatever that means," he said slowly, as if he were no longer talking to Jess at all, as if he'd already drifted out and away, into the night.

Eleven

Gibb and Jess traveled came to Colorado in late September to see Rachel and Jack's new baby, Miranda. The colors were knife-edged, everything honed to glittery, perfect sharpness in that dry mountain air as if two-dimensional—tree trunks, cars and buildings. They looked like they'd draw a line of blood if you slid by too close. And the yellow and red of trees on fire—the world was coming to an end, Gibb thought, and all the time looking so beautiful, too.

They'd walked in the blue twilight, Gibb, Jess and Rachel, a red cast of light coming from somewhere, the sun long down and a crescent moon rising, growing toward quarter, with three rings around it, like frosted glass. Gibb listened, watched, calmly cut vegetables, washed lettuce, changed diapers, looked at baby photographs. Like a man in a rage who turns to a ringing phone and has a genial conversation before turning back to his fury again, Gibb passed the pleasant days. But the dark shadow of the enraged man always stood at the periphery. A week passed and the promised snow never fell. If only it had come and muted that fiery light. He and Jack had sat together in the back yard, drinking bourbon together, talking, until Gibb had convinced himself of something. In the morning his memories were blurry, but Gibb thought he finally believed that Jack was a decent man, and that Rachel loved him. His head throbbed. For Gibb love was not enough to cure a surfeit of anger.

Suddenly they stood together at the airport ticket counter. The days had gone by so quickly. The tinny electronic voices spoke into his ears and people jostled around them. Jess held Miranda, who had been so good, Rachel said, the colic days gone. Miranda made sounds of pleasure and grasped Jess's first finger in a tiny fist. Gibb smiled at Rachel and held his smile against a pain in his stomach that was like a fire; he listened to her voice coming from moving lips, so faint he strained to hear. She looked at him oddly, her face sad. *Don't be sad*, he wanted to tell her, *please please please*. To Rachel's moving lips, because he thought it was the right thing to say, he whispered, *Miranda is beautiful, so beautiful* and Rachel nodded, tears spilling down her cheeks. She wiped them roughly with her fingers. He saw her say, *I love you. Come back soon.*

They walked down the concourse together, Jess in the middle, arms linked, as if they were alone in some great, empty field, the Colgrove children oblivious to the sea of people streaming around them. Rachel laughed. "We really did have a good time. We did, didn't we?" she said, leaning toward Gibb, and he nodded.

Gibb loved to see her face like that, with a flush high on the cheekbones, and her hair, grown long again, swinging free. How he loved her. At the entrance to the concourse he put his arms around her and kissed her. "Goodbye. Thanks for having us." He turned once, as they walked toward the gate—even though he hadn't meant to—for a last look at her where she still stood, smiling. She lifted her hand and he did the same. Then he and Jess turned and walked quickly away.

Back home now, looking at the lighted lobbies of the old hotels, at the lamp-yellow room windows that sometimes turned dark as he watched, Gibb walked along the sidewalk that ran next to the beach, hands in his pockets, glancing from time to time toward the water. He had slept all day. The wind rustled dryly in the trees, like unpleasant voices. He rubbed his jaw, felt the roughness of his face. How long had it been since he'd shaved—three days? Four?

Had he really slept? Laughter and piano music drifted across the street. He'd slept long enough anyway to dream of himself floating toward his father on a flimsy raft, no more than a child's toy and sabotaged, sinking. Later he dreamed of being in an elegant house with thick Persian rugs, heavy dark furniture, French doors that opened onto a vast lawn. Something terrible was happening in the house, but it was necessary to be there, inside, for the danger outside in the darkness—another mystery—was worse. He'd held a long sword with an ornate scabbard in one hand, and in the other hand a common kitchen knife.

The day before yesterday he'd gone to Simpson Park, the forest primeval, or the forest evil; they had found the skeleton of a murdered girl there a few years ago, in this hammock no more than ten minutes from the middle of downtown, dense with gumbo limbo and black gum trees, strangler figs squeezing the life from pigeon plum and sapodillas, golden silk spiders hanging in great webs that caught in your hair and clothes. Light spattered the floor of leaf rot, and silvered the moss-covered limestone. Gibb had watched a man sleeping on a bench near the entrance, his head resting on a bunched-up orange jacket. Gibb stepped on a twig and the man's watery blue bloodshot eyes had popped open. He'd whipped himself into an upright position and waved his arms at Gibb. "Devils," he screamed, the sound reverberating through the silence. "Devils everywhere!" Gibb had stumbled away, down the path onto the sunlit street.

So he had seen them too, Gibb thought, remembering the man's grotesque face. *But I have my own and they make me crazy in a different way from you, sir.* He walked across the street and followed the sidewalk that led to the ocean. When he stepped onto the beach, he took off his shoes and walked toward the dark water. He hadn't been working. He couldn't stay underwater forever, pretend all this didn't exist—the world collapsing in on itself, poisoning itself, people sucking the bones of others. He was too peaceful down there, and he couldn't work if he couldn't sleep, anyway. And he couldn't sleep if he didn't drink. And when he drank too much he wasn't fit to dive the next day. And every day he didn't dive, part of him disappeared. God, the illogic of it made him even more tired. Sitting on the beach, he listened to the water sucking back from the shoreline, no more than a feathery hiss, the night having become unnaturally calm.

His mother had peered at Gibb when he'd reached out, holding the box of photographs as if across the whole long room, across the ancient wood floor that had taken up the sound of a thousand footfalls, and heard the secrets and the beating hearts of five people coming and going, going and coming. His mother's eyes narrowed with suspicion at his careful gesture, more like an offering, really—*Here, look. Take one and remember.* His father had given him the box of photographs. Maybe she suspected that the gathering and giving of the photographs meant more than it did, a father giving his son the family photographs to put in an album. Perhaps she'd heard them talking. She shrank back from his hand and he had seen her pain, but couldn't speak. He didn't know what to say anymore. Hugging them both, he'd left quickly, only looking back to see the old house already shut up tight. He imagined his mother making her slow rounds, locking all the deadbolts, putting the keys in the places they were always kept.

He got into his car, slipped Lou Reed's *Street Hassle* into the tape deck, and drove slowly through the dark back streets. The air smelled fresh and clean with salt. He breathed in great mouthfuls of air, savoring the rich taste of it.

Back in his apartment the air was stuffy and he opened the windows wide. Sitting with the photos spread out before him on the table, he arranged them as well as he could. The rough progression of their lives was easy to determine. His mother's parents first, who'd died before he knew them, a sepia-tinted oval of a couple with faint smiles and collars closed at the neck. In his grandmother's face was Rachel's full, shapely mouth. In his grandfather's amiable, yet direct gaze, in the slight, quizzical cast of his head, he saw Jess. His father's father wore a cap and leather vest, held a scythe and stood knee-deep in fresh-cut rye. His mother and father posed together at the beach, smiling, arms just touching at their shoulders. His father holding baby Rachel, Rachel with Santa, Rachel in a stroller, Rachel's first birthday. Fewer pictures of him, fewer still of Jess. Two years missing here, four years there. His father standing apart, hands in his pockets, touching no one. His mother's face a gaunt, pale mask set off by black hair. He placed the photos in the album carefully, striving to remember each event, each year.

Resting his chin in his hands, he stared out across the room into the shadows, remembering his drive of a week ago, halfway up the state. Like a long-lost relative, she'd shown him snapshots of her own, sipping at her iced tea with the mint leaves swimming near the top, watching him. Ruth Cobb Mitchell, the prosecution's missing witness. Why, she could have been his father's sister, she'd spoken so familiarly about him, nodding under her sun hat, never taking her eyes off Gibb's face, as if his father's features were branded there. He smiled a little, supposing they were. On the last page of the album, he studied a photograph of his father for a long time before closing the book, feeling relieved, finally, of a responsibility that he could no longer name.

Gibb looked at the clock over the refrigerator. Quarter to five in the morning and still it rained. He smelled it on his hands, in his hair. His head throbbed with a stunning, bright pain that made his whole face ache. He rolled a joint and smoked it slowly, feeling the pain subside a little. He'd rarely smoked since Jess's accident, always ready, in case Jess needed him. But he knew Jess would be all right now, without him.

Sitting at the table, he listened to the rain, water flowing through the streets like a flood, cars abandoned, a brown rag-work of debris floating along with the rising water. So dark . To be up against such darkness as he'd seen out there tonight. But darkness wasn't death. One couldn't lose oneself utterly and finally in darkness alone.

He put in a demo tape Jess had given him and remembered the last time he'd seen Jess play with his group, how his fingers had moved over the keys, a quick arpeggio dropped in, his left hand, aggressive on a solo, then his face inclined toward the horn, listening, a few grace notes falling *sotto voce*, the melody coming back offbeat. Gibb had felt something dark in the piano's counterpoint that night. A ballad was playing on the tape now, the grief notes of the horn bending back and swelling out again, and the piano taking on a certain voice, then another, transforming the music tonally. *Transformed. I'll be transformed.* Jess had finally been able to travel alone across the city. Gibb had followed him one of the first times and stood close at the bus stop. He'd sat near him on the bus and seen him deal with clumsily helpful strangers. Jess had been going to a friend's house, and Gibb watched the person Jess had come to see meet him at the door. Gibb had waited, then, followed him home, knowing afterwards that Jess could find his way around the entire planet. Jess would be all right now, without him.

Gibb ran his fingertips over the worn wood of the tabletop, felt the multitude of nicks and mysterious gouges, followed the grain, laid his face against it, listened. He willed the wood to speak, but it was silent. *Please.* Just days ago he had gone to Neoma Kelch's grave at Woodlawn Cemetery. She had lain mute, curled under the grass, under the stone. He willed himself to believe in ghosts, then, just to hear her tell her tale. But he saw that she herself had long ago been transformed, had set roots in the clay, had moldered down into the black earth. She would not speak. The whole world had gone silent on him.

Putting on Jimi Hendrix's "Machine Gun," Gibb let himself be carried back to a time when he had waited for his induction notice. But he'd gotten a hardship deferment just before his lottery number had come up. Funny, if he'd ever been drafted, he'd have been classified 4-F anyway. Unsuitable for service. He'd never considered killing anyone, ever. But the anger that had lived in him so long had become rage after Jess's shooting, violent and unspeakable, like a fire that never died out, but merely smoldered and consumed him, little by little. Jess wasn't just someone he loved, not just his brother, but a person utterly good, no one's enemy. Putting his fingers to his lips, Gibb felt his breath warm against them. He thought of Rachel, who had been and would be with him always.

He listened. The rain had stopped. Tomorrow, then, might be clear, for the dive. But it was already tomorrow. He put on his shirt and locked the door behind him. He didn't want to miss the first light rising at the edge of the sky, where it touched the sea. He was ready for his trip with Megan to Key West and the Cosgrove Shoal dive.

Just after dawn, Megan picked him up. Gibb had gotten Megan to take her boat on the pretense that his own needed plugs. Actually, he'd sold it last week. He counted. Three weeks after his visit to Rachel, or four, he couldn't remember. For most of the long drive, Gibb slept, resting his head on Megan's lap or slumped against the window.

They cast off in a light, cool wind that had died to an occasional warm breeze by the time they approached the Cosgrove Shoal lighthouse. He stared out at the water, hands on the side of the boat, the spray in his face, his tongue tasting salt on his lips. The white plume of the water, stirred to froth by the engines, trailed behind them like smoke, and the sky was pale and fiery.

From a distance the lighthouse looked sturdy, pointing up from the water like a slender finger. But it was no more than a skeleton now, sitting atop a prehistoric reef on the northern edge of the Gulf-stream. If the Gulfstream had moved in today, visibility would be good to 140 feet or more, and he and Megan would go down along the reef slope in search of rare black coral. They trailed a float and secured the anchor. Before Megan put on her gear, Gibb touched her hair and looked south across the water, toward Cuba. Only a few high clouds marked the blue expanse of sky.

She looked at him without smiling. "You know I'd do anything in the world for you."

"I know," he nodded. "You're always doing things for me. Like being with me now. Let's go."

They went down up current from the boat, near the shallowest part of the reef. A cluster of purple sea plumes, tinged with yellow, waved delicately in the current. Around the lighthouse was a maze of ledges and caves where they were sure to see a few barracuda. Within a few minutes, he saw Megan gesture beyond them, toward one cruising near the surface. They headed north, down the slope, across a plain of sea fans. He swam down the coral wall, to about sixty-five feet, and then deeper, toward the terrace of black coral. For a while he rested, watching a cleaner gobie in a depression of fine sand, drifting toward the mouths of a couple of yellow and silver French grunts. He watched Megan, swimming just ahead of him, so graceful in the water. He hoped she would forgive him. The old feel-ing came to him, of the water, continuous with him. The sense of his body's boundaries were gone, and the sea flowed easily through him, surging through his blood, and he thought, *If I could stay here, I'd be safe.* He imagined the time before the first reefs had formed along the ocean bottom, remembering a childish notion he'd had of a pristine place, the earth, sea and land. A world full of promise, he'd called it. A world of light. A world that never was, or was no longer.

*

Two days later, driving out of the city, Gibb concentrated on the road. The massive shadows of late afternoon cast themselves across the asphalt like creatures that had just crawled up from the canal. He shook his head to clear his vision. He was exhausted, but he couldn't sleep. He'd slept a few hours in the car on the way to the Keys and on the way back to Miami, but except for that he hadn't slept in six or seven days at least, maybe more.

Driving past the small Micousoukee villages, to the Shark Valley entrance of the Everglades, he turned left on a road just before the park, where his car couldn't be seen. How easy it would have been on the dive, to have just gone deeper and deeper until his air supply ran out. But that wouldn't have been fair to Megan. He was going to hurt everyone enough as it was. He stepped a short distance down the road. Birdcalls rose up around him and he walked very slowly toward a great blue heron, silhouetted against the sherry-colored sky. He watched for a moment and listened, then went back to the car and sat on the fender, hearing traffic roar past on the nearby highway. Finally it was dark enough to see the stars distinctly. The sound of crickets and bullfrogs began, swelling to a loudness that drowned out all other sounds, and then drifting away on the wind to the soft rustling of trees. He took the length of hose from the back seat, stuck it in the exhaust pipe, and ran it into the car. Getting in the passenger's side, he checked the window to be sure it was rolled up tightly, and moved into the driver's seat, wedging a towel across the top of the window. Turning on the engine, he swallowed the four Halidol tablets he'd taken from his parents' medicine cabinet and drifted, finally, into his dark, coveted sleep.

Part Four

And what of the dead? They lie without shoes
in their stone boats. They are more like stone
than the sea would be if stopped. They refuse
to be blessed, throat, eye and knucklebone.
> "The Truth the Dead Know"
> Anne Sexton

Twleve

Jess's apartment was crooked in the torrential rain. Just as Rachel's cab pulled to the entrance, the building righted itself so that its gray stuccoed walls stood starkly against the dark green trees.

The rain soaked her hair, spilled over the sidewalk and filled her shoes.

"Jess?" she called at the door. "Oh Jess," she said when the door opened. She put her arms around him, her head at his shoulder.

He cupped her skull in the palm of his hand, in the careful way one supported the head of an infant, wrapping his other arm around her as if he might carry her. "You're soaked," he said, touching her from shoulders to forearms until he held her hands in his own. "I didn't think it was raining that hard."

"When?"

"Some hikers...found him early yesterday morning. It took a while for the police to notify me." He clenched his jaw. "There was a note. We, I waited. We need to get his things. I have the address. Megan will drive. She's on her way over."

"I have to sit down," she said, picking up her bag from a puddle on the floor. "I've made a mess, my bag."

"It doesn't matter."

"Let me get some paper towels. Just tell me where they are. I'd better wipe it up. You might slip...or Megan."

"Rachel." He held her shoulders. "Don't worry about the floor." He spoke to her softly. "Let's go sit on the couch and wait for Megan."

"Mother and Dad?"

"We have to go there. I couldn't just call them on the phone."

"They don't know?"

"There was no other way."

She jumped at the sound of knocking.

Jess stood up and walked to the door.

"Jess," Megan said when he opened it. They hugged and walked to the couch together to sit on either side of Rachel.

Megan put her hand on Rachel's arm.

Rachel looked into her dark eyes, irises nearly the shade of the pupils. She took a deep breath and another, fighting the nausea that had come to her suddenly in great shivering waves. "I'm so sorry," Megan said. Her face was calm but her eyes brimmed with tears.

Rachel stared out into the room. "Why? Does anyone know why?"

Megan's bare, brown arms were shapely, the muscles taut. "I don't know. He hadn't worked for a week and a half. He told Jon he had bronchitis. We were diving...three days ago. He said he was better. He seemed...almost happy."

Rachel looked at Jess. His face was blank, drawn. "Jess," she said softly. "What happened? Why?"

"Gibb..." he said brokenly. "Gibb's gone." He swallowed hard and rubbed his face. "We've got to leave," he said after they had sat in silence for a time. "Maybe we'll understand more after we get the papers he left."

Rachel sat without moving, her body heavy.

"Would you like to put on dry clothes first, drink some tea?" Megan asked, her voice half a whisper.

Touching her drenched skirt, Rachel realized she was chilled. She suddenly felt herself shaking with cold. "Yes," she said, willing herself to rise and to compose herself, change clothes, comb her hair, pour her sorrow and grief into a mask that would keep the eyes of the curious from raking her face.

Even after seeing Gibb, his face wearing in death the slightly quizzical, even bemused expression it had so often worn in life, she couldn't believe he was dead. He'd simply played an elaborate trick. Someone would soon tell her everything had been staged, and Gibb would walk into the room with a small, embarrassed laugh. The lingering feeling that Gibb wasn't really dead gave her an absurd hope. She plunged numbly forward.

When she and Jess had told their parents, Noel and Elizabeth had sat at first in dry-eyed silence, exchanging occasional bewildered glances. Crying then, they moved apart on the couch, their father's face streaming with tears, their mother weeping into her hands. Noel had gotten up suddenly, gone to the bedroom and shut the door.

They'd sat together with Elizabeth then, as she cried. "Why?" she asked, wanting to see the note. "When will we have the funeral? What hymns will we have?" Noel came out of the bedroom with his Bible. "The Lord is my shepherd," he read, choking back tears, unable to go on.

"Gibb didn't want a funeral," Rachel told them.

They had been confused. "We have to have a funeral for our son," Elizabeth said, her voice anguished.

"I think we have to do what Gibb wanted. He wants his ashes scattered over a reef where he liked to dive."

"I don't understand," Elizabeth cried. "I don't understand." She hunched over and rocked back and forth, weeping. "I don't understand."

Rachel walked to the couch, sat next to her mother, and gently stroked her hair. "I know," she whispered. "No one does."

Sitting in Jess's apartment more than a week after Gibb's death, Rachel read Gibb's brief note aloud for the third time. To herself, she'd read it over and over, waiting for the words to reconfigure themselves into something plain, an answer.

She held up the paper, her hands trembling, and then laid it on the table. "Forgive me, but please don't use the words 'guilt' or 'blame' in your conversations about me. Please forgive me. I care deeply about all of you. I don't want to hurt you. And I don't consider life meaningless. I believe in its mysteries; I believe in the mystery of death. But all my energy for solving mysteries is gone. All my words for saying the truth are gone. The world doesn't speak to me any longer. I'm empty. I can't live with that—the silence, the loneliness. I'm sorry."

She turned the page and said to Jess, "He put all of his assets into joint tenancy with rights of survivorship so nothing would have to go through probate court. Three savings accounts, one for Mother and Dad and one for each of us. He has a safe deposit box at SunTrust Bank." She read, "'there are some stock certificates, and other items you'll want to keep in a secure place.' He says I'm to take care of his personal effects, in the apartment. Jess, we can do that together." She looked up and Jess nodded.

"All right."

"'The journals are for you, Rachel,'" she read, "'Jess, he says you have an extra key to his apartment." She stopped. Jess sat with his chin in his hands. Rachel moved a little in the chair and Jess turned to her, his expression composed.

"I'm trying not to cry," he said slowly. "I can't explain it, but I loved Gibb so much...I feel...a responsibility to him, to understand what he did. I want..." His voice broke. "I want to respect his right...to do what he did. I don't know if I can...I miss him so much."

"I know," she said. She sat for a while with her arms folded, staring at the wall, her senses dulled from lack of sleep. "I think I'll go to the store, pick up something for dinner." Jess reached toward her as she began to get up; she gave him her hand. "Wait," he said, gently pulling her back down beside him. "I feel your anger—in the way you walk around the room, the sound of your voice. Everything you do and say is so angry. Don't be angry at him, Rachel."

She stood up. "I'm not angry. I'm just so tired and numb I feel like I'll never be able to think again, or laugh, or smile at my baby." Her voice was even and matter-of-fact, as if she were talking about someone else, a story she'd read in the newspaper. "I'd better get out and get us some food. It looks like we're going to have a cloudburst before too long."

Outside, she unlocked Gibb's Valiant, started the engine and sat fumbling in her purse for her sunglasses. She listened to the idling car, a steady, cared-for sound. "Damn you, Gibb," she said out loud. "How could you?" She slammed her hand down hard on the steering wheel and shifted into reverse, pulled out onto a main street and stopped at a red light. When the light turned green, she paused a moment before rolling slowly into the intersection, and the man behind her, in a white Cadillac, lay on his horn and shook his fist as he passed her on the right-hand shoulder. "You stupid idiot," she screamed from the window, even though he was out of earshot. Rage had gathered in her arms and legs, and that current of frightening energy began to move through the whole of her. Her knee shaking as she pushed the clutch pedal, she turned into the dirt lot of a small park that sloped down to a dark canal. A huge old banyan tree shaded the car. The car Gibb had killed himself in. She opened the door and walked away quickly, to the edge of the water, where two geese floated lazily, looking for handouts.

Staring at the water, she thought back over the years, all the letters, stories, parts of Gibb's journals she'd read. For years he had tried to make her listen, tried to get her to understand what he was doing. He had been trying to prove that their father wasn't a murderer. She hadn't wanted to know anything about it. Why hadn't she listened? Why hadn't she helped him? Why hadn't she been able to save him? She was alive. Life sang inside her, nipping ravenously at her like a pent bird, screeching out its presence, all around. She was alive and Gibb was dead. How had he slipped away from her so easily? Severed himself from their love with scalpel ease? Had her own life become so important that she'd *let* Gibb go? She moved her foot back and forth in the rich black dirt, then gazed at the canal, remembering their last visit together in Denver, a series of slow images passing before her eyes. Gibb smiling, drinking too much at dinner, maybe. But he'd laughed and joked with Jack and played on the floor with Miranda.

She thought of her telephone conversation last night with Jack.
"I failed Gibb. I should have...done something."
"You can't blame yourself."
"I miss you both so much. I love you."
"I love you too. Call me tomorrow."
She thought of how Gibb had turned to wave goodbye as he and Jess were about to board their plane. That wave had seemed so positive, the look on his face happy. Or had his expression been one of resolve? How could she have been so stupid? She threw a pebble into the water and watched it break the surface into ripples. The nearest goose stuck his head in and bobbed down, until only his tail feathers showed. His head came up again and he looked up at her, betrayed. "Why?" she whispered. The goose honked, opening his yellow beak so that she could see his blade-shaped tongue. He reached shore and waddled toward her, honking softly. Gibb stood at the gate. She saw them embrace. "Don't die, Gibb," she

whispered in his ear. "Please, please don't die." "Goodbye," he said, "take care." The goose caught the hem of her skirt, pulled at it. Tugging the fabric free, she took a step backwards. "Shoo, go away," she yelled. "I don't have anything for you." She turned and walked toward the car, old, but shiny still, with a brand new coat of wax. As always, Gibb had considered the details, wanting to do everything perfectly.

He had left her his journals. Why had he said "I have no more words"? Would his journals tell her? She had to be alone with them, to share their secrets. They were all she had left of Gibb.

Rachel slipped the key into the lock and swung open the door. She had just paid the landlady a month's rent on the apartment that had been Gibb's. The landlady had shaken her great long head, her wrinkled jowls moving side to side. Gibb, she said, had been a "special boy," a mensch. If only all people cared so much about others. "He brought me presents," she said, "just little things to brighten my day. A chocolate bar. Swiss, always Swiss. A fancy hanky."

From the window, Rachel saw that the sun had gone behind a large, thin cloud full of ragged holes. Light, the sorrowful golden color of watered-down whiskey, spilled over the edges of the cloud and through the holes. She let down the blinds, locked the door and she sat down in an overstuffed chair near the corner of Gibb's desk, a chair, she imagined, marked with the contours of his body. She saw Gibb reading, Gibb writing.

She closed her eyes and slept. She dreamed that she and Jess and Gibb were on a ship, at night, in a storm. She and Jess were clinging to a rope. "Where's Gibb?" she called, over the sound of the wind. Jess pointed. Gibb stood the whole length of the ship away from them. He threw a lantern overboard, cupped his hand to his ear and shook his head. "Wait," she called. She and Jess made their way toward Gibb with their arms outstretched, struggling to stay on their feet. "Take our hands," she screamed over the roaring wind. "We have to save each other." Gibb shook his head again and pointed toward the black water.

Rachel woke up suddenly, her heart pounding as she glanced around the dark apartment, not sure where she was. Waiting for her eyes to adjust to the darkness, she sat for a moment, and then got up to turn on the desk lamp, the image of the dream still with her.

On her brother's desk a blotter with a calendar advertised Jon's business: "Jon's Dive Shop—Salvage, tours, equipment, lessons." The days were marked by lists, printed in Gibb's neat hand. Items were crossed off with a line made by a straight edge. His last list read: "1. Call vocational rehabilitation, 2. Call Goodwill, 3. Go to bank, 4. Go to hardware store, 5. Finish instructions for Rachel."

A photograph album lay on one corner of the desk, and she opened it and thumbed through the pages. Forty years of family pictures. So many old images and faded expressions, impossible to decipher, in an album that looked new. Maybe her mother had arranged the pictures and given the album to Gibb as a present. In a picture taken of her in college, hair down to her hips, Rachel sat with her back against a tree, smiling straight into the lens. A long dock stretched into a lake behind her. Had she ever been that happy since? The smiles of photographs were always a sort of lie.

She moved the album aside and stared at the yellow oval the desk lamp cast onto the desk. Snapping off the light, she walked to the window and raised the blinds to look out at the darkness. The street was empty. What time was it? She had forgotten her watch. The thought came to her like the passing of a ghost, raising goose bumps on her forearms, as if knowing the time would anchor her to living. *A bad lightning storm the other day*, the landlady had said. *The electricity went off.* She walked into the kitchen, and turned on the light, a bright fluorescent circle that hurt her eyes, made the bare counter and gleaming sink obscene, unreal as props in a play. She opened the cabinets, gazing at the neatly arranged glasses and cups, plates and casserole dishes—objects that had been part of the dailiness of Gibb's life. Taking out a bowl, she ran her finger around the rim. But the bowl gave up nothing of Gibb, not a sound, not an image.

A girl's voice sounded clearly below the open window. "I'm leaving," the voice cried out. "It's over!" Rachel walked quickly to the window. The girl had run from sight in the time it had taken Rachel to cross the room. She had disappeared, but the notes of misery in her voice still echoed. Rachel closed the window, dropped the blinds and turned the air-conditioner on high to shut out the night, to mourn alone, to be reminded of no one else's sorrow.

Thoughts swept through her, one after the other with the force of the waves that had knocked them down as children. Laying her head in her arms on the kitchen counter, she wept, her whole body shaking. She cried until she was completely empty.

In the morning, Rachel soaked a washcloth and held it across her swollen eyes. Her hair fell in thin strands around her face. She stepped from her wrinkled clothes and left them in a heap on the black and white tile. She showered, stepped from the tub, toweled herself dry, and pulled jeans and a t-shirt from her suitcase.

She pictured Miranda and Jack at home in the sunlit kitchen, going through the morning routine she'd thought of as a chore, but wished for now, her body in thoughtless motion as the ticking of the clock had urged her on to the next task. Jack had hired a house-keeper. Her name was Alice.

Rachel's blood ran in Miranda's veins, even across an expanse of continent. Miranda's heart beat in Rachel's chest. But she had left her baby and never again would she be the mother-Rachel of the smiling pictures. "Gibb, Gibb," she whispered. It was Gibb she had loved more than anyone, Gibb and Jess, and Gibb had held the three of them together. Together, they had survived. But no. Gibb was gone. Gibb had died. Time had stopped.

After she had walked down to the Mercado Latino to buy a pa-per she called Jess, the wet heat of the street still upon her. He said Cage was dropping him off in an hour or so. "I know the way up," he said.

Putting the phone down, she wandered through the small apart-ment, opening drawers and closets. She found Gibb's journals on a shelf in the bedroom closet. Reaching up, she counted them: twenty similar black loose-leaf notebooks with typed labels on the spines.

She heard a knock at the door, then Jess's voice, the door open-ing.

"Jess," she called, "You got here so fast."

"Cage tends to speed. Where are you?" he asked. "Come give me a hug, please, your hand or something. You sound out of breath. How are you doing?"

"Oh," she said. "You know. I don't think I slept much." They hugged and Jess walked to the kitchen. "Yeah, I know what you mean." He took a glass from the cupboard and filled it at the tap. "It's getting hotter by the minute out there. Rachel?"

"I'm watching you navigate. You know this place."

"Sure. As long as no one moves anything, I can get around here as well as in my own apartment." He touched his forehead and smiled a little. "I don't know what I'll do when my memory goes. What have you been up to this morning?"

"I've sort of lost track. I forgot my watch and the power was off for a while a couple days ago, I guess."

"Maybe you shouldn't stay here alone," he said, "Too much around to remind you of Gibb, too much time on your hands. I've been so busy I haven't had time to think."

"Where did you play last night?"

"Sonesta Beach Hotel. They liked us. When are you going to come hear us?"

"Are you playing tonight?"

"Nope. Not till Thursday."

"I'll come then."

"So you rented the place." Jess put the glass down in the sink. He leaned back against the counter and folded his arms.

"Yes."

"Why?"

She paused, looked down at the floor, then at Jess's face, expectant and puzzled. "Gibb left me his journals. I have to know what he was doing. What he found out. Why...he..." She couldn't finish. Sunlight streamed in through the open blinds and fell in bright shafts across the wood floor and a green rug with a worn flower print.

"Couldn't you take them home with you?" Jess asked softly.

"I *need* to be here," she said, the shrill notes in her voice coming back to her across the kitchen. "I need to think. I can't just go home and get on with my life. I just can't. Do you understand? I don't know if I do."

Jess ran his fingers through his hair and nodded slowly, silent for a moment. "Sure I do," he said finally. "I'll help you any way I can."

"Thanks, Jess," she said. "I want to be here with you, too. I know it's not easy…"

"I manage," he broke in, shrugging his shoulders. "I love what I'm doing, music, the graduate work. Say, speaking of work—today, I'm taking some time off." He faced her. "How about a swim? Gibb and I used to go almost every Sunday, just like when we all were kids." He turned away from her. "I can't believe he's gone."

They walked toward Thirteenth Street, passed Washington and Collins and crossed Ocean Drive, the music of a salsa band drifting from a nearby hotel lobby.

On the beach, Rachel dug her heels deep into the warm sand, watching the waves break all the way down the shore, the line of froth a ragged, pale ribbon fringing the sand for as far north and south as she could see. Looking down the beach, she shaded her eyes; she could just make out the South Beach jetty through the haze.

"How does it look today?" Jess lay on his back with his hands behind his head. "Nice?"

"The sky's beautiful, starting to fill up with cumulus clouds." She stretched, the heat of the sun on her shoulders, and looked behind her. "We're right across from the Waves and the Revere. A couple of hotels just to the north—I can't make out the names—look like pink and green art deco cakes."

"Yeah. Crowded?"

"Well, I didn't see any parking spaces on Ocean Drive, and the outdoor bars are full of people." She turned. "There's hardly anyone in the water."

"What's the water like?"

"The wind's churning white caps farther out, so we might get in some body surfing." Jess sat and faced the Atlantic, his arms around his knees. "Ready to swim?" he said after a minute or two.

"Ready," she said.

"Here." Jess stood up. "Hold my hand till I get my bearings."

They walked over the uneven shoreline and through the trough

184

of shells in the shallow water. Waves lapped their knees, rose to their chests. Jess flinched at a wave that caught him by surprise.

"Let's dive," Rachel called.

Still holding hands they went headfirst through the waves and down. They both came up shaking the water from their hair.

"Still facing east?" he shouted to her over the sound of the surf.

"Yes," she called back, seeing in his face her whole past. She saw the future, too, flowing through them both and through Miranda. A wave crested and broke over her, forcing her to let go of Jess's hand. She scrambled through the water to reach him. But he dove and swam out to sea with a muscular crawl, trusting in something, she couldn't imagine what. In her, perhaps. In himself. The image of her father came to her—a large stern-faced man standing over her with his arms folded. *You take after your father*, people always said when she was small. *I look like my brothers*, she had responded defiantly, as if there were no progenitors; as if they'd somehow made each other up, like characters in a fairy tale. But her mother's blood coursed through her...and her father's. What part of her was like him? Blood was sacred. But the very same blood could poison you, too.

Rachel had forgotten the fierceness of Miami's summer storms. Lightning struck every few minutes, jagged bolts of silver cleaving the darkness. From the sound, each strike halved a tree or cracked a hole in the earth. A strike nearby rattled the window, and the lights flickered and went out. The gray light of the stormy afternoon filled the room.

For the last three days, she'd sorted through things in Gibb's apartment, gone places with Jess, driven all around the city. Taking up with Miami again was like getting together with an old and never very congenial friend, someone haughty and rude, then accommodating by unpredictable turns.

For hours, Rachel had driven along sleepy Coral Gables avenues as the sun winked through a canopy of banyan leaves and made the vibrant colors of crotons and cocoplums, hibiscus and seagrapes, shine as though enameled. The reggae and Caribbean rhythms, Latin and jazz bass beats from blasting car stereos on Dixie Highway thrummed *read, read*, but she was afraid to read Gibb's journals, afraid of the memories and new grief his words would bring. Trying to steel her courage all the while, she had driven on shaded roads in the Grove, down Calle Ocho in Little Havana. She had circled the block where her parents' house stood, blank as a sleeping face, as if she might suddenly park and step onto the front walk, into another time, when she and Gibb were small. Images bloomed and faded like the fireworks she remembered from a long-ago New Year's Eve when she and Gibb had sat together on the front porch, counting the seconds until midnight. *This year will be better*, they'd repeated like a mantra. *This year will be better.*

One afternoon she had pulled to the curb and stared up at the Dade County Courthouse, dwarfed now by towering office buildings. She saw her father put his hand on her brother's shoulder, saying, *it's up to you.* She watched as her father stepped away, leaned against a column and lighted a cigarette. He stood, then, smoking, a once mildly notorious now-forgotten accused murderer who had lived a life of self-pity. Who'd lived without regard for anyone, never realizing that his oldest son had always hoped to set him free by absolving him of suspicion and guilt. Her mother, standing at a distance in the shadows near the courthouse doors, folded her arms as Rachel watched, and like a blindly resolute army of one, closed ranks against the world.

She walked to a window and looked at the rain-drenched street, water flowing in the gutters. As if stepping into air and imagining she'd float, she had come here, cleaving herself for a time from her life—husband, child, rewarding work. But without Gibb, that life seemed a lie, something she could never have again. Reading Gibb's journals, she'd hear his voice in them and he wouldn't be gone. She'd know then, everything he had known.

Thirteen

Rachel began to read Gibb's journals, paging through accounts of their childhood she wouldn't have otherwise remembered. She read about their childhood games, descriptions of their room and of their mother and father, precise accounts of when flowers bloomed in their yard and of each of the birds that perched in their trees on a particular day. She smelled the tall weeds and soil of the vacant lot, felt the cool, dark dampness. Her childhood flooded back to her, with a sharp and painful clarity no photograph could have captured. The last few paragraphs of an early journal set her heart beating hard:

Today is my eleventh birthday. I have an imaginary friend no one believes in. My parents say I am too old to have an imaginary friend. They say it is scary. How can something be scary if you don't believe in it? My friend's name is Rebo. He helped me today remember something I didn't remember before. That was scary. My father's trial. He helped me remember everything from one of the days we were allowed to go.

How long after the trial had Gibb's imaginary "friend" turned into the murderer who stalked Gibb in his dreams? Had Gibb been asleep or awake when he called out to her, "There, in the closet. It's Rebo. See him?" Rachel glanced at the next few lines and closed the notebook. Her hands were cold. Why hadn't they gotten the electricity back on yet? Rain pounded the streets and gusts of wind swept sheets of rain against the buildings. She shuddered. Gibb had described a ride in the car to the courthouse, a suit he'd worn. *My sister had a red mouth,* he'd written. *"A clown's mouth," Rebo called it, and hair teased into a rat's nest. My father and mother argued about whether she could stay that way, and then Mother slapped Rachel.* Rachel took a quick, hard breath. Rachel's mother had never slapped her. She couldn't recall her mother ever slapping her. She saw her mother that day in the front seat of the car, imagined her raised hand, then felt her mother's fingers strike her cheekbone, felt the lingering burn on her skin.

What had Gibb written about in the last few years? She opened a journal from two years ago.

On Murder

At the basis of every murder is power: the power of a weapon, the power to kill without consequence, the power of physical strength, of rage, greed or hate. People murder because they can. Humans are the most predatory of all species, and at the same time, the only beings fully capable of complex thought. Yet humans continue to murder other species to extinction for their own vanity and greed. And to murder each other.

A woman took her eight-year-old daughter to Nauset Beach on Cape Cod late in the afternoon. The beach was deserted and the mother carried the little girl out into the waves. She was known to be a "sweet and gentle" child. That's what the newspapers reported. The mother held the child under the water until she no longer struggled. Ten years later the mother confessed that she'd murdered her daughter—Lynnette was the girl's name—to protect her from the kind of abuse she herself had suffered as a child. She admitted her deed to the elders of her church. Why? Atonement, she cried, redemption, and the child stared back from eternity, unblinking.

On Writing

I wouldn't have survived as long as I have without writing. Shaping my thoughts and experiences in words has been a barrier to pain; it's meant my life to me.

The evening filters down like the settling of dust, at first weightless, but eventually becoming dense as a star collapsed upon itself at the fringe of the galaxy. A man lights a cigarette and thinks of making love to a woman. Has he ever felt or given the kind of love necessary to survive in this complicated world? Cesare Pavese, the great anti-Fascist poet, said "A man doesn't kill himself for love of a woman, but because love—any love—reveals us in our nakedness, our vulnerability, our nothingness." The man on the porch inhales and watches the glowing tip of the cigarette and the expelled smoke. "Nakedness, vulnerability, nothingness," he says with a bitter laugh. "I've risked all three twice—once in loving the world and again in trying to explain my love in words. But the moment I began to explain, I risked the ultimate—not that my words would be misunderstood—but that I'd be overtaken by silence—the ultimate nothingness.

One can't survive it." The man crushes the cigarette in the earth, walks indoors and disappears forever.

A month later he had written about their father's trial:

The following entries are based on my reading of transcripts from the trial of Noel Colgrove, Dade County Circuit Court, Case Number 6896. Noel Colgrove was charged with first-degree murder in the death of Neoma Kelch, and was subsequently acquitted of that charge.

The opening remarks of the prosecuting attorney focused on the fact of murder itself. "A young life has been taken by the deliberate act of another. A so-called 'crime of passion?' No. A carefully planned murder, to dispose of an inconvenience for the defendant, the way you flush debris down a toilet. But Neoma Kelch wasn't an item to be discarded, like a paper container you carelessly throw to the wayside when you finish drinking your fill. No! Neoma Kelch was a vibrant girl. Beautiful. Full of life. She was murdered by a man without a conscience. He should die for his crime. He should suffer the way Neoma Kelch had to suffer."

As its first witnesses, the prosecution called, respectively, a police diver and the examining pathologist to describe where the body was found, its condition and identity. The victim had water in her lungs and contusions on her face and scalp. The prosecution then called Steve (Bix) McGrath, an employee of the Dinner Key Marina, as its third witness. McGrath was one of the prosecution's key witnesses. His testimony placed Noel Colgrove and Neoma Kelch together on the day of the murder. Another key witness, Rhea Kirby, disappeared the day before the trial was to begin. Bill Davis sought a two-week continuance, which the judge granted. Investigators combed the state and followed the few leads they had, but Rhea Kirby—who claimed to have known both Noel Colgrove and Neoma Kelch—never testified. She'd vanished, taking nothing from her Allapattah apartment. There was an extensive search and investigation, but she was never found. For months after the trial, both newspapers printed her parents' heart-rending pleas and offers of a reward for information about her whereabouts. Was she another murder victim?

The following examination of Bix McGrath is taken directly from the transcripts.

"Mr. McGrath, were you working at the Dinner Key Marina on May 30 of last year?"

"Yes sir, I was."

"Now, I know it could just become a blur, all the people you've seen at the Marina. But is there anyone you saw at the Marina that day, May 30, who's in this courtroom?"

"Yeah, the guy at the table over there." (Witness points at the defendant, Noel Colgrove.)

"How can you be sure?"

"He was standin' right next to me while I was gassin' up his boat."

"Was he alone?"

"Yeah, at first."

"What do you mean?"

"He was joined by a young lady."

"Mr. McGrath, I'm going to show you Peoples' Exhibit H, a photograph that previous witnesses have identified as the deceased, Neoma Kelch. Is this the young lady you saw at the Marina on May 30?"

The testimony stretches on, with the prosecutor trying to link Neoma Kelch and Noel Colgrove, through their conversation and "knowing looks." But Sam Lachon's question is obvious: Did you see them leave in the boat together? No? You didn't see the girl afterwards, but you didn't see Noel Colgrove's boat leave either. Is it possible you stepped inside for a time? Maybe you missed seeing the girl simply go on her way and Noel Colgrove take off for his day of fishing. Is it possible?

It was growing too dark to read. Closing the notebook, Rachel sat for a few minutes, then stood again, rubbed her neck. She waited for the thunder, counting silently. The glow came at the glass, a tremor of brightness that shone eerily in the darkened room. A knock sounded at the door and Rachel heard a muffled voice. She opened the door as far as the chain allowed, and saw the top of the gray-haired landlady's head, the face tilted up and dark eyes under wiry lashes regarding her.

"I thought you might need candles, dearie. I called Florida Power but it's a busy signal for half an hour. I gave up."

Slipping the chain free, Rachel opened the door.

The landlady held out a box of Hanukkah candles. "You need some light. You'll ruin your eyes. What're you reading? I hope it's racy."

"I stopped." Rachel glanced toward the desk where her brother's journal lay open.

The landlady slid past her to stand in the center of the room. She folded her arms, her eyes slowly sweeping the apartment. "My poor Gibb. A quiet young man above so many." She turned to look at Rachel, her face in shadows, her voice husky, almost too low to hear. "Why such a man takes his life. Why?" She walked back to Rachel, who hadn't yet moved away from the half-open door. Her pace was surprisingly swift, slippers flopping softly against her bare heels. Taking Rachel's hand in both of hers, she stroked it. "And why are you here, renting? You have a little baby. Gibb showed me the pictures."

Rachel clenched her teeth hard to keep from crying. "I...want to know why, too."

The landlady shook her head slowly. "But death has sealed his lips, hasn't it?" she said kindly. "Let's get some light. You got matches?" She dropped Rachel's hand and turned, making her way to the kitchen with small quick steps. "You got tea?" she called across her shoulder.

The cabinets were open when Rachel reached the kitchen, burner lit, the high blue flames standing like a ring of shining party hats. The landlady squashed them with the kettle, dimming the eerie light they had thrown across the porcelain stovetop.

A box of Lipton tea was whisked from the cabinet's darkness and two sturdy mugs taken from their hooks over the counter. "Your brother called me Mrs. Moriber. It came so naturally, I couldn't change him." The landlady turned and faced her, hands on hips, and looked up into Rachel's face with a little smile. "But maybe you'll call me Rose so I don't feel like your great-grandmother. My grandchildren call me words that mean nothing. 'Nano.' 'Baba.' Nonsense. So call me a name I like, say it."

"Rose."

"That wasn't so hard."

Rachel brushed hair back from her face. The rain's dampness filtered through the closed windows, crept into her like the ache of flu.

"A cruel thing. He couldn't have been as good a boy as I thought, to take away such a fine life. A puzzle isn't it?"

Rachel didn't answer. She brought the steaming mug to her face, breathed in the warmth. The question ran through her like an arrow.

Before Rose turned to swab the already-clean counter, Rachel saw the tracks of moisture on her powdered cheeks.

"Is there anything...you could tell me?" Rachel asked

"The lights on all night for days sometimes. Glad I don't pay the utilities. Your father visited, an older man in a gray suit, maybe your father. He had a mustache. A very distinguished gentleman, I thought."

"My father doesn't have a mustache."

"Dear," Rose sighed, "Have you ever put a puzzle together?"

"Maybe once or twice." Rachel remembered a flower-strewn meadow ending in a jagged line on the rickety card table they usually kept in the cedar closet. She stood over it and pressed a tongue of green into a green-surrounded hole. Then the puzzle lay, unfinished, until Rachel's mother swept it back into the box one day.

"Real puzzle solvers never look at the picture on the box. So you don't even know what the whole picture is till you've finished putting the puzzle together. I'm an old lady. I do puzzles at the Community Center on South Beach all the time. So many little pieces that never fit together the way you think they're going to."

The lights came on and turned the windows black. Rachel blinked against the brightness.

Rose clapped twice. "Hooray for Florida Power. The tea did us good, didn't it?"

Rachel nodded. "Yes, thanks for coming."

Rose narrowed her eyes and peered at Rachel. "Do your business now. I'm out of your way," she said and was gone, her slippers giving a final soft slap as she closed the door behind her.

Rachel stood in the center of the room, listening for the rain. The digital clock at her brother's desk blinked zeros like a pulse beat. She had forgotten to ask Rose the time.

Sitting down at the desk, she began to read where she'd left off.

"*Is it possible?*" she read.

192

"Yes," said Bix McGrath.

"I have no further questions."

Rachel tried to remember Sam Lachon. He had been to their house many times. But only an indeterminate image came to her, of a pale, featureless face, the wavering outline of a chin. Eyes—brown, then blue. A hand gesturing against a blank wall.

The sunlight woke her, the apartment saturated in lemon-colored brightness, so that the desklamp's light no longer showed. She raised her head from her arms. "Bix McGrath," she said aloud, feeling she knew him. Closing the journal, she walked to the telephone, dialed Jess's number and counted the rings to ten, eleven, twelve, hoping for his voice. After twenty rings she put the receiver down slowly.

She lay on the rumpled bed for a few minutes, looking up at the ceiling, arms at her sides. Her neck ached from sleeping at the desk. She felt weak, even lying in bed. Yesterday, she'd gotten a sandwich while driving around, and hadn't eaten dinner.

Digging in her purse for her wallet, she pulled out a ten, stuffed it into the pocket of her jeans and locked the apartment. She walked toward the Mercado Latino where she'd bought the newspaper. The sun had the dazzle of broken glass, making her eyelids ache. She forced herself to cover the distance at a brisk pace, sweat rolling down her neck. She opened the door and a man standing near the espresso counter looked at her grimly. She found a box of rusk-like biscuits, a can of garbanzo bean soup, and, in the small produce section, some oranges.

The man she'd passed stood at the counter, still, staring out into the street. "Cafe?" she said shyly. "Can I get some coffee to go?"

The man turned and looked at her across his shoulder. A day's growth of beard darkened his heavy face. He gestured toward her. "You want some cafe cubano?"

She nodded and he ran a stream of black, thick liquid into a tiny cup and handed it to her, then rang up her groceries on the old cash register.

"Five dollar, thirteen cents," he said, his eyes fastening on hers for a moment as she fumbled the ten from her pants. He laid the change down and turned away, speaking Spanish to a woman who'd stepped up to the outside counter. Rachel took a few small sips of the coffee, and then drank it down in a gulp, as she'd seen people do standing outdoors at the counters along Calle Ocho. Hot, sweet and bitter. She tore open the bag of crackers and chewed one, walking fast, smelling salt in the onshore breeze that had just come up. She needed to get right back, to keep reading.

The afternoon shadows grew long. Rachel read the testimony of Joe Ottawell, her eyes drooping closed more than once. The Ottawells had been their neighbors. They had moved away three or four months after the trial. An earring. A picture of the girl wearing an earring that the witness said looked like the earring on the boat. The earring on the boat that Joe Ottawell had seen once and never seen again. It had dropped, perhaps, into the vast ocean, lost forever. Some of the trial proceedings her brother had reported verbatim. But sometimes he summarized, always noting the difference. She finished the Ottawell testimony. Neoma Kelch's earring…Rachel felt a tingling in her hands, saliva rising in her throat. Gazing across the desk, into the kitchen beyond, filled with shadows, she listened to the voice that came to her over the waves and the sound of splashing, the voice that came to her as if time had never been. "Let's play the drowned girl," cried the voice.

Rachel walked slowly to the couch, and lay down, exhausted. She slept to the sound of water, the murmur the ocean made when you drifted with the sun on your back in a dead man's float. Exhaling, she dropped through the water into darkness. She looked up and saw a speck in the water above her, and she held up her arms as the body tumbled slowly towards her, blue eyes open.

When she woke up, the room was dark. She sat up on the couch and sighed, resting her elbows on her knees.

The phone rang and she made her way to the desk.

"Rachel?"

"Jess, hi."

"Did I wake you up?"

"I...fell asleep, on the couch. What time is it?"

"It's seven."

Seven. When had she fallen asleep?

"Can you meet me at the hotel before our first set at nine? You know where the Sonesta is, right?"

"Sure. I'll come over. To the bar?"

"Yeah, eight-thirty'd be good." Jess paused. "You sound so ragged, every time I talk to you. Are you sure you're doing okay?"

"I'm fine," she said quickly. "I've been reading so much, that's all. It's hard...it brings memories." She kept her voice light, but when she hung up, fear shivered along her spine. From what? She'd felt such relief at the sound of Jess's voice. After she hung up from talking to Jess, she would call Jack. He was the only one who would understand how she felt, reading about her father's trial. Before she'd left Florida, she'd told him everything—how badly she wanted to forget the trial and its aftermath, a childhood tainted by her parents' cold silences. Her father had been acquitted, and that had been enough for her, but not for Gibb, not ever. The crime was unsolved. Who was the murderer? Gibb had needed to know.

Rachel swirled the ice in her glass, took a small sip of her vodka tonic, and glanced around the dark bar. The band was on stage, her brother on piano and his friend Cage, playing a darkly lustrous bass. The vocalist doubled on sax. He wore a fedora with a slightly over-large brim and his coffee-colored face reflected the spotlight. His full, sensuous mouth formed the words of the song and his hips moved slightly to the beat.

Someone touched her elbow and she turned, startled. A man leaned over from a nearby table to face her.

"I'm sorry," he said, his voice a thick whisper. "Excuse me if I intruded on your thoughts. Do you have a match?"

"No," she said, shaking her head, "I don't." From the corner of her eye she saw him watching her. The tables were close and with a few quick movements he swung his chair around to join her. "Excuse me again," he said with a slight nod, his eyes flickering closed briefly, in the gesture of a very old man. "Would you dance with me once?" But the man was not old, no more than a few years older than Rachel, perhaps. Strands of pomaded dark hair fell across his forehead and heavy eyebrows.

She glanced at the empty dance floor. "No," she said, facing the small stage, his gaze upon her still.

The man stood up and took a step away from her table. He was tall. For a moment, he held out his hands toward her, then bent down and laid them flat on the table. He was so close that his breath was warm in her face, and she smelled the sweetish powdery odor of alcohol and cigarettes. "Leave me alone," she said. "I don't want to dance." Picking up her purse and drink, she walked to a table near the stage, feeling the man's eyes at her back. She sat and looked up at the band. Cage nodded at her and jerked his head to the right. Turning, Rachel saw the man walk slowly out of the bar.

The number closed with a series of pure, sustained notes from the sax, and the sax man smiled out into the darkness. "Thanks. That was a Johnny Hodges tune, 'Tonight I Shall Sleep.' We're gonna take a little break now. Don't ya'll go away. But before we step down, let me take a few minutes to introduce the folks that make the sound of Ikat." He gestured behind him. "Here's Marty Russell, Mr. Drums." Marty brushed the drumhead while Cage took up the beat on the bass. Jess ran his fingers along the keyboard in a riff. "Brother Cage Evans on bass, and the best piano man to come our way in a long time, Dr. Jess, Jess Colgrove." He raised the sax to his lips and played the last few notes of the song again. "I'm Tommy Hopkins, and we're Ikat."

A ripple of applause died to silence and the stage lights dimmed. Putting his hand on Cage's shoulder, Jess stepped off the stage. Cage looked at Rachel and shook his head slowly.

"Jess, Cage," she said. "You all were great."

"Sure, thanks."

"Hey, I like your sound," the bartender said when he brought their drinks.

"Thanks, how's the crowd?" Jess asked. "Anybody alive out there?"

The bartender laughed. "Yeah, well don't forget where you are. We usually get the Black Velvet and Four Roses crowd. But you're doin' okay for a Thursday. You must have a following."

196

"I gotta hit the john. Anybody going that way?" Jess asked.

"Yeah." Tommy put down his beer.

When Jess and Tommy were out of earshot, Cage shook a cigarette out of his pack and offered one to Rachel. "Smoke?"

"No thanks."

"Hey," he said. "Looked like the tall dude was putting the moves on you."

She nodded.

"Yeah, I figured not sayin' anything to Jess would be better. I like to save him grief." He turned away from her and took a deep drag from his cigarette, blew the smoke up toward the ceiling. "He'd report the guy, you know, track him to his room or something and give him hell." He looked at her and laughed dryly. "I'll be honest with you. Jess is like a brother to me, you know what I'm sayin'? He thinks 'cause that bullet didn't take him down he's got eight more lives. Jesus, he won't tolerate shit from anybody." He laughed again and finished his beer, gestured toward her glass. "Want another?"

"I'm okay," she said.

"He's fucking bull-headed." Cage sighed and stubbed out his cigarette. "Look, I'm sorry to lay this on you, but I want you to know. I can't get into it all here. They think they caught the guy who shot Jess. They want Jess to testify. He says no way."

"He doesn't remember anything."

"That's the idea, see. Just go to court, say you don't remember instead of getting slapped with contempt or something. I don't know. I need some advice here. I want to make sure what comes down is the right thing for Jess. Meet me for lunch someday next week if I can get up that early and we'll talk about it."

"Tuesday?"

"Tuesday's good. Here's my number. Call me late tomorrow afternoon." As Jess and Tommy were walking back, Cage scribbled on a napkin and handed it to her.

"Jess," he said. "This woman likes our sound. She must be one educated person."

"Yeah," Jess said, turning toward her and putting out his hand. "And more, you know?"

Rachel laid her fingers on his palm and Jess closed his hand around them. Groping for something to say, she thought of what Cage had just told her, recalling the tall man's slow stride from the room, a figure in silhouette from the light outside the bar. She would have told Jess. A blunder, not knowing the part of him Cage had described. I don't know that much about jazz...," she said awkwardly.

"That's okay," Jess broke in, "you'll learn, right?"

"Yeah," Cage said, "just keep tuned in to our gigs."

Jess took a swallow of beer, and gave Rachel's hand a slight squeeze before letting it slide from his own. He touched his watch. "About five more minutes?"

"Right." Cage lit another cigarette and glanced toward the stage.

"Call me tomorrow," Jess said to Rachel without turning around, his elbows on the bar. "Let's go somewhere together. Talk."

"I will," she said.

He nodded and squeezed his hands into fists, shook out his fingers. "Ready?" he said to Cage.

"Let's do it."

She walked back to her table. Tommy and the drummer were already on stage. When Jess and Cage joined them, Tommy started the first number with a low three-count.

"Can I get you something?" A waitress leaned down to her. "Vodka tonic."

"Say," she whispered, "is that your boyfriend on piano?"

"My brother." Cage's words still echoed—*'cause that bullet didn't take him down...He thinks he's got eight more lives.*

"He's amazing," the girl whispered. "An amazing musician."

Rachel nodded, trying to smile. "Thanks," she said awkwardly. The waitress left and Rachel looked at the tables of mostly couples, some holding hands, others gazing absently across the bar, as if their partners had ceased to exist. Who was troubled, happy, lonely? Their expressions were blurred in the half shadows. But even if she'd seen their features in a merciless light, heard invitations to seduction, gibes or words of anger, what would she have known? What had she ever learned about anyone that she could really trust?

She left money for her drink, waited until no one in the band was looking and slipped away, to an outside patio. A couple sat at one of the tables, their heads close, tall, opaque glasses in front of them. Rachel hurried past them and walked down wooden steps leading to the beach. The moon rippled light across the water. She remembered a song on a record her father had played, years ago. "Where the sea is dark and cold, my love has gone and our dreams grow old." She saw her father's lips move to the words, a young face. The song reminded her that her parents had once danced to music on the record player, had once been in love. Good and evil, love and hate were interwoven in all of the stories of the past that made her who she was.

Edging close to the surf, she gazed out across the water and into the luminous sky as if the silent landscape might yield a message— anything that might relieve her despair. But the sky was blank. The water hissed onto shore, and suddenly she craved dreaming and the austere apartment where the journals lay *full* of messages—spanning so much of Gibb's life. Walking to the parking lot, she thought she heard someone following her. But when she glanced back, she saw nothing but the dark shapes of bushes moving in the wind. As the sax started into a mournful-sounding solo, she unlocked her brother's car and drove quickly away.

The next morning Rachel turned to a journal entry Gibb had written a few months before he died:

The boat rocked gently on the calm sea, glittering with noonday light. The man's face was tight and drawn in the sun. When he looked out across the shimmering water, the light hurt his eyes. Nothing broke the sea's long expanse. It met the horizon at an undefinable place, as if the man floated in a giant glass sphere.

A fishing pelican, the only living thing he'd seen for the last half hour or more, dropped suddenly from the sky, cleaved the water and surfaced, the fish already swallowed. Then the bird floated near the man and regarded him with its black eyes. A panic ran down his breastbone to his groin. The man raised his arms and waved them. "Go!" he said loudly, but the pelican simply drifted serenely, a figure of majestic silence.

He checked the knot that secured the concrete block around her ankles. It would hold. He had already turned her face away from him. He took

out his binoculars for a last careful look around. He was still alone, ex-
cept for the pelican. Picking her up, he half-rolled, half-threw her over the
side of the boat. The water was clear. He watched her sink, her hair drift-
ing up, toward the surface. He looked down until he saw nothing more
than the silver-rippled water.

How long, how wholly had the imagined event lived inside of him? When had Gibb's obsession with their father's innocence transformed itself into an obsession with the murdered woman? He had recreated her in his imagination. Rachel turned the page. Gibb had written in pencil: "'Murder itself isn't as important as what leads up to the terrible moment.' Ask Tom Mullen source of quotation." Who was Tom Mullen? She had begun to skim the journals now, to sift them for clues to Gibb's suicide, to who the murderer might be, but she'd paid less attention to searching through Gibb's things. She needed to go through everything, so she could start to pack up his apartment, to get things in order so that she could go home.

Pulling open the desk drawer, she looked at its neat arrangement of pencils, pens, paperclips, the address book lying in a corner of the organizing tray. She thought of the chaos of her own desk drawer, its jumble of business cards, pennies, pencil stubs. Her brother's drawer had been arranged to betray no disorder. She thumbed through the small address book. Numbers and addresses were printed in the same color ink, lately copied from another book, perhaps, with a history of friends come and gone that she'd never see. She flipped to the M's where there was the listing:

"Mullen, Tom/18649 Bel Arbor Drive/Ft.Lauderdale/ 1-682-5676."

She picked up the phone and dialed.

Tom Mullen had agreed to meet with her and Jess on Saturday. On the interstate, Rachel felt the highway drumming under her wheels, the glittering cars around her a confusion of light and color.

She looked over at Jess, who leaned forward a little in his seat, hands on his knees. "I'm nervous about meeting this guy. I'm glad you're with me."

"Yeah, I'm glad to come. Let's see what we can find out," Jess said.

She rolled down the window. The air smelled of diesel fuel and of wet marsh. A rare wind blew in from the Gulf. It was hurricane season.

"Rachel?"

"What?" She slipped into the center lane, suddenly remembering Jess small and the long-ago nights of music and dancing. Rachel, play "Hound Dog," please, Jess had begged. Play "I Want to Hold Your Hand." Play "In the Midnight Hour." He'd never gotten tired of the music or of watching Gibb and Rachel dance.

"How're you doing, really?"

"Okay."

"You're lying."

She signaled and took another lane, slowed for the exit and stopped at the light. "So," she said finally. "I suppose you're going to tell me you can hear it in my voice."

"I'd have seen it on your face, too."

He was right. She didn't have a liar's knack.

"What can I do?"

"I don't know," she said.

"Rachel."

"Wait," she said, pulling into a gas station. "I'm lost. I missed the Wilton Manor turnoff." She felt her voice rise.

"Give me your hand."

She switched off the ignition, turned, and put her hand in his.

"Relax," he said. "You're shaking."

"I'm so angry. Gibb gave up. Why didn't he let us help him?"

Jess shook his head. "I don't know. He couldn't, that's all. He didn't know how."

Rachel and Jess followed a paving-stone walkway to the concrete block steps of Tom Mullen's trailer, a fine old Silverstream in immaculate condition. Shiny as a mirror, the trailer's metal skin glinted in the sunlight and reflected the colors of the hibiscus bushes planted along it, in wavering shapes of green and pink. A tall man appeared against the dark screen and stepped quickly out the door to stand haloed in sun on the top step.

"Tom Mullen," he said heartily, first taking Jess's hand and shaking it, then extending a hand to Rachel.

The soft palm and fingers betrayed his deep, leathery tan as one acquired by leisure, not outdoor work. He looked long at each of them and shook his head. "Forgive me," he said, "for feeling I know you both well. Your brother was a man of few words but what he told me about you counted. I never thought I'd have to say I miss him. I'm sorry."

"We'll appreciate any help you can give us," Jess said.

"There's a little patio around back, with some shade. Let's talk there instead of inside with the fishing rubble," Mullen took a step toward Jess. "Why don't you walk with me, since I know the way, son. How do you like to do it?"

"Let me take your arm," Jess said, and they walked together through a tiny plot of grass that lay like a patch on the gray dirt surrounding the trailer, Rachel a few steps behind them, thinking that Mullen seemed a familiar uncle they'd been visiting for years.

"Gibb's kept me posted on you both," he was saying. "I did some private work on the investigation of your...accident, Jess." He paused almost imperceptibly, to find the word. "As a favor to Gibb."

Jess nodded, his expression benign.

Rachel watched Jess's face for some flicker of discomfort, thinking of her meeting with Cage tomorrow, but saw nothing.

They moved around back to sit under a faded green canvas awning. A patch of grass and stretch of dirt separated them from the next trailer.

"Okay," Mullen said to Jess, "you've got yourself one of those Target chairs right behind you."

After Jess sat, Mullen pulled up two more webbed chairs for Rachel and himself. The aluminum frames scraped the concrete and squeaked with the settling of their weight. Mullen put his elbows on his knees and leaned toward them both, speaking softly. "I used to be a Miami homicide detective. I've known your family for going on thirty-five years. I was one of the detectives on the Neoma Kelch case. I questioned your neighbors, your dad's boss, everybody I could. Gibb came to me years ago. He was a pain. He wanted to know everything. He thought I'd have instinct if I didn't have information. I sure never had much information. I thought I had instinct. But now I wonder. I'm feeling kicked to know Gibb's gone." His voice settled into the faint noises of the afternoon.

Rachel heard the buzz of a fly, rumbling somewhere in a fold of the canvas above them, a sound of distant voices, the soft clatter of dishes. Perspiration started at her temples and trickled slowly down the sides of her face, through her hair.

"*Gibb* had instinct," Mullen said suddenly, smacking a fist into the palm of one hand. "He was crack at his work. A fine, fine man." He paused and looked down. "I wouldn't have figured he'd have killed himself," he said softly. The last sentence seemed not meant for them, and he shook his head, as if to take it back. He stood up, sending the light chair skittering backwards a little. "I'll get us some sodas," he said, his voice husky, "then I'll tell you everything I know." Without waiting for their reply he turned, walked up the steps leading to the trailer's back door, and disappeared into the shadows beyond the screen.

"Rachel," Jess half whispered, hissing out the last syllable of her name.

She reached for his hands. She squeezed her eyes closed for a moment as their fingertips touched. "I'm here."

Mullen came back, handed them drinks and sat down. "I found out a few things for your brother over the years. Not a whole lot. Gibb mostly liked to follow up on my leads himself." Mullen sat back in his chair. "Do either of you know much about the case? "

"Only from Gibb's journals," Rachel said.

"He told me some things about it once in a while," Jess added.

"The evidence was circumstantial. Weak enough that your father got out on bail before the trial. Both lawyers were ambitious guys. Even more than usual. They were both set on winning the case. Then the prosecution's key witness disappeared."

"Rhea Kirby," Rachel said.

"Okay, you know about her. I gave Gibb some pretty good leads on her not too long ago. He never got back to me. Now I know why." Mullen turned away from them and mopped his face with a handkerchief. "I found some physical evidence that didn't turn up during the investigation, an earring. We searched your house, car, your father's boat. Didn't turn up anything linking him to the dead girl. Would a little earring have tipped the scales to convict? You never know. Searching the boat again was Gibb's idea. He brought me a picture. Your father's boat wasn't big or fancy—Lapstrake design, Johnson seahorse—but your father or somebody about ten years ahead of the times had customized it—used steering cables to mount a center console. I put an ad in the *Herald* and tracked it down. I paid the owner fifty bucks to pry up the floorboards. He was already doing some hull work. The earring was aft, way back by the motor. Did Gibb tell you about it?"

Rachel was silent. She remembered Joe Ottawell's testimony.

"Gibb mentioned something about an earring once, but he didn't say he had it," Jess said.

Mullen leaned toward them, his voice quiet. "Once your brother told me that he didn't like cops. But somehow we ended up getting along real well. I didn't find that much, but me and Gibb liked to talk. He always had questions. Crime questions, questions about the other homicides I'd worked on. One day he asked me straight out, 'do you think my father's guilty?' 'I don't know,' I said. 'We have to face the fact we might never close this case. There's so many homicides,' I told him. 'If you can't solve one, you just go on to the next.' That didn't set with him. I was thinking like a cop and he was thinking like a kid who wanted to know whether his dad, a guy he loved, could've killed somebody."

*

Rachel walked slowly to the restaurant to meet Cage. If she hadn't been worried about Jess, she would have canceled. She needed to search more carefully through Gibb's things. Had Gibb found Rhea Kirby?

She turned on Washington Avenue. The temperature on the bank thermometer read ninety-one. Car windshields glittered with fiery light. Sweat rolled down her bare legs. The humidity was suffocating. Pushing open the restaurant door, she welcomed the cool air that suddenly flowed around her. Cage was sitting in a booth in the back. He lifted his hand. She slid into her seat, feeling shy. She had spent so much time alone these past weeks...

"Hey," Cage said. "How're you doin'? This place okay?"

"It's great."

"Florida cooking. Say," he dropped his voice. "I'm real sorry about Gibb. He was a good guy. He wanted to take me out diving. I told him, 'You'll have to teach me to swim first.' He couldn't believe I'd lived in Florida all my life and never learned to swim." He paused. "I'm real sorry for both you and Jess."

She bit her bottom lip and turned away. A waitress brought them water and menus.

Rachel opened her menu. "What's good?"

"Conch fritters, conch chowder. You like conch?"

"I've never had it."

He cackled. "You're *no* Florida girl. But you were born here, weren't you?"

She nodded and felt herself blushing.

"Don't mind me," he said. "Look, can you talk to Jess? He's ragin', 'they're not gonna parade me around to get the jury to hang somebody. Look at the poor blind man.' I have a different opinion of the matter. I say, crush the guy they think did it. Put him away." Hey darlin'," Cage called to a passing waitress, "we're about to croak from hunger here."

"I probably won't be able to change his mind if you can't."

"That could be a fact," Cage said, lighting a cigarette. "You know," he said, grinning at her, "you've been away a long time, but ever since I've known Jess, it's been 'my sister this, my sister that.' He respects the hell out of you. It's good you can be here for a while.

I've got a couple sisters, and I don't know what I'd do without them around. Jess and I usually go over to my mom's place every other Saturday or so for dinner. My mom and sisters look at Jess like he's a movie star, you know, like this." Dropping his jaw, he opened his eyes wide and dreamy. "I could get jealous," he said, screwing his face into a mock frown.

"I was thinking about what you told me the other night," she said awkwardly, half-ashamed she needed someone else to explain her own brother to her. "About Jess, you know."

Cage broke in, raised a hand. "Hey," he said. His grin fell away. "I don't want to worry you, but Jess is no happy-go-lucky kid anymore. Should he be? He's suffered, you know?—he'd be pissed if he knew I said that—a mother-fucker tries to off him for no good reason. Gibb…dying." He fell silent and shook his head. "Jess is one strong dude. Nothing's gonna stop Jess from doing what he has to do and saying what he has to say." Cage stared out across the restaurant, toward French doors that gave a view of a courtyard garden filled with white and peach-colored hibiscus and a brilliant purple bougainvillea. "From that time he went diving with Gibb and Megan—you probably didn't even know about that—to canoeing in the Glades, working with this justice group at the school, whatever. That's why he doesn't want to testify. He thinks it's the wrong thing to do." Cage shrugged and looked puzzled. "Sounds like I'm talking myself out of wanting him to…I don't know."

"I don't know either," she said. "I'll bring it up anyway."

"I desire revenge," Cage said, opening his hands, "plain and simple, for what some fucker did to Jess. Okay? I admit it. The guy should be punished, not walkin' around free." He paused, glanced away and drummed his fingers on the table. "I'm sorry," he said when he finally turned back to her. "What do you think? Will you talk to Jess?"

What *did* she think? Someone had tried to kill her brother and had blinded him instead. Cage was right. "I'll try to get him to testify," she said.

"Keep me posted. Thanks for coming over to the Sonesta the other night. You like our music?"

"I really do, especially when there aren't any menacing characters hanging around." She smiled. "What do you do besides playing music?" she asked.

"That's all," he said, "play it, write it, listen to it. Like Mingus said, 'stay inside the beat.' I'm always tryin' to figure out exactly what he meant by that, so I have to be working on it all the time."

"Like living in the present?" she offered hopefully.

"Nah," he said with a burst of laughter that made the people at nearby tables turn to them. "It means more. Much, much more." He leaned close, dropping his voice to a husky whisper, his eyes locked on hers. "See why it's hard? You can't use music to think your way out to some other, bigger planet. Music can take you traveling all right, but you gotta know what planet you're on first, before you go space traveling. You gotta stay inside the music."

Fourteen

Jess rewound the audition tape they'd made in the studio in the morning. He wanted to listen to it again and see if it was as good as they'd all thought. "We're on the verge, man. Almost there," Cage had said after hearing the tape. Tommy was close to getting the group a contract with a small record label.

Jess's work was good, but too calculated on a few numbers. But overall, everyone had clicked, ad-libbing breaks, and soloing against broken rhythms.

A contract with Blue Cat or Reef would mean touring, quitting graduate school, a blur of clubs and hotels. He'd never have an orderly place to think or write. Jess stepped to the door and picked up his cane. He needed to walk, to think. The air outside was steamy and smelled of cut grass. Walking down the sidewalk and along the hedge of Florida cherry, he rubbed the shiny leaves between his thumb and forefinger. The leaves were warm; they'd taken up the afternoon sun, and he felt that heat in their fragile veins. The click of his cane on the concrete was resonant against his palm as he walked. He thought of Gibb, how keenly he had come to know his brother's voice, finding in its pitch and timbre, his pauses between sentences, his every nuance of pronunciation, more than Jess had ever noticed in Gibb's face. Yet all his knowledge of Gibb hadn't been enough. Jess touched his watch. In another fifteen minutes Cage would be at his apartment to practice. His cane struck an obstacle on the sidewalk where yesterday there'd been nothing. It must have been a barrier, warning of construction or a ditch. It rang of metal. He found its legs, then its top.

"Hey." A woman's voice, beside him.

"Yes, hi," he said politely, but dreading a good Samaritan who'd drag him halfway down the block before he'd be able to convince her he could make it home on his own, just the way he'd come.

"Take two steps to your left, walk on the grass for about ten steps, and then you can get back on the sidewalk. They're replacing a section."

He laughed. "Sounds like I can trust you."

"You can," she said matter-of-factly.

He heard no hint of discomfort in her voice, no hesitation. Like the detective, Mullen, she didn't speak to him as if he were an imbecile or small child, or lose all common sense in his presence. She stood so close that he caught the light scent of freshly shampooed hair.

"Is this your neighborhood?" she asked.

"Yeah, I live in the next block. How about you?"

"The house with the dog. The one you just passed. He's not mean."

"It's probably the cane."

"The barriers," she said. "He's been barking at them all day. He's not mean but he is a little dumb."

"Thanks for the directions." He stepped onto the grass and passed her. Cage hated to be kept waiting.

"Come by again and I'll show you the garden," she called. "We have an orchid house."

"Yeah, okay," he said, remembering suddenly they'd once had a neighbor who had raised orchids. When Jess was small, the neighbor had painstakingly named them for him, each plant, told him the rare ones and the common, pointed out the subtleties of their blooming times, their scents. He'd take her up on her invitation, the girl with the orchid house.

Before Jess reached the hall he heard the bass. Cage had a key.

Cage's laughter sounded at the door. "I passed you and the neighborhood babe. Holding out on me, huh?"

Jess gave Cage a little shove and walked by him. "I never saw her before."

"Hey, you listen to the tape again?"

"Yeah, it's pretty outrageous. Gritty."

"Oh," Cage said, snapping his fingers. "Sweet record deal. I think Reef wants us, bro. So let's get down, do some tunes. How about 'I Could Care Less'?"

They started into the number, but Cage stopped before they finished the piece. "What the hell's wrong with you, man? I thought we had this tune down."

Jess ran his fingers over the surface of the keys. A sudden gust of afternoon wind shuddered through the palms. He thought of Gibb coaching him through a score, the sound of Gibb's voice reading.

Cage walked over and put his hand on Jess's shoulder. "You thinking 'bout that chick?"

Jess struggled for a moment to find her voice, remembered suddenly the sickly sweet scent of a purple orchid he'd pinned to the dress of a girl he'd taken to a junior high school dance, his first date.

If you touch the petals, she'd said, they'll turn brown. "Yeah," he said, lying, Gibb's laughter in his ear, Gibb teasing him gently that night, before the date. She'll want to dance close, Gibb had said. And to kiss you, right on the lips. "I am. I am now."

"Don't be angry," Rachel said, standing by the window.

"Why didn't you tell me right away that Cage was trying to get you involved in this court thing?" Jess sat at the piano with his back to her.

"You really are angry."

"Yeah, I'm getting there," he said, raising his voice a little. He played a few chords and turned around to face her. "Look," he said. "I want you both to stay out of this."

"Jess..."

He interrupted. "I mean it." His voice was low and even. "Let them fine me, put me in jail, I don't care. I'm calling the district attorney and telling him I'm not going to testify, the same thing I said in our first conversation."

"But what if it would help, having you there?"

"Sure. It'll help a corrupt system maintain itself. The pressure's still on after two years to get a few more convictions, to nail the vicious blacks who hurt white people during the riot. They'll parade me through the courtroom—can't you just imagine it?— 'The defendant shot a man in cold blood. He intended to kill him but instead left him blind." He stood up. "'Mr. Colgrove, what kind of adjustments have you had to make? How has your life changed?' They want to make me out to be a pathetic victim. I'm not going to be used like that," he said.

"But there should be consequences," Rachel cried. "Why even have laws if people can just go around murdering each other? Jess, somebody stalked you with a gun and shot you in the head. Whoever did that to you should be punished."

"That's not going to bring my sight back." He raised his hands. "Time out," he said softly. "Victim, crime, criminal, punishment, it all sounds so simple. Let me try...to say the same thing to you I said to Cage yesterday." He smiled wryly. "I think I convinced him to change his mind about my testifying. Maybe I can convince you too. If I could go to court and say to them what I'm about to say now..." He trailed off and sat in silence for a minute, then shook his head slowly.

Rachel took a quiet breath. A mockingbird sang insistently in the tree outside the window and a pink blossom from a hanging impatiens twirled silently to the floor.

"Do you know who Arthur McDuffie is?" Jess asked.

"I don't think so."

Jess walked the length of the room and stood near her with his hands in his pockets. "Do you remember what happened a couple of days before I was shot?"

"Sure. The Liberty City riots. Is McDuffie the one police beat to death?"

"Yeah."

"Gibb and I talked about it at the hospital," she said. "They tried to cover it up and make it look like a motorcycle accident, right?"

Jess nodded. "The cops were white. Same with the Tampa jury that acquitted them. All white."

He walked over and sat beside her on the couch. "What was the relationship between crime and punishment then? The day that judgment came in? And now? The guy they've charged with my 'attempted murder' is seventeen years old. That means he was fourteen when he shot me—if he shot me. He bragged to some friends about offing a white guy the day after the riots were pretty much over. An informant heard about it. No witnesses. Inconclusive ballistic tests. A lot of hate." Jess shrugged his shoulders. "I'm trying to find words for this. I live in a city that's hot as a tinder box...the murder capital of America." He ran his hand along the arm of the couch. "Last year the morgue was so overcrowded they had to store the bodies in refrigerated trucks. We've got all kinds of crime here, big time stuff. Throw in your politically ambitious prosecutors..."

"I guess they'll do anything to get a conviction," Rachel broke in softly. "Even if they're trying the wrong person."

"Yeah," he said. "You've got it. It's a house of cards. A whole phony system. Crime and punishment. As if it were that simple."

I want it to be that simple, she thought. *I want the guilty to be punished.* The world had gone topsy-turvy on her. As she watched the sunlight pour into the room, glitter in a blue vase on a shelf and turn the leaves of the philodendron translucent, she wondered if Jess could sense that imperious light, washing over everything.

"I feel so helpless," she said finally. Gibb had put his life in order, dying. Now she was the one gone out of control. The careful world she thought she'd built for herself was coming apart.

"I know," Jess said. "Listen. It does mean something to try to get to the truth. But the process is complicated," he said softly. "Gibb thought it was possible to set things right. He thought it would be simpler than it was. He just got in deeper and deeper. He stopped working. Did you know that? The murder and the murdered girl was all he thought about. At the end...I should have known. But he was very careful not to say too much." Jess sighed and ran his hand through his hair. "Victim, crime, criminal, punishment. They're not absolutes. They're words. They can mean different things, depending on who's saying them."

"Were they absolutes for Gibb?" she asked.

"Maybe not always," Jess said, "but at the end...I think they were."

The next day, back at Gibb's apartment, Rachel got up from the desk and walked to the window. The brittle rustle of palm fronds came from somewhere out of sight.

Thunder rumbled overhead, like the passing of a too-close jet. A hurricane had formed off the southeast coast of Cuba and was slowly moving northwest. The latest weather report predicted Hurricane Allen would strike the island during the night and gather power when it was over the Atlantic again. For the last few days, the weather had been hot and overcast. She walked downstairs to get the mail, hers and Rose's. Rose had been visiting her son in New York for the past week, and wouldn't be back until Wednesday. That was tomorrow, Rachel reminded herself.

Letting herself into Rose's apartment, she laid the day's mail on the table. She pulled Rose's door closed behind her and flipped through her own mail, a Florida Power and Light bill and a flyer advertising an Italian restaurant. Maybe she should go out, bring a book, get her mind off things for a while. But all she wanted was to stay focused on Gibb's journals.

Rachel walked to the bathroom and looked at her face in the mirror. With her fingertips she gently traced the curve of her nose, the outline of her lips, features she and Gibb had shared, the features her daughter bore. New strands of gray marked her black hair and she hadn't worn makeup in weeks. Closing her eyes, she saw Miranda's face as clearly as if she were in the room before her. Neoma Kelch had been someone's daughter. Gibb had cared enough about her to try to find out who'd killed her, to try to absolve their father of a heinous crime. Gibb had tried to set things right, as Jess had put it. But Gibb was dead and nothing had changed.

Rachel picked up the letter she'd received yesterday from Sarah Jauss, who was now the chief psychiatrist at Chautauqua Institute. She had told Rachel about changes in the staff, and how Rachel's temporary replacement was handling her caseload. She said that hail had shredded the blooming columbines she and Rachel had planted in the secluded backyard patio. "They'll come back," she wrote. "I'm hoping you will too. Thanks for your letter. Are you all right? Can I help? What you're going through is so difficult. It sounded in your letter as if you were taking some of the blame for Gibb's suicide. As hard as it is at a time like this, remember what you know from your work. Forgive Gibb. He had more reasons for wanting to die than you'll ever be able to understand. If he'd wanted to live, you could have saved him. Please call if you want to talk. Affectionately, Sarah."

Rachel stared out the window and listened to the wind, imagining the whitecaps stirred by now into a choppy froth all along the coast, a swath growing broader as the wind blew harder. Feeling the exhaustion gathered in her arms and legs, she decided to lie down for a while to rest before reading more; just a minute or two with her eyes closed would be enough.

When she woke, she knew she'd slept for hours. The light of a waning moon streamed in the window. She usually liked moonlight, but tonight its color was sickly, a weak yellow strained through shredded gray clouds. The air was so still, she wondered where the storm was, if it had roared its way north to the Keys by now.

She rubbed her eyes and switched on the desk lamp. The clock on the desk read ten minutes past midnight. She opened to the journal she'd been reading, anxious to find the next story, for Gibb never missed a detail. He kept her turning the pages with descriptions that she gave herself over to completely. They were so real— honed images, scenes from her own life burning under glass. As long as she could keep turning the pages to find one more story, until the whole story was told, as long as she could touch these pages and read Gibb's words, it would be as if Gibb himself were with her, as if they worked together and their work had a consequence. She was grateful for her friends, for Jack. They had tried so hard to console her and help her through this. But it was time for her to finish what'd she'd begun here. Time, she knew, to go home.

She ran her finger under the first line of the entry she was about to read, feeling the density of the words, the shapeliness of each letter.

The account that follows, Gibb wrote, *is based on the testimony of Bertha Kelch, the mother of Neoma Kelch. As a result of my own research, which included reading newspaper stories on the trial as well as talking to Sam Lachon, attorney for the defense, I was able to construct this courtroom scene.*

Bertha Kelch was a major witness in a weak case, in which the evidence was wholly circumstantial. The prosecuting attorney began questioning her on the third day of the trial, after Joe Ottawell had given his testimony.

"Can you tell us exactly what happened on the last day you saw your daughter?" Bill Davis asked.

"We all got up and had breakfast—me, Neoma, my husband and the baby. My husband went to work but Neoma and I had the day off. She asked could I take care of the baby. Said she was going to ride the bus to the beach. I never saw her again except, you know..." Mrs. Kelch started to cry.

"Was your daughter dating anyone?"

"I wouldn't call it dating. She was seeing some fella who parked down the block when he came for her, wouldn't come up to the house."

"How many times was your daughter picked up this way, Mrs. Kelch?"

"Once or twice a week for a couple months, maybe longer."

"Were you able to see the kind of car that picked her up?"

"Sure, same car every time, same man..."

"Objection."

"On what grounds, Mr. Lachon?"

"Your honor, there's no foundation this evidence is relevant."

"Overruled, proceed with your answer, Mrs. Kelch."

"Same car, same man. Fifty-two four-door Ford, powder blue."

The prosecutor took a step toward the jury, "I'd like to note evidence has already been introduced in the form of Florida Motor Vehicles Department records that the defendant owns a 1952 Ford, color light blue. A copy of that registration is Peoples' Exhibit M."

"Objection. There are hundreds of 1952 blue Fords in Miami. It's a very common car."

"Overruled."

Rain had begun to splatter the windows. Lightning struck, thunder following within a heartbeat. Sirens wailed in the distance, several together, a mad yowling that became fainter and fainter then rose up in a crescendo before dying out. Mr. Lachon visited them, she recalled, as if he had been her mother and father's old friend. The sad face of her fifth grade teacher, Mrs. Lowry, swam into her mind and shivered into clear focus. She had turned eleven that year, the year of the trial, but she remembered no judge, no jury. She wished her banished memories back for Gibb's sake.

*

Rachel didn't know what time she'd finally gone to bed, or what time it was now. Gray light filtered over her. Somewhere, someone was pounding in a nail, pounding, pounding. She sat up in bed. Rose's voice was at her door.

"I know you're in there, dear. I saw the car. Are you all right? I waited. It's afternoon. I've been back hours."

Rachel pulled on her jeans and a shirt. "I'm coming," she called.

When she opened the door, Rose thrust a wrapped package into her hands. "It's from New York. Don't open it now. Do it in privacy. Can I come in?"

"Sure. Thanks. How was your trip?" Rachel put the package on the table and brushed her hair back from her face.

Rose squeezed her forearm. "You aren't awake yet. Come sit at the table. I'll make us some coffee. I'm in the mood. Shirley, my daughter-in-law, waited on me too much. I think she didn't want me rummaging in her kitchen. Mitchell worked all the time, and my grandchildren, Stevie and Lynne were starting to drive me crazy— 'buy me this Nano, buy me that.' That puzzle is ruining your eyes. You got big dark circles."

"I look a mess, don't I?"

"No comment." Rose turned toward the counter.

"Rose, did Gibb ever talk to you about...our father?"

Rose pivoted around to face Rachel and put her hands on her hips. "No," she said, her voice oddly stern. "We talked. We talked about Jess and you. He showed me pictures of your baby. He told me about diving. He never talked about his father. But I knew," Rose said suddenly, her eyes growing wide. "All the years and I still remembered the name from the papers. Miami seemed like a small town back then. I saved clippings. I'm always cutting stories out of the news. Terrible," she said, shaking her head. "Such a pretty young girl. The fish had already started to get at her. If those divers hadn't found her when they did...But now people get murdered here every day, don't they? Thank God your father didn't do it." Rose took down two cups and poured. "What a thing to live with." She walked to the table with the cups in hand. Steam curled up toward the ceiling like smoke. "Your father's still with us, isn't he?"

Rachel nodded.

"Feel this suffocating air. I should have made us a cold drink. You can tell a hurricane's coming."

"It is?"

"Yep. On its way. Forty-eight hours. They veer sometimes, but something's about to happen. I feel it in my bones."

She should go to Jess's, Rachel thought. She hadn't spoken to him since the day before yesterday. And her parents. They seemed to fend for themselves perfectly well, most of the time, but if the hurricane hit there might be things they couldn't do alone. She sipped at the coffee. Since last night the wind had picked up even more. A sudden gust whipped the palms and sent a garbage can lid banging down the street.

"Whew, listen to that. I've got to go back to my place and put the TV on." Rose put her cup in the sink and sprayed it clean.

After Rose left, Rachel called Jess. "Hi, it's me."

"Have you been listening to the news?" he asked. "Allen could be a big one."

"No," she said, "not since early yesterday."

"Why don't you come over here? We'll take on Allen together."

"Okay. I'll be there in a little while. I just need to finish one thing."

"What about Rose? Will she be all right?"

"I'll ask her."

"Call me back if you think you need to stay. Otherwise I'll see you soon," Jess said.

Rachel took the stairs two at a time and knocked on Rose's door. "Are you okay, Rose?" Rachel asked when she was inside Rose's apartment. "Do you need anything?"

"I'm a hurricane veteran, don't worry." Rose began to count on her fingers. "Let's see, there was Diane in '55 when Mitchell and I first moved south. We put the awnings down and filled the bathtub with water and wished ourselves back in the snow again. Donna in '60, then Betsy in '65—or maybe '66—Inez, that was '66. My friend Sam Levinson the socialist will come and read Carl Sandburg poems by candlelight, and I'll be happy as a clam at high tide." She smiled.

"Go stay with that dear, handsome boy. I wish I was fifty years younger."

Back upstairs, Rachel gathered some things to take to Jess's. Before she left she sat down to finish the entry she had started to read last night. How odd it was: Gibb had actually met Bertha Kelch a few years ago. Even stranger, he'd been dating her granddaughter at the time.

I felt exposed, she read, *as if this woman I know more intimately than she'll ever realize has seen through me to my wildly beating heart. I have a feeling Bertha Kelch—the confused, frightened woman who testified that day so many years ago—has been consumed by the creature of contained rage I've just visited. Rage is a scent on her. It's supplanted her grief. Had she seen the Colgrove features in my face? I've lied to her granddaughter, about my name, if nothing else. I wondered if this woman with the fierce black eyes would suddenly expose me. As Bertha Kelch handed me a glass of limeade, a gray cat snaked around my ankles and an ancient clock struck the hour. Four o'clock. That's not the right time, she'd said with a strange, haughty pride. That clock appears to work but it don't keep time. You never get over heartbreak, sir, she said, no sir. My only daughter drowned while swimming, and my husband died of his grief soon after, leaving me to raise this girl alone. She walked to a glass-topped table. A piece of heavy lace with a complicated network of lines, knots and spirals hung over its edges. She picked up a large photograph, gazed at it, then turned it toward me. Look at her, she said, thrusting the photograph into my hand, insisting by her gestures that I take it. Look at her. In my imagination, I heard her say those words twenty times. She could have been somebody, she said so loudly that her granddaughter stepped between us and put her hand on the old woman's arm. Grandmother, please.*

Why had she lied to Ama about the murder?

I'll learn only so much from her and Ama. Maybe I've already found out all I can.

Rachel thought about the entry, the old woman's words. She felt Bertha Kelch's bitterness like the taste of something vile, something spoiled. Rachel closed the notebook, hair tingling at the back of her neck at the thought of the dead girl, like herself, someone's daughter, a mother. A photograph in a too-ornate frame. Gibb in the woman's suffocating living room.

Glancing around the room, she thought of Gibb's life here. The furniture was old—an overstuffed couch of a faded gray material. A kitchen table with four mismatched chairs. He owned almost nothing of value except his books, old books on the history of Miami and the Seminole Wars. Gibb had needed so little, it amazed her. Rose's present still lay unopened on the table. Rachel walked across the room and slipped the ribbon free, tore off the white paper and opened the box. Rose had bought her a silver charm of some sort on a chain. A note was folded underneath.

"To Rachel," Rose had written, "whose name means gentleness and innocence. May this mezuzah—'scroll of the law'—protect you from all evils and bring you good fortune. Love, Rose."

The windshield wipers clacked frantically across the glass but still Rachel could barely see. She'd already changed her route twice to avoid flooded intersections. Rainwater nearly covered the sidewalks, and passing cars caused wakes that flowed deep into the soaked yards of the houses and apartments along Jess's street. Gust-rippled sheets of rain shook the trees and jolted the car.

She touched the mezuzah. On her way out Rachel had stopped to thank Rose. Rose had smiled a little. "You need it, hon," she'd said.

Rachel parked on the street in front of Jess's apartment, opened her umbrella and ran through the rain to his door. She let herself in to the sound of a few notes played slowly along the keyboard.

"It's me," she called out. "I'm going into the bathroom to dry off."

When she walked into the spare room Jess had made into a studio, a young woman who'd been standing beside the window came over and put out her hand.

"I'm Martha," she said, smiling. Her wet, dark hair was combed straight back and held with a barrette. She had a small gap between her two front teeth that complemented the delicacy of her features. Martha met Rachel's stare without embarrassment. "I live around the block."

"I'm trying out a new piece on Martha, something I just wrote," Jess said.

"I like it," Martha said. "It's almost more blues than jazz."

Jess moved away from the keyboard toward Rachel. "Let me give you a hug."

"I'm still soaked."

He slid his arms around her waist.

"I'm going, Jess, before the rain gets any worse, if that's possible," Martha said.

"Wait," he said, taking a few quick strides to the piano. "Listen to the beginning again. Rachel, I'll play it all for you later." He played for a minute or two, and then turned to them. "That's the first nine bars—to set up the feeling of the whole piece. What do you think?"

Martha looked at Rachel and slowly nodded. "Sounds great to me. I want to hear it again. But I'm going to make a run for it now."

"Where's your raincoat?"

"I've got it."

"I'll walk you to the door."

"No, that's okay. I'm glad to know you," she said to Rachel, putting out her hand again.

"Yes, same here." Martha's handshake was strong. She met Rachel's eyes for a second or two, her face serious. Rachel wondered if Jess had told her about Gibb.

Then she turned and was gone, the door closing quietly behind her.

"Well," Rachel said after Martha had left.

"What?"

"Martha."

Jess smiled. "What are you thinking? Come on."

"I don't know. She's pretty. Serious. Sort of offbeat. What's with the overalls?"

"She works in her parents' greenhouse. Here, let me show you something."

"How did you meet her?"

"On a walk. I want you to hear more of this. I've laid down the basic melody line. I need to work at creating texture. That'll be where the tension comes from." He had his hands on the keys. "You heard the beginning, now here's how it goes from there." He played, stopped. "What do you think?"

"Good. Different. Kind of dark somehow."

"I know it's off-the-wall. It's supposed to be. Heavy bass ostinatos and dissonance in that series of descending chords you just heard."

"I'm lost."

He went to the desk and made some notes on the Braille type-writer. "I write out the basic things I want to remember, and then tape-record the instructions for standard musical notation. My student assistant works from the tapes."

"What's it called?"

"I haven't decided yet. Hang on here while I get this down." He typed several more lines and checked what he had written. "I've gotten some good ideas from Martha. Either she knows something about music or she's very intuitive." He paused. "Gibb would have liked it. To be honest, I wrote it for him. So I really don't want it to be dark. Eccentric, yes, but not dark."

"Don't pay attention to me. Lots of things strike me as dark these days." Even in the air-conditioned room, she felt the oppressive heaviness of the air, the barometer slowly falling.

"No, you're right." Jess walked to the piano and ran his hands along the surface of the keys.

Rachel studied his face. His expression was distant. Was he thinking about the piece he'd written, or the woman, Martha? "Can I read you some journal entries tonight?" she asked suddenly.

"Sure," he said. "I'd like to know what you're finding out Rachel?" His face was puzzled at her silence.

"I'm sorry. I was just thinking about the storm." But she had really been thinking about what it would be like, reading Gibb's words aloud to Jess.

"We're safe here. Are you all right?"

"I'm tired, that's all."

"Let's sit down on the couch." He took her arm and gently half-propelled her there.

"I want you to know what I've been reading," she said.

"Yeah," he said, "I want to know. I want to know if something's

222

wrong, too, if there's something you're not telling me. Have you found anything new?"

"No, not really. I have more to do. Things I have to look into." The wind changed direction as she watched, whipping the leaves of the trees into spirals of dark green.

"You sound like you're ready to jump out of your skin."

She sighed. "I miss Jack and Miranda. I miss...Gibb. Every day. I've spent years imagining I was strong and rational. Now I look back and I don't know why I believed that. Being here, reading the journals...it turns my stomach to read about the trial. I feel like I've started my whole life over, that I have to think about things I never let myself think about before." She took a quick breath.

Jess rested his hands on his knees. "I've had to do that too," he said quietly. "But it's been almost a year since the last time I wanted to put my fist through a wall." He laughed a little. "I still throw things."

She turned to him. "We wanted to keep you safe, Gibb and I, and...we couldn't," she started to cry and put her hand over her mouth, but the sound of her heart was what she really wanted to stop—that thin fluttering—light and sharp-beaked as a paper bird.

"Don't," Jess said, touching her arm, running his fingers gently to her wrist. "Please. Don't blame yourself for something you can't change." He turned away. "At first, I used to wake up, sit on the edge of the bed, and think 'I'm just one step from not existing.' I was really scared. Now I get up, go to a window and listen—to the traffic, birds, wind, dogs barking. Anything. Then I play something and I'm back into the world again." He paused.

Rain battered the trees. A branch crashed below the window.

"I want to make music. I want to have my own family and other people in my life I love, like Cage. People I can love like you and Gibb. I want to live a long time and make outrageous music, music that sets people's teeth on edge, or brings them a little wild joy."

"You sound like Gibb in the journals, when he talks about...finding the right stories."

"The right stories. The *just* telling of events," he broke in. "What he couldn't handle was *not* thinking: hitting the golf course, turning on the tube, keeping his mind numb. Nothing like that worked for Gibb. Maybe he thought too much, but he wanted to *connect* with things—the sea, the earth, people he loved."

"Yes," she said, remembering suddenly a summer day in late spring when Gibb's strange whistle had surprised her, echoing out-side the bedroom. She'd gone to the window and seen him there, smiling. "Yes," she said again, absently. "I need to know…everything about Gibb, what he was doing, what he wrote about us, our family."

Jess put his hand on hers again, his voice low. "You've got to be prepared, Rachel. You've put so much into this. What's it going to be like when you've finished reading Gibb's journals and there are things you still don't know?"

"I can't think about that yet." She studied Jess's face in profile, remembering the visit he and Gibb had made to Denver after Mi-randa was born, how Jess had touched her baby's face so delicately, stroked her ears and tiny nails. Gibb had surprised her in her watch-ing. She'd turned to find him suddenly standing in the doorway, an aura of yellow afternoon light around him. She had stepped away then, and joined him in the other room. "He's doing all right," Gibb had said. "In fact, he's doing fantastically." He gave a harsh laugh and fixed his eyes on hers, his expression cutting deep ugly lines, like scars, a look of grief she wanted to forget she'd seen.

"What does it look like outside?" Jess asked. "I can't believe the sound of the wind, even with the windows closed."

"Do you remember Hurricane Donna? You were about three, I think, so you probably don't."

"Did we play in the water afterwards? I remember water up to my waist once, after a storm."

"Yes! All three of us went to the corner, across from the Nelsons'. They had that boxer. You used to ride on his back."

"I remember."

She herself had forgotten until this moment that gentle, enor-mous dog she had petted as he sat docile in his front yard, despite her mother's warnings of rabies and germs.

"Open the window," Jess said

She cranked open the window and was caught in the face by a gusty spray of rain. "The grass is weirdly green," she said. "It's been so soaked the last few days. A few clouds are rolling through, but mostly the sky's just solid gray."

"We should call Mother. She always asks me why you never call."

Rachel was silent, looking out into the pounding rain. *Because you're dead*, she thought. *Because you're both dead to me and I hate you*. "The bushes are really getting whipped around, like tattered cloth. I'll bet the water's a foot deep out there." She didn't tell him the story of how the Keys had been ruined in the hurricane of '62, trees scattered like sticks from winds a hundred and ten miles an hour, and the damage to the coral reefs that took years to heal; she didn't ask if he remembered the way a house filled with candles shimmered with light after the power lines had blown down. Why pile memory upon memory? Weren't they all distorted by pain or yearning for a certain kind of past? Jess wanted the world as she saw it now, firmly rooted in the present.

"I'll call," Jess said.

While he went to the phone, she stayed near the window. She hadn't told him how ominously dark the clouds had become, the sky descending as she watched, how the flotsam of leaves and trash on the higher edges of the yard swam along with the moving water like a slithering living thing.

Until she heard her name, she didn't listen to him talk to their mother. "Rachel," he said. "Rachel's here."

She walked across the room and took the receiver. "Hello. How are you? Can we come over and help you get ready for the storm?"

"The last weather report said it's turning away from us. What do you mean 'we'? What could Jess do?" Her mother's voice had the ring of steel to it, resonant and cool. "Come over if you want but the Dowds next door have been helping us. We've been doing this for years, you know."

"I'll come see you this week," Rachel found herself saying. "I wanted to ask you...about some things."

"Don't drag up anything from the past," her mother said as if she'd read Rachel's thoughts and laid them bare, opened to pain, like exposed nerves.

"I have to go now. I'll call you back." Rachel hung up. Once her mother had convinced herself of something, Jess's helplessness in

225

this case, no logic would persuade her otherwise. She wondered if her father had been sitting listening. A part of her longed to have heard the drawl of his voice. *Ray-chul*, he had called to her from the doorway, just home from work. *Come sit on Daddy's lap and tell him what you did in school today.*

The six o'clock Hurricane Center report said that Allen was veering back into the Atlantic, losing force, but still cautioned people about flooding and downed power lines.

By the time they left Jess's apartment to get something to eat, the rain had already started to let up. Traffic lights and brake lights left garish, rain-distorted swaths of color on the dark pavement. They grabbed a take-out pizza and hurried back to the apartment.

"When are you going to SunTrust?" Jess asked as she took some plates from the cabinet.

"What?"

"That's where the safe deposit box is, right?"

"I think so. I'll go tomorrow. Do you want to come?"

"No, I need to study in the morning before class. Why don't you stay tomorrow night, too? Did you bring extra clothes?"

"I left them in the car. I'll go back out later and get them."

"Whenever you're ready to start reading is good for me," Jess said.

Rachel turned to the journal page she'd marked. "All the entries are typed. He must have gone back and typed everything. I remember him writing in these big notebooks, oh, for years. He'd sit up in the poinciana or the jacaranda sometimes. Did you ever read anything he wrote?"

"Sure, once in a while, mostly descriptions of dives, part of a science fiction story he started. I asked him once why he didn't try to get some of his writing published."

"What did he say?"

"'Maybe I should,' he said, 'maybe I should have done that from the beginning, just been a storyteller, told other people's stories.' Then he changed the subject. I remember, because it made me feel uncomfortable for asking, the way he started talking about something else so abruptly, the size of a grouper he'd just seen or something like that, totally unrelated. You know, now that you bring it up, I talked to him more than once about his writing. He had a strange answer for me the last time I mentioned it. He said something like "I can't even figure out the plot of my own life." Jess paused and shook his head. "Do you want a beer or some wine?"

"Sure, I'll have some wine."

Jess brought two glasses and a bottle to the table and sat down. "So how does this one start?"

"Okay, 'As I've explained earlier,' he writes, 'for reasons of expense and other bureaucratic complications, I didn't have access to all transcripts of the trial. The following testimony is cast partly in the form of a narrative, in order to capture our father's character, his tone of voice, the confident way he handled the questions he was asked.'

"That's the end of his explanation. The narrative starts on the next page.

"'I woke up early,'" she read. "'I couldn't sleep. I decided to go fishing. The sky was pale, a washed out, hot-looking color. The temperature was already in the mid-eighties. I'd heard where the mackerel were running, out about twenty miles from the 24th buoy. I wrote my wife a note and left the house around 6:30.

"'I remember thinking, 'It's not too windy, that's a good sign.' I got gas at Dinner Key Marina and talked to a guy who worked there. Said nobody'd caught much since Wednesday. That was a bad sign. I bought a six-pack of Schlitz and some bait. I'd made a couple sandwiches and hauled the boat all the way from home, so I figured what the heck and went out. I should've woke my boy, I guess, then none of this trouble would have happened, you know? I would've had someone with me...to know what I did. He likes to fish.

"'Well, it was pretty calm at first and I headed out to the place I thought would be best and put down the anchor. I let out my line and waited for a strike, nibble, anything, but it was no go. I was frying out there. Also, the water was getting rough, and the clouds were gathering up along the horizon. I thought I'd troll and move on.

"'I'll be darned if the engine wouldn't start. Heck, I'm no mechanic but I fiddled around like to snap the rope and pulled my shoulder out trying to get the damn thing going. I must've been at it on and off close to an hour when some joyriding kids came by. They stopped. There were three of them, and one kid hopped on and tried to help out. Nothing doing, he couldn't get it started either. I asked them for a tow, but their boat was even smaller than mine, so the only thing we could think of was for me to go with them. I dropped the anchor and hoped for the best, as far as the boat went. The wind and chop were coming on strong by now. I figured when we got to the marina I'd call my friend Joe to help me out, and my wife, to let her know I was okay.'

"'Mr. Colgrove,' Sam Lachon asked, standing close to the witness box, 'did you meet Neoma Kelch at the Dinner Key Marina on the morning in question?'

"'No sir, I did not.'

"'Did you know Neoma Kelch?'

"'No, I didn't.'

"'I'd like to show you a photograph, Peoples' Exhibit H, and ask you if you've ever met the woman in this photograph.'

"'No sir, I haven't.'

"'Have you ever seen the woman in this photograph?'

"'No sir.'

"'Not even at the marina that morning?'

"'No sir.'

"'Please recall that Mr. Bix McGrath testified under oath that he observed you in conversation with a young woman he identified as Neoma Kelch. Tell me again, did you speak with Neoma Kelch that morning at Dinner Key Marina?'

"'No sir, I never spoke with her, never saw her in my life. I didn't talk with Mr. McGrath either, so maybe he's mistaken about my identity.'

"'Objection. Speculation.' Bill Davis stood.

"'Sustained.' The judge leaned down toward the witness box. 'Just answer the questions, Mr. Colgrove.' He glanced at the court stenographer. 'Strike the last sentence.'

"'Mr. Ottawell told us about finding an earring in your boat. Do you have any idea what happened to that earring?'

"'No, I don't.'

"'Do you have any idea how that earring got into your boat?'

"'Sir, to tell you the truth, I remember Joe handing me something. I thought it was a piece of wire but if he says it was an earring, it could've been. I don't remember.'

"'Mr. Colgrove, have you ever been unfaithful to your wife?' Sam Lachon asked.

"'No, I have not.'"

Rachel closed the notebook. "That's it," she said, taking a sip of wine, thinking of an entry she'd read a week or so ago, her brother's description of a watching pelican and a body thrown over the side of a small boat. The tips of her fingers went cold, as if she'd just plunged them in icy water.

Jess rested his chin in his hands. "I don't know." He shook his head. "I'm not sure of what I can get from just that entry, one person's testimony. Does it convince you of Dad's innocence or give you any more clues? Do the details fit with anything else the journals tell you?"

"He sounded credible, I guess."

"It's such a small piece of the whole."

Rachel walked the length of the table and back, still holding Gibb's notebook. She laid it down. "Gibb tried to tell me, and I'm finally getting the idea. He tried to show us something complex—a whole system, I don't know the right word—a web of connections?"

"It's never just been a question of who killed Neoma Kelch, it's about us," Jess said.

"Maybe Gibb thought that if our father was guilty, then we were guilty too. If he could have proven our father's innocence...well, Gibb thought everything would have been different. For all of us."

"Dad's never wavered. That's what I get from everything I've heard, anyway."

Rachel poured herself more wine. "No, he never has."

By morning, like dirty wadding that had covered something rare and beautiful, the clouds drifted apart to show bright stretches of the porcelain-blue sky. Ragged strings of debris marked the waterline on sidewalks and yards. Black water still rushed along the streets. Rachel drove to SunTrust Bank.

She walked to the information desk where a young, dark-haired woman with very long red nails sat. "Yes, can I help you?" she said in accented English.

"I need to get into a safe deposit box."

Pointing a finger like a small sword, the woman said, "You go over there and the gray-haired lady will help you."

A woman with steel wool curls examined Rachel's key and scanned the papers she'd brought—Gibb's death certificate and a paper from the Dade County court showing that she was the executor of his estate. The woman showed Rachel to a large steel-walled vault. "You can use the private room to decide what you want from the box," she said.

Rachel took the drawer into the room and closed the door. The room had the dank smell of a little-used space. The laminated top of the oval table was slick as ice. In the box were several sealed envelopes, nothing more. Rachel scooped them out and put them in her purse, replaced the safe deposit box and walked quickly out of the bank.

A delicate pain needled its way across her forehead as she hugged her purse to her side and hurried to the car. She drove back to Jess's, a ferocious heat rolling through the open windows.

Fifteen

Jess's apartment was cool and dark, the curtains drawn. Closing the door, she locked the deadbolt and walked into the kitchen. Jess had left a note: "Glad you're staying another day. Back at one or so." The kitchen clock read 11:45. It was two hours earlier in Denver. She walked to the telephone and dialed her home number. It was busy. Although she called Jack almost every day, she hadn't talked to Alice, the housekeeper Jack had hired, for almost a week. She'd phone Jack later, she decided, after she had looked through the contents of the safe deposit box.

She went back to the kitchen and laid her hands on the cool tile. The silent second hand moved round the kitchen clock. She turned and circled Jess's living room as he might have, running her fingers along things she passed, the chair backs, the smooth fabric of the couch, the desk's cool, slightly rough wood. When she came to the phone, she lifted the receiver and dialed her home number again, listening to the ring that was so familiar.

"Kellogg residence," a woman's voice announced. "This is Alice."

"Alice, it's Rachel, how are you?"

"Hi, Mrs. Kellogg. I'm fine."

"How's everything been going there? Jack said he thought Miranda was running a temperature the other day."

"Oh, she had a little fever, and I gave her baby aspirin. She's okay now. No sniffles or anything. She's eating good too."

"Is she awake?"

"Sure, she's right here with me." Alice's voice grew fainter as she turned from the phone. "It's Mommy," she said. "Look here, it's your mommy."

Miranda cried out in sounds that were almost words, if only Rachel had known the code. "Hi, sweetie," she said. "I miss you."

Alice was back on the phone. "She's been laughing so cute."

"The weather's been bad, hasn't it?"

"Yeah, sort of. It's been raining a lot."

"I'm going to give Jack a call later this afternoon. He's in a staff meeting Friday mornings."

"Okay, I'll tell him I talked to you if he calls here. I've never been to Florida. Is it pretty?"

Rachel hesitated. "Yes it is, it's very pretty here. I'll bring you some photos."

"That'd be great."

"Talk to you soon." Rachel hung up, slipped the apartment key into her pocket and walked around the building into the large yard. She didn't feel ready to open the envelopes. A painfully bright sun had come out, its dazzle reflected in the still-wet grass and shrubs. A bougainvillea climbed a trellis at the building's corner, each purple bract cupping a cluster of small white flowers. Grapefruit trees, a banana tree and a high hedge of jasmine grew together in thick profusion. Kneeling down, she saw a patch of clover, three-leafed, all of them. She pinched a seedpod until it burst, spilling the unripe seeds like tiny pearls.

Once, as a child, she'd found a stunted four-leaf clover, the fourth leaf a freak of division like an extra toe on a kitten. What was the difference between chance and luck? She hadn't known then and she still didn't know. She'd taken the clover and pressed it in her confirmation Bible until its leaves grew brown and thin as parchment, and the luck seeped away through the pages.

Standing up, she peered into the yard of a pink house. A woman in a large straw hat and flowered garden gloves scooped twigs and leaves into a bag. As Rachel watched, the woman turned to her and lifted her hand in a fluttery wave. Rachel waved back.

"Quite a storm," the woman called, walking over to the fence.

"At least the hurricane missed us," Rachel said as the woman approached.

The woman raised a gloved hand to shade her eyes even though the big hat already shadowed her face. "I'd have been in a pickle if that thing had hit us."

"You have a beautiful yard."

"Thank you. I prefer to think of it as a garden. I've been patient with each and every plant and tree. Do you see that trumpet flower over there?" She pointed to a shrub with glossy green foliage and apricot-colored, tubular blooms. "I almost lost that twice and now it's growing just fine. It's a survivor. Maybe that's why the black people call it 'Nassau lucky plant.'"

For luck, Rachel ran her fingertips along a leaf's vein.

"Over by the house I've got a night-blooming cereus. The flowers only open during a full moon. Come over and see it, will you? The next full moon's only a few days away."

"Thanks. I'd like that. Nice talking to you."

"You too, dear."

Rachel turned and walked back through the yard. When she glanced behind her, the woman was on her knees, pulling weeds. She turned the key in the lock and walked over to her purse. She tore open one of the envelopes, a small one, no larger than a business card, and a gold hoop earring fell into her hand.

Looking at the tiny ornament, for a few seconds she ceased to breathe. As she tilted her hand, the gold glinted. She stared at her palm, the intricate network of lines, like a cutout from a map, with all the place names removed. She put the earring back inside the envelope and glanced at the clock, five minutes to one. Jess would be home soon. She flipped through the other envelopes, her hands shaking a little. She'd wait until Jess got home to open them. She walked to Jess's study and lay down on the foldout couch that served as her bed, her knees curled towards her chest, cool air blowing over her from a nearby vent. Last night she'd woken up every hour or so, her dreams slipping just below consciousness as she'd opened her eyes. At dawn, she had heard the jays screeching messages to one another across the yard.

She closed her eyes and dreamed. She stood on the edge of a huge outdoor aquarium; she was the caretaker, cleaning up with a hose and long-handled brush. Meleleuca trees towered up over her. Even in the daylight their white, papery trunks were ghostly, their gray-green leaves flat-colored and somber. A man pushed through the shrubbery and walked towards the edge of the aquarium, as if he were in a open field. It was Jess. *Jess*, she called, *Jess*, but he didn't answer. Just at the aquarium's edge he stopped, ran his hand along it and sat. The dull leaves of the meleleuca trees suddenly sprang into a multitude of black and orange blossoms that fluttered in the wind, then alighted, hundreds upon hundreds of Monarch butterflies, broken from their chrysalises. *Jess*, she shouted, and the man turned. But it was Gibb, his hand lifted in a wave. He slipped over the edge and into the green water. "Goodbye Rachel," he called as he disappeared below the dark surface.

Rachel opened her eyes as Jess walked into the room. "Jess."

"You're awake. Martha dropped me off and was going to stay for a while, but when she saw you were sleeping we didn't want to bother you."

"Martha." Rachel sat on the edge of the couch. "Martha was here? I thought you were at school this morning."

"I was. I took the bus, and Martha picked me up. She had a wholesale delivery of carnations out that way. It's a forty-five minute bus ride and I wanted to be back when I said I'd be."

"I'd have picked you up."

"I know, but you have enough going on. Did you go to the bank?" he asked.

"Yes, but I waited for you. Almost. I opened an envelope that was in the box."

"What was in it?"

"Put out your hand," she said.

Jess held his palm open and she dropped the earring into it. He picked it up with the other hand and felt around its circumference with his thumb and forefinger. "An earring."

"Yes." For a year or so after the trial, their father's boat had sat unused along the side of the house. Sometimes they'd sneak into the boat to play, even though that was strictly forbidden. Gibb had gotten the belt once, when their father had seen him scrambling out of it. He'd spanked Gibb so hard, she remembered, that Gibb could not sit down the next day. Over the damn boat. One day, the boat had been gone after she'd come home from school. Indentations in the soil and fringes of yellow grass where the trailer had stood were all that was left to remind her they'd ever had a boat.

"So what does this mean?" Jess closed his hand around the earring.

"It doesn't mean anything. That's why no one cared in the jury. It's a common piece of jewelry," she said firmly, using the line as if

234

she'd been the first to think of it. "There are a hundred ways it could have gotten in the boat. Even after Dad sold it."

"Maybe you're right. Is there more?"

She opened the first of the other envelopes. "This is a list of names and addresses," she said. "Two people in Miami, one in Homestead, one in Brooksville. That's up north of Tampa, right?"

Jess nodded.

"Samuel Lachon, Attorney-at-Law; Bertha Kelch and Amanda (Ama) Kelch. The person in Brooksville is called 'Ruth Cobb.' There's a little note by her name— 'prosecution witness, never testified.'" She looked up.

"She's got to be that witness who disappeared before the trial started," Jess said.

"Could be. Maybe Cobb's her married name."

"So is that everything?"

"No." She took a deep breath. "Three more envelopes. Let me see what's in them. Here's a stock certificate, for that ConEdison stock Gibb bought years ago." In another envelope she found an eight-by-ten print of a young woman, wearing small hoop earrings like the one Jess still held in his hand. On the back Gibb had printed: *Neoma Kelch, age 23—made from a snapshot given to Mother by Sam Lachon.* "A photo." She described it.

Jess pushed his chair away from the table and sighed. "What are we going to do with all this?"

She pulled some papers out of the last envelope. "These look like the old style of photocopying. You know, dark and shiny. What was that called?"

"Photostats?"

"Right."

She saw the City of Miami seal and the city logo. "'Dade County Coroner,'" she read. "It's the autopsy report, on the girl." Remembering the summary of the pathologist's testimony, she slumped in her chair and leaned her head back. "I feel like I'm tangled in a net."

"Gibb had a reason for wanting that autopsy report, I guess," Jess said gently. "It's one thing to say about someone who's been murdered, 'oh, she drowned,' or 'he was hit on the head.'" He spoke

slowly, almost to himself. "It's something else to know the details...
the visceral reality of death. Read it if you want."

"No," she said, hearing Rose's voice. *It's a good thing they found her
when they did.* "Not now. Later this afternoon, maybe." She took a
deep breath. "I'm ashamed of who I am."

"Why?" Jess asked.

"How could you know? You weren't even born," she said. "Why
should you even have to go through all this?" She put her hand on
Jess's arm.

"You're my sister." He shrugged. "We're in this together. What do
you want to do? You don't have to do anything, you know."

"Yes...I do. At least I'll try to find the people on the list and talk
to them." She picked up the hoop and held it between her thumb
and forefinger. The gold was worn. They had played "shipwreck"
and "storm" on the boat, she and Gibb, crouched in the bottom
whispering, so they wouldn't be caught. Closing her eyes, she remembered how the saltwater smell grew stronger when the sun crept
across the house and shone down full into the boat.

"What are you thinking about?"

"I don't know," she said. "I want to be out in the woods, near
the tree line looking up at a cloudless sky. I want my mind washed
clear as a sky like that." She tried to remember that deep blue, the
way the sky in Colorado looked when you were in a niche of rock
at ten thousand feet and a hard wind was blowing. But she couldn't
imagine the color, as much as she tried. Only the blank, white-hot
tropical sky came to her, as if she had been no other place but here,
ever.

Slipping the key into the lock, Rachel pushed the door open. It
was hotter inside than out. The air conditioner needed a new coil.
She opened all the windows wide and turned on the small rotat-
ing fan she'd pulled from a closet last night, positioning it so that
the blades would stir a semi-circle of air near the desk where she
worked. As she'd walked from the car to the apartment, the sidewalk burning under her feet, she thought of the things Gibb had
done just before he died. *Before he died.* The words reminded her
of Gibb's story, of the time out of time—*Before the Reef*—when the

236

world had been pristine. *Call me a utopian…* he'd written. *A crazy utopian.*

At Gibb's desk, Rachel opened a journal to a place she had marked earlier, an entry on Sam Lachon. She ran her fingers down the page. The words weren't a map anymore, or a road to a certain destination. The words were the labyrinth itself.

Just a few days from my birthday, I kept an appointment I'd made a few weeks earlier with Samuel Lachon. His office is in a building on Brickell Avenue, a highway originally built of coral rock through the jungle thicket from Coconut Grove to the Miami River, a street of mansions and the shade-filled privacy of the rich.

The brass plate at the door read Lachon, Lachon and Beaumont. He was gracious, but he should have been. I wasn't taking up his time for free. I sat with him in an elegant room that seemed intended only to receive visitors. The walnut desk was clear, the lights indirect, dimmed to a soft golden. I told him I was interested in details of his defense strategy, if he could recall them. He smiled genially and straightened his tie with a fluid, practiced gesture. He was a vigorous man in his late fifties, carefully groomed.

"Of course, I remember," he began. "The Colgrove case was a very important one for me and another young lawyer by the name of William Davis. Bill and I had an adversarial relationship. It wasn't the relationship of enemies, but—as I said—adversarial. That's healthier," he chuckled. "I encourage my clients to tell the truth. Of course they don't always, but I can represent the people who do tell the truth better than those who don't." He paused and rested his fingertips for a moment upon the polished desk.

"How can you be sure you've made a correct distinction…between truth-telling and lying?" I asked.

"I'm not always sure, but I've built my reputation upon being right most of the time."

"What about my father? Did he tell you the truth?"

"Your father steadfastly maintained his innocence. Isn't he steadfast to this day?"

"Yes."

"Then why are you here, Gibb?"

"The murderer's never been found."

"Oh," he said, his eyes cast upward for a moment. "Unsolved crimes are the order of the day…the millennium. We'll always have unsolved crimes. Chance plays a part, careful perpetrators, sociopaths."

"How did you persuade the jury of my father's innocence?"

"The objective of my final argument was to make them uncertain. I wanted them to be troubled. To be afraid of making a mistake that might send an innocent man to his death. I reminded them explicitly of the instruction which says you mustn't vote to convict a man if there is any reasonable doubt of his guilt." He paused and fixed his eyes on mine until I had a sense of what it might be like to have him stand before me, a listening jurist, about to make a critical decision. His eyes were a pale blue, the color of my mother's eyes, except they had rings of gray around the irises that intensified their paleness. He went on, breaking his gaze and looking around the room. "It was a shaky case to begin with and the state knew that. I was more eloquent than my opponent who argued there were no reasons to doubt Noel Colgrove's guilt, he was surely the murderer of Neoma Kelch."

Hearing my father's name mentioned this way really chilled me. I can't fully describe the feeling—the way his name was linked to Neoma's.

"Thank you," I said. "I understand your strategy now." Before I'd entirely finished my sentence Lachon began to rise slowly, gracefully hastening the conclusion of our talk.

"'Steadfast.' Isn't that a wonderful word, Gibb?" he said as he saw me to the door of his office.

I didn't respond.

"Goodbye. Good luck to you." He closed the door gently.

After she'd finished reading, Rachel pulled out her notes. "Lachon strategy," she wrote, "reasonable doubt. The entry seems guarded. So does Lachon. Holding back."

She walked to the window, watching as a mass of clouds knotted into the shape of dark fists and blocked the sun. The soggy air and darkening sky made it certain: the weather would be violent again that afternoon. She took out the phone book and looked up the number for Lachon's firm. She dialed, asked for him and gave her maiden name. "I'm not sure if you remember me," she said awkwardly, when he was on the line. "Excuse me," the voice interrupted politely, "I think you have me confused with my father. I'm sorry. He passed away last year." She mumbled her apologies and crossed out the name. Another ghost. Another corridor in the maze that ended in a wall.

As Amanda Kelch lit another cigarette and took a deep drag, Rachel watched the ash glow and lengthen. Amanda's face had been pretty, Rachel thought, until something had starved it to unhealthy thinness. Worry or pain. The skin clung around her fine bones, and static from an unseen source stirred her wispy blonde hair to a fullness it wouldn't otherwise have had. Perhaps Rachel had looked at the photograph of Neoma Kelch one time too many, she found her sense of knowing Amanda so striking.

They sat together in the break room of the clothing store where Amanda worked and where she had agreed to meet Rachel.

"Explain to me again exactly who you are and why you're here," Amanda said, her voice practiced in its wariness.

Rachel's trip down Dixie Highway in rush-hour traffic had given her senses a keen, nervous edge. "You knew my brother," she said and Amanda stared at her, unblinking. Rachel paused. Should she tell her the truth, now, of Gibb's identity, and risk Amanda's anger? That might jeopardize the whole purpose of her visit. "Gil Conover," Rachel pronounced the words slowly.

Amanda tilted her head and smiled slightly. "Oh yes," she said. "Gil, the man of a thousand faces." She frowned and chewed on a nail. "I don't know why I called him that. Because he pops up in my dreams so much, I guess."

"Are you still studying art? Gil described your work in one of his letters."

"Art?" said Amanda incredulously, shaking her head. "Boy, was I a fool, thinking I could live in San Francisco and be an artist. Look at me," she gestured. "In Homestead working in this lousy store. I only lived in San Francisco for two years." She shook another cigarette loose from the pack and stared at it for a minute, then looked up at Rachel. "How's Gil doing? I always meant to look him up, but I figured I'd find out he was married and make a fool of myself."

"So you haven't been in touch with him since...you moved?"

"No, unfortunately. Is he okay?"

Rachel was never prepared for the surge of pain she felt, telling people about Gibb. "He died...several months ago."

For just a moment, Amanda Kelch's expression was blank. Then the color drained from her face, and she bit her bottom lip. "No." She shook her head slowly back and forth. "Oh, my God," she said, her face crumpling into tears. She pulled a wadded Kleenex from her pocket and dabbed at her eyes. "How?" She stared at Rachel. Her face was blotchy and wet, mascara smudged under her eyes.

Rachel moistened her lips. She wondered how Gibb himself would have talked about his death. "He took his life," she said finally.

Amanda laughed bitterly and turned away. "Gil, you jerk. Why." Taking a compact and lipstick out of her pocket, she wiped around her eyes, put on powder and applied the lipstick until it was glossy and dark. She faced Rachel. "He was one of the kindest guys I've ever known. I don't understand," she said sadly, standing and peering down at Rachel. "I feel bad, awful. I've got to go back to the register. Meet me in an hour, please. Please," she said. "Out front."

An hour later, they sat on a bench in a meager park, the overhanging branches of a nondescript tree shading them. Across the sidewalk, a playground stood silent in an inverted dome of dirt. "Why are you here? You didn't come here just to tell me Gil was dead, did you?"

"He...was writing a book when he died. He'd almost finished it. I thought he might have called you...with questions."

"Hang on," Amanda said, putting her hand on Rachel's arm. "Are you conning me? I hope it's not for money 'cause I don't have any."

"Gil was looking into the circumstances of your mother's death."

"Hey, if his big news was that my mother didn't die by accident, I've known that for a long time. I used to be sweet and innocent and protected, but I was never stupid." She pulled the crumpled cigarette pack from her purse, took out a cigarette and cupped her hand around its tip to light it. "I went to the Miami Public Library and searched through '58 copies of the *Miami Herald* on microfiche, just before I left. I read all the stories, about my mother and your father, so you can drop the 'Gil Conover' b.s." She inhaled and blew the smoke up over her head. "Your brother wasn't as good a liar as my grandmother. He used to ask me a lot of questions, spaced out real casually, you know? One day and another a couple days later, then a week later. I checked his wallet once when he was sleeping, right before I decided to see if I could find out anymore about my mother myself. Colgrove and Kelch, two plus two equals four. I was real angry at first, but I sort of understood that Gil—Gibb—had ended up really caring about me. He didn't mean to, but it happened. I just hated it that he was one more person who lied to me," she said softly.

"What did your grandmother tell you?"

Amanda laughed her low, mocking laugh. "Everything but the truth, probably. My mother was so popular, so beautiful 'she could have been a beauty queen'—my father was the son of millionaires who didn't want anything to do with us because we were poor. They disowned him when he married my mother. Please," she said scornfully. "My grandmother never got over my mother's murder. It's all she ever thought about."

"What *did* happen to your father?"

"Well, as my grandmother's story goes, my father died too—before I was born—in a car accident. The newspaper stories said Neoma Kelch had a baby 'out of wedlock.' That would be me, wouldn't it?"

"Unless all your grandmother was lying about was that your mother and father were married."

"My grandmother lied about everything. That's why I had to get out. One day I was a slut to her and the next day a virgin princess. I looked like my mother, I was wonderful, I was 'fast' and was going to get in trouble like my mother." Amanda put her hand to her forehead. "It made me crazy," she said. "But I thought of that—maybe finding out about my father—and I started looking for some of my mother's high school friends."

"Did you ever find any?"

"Nobody who knew anything. One of the newspaper articles talked about some mysterious girl who disappeared before the trial started. Supposedly she was ready to testify. The article said she knew who my mother was going out with when she was killed. I wish I could've found her."

"Do you have any idea what happened to her? Did your grandmother ever mention any of your mother's friends?"

Amanda shook her head. "No. All I know is what I read in the paper. One day this girl was living in an apartment in Allapattah and the next day she was gone. Nothing in her apartment had been touched. She didn't even take her clothes. Eerie. She got scared, I guess. They printed her name in the paper, but I don't remember it—'Somebody Somebody, star witness.'"

"Rhea Kirby," Rachel said.

"Yeah, sounds familiar. Rhea, that's a name you don't hear everyday." Amanda held up her arms and stretched. "I wish we could go out to dinner and talk more," she said, "except I have a date with a creep who's taking me to an expensive restaurant in Coconut Grove. He'll probably try to get his hand up my skirt by the time the wine comes." She narrowed her eyes and stared at Rachel. "Say, why did you come anyhow? To hear me tell you you're doing the right thing, taking all this on? Well, you are. You have no idea what it's like—not having a father, not even knowing who your father is."

But I do, Rachel thought. In a way, I do.

"How lucky we were to share a little part of Gibb, huh?" Amanda said softly. "You're a beautiful woman, you know that? You remind me of your brother so much it hurts. Your expressions. The way you talk." Amanda looked away. "We really did love each other. For a short time, I had a perfect life. Say," she said, meeting Rachel's eyes, "the murder mystery, that's only the half of it. You didn't come here to be convinced to go on, because the mystery that's got you by the throat isn't who killed my mother, it's Gibb. Now that he's gone, you want to find *him*. You want to know him totally, but you'll never be able to."

"He was my brother," Rachel said numbly.

"It's terrible how death steals people away from us, isn't it?

Gibb had a secret life, everyone does. But Gibb had more secrets than most of us. Find Rhea Kirby. Find out what she knew, *her secrets*, why she was such a *star witness*." Amanda said the last words mockingly and put out her hand. Rachel took it in her own. For a moment they stood that way, their eyes locked, as if they had made a silent pact.

Jess walked with Martha among the orchids and bromeliads, the greenhouse hot as a steam bath, full of the smells of growing things and rich, dark earth. Martha took him to the plants, one by one, beginning with the bromeliads. She guided his fingers to the tips of their broad leaves, and he traced them down to the deep hollows where they caught water and nutrients. He touched the spiky flowers that rose in their centers.

"Air plants, that's what people call bromeliads, as if they'd just drifted in from another planet." She laughed a little. "They are pretty weird-looking. And they seem to live on nothing," she said. "But they need food and water just like every other plant. They're clever survivors. After millions of years on earth, bromeliads are pretty well adapted to survive. I'm getting boring, aren't I?"

Jess shook his head. "No," he said. "Really. Tell me more. Everything."

"Okay, let's go on to the orchids. Some of them are the opposite of bromeliads. They need pampering. Here," she said as they walked on the slatted floor between the rows of plants, "smell this moth orchid, *Phalaenopsis*."

Touching the stem, he ran his fingers carefully upwards and brought the spray of blossoms gently toward his face until he caught the orchid's delicate fragrance. "Not like any flower I've ever smelled." The stem was cool and the petals brushed his lips as he brought them to his nose. They had the texture of smooth, damp skin.

"This one over here, *Rhynchostylis coelestis*, is rare, mainly because of the color. It's pale blue. Blue's a very unusual color in orchids." Taking his hand, she let the bloom rest lightly in his palm, her own hand beneath his.

"Not something you'd want to break off and pin to your shirt, right?"

She laughed. "No. But we have lots of those, too—*Cymbidiums* and *Vandas*, various species that we grow for florists."

He turned his hand over, the edges of the orchid brushing his knuckles, and caught her fingers. "Thanks."

"You're welcome."

Jess held her fingers a few moments before opening his hand, then she slid her hand gently from his, but didn't step away. For minutes, they stood close enough for him to hear her breathing. His heart beat in his throat. Floating near his face was the scent of her hair that he could pick out from all the intertwined smells of the greenhouse. He pushed from his mind everything but the dirt-rich perfumed air, forcing himself to forget for a while the cool earring that had lain in his hand, and the grief he always heard in Rachel's voice. "Do you like working here?" he asked finally.

She answered from just beside him, the bare skin of their arms brushing as she turned, slightly, to face him. "I do," she said softly, "more out of habit than real attachment to the plants. But my parents are passionate about every single thing they grow, total perfectionists. I did get a master's in botany. I specialized in plant pharmacology. On the other side of the yard I have a little green-house of my own...where I grow a bunch of medicinal plants." She paused and took a light breath. "Would you like to see them?"

"I'd like to." *Yes,* he thought, *I'd like to spend hours more with you. And days, whole languorous days.* "But I can't," he added quickly. "I've got some things to do before I play tonight and I need to give my sister a call. Say, why don't you come out and hear us? We're playing at Montana's. I'm going to ask Rachel to come too if she's back from Homestead in time."

"I'd like that."

"First set's at nine. Do you know where it is?"

"I can find it."

"I'll see you tonight then. Thanks again for the tour."

"Thanks for coming."

She walked him to the gate and he headed back around the block to his apartment. He knew the neighborhood perfectly now, where the shrubs drooped too far over a fence, where the sidewalk was uneven or broken. The smell of salt drifted on the breeze. The sun was fiery on his bare arms and neck. Mockingbirds screeched somewhere near him, the sound falling as they swooped down upon the neighborhood cats. Remembering the feeling of holding Martha's hand, how without awkwardness they had stood close in the greenhouse, he imagined the curve of her neck and the hollow of her throat. He'd barely stopped himself from touching her, pulling her near. He brushed past the hedge of Florida cherry that reminded him to turn down the walk to his building and he did, smiling idiotically all the way to his door.

"We're Ikat and we don't mess around, so we'd like to start off with a song I wrote called 'Show Me,'" Tommy told the audience. "Then we're gonna do a standard, 'Limehouse Blues.' If you've followed our sound and you think we're slidin' from time to time into the blues, thanks for listening, 'cause you're right. We like to surprise you."

Tommy started off with a riff on the sax that led into Jess's solo. The piece was tight, all the way through. Over the last few months, Jess's playing had become at once resilient and clean in a way he couldn't quite put words to. He connected with the music more viscerally than he ever had, listening all the way through a tune with his fingertips, the muscles in his hands and arms, the bones and tendons of his wrists, his whole body listening and responding.

Cage pulled the number to a close on the bass. Applause was light. There wasn't much of a crowd yet. He heard the sounds of laughter and footsteps, the scrape of chairs, and smelled the sweet-stale, intermingled smell of beer and booze, the mark of every club or bar that the most sophisticated ventilation in the world could not disperse. He wondered if either Rachel or Martha had come yet.

Between numbers, he imagined the couples, faces close, conversations over drinks. All the words wouldn't be so romantic. Jess heard the voices over-loud sometimes, public voices, falling just short of anger, the too-loud laughter of someone drunk, someone whose date wasn't working out, whose marriage was crumbling, that bitter laughter the backdrop of its decay. His thoughts drifted to his father and mother, the Sunday visits that had become habit with him and Gibb, every other week, remembering Gibb's restless urgency, in everything he did. Unexpectedly, grief coursed through him like a strong, raw drink. He missed Gibb with an aching clarity he could not push from his mind.

"This is our update of a tune Lenny Tristano made famous way back in '49, called 'Crosscurrents.'" Tommy's short, deep laugh caught Jess's attention, and brought his focus back to the music.

"We got some snowbirds here? Some landlubbers? Listen up now, ya'll, and hear the surf, feel that old tropical sun, hear the sweet tinkling of ice in a cool drink. Think of some loving times under the palms. Crosscurrents."

Laughter, clapping. Jess played, keeping Tristano's cool edge. The applause was strong at the break and Jess knew the last set would be ultra-tight. "Bad," as Cage would say later, when they'd all be wired, talking about the gig.

As they got ready to leave the stage, an image of Gibb came to him again, Gibb's voice, suddenly, reminding him that he was Jess, the youngest, the free-of-pain, the unscathed. How ironic Gibb's ideas about him had been, Jess thought, without bitterness. But the familiar voice was comforting, and Jess was grateful.

Sixteen

The day after Rachel had met with Amanda Kelch—even after hearing Jess's group play better than she'd ever heard them—she couldn't calm herself. She'd been driving to Jess's when the thermostat had gone out on the Valiant, right on Collins Avenue. She had to have it towed to the nearest garage. The mechanic had promised that it would be ready today, before the shop closed. Was he sure? she asked. She needed the car back right away. She'd been ready to go on a trip upstate.

She walked to the beach, stripped to her swimsuit, and plunged into the sea. She swam away from shore with an urgent breaststroke, fighting the tension that had gathered painfully in her arms and legs, her whole body. Never having learned a very good frog kick, she put just enough energy into the kick to keep herself from sinking, but the outward thrust of her legs wasn't enough to propel her far. For all the years she'd been around water, she had never developed much grace or power as a swimmer, just endurance. She had plenty of that. The water was bath-warm and calm. Sun rippled across the surface and she shaded her eyes to look at a scattering of swimmers near the shore and the sunbathing tourists, laid face up to the sun as if pegged in place, their bodies slick with oil, already brown and burnished. Still they wanted more. More rest, more fun in the sun, the idle passing of the hours. That was their idea of paradise. Breathless, she swam the crawl back to the shore, walked up the sand to where she had left her things and toweled herself dry. Slapping the sand from her thongs, she pulled on her shorts and carefully made her way between the nearly naked bodies. Which of these closed eyes were turned thoughtfully inward and which fixed, simply, on the blank, indeterminate brightness?

At the beach shower, Rachel washed her feet and legs in the cold water. She put her thongs back on. A line of cars moved slowly down Ocean Drive, glittering in the sun. She shaded her eyes and waited for a break in the traffic, half-running, finally, between two cars. Someone honked and shouted something, but she didn't turn. Was Ruth Cobb Mitchell the same person as Rhea Kirby? Turning the key in the apartment lock, she pushed the door open.

She walked slowly from room to room in the small apartment, trying to slow her jumbled stream of thoughts. She stopped and looked at Gibb's books: *History of Southwest Florida, Miami Pioneers, Early Settlers of the Ten Thousand Islands, Hunted Like a Wolf: The Story of the Seminole War*. In a labeled box were several old Chamber of Commerce booklets, one from the fifties called "Highlights of Greater Miami." She took the last two books and the pamphlet off the shelf. Flipping through the pamphlet, she read, "Arrival of the railroad brought many of Miami's pioneers; among Flagler's 'Men of Action' were the Sewell Brothers, from Georgia, who worked Negroes as their specialty. With hundreds of them, they accomplished wonders in clearing land so that buildings could be erected." In the margin Gibb had written, "Wonders, indeed. The history of Miami, written in blood, a history of exploitation, greed and violence." The front of the pamphlet showed a garishly colored aerial photograph of the skyline and bay, a skyline long since changed, now full of office buildings and towering condominiums.

Gibb had also made notes in the book on the Ten Thousand Islands. "Where is his description of the Calusa? They built Chokoloskee from shells. That's what the word means, 'shell mound,' but they were driven away, a 2,000 year-old race of giants (Literally. Both men and women averaged 7 feet tall.). They tried to hide in the mangrove swamps, but they were chased down and massacred by the United States Army," he'd written on the first page. She opened the book on the Seminole Wars and scanned the author's words on the book jacket. "Four thousand Seminole were exiled by a mighty nation that boasted of its justice, its honor, and its love of liberty. The Florida Indians and blacks defended their home and their freedom with a desperate tenacity that has few parallels in the annals of colonizers and conquerors." Closing the book, she sat for a minute. She had lived so long, understanding so little.

She hugged the book to her chest and looked up through the window at the part of the sky she could see, that streaming brightness, all promise. She wanted to feel Gibb's passion, like a coursing of blood through her own body. She breathed his name into the still air, imagined him moving through the silvery bubbles of his beloved ocean, the sea that had always borne him up. Gibb, who would be with her always. Soon, she would leave this place and take his journals with her. But she wouldn't go until she knew what she'd come here to know, how this part of the story ended.

The Valiant was indeed ready on time, and early the next morning Rachel climbed in and headed northwest. Outside Tampa, she passed the exit signs for a half a dozen small towns she'd never known existed—Lutz, Pasco, Darby, Spring Lake, until finally she saw the Brooksville exit sign--eleven miles to go. She felt the hum of the wheels against the miles of highway in her whole body. Early in the trip, a pink sunrise had given the colors of the grass and flowers a vibrancy that contrasted with the silent streets and darkened houses. Night had cooled the air a little, and she tried to savor the fresh, marshy smells of the Everglades and watch for heron and snowy egrets. Only the Everglades was as she remembered it, so large and congested had the cities along her route grown. Rachel thought about nothing but the passing landscape, those first hours of driving, the expanses of sawgrass flowing by, the cypresses off in the distance and the Tamiami Canal glittering through the row of Australian pines that fringed it.

But now fear plucked at her with insistent fingers. If Ruth Cobb Mitchell was who Rachel thought she was, Rachel was calling on a woman who years ago had disappeared and hadn't wanted to be found, not by anyone. Had Gibb been here before her? Past a small, wood-frame post office she turned onto a dirt road marked with a leaning, faded sign: *Citronelle Way*. She wound past orange groves on the right, dozens of rows of trees snaking off like green caterpillars into the distance. Fields of okra and beans were planted on the left. Up the road, she saw a white frame house, surrounded by a picket fence. That would be the one. She parked on the grassy shoulder and opened the gate, expecting at any moment a dog to come snarling at her, but only bees sounded in her ear. The stillness of late afternoon had cast the deep lot into silence and shade. A big live oak spread over part of the front yard and a tangle of flamevine grew up a trellis along the side, near a birdbath. Taking long steps, a very tall woman came towards her from behind the house, wiping her hands on a white dishtowel.

"What d'you want?" she called.

Rachel's voice froze in her throat and she stood by the gate unmoving as the woman approached her.

"I said, what d'you want?"

"I...I'm looking for Ruth," Rachel stammered.

The woman peered at her.

"I...must have the wrong house." Rachel turned and put her hand on the gate. "I'm sorry."

"Wait," the woman said. "Ruth's my sister. What d'you want with her? She's an invalid. She doesn't know you, does she?"

"No. I'd like to ask her a few questions. I'll try not to take long."

"Questions," the woman sniffed. "You're the second stranger who's come by wanting to ask questions."

"Irma? Who's there?" A voice came from behind the house. "I need to get back in. I'm roasting out here."

"Come on," Irma said and turned, muttering something.

At the back of the house was a small, old-fashioned verandah where a woman sat in a padded wicker chair. As Rachel approached, she could see that the woman, Ruth, was younger than her sister Irma. She fanned herself vigorously with a straw fan.

"Who's this? Get me inside."

Ruth was an attractive woman in her fifties, her dark hair showing only a few streaks of gray. She wore dangling silver earrings of a modern style that sparkled in the sunlight, and a colorful loose dress of Indian cotton. Irma unfolded a wheelchair that leaned on the verandah railing and locked the brakes. Ruth lifted herself from the wicker chair to the seat of the wheelchair. Her withered feet dangled awkwardly, until she raised her legs from the knees and pulled them onto the wheelchair's footrests. Patting her thighs, she looked up at Rachel and sighed. "Can't move from the hips down. I drag myself around with crutches when I feel like it, but it's too much work in this ungodly heat."

Irma helped Ruth guide the chair over the doorsill and Rachel followed into a large kitchen, dining room, and then into a small living room furnished with dark heavy chairs and a walnut sideboard.

Ruth gestured for Rachel to sit and she leaned forward with her elbows on the armrests of her chair. "You seem to be here to see me and you've met Irma. Who are you, barging in on us like this?"

Irma and Ruth's eyes met for a moment and Irma walked back into the kitchen.

Rachel heard the rattle of dishes. The living room was cool and dark. All the shades were pulled down tight. She took a breath. "I'm Rachel Colgrove, Rachel Colgrove Kellogg, now. You might have met my brother." She paused.

"I might have met him or not. Go on."

"I'm here to ask you...Were you once subpoenaed to testify in a murder trial?"

"Not too many people we don't know come out to visit. I'm surprised you caught me. I'm usually working in my husband's office. Some of the groves you passed are ours." The woman spoke quickly, matter-of-factly, watching Rachel all the while. "My sister lives down the road. We've lived here since 1957. Why are you bothering us?" She pulled herself up in the wheelchair, straightened her legs again and wheeled herself to within a few feet of where Rachel sat, waiting for her answer.

"You're Rhea Kirby, aren't you?" Rachel said finally.

"Maybe I once was, if it's any of your business. But I'm not her now, not anymore. I always liked the name Ruth and now I'm Ruth. What do you want?"

Rachel broke the woman's gaze and looked down at her hands, groping for words. More than one clock ticked in the room, in a jagged counterpoint. "I need to know what you know," she said finally.

Ruth Mitchell rolled past Rachel, down the length of the rug and back, like someone pacing. Ending up where she began, she fixed Rachel with a fierce stare. "But do you *want* to know?" she asked, her Florida drawl exaggerating each word. "Because once I start, I may tell you things you wished you didn't know." She glanced away, toward the kitchen, and then looked back at Rachel. "*Was* it your brother who came here? Jeb, wasn't that his name?"

"Gibb."

"Gibb. I don't know how he ever found me. He said it took a detective. Maybe I was ready to be found, I don't know. But his coming here started me thinking about things I've been trying to forget forever. Even she don't know it all," she whispered, jerking a thumb toward the kitchen. Nor Del, my husband, or my own children." She squeezed her thighs until Rachel saw the cords in her hands stand out white. "I can't feel that." She poked a calf. "Or that." She lifted her skirt to the knees to show her wasted legs, thin as poles. "I'm punished," she said dropping her voice again. "I used to be a looker. I used to bop and twist better'n any girl in Miami. Before spinal tumors and three operations. Thank Jesus it wasn't cancer. Fifteen years ago. And now I can't even walk in the groves no more. I'm punished for what I didn't do." She looked away, calmer, and patted her hair. "At least I'm alive," she said, "but I know things I don't want to know," she hissed. "Why do you want to know them? I knew I shouldn't have shown your brother the pictures."

"What pictures?"

She reached out suddenly, grabbed Rachel's hand and squeezed her fingers so hard that it hurt. "Oh I'm sad for you," she said. "I feel for you and your brother. Is it just the two of you?"

"It's just the two of us now. My younger brother Jess and me," Rachel said softly. "Gibb killed himself. A month ago."

"No!" she gasped, shaking her head, "Oh no, my God," she started to sob, her hand on her chest. "Oh my God," she said. "Sweet Jesus, will it ever end? I told your brother that the last night I ever saw Neoma she told me she was going on a boat ride with Noel. After that, she turned up...murdered."

"What about the pictures?"

Ruth Cobb reached into a pouch behind her chair and pulled out an envelope. She handed it to Rachel.

Inside were three negatives and three black and white photographs. On the negatives, shadows on the faces showed as puddles of white. The figures stood in shade, pale as vapor. Rachel put them back into the envelope and the nicked edges caught on her fingertips like corrugated blades. She stared at the first photograph. A man and two women on the beach. Young, slender bodies. The man looked down. Although the man's features were distorted by the angle and the shadows, Rachel recognized him as her father, standing with Neoma Kelch and Rhea Kirby.

Rachel saw the room swim. The edges of things turned silvery, then dark. She felt as though someone's hands were around her throat, squeezing her breath away. As she was putting her head down, she heard Ruth's voice from a distance.

"You all right? Irma? Irma? Damn, she's headed home already."

Ruth peered into her face. "You're white as flour. I'll get us some ice tea." She wheeled herself into the kitchen.

Rachel started to get up, her arms and legs feeling too heavy to move. She stood finally, her knees trembling, and walked slowly to where Ruth was, in front of the refrigerator. Ruth handed her a pitcher of tea.

"Here," she said, "reach up into the freezer for some ice. There's some clean glasses on the counter. Let's go back outside. We'll have shade and a breeze now. Take the pitcher and glasses out."

Rachel walked outside and put the pitcher and ice-filled glasses on the table. As she bent down, the mezuzah Rose had given her clinked against the edge of the pitcher. Rachel caught the charm and held it a moment in her hand.

"Stand here just to steady me," Ruth said, lifting herself into the wicker chair, "and put that wheelchair somewhere out of my sight. You don't have to fold it."

Rachel pushed the empty chair back to where it had been when she'd first come. She sat down beside Ruth and stared out into an expanse of green yard. A rabbit hopped across the grass.

Ruth leaned forward, waving her hand. "Scat, scat. Damn things eat all my lettuce." She turned and looked at Rachel. "Isn't that what you come for?" she said quietly. "That's what you said, 'I need to know what you know.'"

"Yes," said Rachel, "I'm all right." She struggled to get the words out, her heart pounding. She looked at the other two photos. Rhea Kirby and a man she didn't recognize, standing arm-in-arm. Her father with his arm draped over Neoma Kelch's shoulder.

"Jimmy Youngblood took the one of the three of us. I took the one of Noel and Neoma, and Noel took the one of me and Jimmy."

"Why didn't you testify?"

Ruth took a sip of her tea and picked up the straw fan. "The story starts way before that. Neoma and me, you know, we were best girl friends at Edison High School. Passed notes, went to football games, talked on the phone for hours." She glanced at Rachel and Rachel nodded. "We graduated and I got a bookkeeping job at Jensen's Hardware. I took up bookkeeping in high school, so's I got an office job. That made everyone so proud. I didn't have to go to work in a factory or waitress. It was the cat's whiskers to have an office job—I do the books for our groves now, I told you that." She paused. "In two years I got my own apartment and took up with Neoma again. I hadn't seen so much of her since high school. She worked in the Mercy Hospital laundry." She lifted her hair up off her neck and fanned her throat. "We started to go out dancing, oh, two, three times a week. Believe it or not there was some nice clubs along the Miami River back then. I hear it's not so nice nowadays. One night, just a hot old night like tonight's gonna be, Neoma leaned across the table—I remember as if it happened yesterday. 'Maybellene' was playing on the jukebox—and whispered in a tiny little voice: 'Can't you tell?' she asked me, 'can't you tell how much weight I've put on? I'm pregnant.' I clapped my hand over my mouth, I remember. I was so surprised. I never knew her to go home with anyone or sleep around. 'Are you getting married?' I asked and she just shook her head real slow and sad like, back and forth. I pleaded with her on our friendship to tell me who the father was, but she never would say. After her little baby girl Amanda was born she was back to dancin' and havin' fun harder than ever. Left the baby with her folks. One night she comes to a place we liked to dance at especially, with a man. That was the first time I met Noel Colgrove." The sky had paled. Soon it would be twilight. Crickets had started up in the distance. Ruth glared at Rachel, her eyes bright. "You listening to all of this?"

"Yes," Rachel said, "I am."

"I'm almost finished. Del's about to be home and he'll be upset to see us sittin' out here in the dark. Well, anyway, they seemed to be a couple, though she'd come alone more often than not to the dancin' joints we liked. Three months or more it went on. Noel was quite a bit older, of course, but handsome. We both thought he was so handsome, and we'd never danced with anyone better. But they both had hellcat tempers. I seen them on the dance floor more than once where he'd have her arm pinched back, and her mad as all get out. We went places together once or twice in the day, to the beach and such, that's where we took the pictures. I had a boyfriend by then, Jimmy Youngblood, the one who took the pictures." She looked out into the night. "Jimmy was the kind of fella the girls flocked to. Something wild and dangerous about him. Noel wasn't like that. Neoma told me from the first, 'don't ever breathe a word, don't tell nobody about Noel and me.'" Ruth shrugged her shoulders. "I never told this much till now. Only that I knew him and that I'd seen them together, that's what I told that lawyer for the state. Under oath I would've told what I'm telling you." She fell silent and smoothed out her skirt. "I told your brother that the last night I ever saw Neoma she said that the next morning she was going on a boat ride with Noel." She paused and took a breath. "After that, she turned up...murdered. So did Jimmy. A day before they found Neoma, he bled to death in the parking lot of a bar in the Keys. Stabbed. I guess his gambling finally caught up with him. I was terrified. Jimmy flashed money and got himself killed. The police asked me all kinds of questions. My girlfriend murdered. More questions. Land. I'll be plain, I was afraid. Two murders. Maybe I'd be next. I didn't know what Jimmy'd been mixed up with. Cops, judges, lawyers. I decided not to testify." Her voice had fallen to a whisper.

"Before the trial, in the middle of the night, Irma picked me up from my apartment in Allapattah and her and me drove up here to stay with a friend of our momma's. They questioned my folks black and blue but everyone was real careful. My momma and daddy, they even advertised a reward to find me. I pushed Noel and Neoma and Jimmy out of my mind, the way people do with bad things. I met my Del, had three babies—all near grown now. I didn't think about what happened again until I got my disease." She stopped and rubbed her arms. "I woke up one morning with my feet numb. I had three operations before they were done with me—I told you that. I thought about Neoma all the time then, that I did wrong, not speaking up, and was suffering a punishment for it. Please, God, I used to pray, I'm punished enough." Her voice broke a little and she started to cry. "I'll testify now, if anybody wants that. Course they can't try a man twice, anyhow. And they won't put me in jail, after all these years, a crippled woman." She sighed and picked up the fan again. "Look at that moon coming up. Did Neoma really go on the boat that morning? Did Noel kill her? Only he knows. Why don't you ask him," she said, looking at Rachel, her face turned ivory in the dwindling light and her eyes glittering with the last of her tears. "I was young," she murmured, looking out into the darkness. "They made me out to be so important, what I'd tell, but I never saw Noel hurt anybody, much less kill Neoma. He loved her. Looked at her like he did anyhow. She was a pretty girl, for sure, but she had a mean streak wide as a road. Oh, they fought," Ruth said sharply, her eyes widening a little. "She spoke her mind, Neoma did. At the end, you know, she had real nice clothes, expensive clothes. Maybe she was taking money from Noel to keep quiet. Maybe, maybe, maybe. I tried to tell your brother...'Maybe it was by accident,' I said. But that set-hard face of his told me he'd made up his mind otherwise, just seeing those pictures." She glanced at her hands. "Those lousy pictures. Why did I show them to him anyway?" Shaking her head, she started to cry again. "I didn't know better, that's why." She twisted her wedding band around on her finger, looked up at Rachel. "What if what I'd said put your daddy in the electric chair?" Her voice grew softer and she gazed away. "He was so handsome. He had you kids. Wouldn't havin' your daddy die like that have been worse than what you been through? Your daddy put to death? The shame of it and more, your momma having to raise three little ones alone?" Her voice dropped away into silence. "I couldn't take the risk," she said finally, her voice half a whisper. "I had too much doubt for what rested on me, the punishment Noel could get. If I'd known for sure," she said, shaking her head slowly. "For sure."

"She gave me the pictures," Rachel told Jack, crying.
"I'm coming out, Rae. Don't do anything till I get there."
"Can you get time off? What about tickets?" She felt raw with anger and fear.

256

"It doesn't matter. I want to be with you. Right away. When will Jess be home? I don't want you to be alone. I'll call you back as soon as I have our reservations."

"If I'm not here, don't worry. I've got to get some air."

"Okay. Be careful."

"I'm all right."

Rachel walked through the backyard of her brother's apartment building in the moonlight and leaned across the fence, catching the scent of the night-blooming cereus. Jess was playing at Montana's and wouldn't be back for several hours. After calling Jack she had paced through the apartment, thinking of her meeting with Ruth Cobb Mitchell, who'd never told anyone, before Gibb, what she knew. How had she kept such a secret? When Rachel reached the fence, she put her hands on a post and looked at the dusty sky. A face floated up, ghostly, and Rachel jumped back with a little cry. She saw the woman she'd met after the near-hurricane. She took a deep breath, feeling her thumping heart.

"I didn't mean to scare you," the woman said. "You've come back to see the flower, haven't you? You said you might. You won't be sorry. What's your name, dear? My name is Helen."

"Rachel."

"Rachel. What a lovely name. You're very lucky to have such a name. Unless you want to climb the fence, there's no way to get in the yard from here. Why don't I meet you out front. Walk around the block. You'll see me on the porch."

Rachel walked slowly through the yard and down the sidewalk, her arms and legs heavy and aching. She passed the houses, some with lighted windows and some dark, and thought of the lies cheerful pictures on the wall told, the things the houses had heard that no one outside the houses knew, stories beyond her imagining, even now. Light spilled over a man sitting near a window, watching television. A bright orange seeped from some of the windows, as if the houses were on fire. All the houses had secrets. The walls and floor joists and roof beams held bitter stories of secret selves and desires. She looked back toward Jess's apartment, at the small light burning in one window, and remembered Jess and Martha a few nights ago, holding hands during one of the breaks. So in some of the houses, then, there might have been happiness—the pleasure of simple companionship, the joy people gave and took in loving one another.

Helen sat on her front stoop. She stood when she saw Rachel. "I like to be in the garden late at night," she said, "especially with a full moon." She gestured across the yard. "Everything seems to glow with a light of its own." She trotted off, under a tree, and signaled Rachel to follow her. On the side of the house was the plant, more tree than bush, about seven or eight feet high and climbing up the house along a lattice. The blossoms were large and a luminous white under the moon, and their fragrance filled the surrounding air.

"Here's my 'queen of the night.' Do you like her?"

"She's beautiful," Rachel said.

"I'm glad you think so. Gardens are a joy. There's not enough time in the day to garden, so I do it at night, too. I'd invite you in for tea but it's late and you're a young woman with things to do." Helen looked at her earnestly. The moon bathed Helen's face with clear light. "Oh," she said softly. "You look so sad, dear. Some terrible things have happened in your life, haven't they?"

Rachel nodded, holding back tears.

Helen stepped close to her and wrapped her thin arms around Rachel's shoulders. "I'm sorry," she said quietly. "I'm so sorry. If people have hurt you, try to be forgiving. It's too hard to go on otherwise." She paused. "Don't forget, though. Don't confuse living in the past with remembering it…hearing its messages." Helen touched a white blossom with her fingertip. "You can look at the past the same way you look at a garden…to get ready for the next season, the next planting." She stepped back and looked up at Rachel's face. "I'm very old," she said. "I've learned the hard way."

They walked together back to the front yard.

"Thank you for spending time with an old woman. Good luck. I hope you'll come back."

"I'm glad I got a chance to meet you," Rachel said before turning away. Exhausted, she followed the sidewalk, the way she'd come, back to Jess's apartment, the moonlight flowing across her path like water.

When Jess came home it was almost three. Rachel told him that Jack was coming and then began to cry while she described her visit with Ruth Mitchell. "How could our father have killed that girl?" she said, her voice breaking.

"What about all the 'maybes'?"

"He sacrificed Gibb so he didn't have to face killing Neoma Kelch. Gibb took the whole burden of her murder on himself."

"Don't," Jess said softly. "Listen. Gibb died of despair. Of anguish. He struggled so hard. He...struggled against the violence in his own life. He understood the larger struggle, too. But he couldn't...make the connection between the two that might have saved him."

She felt herself shaking.

"Rest," Jess said.

"Gibb gave us so much," she said angrily. "He was committed to everyone but himself. He took all the pain inside, from our father's trial, our childhood, what happened to you."

They sat in silence. The first birds had begun to sing in the darkness. "I'm going to confront our father with all of this," she said finally.

"You need to rest before you decide what to do next. Wait till Jack gets here. We can all talk more then."

Jess went to bed and she sat in a chair until the sun came up, streaking the clouds with faint color. She'd brought Gibb's last journal entry with her and she read it before she went to sleep.

Unlike the million-year-old Pacific reefs, the reef where I've spent so many of the good hours of my life is less than 20,000 years old—a young reef, then.

Before the first reef formed, glaciers swept the earth and all human potential was locked in bits of protoplasm in the frozen seas. But in the young reef, time is finally within our grasp, in the workings of its complex ecology. The fragile symbiosis of reef life is a microcosm of the human. It doesn't belong to us, but it is our mirror. I've watched other divers, spears in hand, push back delicate sea fans and strands of elkhorn as if they were hardy as scrub palmettos, just for the biggest and best fish.

What will happen in the next decade, when there's more garbage and poison in the water? When there are more people?

Before the reef. Before the reef was the promise—that a civilization would be built by what we now imagine to be the most intelligent species in the universe. After the reef, nothing will be left but bare rock auguring death—the death of that "noble" species and of the planet that was our home. After analyzing every element of cause and effect, and pursuing the players in a single murder, I've found my efforts to be purely symbolic. It's not the destination that matters, but the journey. Journey wisely, Rachel.

This was the last thing of Gibb's she'd ever read. She felt the emptiness Jess had warned her about, the room gone still, become a vacuum. Shadows flickered all around her. *How could you have killed yourself? Why?* Her head was full of voices. *Just ask him*—Ruth's voice, echoing—and Gibb's voice and Jess's.

Rachel stood on her parents' front porch. Jack and Jess were on the sidewalk behind her. She hadn't called. Her hand trembled as she lifted it to ring the bell. Her mother opened the door, wearing a faded duster. They stood face-to-face for several seconds until her mother stepped back into the shadowy house. "Come in," she said quietly. "I'll get your father." With her brother and husband, Rachel entered the house and looked around the living room, hardly changed since her childhood. The house was hot and stuffy. All the windows were closed and the air smelled faintly of insecticide. She watched her mother disappear into the bedroom, bent and tiny. *You abandoned us by aligning your self with him. A murderer*

Her father came out of the bedroom wearing a white T-shirt frayed at the neck, and grass-stained tan Bermuda shorts. His legs and arms were thin, and his once-tan skin had faded to an unhealthy-looking yellow.

"Sis." He nodded in Rachel's direction, walked over to Jess and clung to him for a moment without speaking. Jess towered above his father, a man she'd remembered as so tall. Then he turned to Jack and offered a trembling hand. "Mother," he called. "Bring us some iced tea." He gestured toward the dining room. "Why don't we all sit?"

Rachel's mother put on an apron and brought a pitcher of tea to the table. Rachel walked into the kitchen. She heard her mother's voice behind her. "Do you remember where the tumblers are?"

Rachel turned and nodded. Her mother's eyes, bright behind her glasses, searched Rachel's. "Where's your baby?" she asked softly.

"Gibb's landlady's taking care of her."

Her mother put some vanilla wafers on a plate and Rachel found five glasses. At the table, Jess spoke quietly to their father. Jack glanced in her direction. Rachel sat down and reached in her purse. She looked at her mother. "You knew all along, didn't you?" Her mother's face turned stony and she glanced away toward the Florida room where sunlight had washed the color from walls, the sofa, everything she could see.

Rachel put the photographs she'd gotten from Rhea Kirby on the table.

"She gave them to you," her father said flatly.

"You killed someone."

Noel began to cry, the tears rolling down his wrinkled face. His eyes met Rachel's. The man of tears and biblical rages. "Yes. I killed Gibb. I killed my son." He sobbed. "I killed the girl, too, by letting her go with Jimmy," he said, his voice rising to a cry, his ancient-looking eyes fixed upon them.

"What are you talking about?" Rachel asked, glancing at Jack and Jess, their puzzled faces.

"Your brother came over…that night. He told me he'd found Rhea, seen the pictures. 'Tell me the truth,' he said. I said, 'You were always right, Son. I'm not a murderer. I never killed anybody.'" The tears ran down his neck and seeped into the thin cotton of his T-shirt. "I told him what happened…He didn't believe me."

"What *did* happen?" Rachel asked. The Seth Thomas clock struck two pure notes. Nothing else stirred in the house. The close air choked her.

"I lied about Neoma. I cheated on your mother and lied about it again and again. Before I met Neoma, she'd gotten in trouble, and her mother never let her forget it. She always told Neoma what a slut she was." He laughed harshly. "Neoma thought I was the one who'd make her respectable. She started off with hints. 'You and me could go away together. Start fresh.' She talked more and more about our being together. One night she said, 'I want to get married, Noel.' I said, 'I got kids, a wife. Why spoil things? Let's just keep having fun.' We were in the car, out in the woods at the lighthouse on Key Biscayne." He glanced at Elizabeth, whose eyes were fixed on her folded hands, resting on the table. "Your mother thought I was in night school and I was. Afterwards I'd spend an extra hour…with her. That night she raised her voice to me in the dark car. 'I'll tell everybody you're Amanda's father. Your kids, your wife, my mother. Everybody. I'll take you to court.' It wasn't true. I'd met Neoma after Amanda was born. I lied to my father, told him I was starting a business. I told him I needed five thousand dollars. I arranged our boat trip that morning. Neoma was always nagging me to go out on the boat. I called Jimmy Youngblood—Rhea's boyfriend. 'There's five hundred bucks in this for you,' I said. 'Just take her to Key Largo and drop her off. Show her a good time, but make it clear I want her out of my life for good. I never want to see her again.' Jimmy met us at the channel buoy in Turtle Harbor. I'd already given Neoma the money by that time and told her to leave me alone. We were drinking rum and coke, her favorite.

"When Jimmy boarded, she was drunk. She threw her arms around his neck. She started kissing him and dancing around. That must have been when she lost the earring. 'Let's go party,' she said, 'My treat.' She stood aft in his boat when they pulled away, waving. 'I don't need you any more. I got Jimmy and I got money,' she yelled to me across the water. The wake pointed to her like an arrow. I tried to start the boat. The rest is what I told in court, what happened. I read about Neoma in the newspaper, like everybody else. I guess Jimmy wanted all the money. He didn't count on the divers finding her. Nobody dove Carysfort back then. He thought he'd get away with it. Got himself robbed and stabbed to death before they even found Neoma." He started to cough, a deep phlegmy cough that shook his whole body. "Jimmy murdered her! I let that happen." He put his face in his hands, then raised his head and it bobbed slightly, like the head of a cowering animal. "Gibb didn't believe me. He thought I was Amanda's father. 'No Son,' I said. 'I didn't even meet her until after the baby was born.' He turned his back on me and closed the door. I loved him. I wanted him to forgive me." He looked at Rachel. "Will you forgive me?" he whispered.

She stood, her own tears brimming, filling the room with jagged stars. How could she answer? "You could have told Gibb sooner," she said. "You could have told all of us." She looked at her mother. "Why didn't you tell us?"

"She kept quiet because I made her give me her promise she would. I didn't want you kids to know I was a liar and a cheat. And worse, that I sent a girl to her death."

Her mother was silent for a time, twisting her dress in her hands. She glanced at Noel. Finally she spoke in a trembling voice. "I loved him more than my own children. That's the guilt I'll carry with me to the end."

Jess touched his father's shoulder.

Jack put his arms around Rachel. "Easy," he said softly.

"I have to go," Rachel said. She walked through the living room and out the front door and stood with her back to the house, leaning on the car, feeling sick and dizzy. The sky above her was filled with color, spectacular fiery hues of orange and pink, mockingly beautiful and frightening at once, as if she might hold up her arms and burn, burn completely away except for her stone heart.

Back at Jess's apartment and the three of them sat together on Jess's couch, Rachel in the middle. "We need to pick up Miranda," Rachel said after a moment.

"I called Rose and told her we were going to have some dinner together and then come by," Jess said. "I hope that was all right. She said she and Miranda were having a great time together."

Rachel looked at Jack. "Okay with you?"

"Yeah," he said. "I'm exhausted. I'm so sorry for everything that's happened...to all of you. What I saw this afternoon was a pitiful old man who fell into something a long time ago that he didn't know how to get out of."

"He's a coward. He and Mother are both cowards." Rachel thought of her mother's face. A face full of sadness and pain that had simply grown older without changing expression.

"What would you have done in Mother's place?" Jess asked, his voice careful.

"I would've left him."

"Mother's not as strong as you are."

Rachel put her face in her hands. "I always thought she was stronger than I am," she said through her tears. "They lied."

"They've suffered for it." Jack took her hand. "They lost Gibb too."

Her brother. Her wonder. Part of her was gone. "I'm lost without him."

Jess put his arm around her. "You're sad...But you're not lost." After a while he stood up and walked to the piano. "Do you think it's time we scattered Gibb's ashes? He wanted us to do that...out by French Reef."

She looked at Jack.

"I'd feel honored to be a part of it," he said.

"Megan and Jon will take us out," Jess said, playing a few bars. His hands were easy on the keys, all concentration in his shoulders.

"That was the beginning of 'Epistrophy,'" he said, turning. "A Thelonius Monk number Gibb loved even more than I do. He always wanted to hear it when he was down. I've got it on tape. I'll play it out on the water."

They planned to go out with Jon, and two days later they set out from Key Largo in the afternoon. Rachel looked aft at the foamy wake. The boat was full of flowers. Martha had brought dozens of carnations from the greenhouse, and Megan had brought a huge bouquet of white roses. The sun was close to the horizon. They'd decided to wait until sunset, Gibb's favorite time of day. Rachel looked at the simple urn. Jon cut the engine and attached a rope to a mooring buoy. As the sun neared the horizon, Jess started the tape of his arrangement of "Epistrophy." Megan and Martha gave them all roses and carnations. Megan read the love chapter in Corinthians, tears streaming down her face. As the sun touched the water, Rachel opened the urn and read a few lines from a poem by Dylan Thomas—"And death shall have no dominion....," she began. "They shall have stars at elbow and foot..../ Though they sink through the sea they shall rise again; / Though lovers be lost love shall not..../ And death shall have no dominion / Under the windings of the sea." She scattered Gibb's ashes as the burning sun cast its light over the bright water before extinguishing itself. The surface of the water was covered with flowers, and the ashes floated a few seconds before they disappeared into the strong tidal current.

A week later, she was ready for her journey west, back to Colorado. She and Jack and Miranda had a flight the next morning. She sealed a letter to her parents. She'd described the flowers, the sunset streaming color across the water, and enclosed a copy of what they'd each read for Gibb before they'd given him to his beloved sea. In her last paragraph, she'd asked them, "Did you think you were protecting us from something worse than we've had to go through, by not telling us the truth? I'll write more when I can," she closed. She wanted to know what had happened to all of them. She wanted redemption. She had neither. But the puzzle was solved, and she was going home, where the story of her life would begin again. She heard Gibb's voice—*Journey wisely, Rachel.* She remembered Helen's words—*Don't confuse living in the past with hearing its messages.*

She stepped outside to mail her letter, a woman under a yellow sun that had shone before the reef and was still a pitiless, powerful light shining alike on the living—who both gloried and smoldered in that radiance—and on the dead, who lay expectantly, looking up, waiting to be blessed.

About the Author

Eleanor Swanson's work has appeared widely in publications such as *The Missouri Review, Black Warrior Review, High Plains Literary Review, The Denver Quarterly,* and The *Southern Review.* Awards include the A. E. Coppard Prize for Fiction, a Fiction Fellowship from the National Endowment for the Arts, a Colorado Council on the Arts Fellowship in Literature (fiction), and first place in the Plum Review Fiction Competition. Her  first collection of poetry, *A Thousand Bonds: Marie Curie and the Discovery of Radium,* was a finalist for the 2004 Colorado Book Award. A native of Miami, Florida, she now lives in Denver and is a Professor of English at Regis University.

Printed in the United States
107344LV00001B/52-78/A

9 781891 386961